'Anton Svensson' is a pseudonym for Stefan Thunberg and Anders Roslund.

Stefan Thunberg is one of Scandinavia's most celebrated screenwriters. His body of work spans popular TV series such as Henning Mankell's *Wallander* and Håkan Nesser's *Van Veeteren* as well as two of Sweden's biggest box office successes in recent years: *Hamilton* and *Jägarna 2*. While Thunberg achieved fame as a screenwriter, the rest of his family became infamous in an entirely different way: his father and brothers were Sweden's most notorious bank robbers, dubbed Militärligan (The Military Gang) by the media.

Anders Roslund is an award-winning investigative journalist and one of the most successful and critically acclaimed Scandinavian crime writers of our time. Roslund is part of the *New York Times* bestselling author duo Roslund & Hellström, who are recipients of many prestigious awards, including the CWA International Dagger, the Glass Key and the Swedish Academy of Crime Writers' Award, and who boast sales exceeding five million copies. Films and TV series based on Roslund & Hellström's novels are in the works, both in Hollywood and Europe.

'Vividly portrays perpetrators, victims and police'
Upsala Nya Tidning

'Captivating . . . about the inner workings of a gang of robbers'
Borås Tidning

'More than a traditional suspense novel'
Mariestads-Tidningen

'Something much more than a book you can't put down'
Tara

'Flawlessly constructed'
Femina

'Seductively well-written'
Kristianstadsbladet

THE NETHERLANDS

'Bring on the stellar reviews and the millions of readers'
de Volkskrant

'A must-read for every crime lover. Actually, a must for anyone who likes to read'
Hebban

'An incredible crime novel'
Brabants Dagblad

'The robberies are depicted stunningly'
NRC Handelsblad

'It is amazing how much tension the authors create'
VN Thriller & Detective Guide

'Never before have I read a book that so successfully explains how people can end up as criminals'
Het Nieuwsblad

'Provides an intriguing insight into the criminal life'
De Telegraaf

ITALY

'Crafted with breathtaking cleverness'
Corriere della Sera

The
SONS

MADE IN SWEDEN: PART 2

ANTON SVENSSON

Translated by Hildred Crill

sphere

SPHERE

First published in Sweden in 2017 as *En Bror Att Dö För* by Piratforlaget
First published in the English language in Great Britain in 2018 by Sphere
Published in agreement with the Salomonsson Agency.

1 3 5 7 9 10 8 6 4 2

Copyright © Anders Roslund & Stefan Thunberg 2017
Translation copyright © Hildred Crill 2018

The moral right of the authors has been asserted.

A CIP catalogue record for this book is available from the British Library.

Hardback ISBN 978-0-7515-5777-0
Trade Paperback ISBN 978-0-7515-5779-4

Typeset in Sabon LT Std by Palimpsest Book Production Limited,
Falkirk, Stirlingshire
Printed and bound in Great Britain by Clays Ltd, St Ives plc

Papers used by Sphere are from well-managed forests
and other responsible sources.

MIX
Paper from
responsible sources
FSC® C104740

Sphere
An imprint of
Little, Brown Book Group
Carmelite House
50 Victoria Embankment
London
EC4Y 0DZ

An Hachette UK Company
www.hachette.co.uk

www.littlebrown.co.uk

What constitutes the past in this book has been inspired by real events (while the parts in the present are pure fiction).

Black Gaps

BLOOD.

He has never thought about how red it is.

How much there is in a woman's body.

Enough to colour an entire kitchen and an entire hall and, step by step, three storeys down to the outer door. And still there's enough left that she's able to keep on running away.

The rag in his hand becomes darker and darker. He forces his spine outward and braces himself with his feet. He presses all his weight against the plastic rug on the kitchen floor as he rubs away the last patches of blood, rinses out the cloth in the warm, bubbly water in the bucket, and crawls to the doorway and the sticky stuff in the cracks.

What happened here has to stay here. That's how it works in a family.

Mamma whimpered like a wounded animal and, without turning back a single time, ran out, away, pursued by the tracks of blood he rubbed and rubbed until they were nothing at all.

Leo gets up and stretches his legs that have been cramped for so long, not changing position. That's strange. He should be exhausted. But he somehow feels exhilarated, restless and calm all at the same time. Stronger than ever. Every thought clear. He knows exactly what he should do. There's nothing he can compare it with, apart from maybe the first time he drank alcohol, that instant before he became *too* drunk. But this is better, soft inside and hard on the outside.

The kitchen window has striped curtains and faces the street. Leo peers out, and looks for Mamma who's not there. Of course, it's just the spatter in the hallway that remains.

And Pappa.

Is *he* still here? Why is he sitting down there in the car as if nothing happened? What's he waiting for? Police, shit – they could come any minute.

Pappa drove here all the way from the prison outside Stockholm and barged in intending to kill her. His eldest son jumped on his back and pressed his arm around his father's neck, fought him and forced him to stop hitting.

3

The kitchen is done, not a trace. It smells clean.

The hallway is worse. She slipped several times there, and the patches are bigger – like pools. But finally it is less when he has rubbed and scrubbed a bit out into the stairwell and the water has become more of a cloudy red than clear.

He sneaks back to the curtain again.

The yellow Volkswagen van is still down there, parked. With Pappa in the driver's seat and the front door open and his left leg sticking out, the wide grey trouser leg flapping in the wind and the brown shoe tapping the asphalt.

Pappa must be waiting for someone. Why the hell else would he be there?

Does he think Mamma will come back?

Or is it that Pappa is angry and disappointed that Leo stopped him, just as he got hold of her head and kneed her again and again – has he decided to come back into the stairwell and up to the flat on the third floor? Is it his turn now? Leo is the one who saw to it that she escaped, that she's alive.

But the rattled, hyped up, alive and almost happy feeling inside takes away the fear. He is not afraid, not even of his father.

In the bathroom, the nurse's bag with Mamma's medical paraphernalia is spilled out on the terry cloth bathmat, and the lid with a white cross is ripped open – someone has been rooting around in it. He lets it be. First he must get rid of the cleaning cloth in the rubbish and wash off his mother's blood. The warm water rinses away the scum from his skin. It becomes a beautiful, light red whirl just before it vanishes down the drain.

Felix was worried. He often is, but this time it was particularly clear that he was not well. And Vincent, his youngest little brother, didn't say a word. He just closed the door to his room and stayed there.

He checks a third time through the window. And now, now the police are coming. Fucking Pappa just sat there and waited for them! They've done it before, picked him up. Four years ago. The time Pappa threw a Molotov cocktail and burned down Grandma and Grandpa's house because Mamma was hiding there, but that was like the other way around. This time it's Pappa who is waiting for the police.

Right away one of them is standing on the stairs, ringing the doorbell. A tall, rather young one is visible through the peephole. And when he steps in onto the doormat, he doesn't see shit. The blood is completely cleaned up.

'Hi, I'm Peter Eriksson. Constable. I just want to say someone's on the way here. From social services. You don't need to be worried.'

'I'm not worried. Why would I be?'

'What's your name?'

'Leo.'

'And how old are you?'

'Old enough.'

'*How old?*'

'Fourteen.'

Now the cop looks around, inspects the hallway and leans forward a little to be able to see into the kitchen. But there's nothing to find; everything is put back. The table stands in its place again, both chairs are picked up and pushed in under it, and even the rag carpet that he turned over to hide the blood spots lies without a crease between the table legs.

'Was it here that it happened?'

'What do you mean "happened"?'

'Your father has already confessed. So I know *what* happened. I'm here to examine the scene.'

'It was here.'

'Where?'

'It began in the hall. Ended in the kitchen.'

The cop-gaze sweeps through the flat – along the hall floor, through the doorway into the kitchen.

'I see you've cleaned up. I can even smell the cleaning products. But that's not important right now. Still, I do want to know if your father has been here before.'

'He hasn't lived with us for a few years now.'

'So he's never been inside this flat?'

'No. We moved here from Stockholm four years ago. When Pappa went to prison.'

The cop's hand is on the door handle. It seems as if he'll go. No more questions from someone who shouldn't be meddling.

'There's one more thing.'

'Yeah?'

'The woman coming from social services soon is Anna Lena. She'll see to it that you and your brothers get help.'

5

'We don't need any help.'

'Everyone needs help once in a while.'

And so he leaves. Not a bloody word about what happened to Mamma. Pappa gave himself up, maybe that's why.

Felix is still hiding behind the sofa in the living room, but crawls out as soon as Leo waves at him.

'Is she . . . dead? Leo, is she? Say it, if it's true.'

'Of course she isn't dead.'

'Where is she then? Where, Leo? She must be really hurt.'

'She's a nurse. She knows what to do. Where to go.'

'Where to go? So can he find her there too?'

'No. The police have Pappa.'

'I don't understand.'

'What do you mean, you don't understand?'

'Why he came here. And wanted to kill her.'

'Because Mamma split the family up.'

'You're just saying that because Pappa said that.'

'No, I'm not. But I know Pappa better than you do. He just is like that. He operates that way.'

'But if he—'

Leo traps his little brother's agitated, flailing, swinging arms, a torrent that must be shut off.

'Felix – I get it that you are worried. And scared.'

'I—'

'But I *know* that she's all right. I saw it. And now I need your help, Felix – with Vincent. OK?'

Leo lets go of both arms, which seem to understand now. They aren't flailing or swinging any more.

'OK.'

And together they go towards the closed door.

'Vincent?'

Their little brother doesn't answer. Leo carefully turns the door handle. Locked. He looks in through the keyhole. Blocked, the key in the way.

'Vincent, open up.'

They both lay an ear against the door, hear him breathing heavily in there.

'The nurse's bag.'

'I saw it. On the bathroom floor. But, Leo, what if he's hurt himself. If he . . .'

'I'll take care of it.'

Leo is already on his way. Somewhere. Through the hall, towards the stairs.

'Where are you going?'

'The drainpipe.'

Felix doesn't like being alone when it's not his own choice. He looks at the locked door to Vincent's room, at the wood surface, which has peeling paint at the bottom, and at the door handle that doesn't move – as if he could make it turn by staring. He knows exactly what Leo plans to do. He knows that when he's rushed down the stairs, he'll continue out to the garden, to the back of the building. They climb up there to the balcony if they've forgotten the keys. But that won't help now; it's Vincent's door that's locked. So Leo's going to climb up the second drainpipe, the one rising to the heavens between Mamma's bedroom and Vincent's room, near the window that Vincent usually wants to have open. That way is much harder. A metal railing runs around the balcony that you can grab onto and lift yourself over. Vincent's room has only a small window ledge and it's extremely dangerous – slippery with edges that cut up your fingers. Leo has to hold onto the drainpipe with one hand at the same time and reach out and grab the ledge with the other. And then, with a jerk and a swing, he throws himself over. It's not easy. And what if . . . surely it rained a little before? Then the whole drainpipe gets sticky and slippery like really wet brown leaves in the autumn. He doesn't know what frightens him most: Leo climbing straight up and maybe falling down, or Vincent, who may have hurt himself behind the locked door.

He kicks the door handle and regrets it; he might frighten Vincent.

He should probably just look at it. There's nothing else to do. Stare. And count the seconds. Until it moves and Leo is standing there and Felix can also go in.

Two hundred and forty-eight seconds.

Then it happens, it is actually moving and the door opens.

He has never seen anything like it.

Ever.

He walks forward to the bed. Vincent is lying down and Felix doesn't know if he should touch him. He doesn't. Instead he tries to catch Leo's gaze.

'What . . . So Vincent has . . . Why did he bandage himself?'

All over the floor, among toy cars and soldiers, are empty paper boxes that otherwise belong in Mamma's nurse's bag – and should contain bandages. Now the chalk-white cloth is wrapped all around Vincent. His whole body covered, from his ankles to his thighs to his stomach to his shoulders to his throat to his face. The work of a seven-year-old. There are narrow spaces between the edges of the bandage and his underpants and T-shirt plus his naked skin sticking out through the gaps. Most obvious is the intended opening for the mouth, his breath wetting the woven edges.

'The blood out there . . . shit, Leo . . . it's . . . Mamma's, right? Isn't it?'

'Yes.'

'Just Mamma's?'

'Just Mamma's.'

Leo squats down by Vincent's unmade bed and grabs a bit of bandage that dangles loose from his wrist.

'We're here now, Vincent, with you. And Pappa is far away.'

One hand around the loose cloth and the other on Vincent's bandaged cheek.

'So I think we'll ease this shit off now.'

He doesn't even manage to loosen the first layer. With all his strength Vincent jerks the bandage out of his brother's grip, and his scream is muffled in the way screams are if you press your face hard against a pillow.

Felix is standing just past the doorway, not really understanding what he's looking at, when the doorbell rings. Again. And waiting on the other side of the peephole is the woman the police officer talked about. The social services lady. And that . . . he knows exactly what *that* means. So he hurries back to his big brother.

'If she sees that goddamn little mummy, Leo, everything will go to hell.'

'Fix it then. And don't talk so loud. I'll answer the door and you can take care of him.'

Vincent has managed to sit up in bed. He has got the red felt-tip pens and drawn round spots on his bandaged left arm. Felix hears Leo opening the door out there, the social services lady stepping in and the rattling of the hanger when she takes off her coat, and he whispers to his brother, who is just about to begin a rather large spot on the middle of his stomach.

'You have to lie down. Know what? Pretend you're sleeping.'

8

'I'm not tired. And *you* aren't lying down.'

'The woman out there, Vincent, you hear her, don't you? She can't see you now.'

'Who?'

'It doesn't matter. But if she sees you . . . with all that shitty . . . with all of that on you, then she'll take you with her, don't you get it?'

If he fixes the sheet, unfolds the blanket . . .

'Come on, for fuck's sake!'

If he turns the pillow and the wet patch of sweat disappears . . . maybe Vincent will lie down then.

'She's coming soon!'

He does it – Vincent gives up, he crawls in and Felix hides him almost entirely. The blanket is tucked in around the bandaged head.

'And now you breathe exactly like you usually do when you're sleeping. In, out. In, out. Slowly.'

Then he hurries out and meets Leo and the social services lady in the hall. They say hello and she smiles.

'And your little brother? Where is he?'

'He's asleep. He's entirely under the blanket. It looks comfortable.'

They let the lady peek into the room and she sees what she ought to see, a child who's sleeping deeply and shouldn't be disturbed. And that works out well, she explains as she looks at Felix, because now she wants to talk alone with Leo.

'If you tell us how Mamma is first.'

'She's in pain, Felix. But at present she's in hospital – they know how to take care of this kind of thing.'

And when they are alone, she and Leo, when Felix is sitting on the sofa and looking at some television programme, she makes an attempt to talk and explain.

'I have visited your mother in the hospital ward where she is staying. The doctors check on her every hour – and she has to remain there for a few days.'

She puts a hand on his shoulder. He twists downwards and steps backwards until her hand slides off.

'Your mother wants you and your two brothers to stay here. But it isn't really possible, is it? Not if you're alone.'

He doesn't nod or shake his head. He heard what she said but he's not planning to leave the flat. Not now. Vincent, shit, they can't go out with a mummy. And if they yank the bandage off him he would get hysterical. Not a fucking thing would be better.

'Felix is eleven. And Vincent is seven. Do you understand what I'm saying?'

I understand what you're saying, he thinks. And I remember what Pappa said.

You have the responsibility from now on.

'I can take care of my little brothers.'

'You're fourteen years old.'

'Look, there are fourteen-year-olds who experience a shitload worse things. A boy I read about, in Brazil I think, he harpooned fish to get money for his family, but then one day he harpooned himself in the foot, and then—'

'Listen to me. I reasoned with your mamma a long while.'

Her hand is on his shoulder again – and it stays there even though he twists his body.

'Leo, how are you? Now?'

'Now? I don't really know . . .'

He knows exactly how he is. But he doesn't know if that's the right thing.

'. . . or, it's all right, I guess.'

The right thing to feel so incredibly strong. Almost happy. That should be wrong. How can that happen when his inside explodes with the image of Mamma bleeding and running away?

'Your mamma told me about everything that happened.'

The social worker's voice. Serious. She wants to know. Now come the questions.

'I don't want to talk about it.'

Not a word, to anyone, about what happened. It would just be worse.

'What is it you don't want to talk about?'

'What you want to know – what Pappa did.'

The hand is still on his shoulder.

'Your mamma didn't need to tell what he did – I could see that myself. Her injuries. But she said what *you* did. About your courage. That it was why she was able to run away.'

Everything is released, suddenly. He isn't at all prepared.

The lovely throb through his body sort of comes to a standstill and is washed away; the happiness and softness leaves every little joint and muscle

10

and thought. And it feels as if he's going to cry. His whole damned chest is pressed by shit that has to come out. But he has no intention of letting out a drop. To cry now, before her, would ruin everything.

He twists himself loose, again, and rushes to the kitchen. But she doesn't give up and follows him. The food they never ate is still there on the round table, cold. He picks up one dish at a time and opens the oven door; 150 degrees is usually about right.

'Where is Pappa?'

His voice is steady, nowhere near crying.

'He isn't coming back.'

'I get that – I asked where he is.'

'At the police station.'

'In custody?'

'Yes . . .'

He notices her look. They usually have that look – those who think that he shouldn't be familiar with that word.

'He's been that before. In custody.'

'You don't need to be worried that he'll come back – it's going to take time.'

'I'm not worried. Why would I be? So I don't understand actually why we can't stay here at home a few lousy days.'

'Because you are fourteen years old. Because you and your *even younger* brothers have experienced something that children shouldn't have to experience.'

You don't have a fucking clue what we cope with. Or what shit we've seen, he wanted to say, but that wouldn't be especially smart.

'Leo, listen. This is important. If your mamma is away for a long time – we don't really know yet, do we? – then you'll have to live with another family.'

'What do you mean . . . another family?'

'But that might take a little time to arrange. So until that time someone will come here instead and look out for you.'

'Come here? Who?'

'I don't really know yet. We have an on-call list with decent people who help when things like this happen. It will be settled this evening.'

Another family. Leo adjusts the cutlery that has been waiting for a long time on the kitchen table and that must have rattled when Pappa kneed Mamma in the face. *We already have a mother, even if she is lying in a*

11

hospital bed. He puts out glasses and iced water in a plastic pitcher – she never managed to bring that out. *We already have a father, even if he's in custody.* And last of all he folds the ripped-off paper bits from the paper towel roll ceremoniously, runs the top of his hand over them and strokes them. *And that is why I make this decision now.*

'Listen.'

He tries to catch her gaze.

'Social services lady?'

He still has no idea what her name is because he doesn't care.

'Yes?'

'It's like this . . . If that's the case, can't Agnetha look in on us instead?'

'Who is Agnetha?'

'She's on the second floor. Mamma's friend. She's up here often. And she's decent, like the people on your on-call list.'

VINCENT IS SITTING in bed – or rather, he's arched backwards. As soon as the social worker disappeared down to the second floor, he sneaked out and ran to the toilet. And now, afterwards, he has to bandage his entire stomach again.

Felix seems to have given up. He is breathing more peacefully and leaning against the edge of the bed. A bandaged little brother perhaps doesn't alarm him so much any more.

'What the hell happened out there, Leo? Has she gone? It sounded like it.'

'She's coming right back.'

'Did she say anything else about Mamma?'

Leo sinks down by his younger brothers, against the same hard edge of the bed.

'Felix – Mamma's going to be gone a few days.'

'How many?'

'A few.'

'How many?'

'I don't know.'

'How many?'

'*I don't know.*'

Felix isn't satisfied. Leo sees a facial expression that is so familiar, knows that his brother intends to keep asking until he gets an answer. There isn't one. And it's as if Felix senses that. Instead of keeping on repeating *how many*, he starts to laugh – a sort of laugh none of them has heard before. More like a giggle, it doesn't take shape on the inside where it usually does. It comes into being right at the front of the mouth, at the lips, comes from nowhere and isn't connected to anything. It slowly gains in strength and he starts to talk at the same time, half giggling, half speaking, about the mummy in the bed and the cop and the social services lady and then all the blood spots on the floor – *Leo, the blood must have spurted – spurted!* Felix is giggling and Leo doesn't have the energy to listen any more. He climbs up into the bed, next to Vincent.

'Everything OK, my littlest brother?'

The stomach is finished. Rebandaged in new, careful layers. But the fingers of his right hand are free and Vincent brings these to his mouth before he answers by drawing the loop of the bandage up, a little above the upper lip.

'Yes.'

And then he draws the next loop of bandage down, a little below the lower lip.

'No.'

And again, up. And again, down.

'Yes. No.'

Up and down, the small opening in front of his mouth is closed and opened.

'Yes. No. Yes. No. Yes. No.'

Until Leo gingerly strokes the bandaged cheek.

'Excellent, little brother. That's really good.'

Then the doorbell rings out there, again.

He closes the door carefully and hurries towards the monotonous signal. It's the social services lady and behind her, Agnetha. They are smiling.

'We'll do what you suggested.'

The social services lady is maybe smiling the most; she's the one who's talking.

'So, Agnetha will look in on you, at least this evening and tonight and in the morning. And then we'll take it from there.'

Her coat is hanging on one of the hooks under the shelf for hats. She buttons one button after another and looks for a long time at Leo, who hopes that they remain at a distance so that the giggling won't erupt.

'But – there's one condition.'

'Yes?'

'That Agnetha can come and go exactly as often as she needs to. She and I will stay in contact the whole time. OK, Leo? OK, Agnetha?'

He nods and they both wait for Agnetha to do the same. But she doesn't answer. And they soon understand why. Her gaze has become fixed a little further off in the stairwell, just where Mamma stumbled and hit hardest. The only patch he didn't really wipe away. There was quite a lot of blood there and he was in a hurry.

He waits until they've gone.

The cleaning bucket is still in the bathroom where he left it. He fills it

14

with warm water and a dash of washing-up liquid, wets the rag and rubs with the whole weight of his body pressed against the stone floor until the last drops that hadn't been mopped up are gone.

Now he knows exactly what to do.

He opens the door leading to his two brothers – one giggling hysterically, one hiding in bandages – and plops down like before, on the floor with his back against the side of the bed.

'I still don't know how many days, Felix. But we'll fix it all the same.'

'What do you mean, fix it?'

'I have thought it all out. And you're going to help me.'

'Oh, yeah?'

'Do you still have the blue case? With the maps?'

'Yes.'

'Get it.'

'Why?'

'The social services lady has got the idea that we shouldn't live here any more. But that's not going to happen.'

Felix is already giggling less as he gets up more slowly than ever before in order to illustrate how unwilling he is.

'Felix – just get it.'

The blue map case isn't larger than a postcard but it's as thick as a box of chocolates and it flies in a nice arc as Felix throws it from the doorway to the bed, nearly hitting both Leo and Vincent as it crash-lands.

'Satisfied?'

A compass is shoved down in an open pocket on the outside of the case. It gets in the way as Leo scoops up and unfolds the map, which has shrunk all the cycle paths, minor roads and lanes of Falun to a scale of 1:5000.

'Look here.'

He points somewhere in the middle of the map and Felix tries to do what he says, look, but he doesn't understand what he should look at.

'What?'

'The roads from the city centre to the forest.'

Leo's index finger dives down to a little section in the outskirts of Falun, not particularly far away. The angular letters form S-L-Ä-T-T-A. Felix knows exactly how the map looks in reality. He has been there a couple of times; they have a really worthless football team.

'And? What about it?'

15

'I will explain it all, later. When we get there.'

'Where?'

Leo is in a hurry to fold up the map and Felix almost feels in his body how there'll be new folds that weren't there before.

'Where, Leo? And, listen, I want that back when you're through with it. Don't ruin it – it cost fifteen kronor.'

'You can have ten shitty maps just like it when I'm done. Come with me now and I'll show you.'

'Show me what?'

'What you'll get to see.'

'And the mummy?'

'He said he wanted to be alone. Now he can be. We won't be gone long.'

LOOKOUT POINT. The little hill behind the thorn bushes that frame the square. Now they are squatting on the top of it, close to each other. Their hair is blowing and the fallen leaves are dancing drowsily over the open asphalt surface. They can almost forget this lousy day for a short while.

'Hey, Leo?'

'Yes?'

'What are we doing here?'

'You'll see in a minute.'

Then Leo's cheeks tighten, which means he is entirely focused and peeling away everything around – he does that sometimes, crawls inside himself. Felix follows Leo's gaze. A woman, about their mother's age, strolls across the square. It's her Leo is studying. Or it might be the leather bag she's carrying in her hand.

'Do you see it?'

It *was* the bag. A brown one, which seems not to be especially heavy.

'Yeah.'

'Do you know what it contains?'

'And you know that?'

'Mmm.'

'What?'

'Twenty-five thousand. Sometimes forty. Sometimes even fifty.'

'Fifty thousand . . . what?'

'Kronor.'

The woman is on the way from the ICA supermarket on one side of the square to the bank on the other side, with long, determined strides in leather boots with high heels that clatter. The wind carries the sound up to Lookout Point.

'Every day she does this walk, just after the shop closes – the same route, across the square with the bag in her hand – and when she gets there, she puts all the shit in that over there, do you see?'

She pulls out a metal box on the bank's brick wall, tilts it and lets the bag drop down, a toothless mouth that gobbles it up.

17

'Money they made. And that goes into their account.'

'How do you know that?'

'The owner's son usually brags about it in the smoking area.'

Now she's finished – on the way back, without the bag, to the area's largest ICA shop.

'Are we done? I want to go home.'

'Don't you even get why we're here?'

'Vincent is alone. We're leaving now, Leo.'

'The leather bag. I'm going to take it.'

'Take . . . it?'

'Yes.'

'What do you mean . . . take?'

'Swipe. A heist.'

'Heist?'

'That's English. It means a supercool robbery.'

'That's not supercool – you know, it won't work.'

'It'll work. And I know how. Just before she drops the money down I'll snatch it.'

'But . . .'

The woman who has high heels on and is Mamma's age has company, so Felix falls silent. A guard in uniform. He is employed to watch over the city centre. He marches loop after loop from morning to evening and he meets her now in the middle of the square.

'Shit, Robbie's big brother. *He's* the guard.'

'I'll take care of it.'

'Click. They call him that. Click with the baton. Click with the big radio. Shit, he knows who you are!'

'I'll take care of that too.'

Felix looks for a long time at the guard, at Robbie's big brother. If Leo snatches the bag, then Click would easily catch up with him. Just two or three steps.

'It won't work. Do you know how quickly Click runs? And *if* he doesn't manage to . . . then he'll recognise you.'

'I'll never get sent down.'

'How can you know that? Bloody idiot! You can't know that!'

'I said I'll take care of it. OK? Masked. That's what you have to be. And before you strike, you put out false leads.'

The guard seems to be growing. Or maybe it's that Felix only sees a uniform and a baton and a walkie-talkie. While Leo, at the same time, doesn't seem to see him at all.

'I want to go home.'

'Just a little while longer.'

'Leo – we're leaving now. The guard. Robbie's brother. And—'

'A little longer.'

Felix pulls on one of the sleeves of Leo's jacket.

'You are exactly like . . . back then! When you wanted to . . .' He pulls a little more, 'fight with Kekkonen. When you took Pappa's knife. You don't listen and you disappear into yourself. When you aren't with me – only with yourself.'

Felix gets up and starts walking. Soon he hears steps: Leo's running gait.

'Felix . . . stop now!'

Until he has managed to catch up and they are walking side by side.

'You *have* to go along with it.'

'Leo – you can forget it.'

'You're the one who's going to lure the guard away!'

'Don't you get it! I don't *want* to be a part of it! And I don't *intend* to be a part of it!'

Leo grabs hold of his brother, not hard, but friendly hands around the tense shoulders so that they both have to stop. And he smiles, even laughs a little, like when they have a laugh together sometimes.

'Felix? You and I can do what we want. If we just do it together. And together we'll easily hoodwink Click. A diversion tactic. That's what it's called. The fucking guard won't understand a thing.'

'I don't want to. Don't want to. *Don't want to.*'

'Listen, I've planned it all out, OK . . .'

Felix looks away, covers his ears and starts to walk again. Leo follows him, like before.

'You don't need to be afraid. Not a bit. That square, it's ours.'

And he points, arm outstretched.

'See that fucking bronze statue that stands right on the edge between the benches? Do you see it, Felix? That's us, afterwards! We are going to stand there and shine.'

Felix presses his hands even harder over his ears.

'And do you know what's best of all, Felix? That this is just a one-shot deal. Thirty, or even forty thousand in the leather bag. One single time.'

Every time the same thing – when Felix makes up his mind, he has made up his mind. Maybe he . . . went too fast. Maybe that's it. So much else has happened. Maybe he needs to take care of that first so that everything will work out. Time to change tactics.

Social worker. Cop. On-call list. Blood. Custody. Another family. A day filled with words he hadn't imagined he would need to explain to someone covering their ears. Words, which, if you think about them, if you try to understand them, put all together mean *a long time*.

A long time for three brothers to be alone in a flat.

A long time for Mamma to lie in a hospital bed and heal. He knows that makes Felix all the more worried, even sadder.

But also a long time for Pappa to be locked up in a cell. He knows that will calm Felix down.

Because of course he needs his little brother to succeed.

'If I can change, you can change'

THE INSIGNIFICANT SIGN greeted him from a few hundred metres away – mounted on metal legs, it stood there and pointed stubbornly to the left.

CORRECTIONAL FACILITY 2 KM

He leaned back in the sagging, far too soft driver's seat, which seemed to become bottomless as his heavy body sank deeper in. A tap on the brakes, a sharp turn, and he was gone.

Change. When you can't run any more, when you don't make your way home, or even know where it is – sooner or later change is the only road to travel, he was absolutely convinced of that.

He parked at the far end of the prison's empty visitor parking and rolled down the side window for some fresh air. It wasn't enough. He needed more. He opened the front door and let his left leg slide along with it and stick out while the dry-cleaned suit's wide trouser leg flapped in the mild April breeze and the newly shined dress shoe tapped on the dry asphalt.

The muzak on the radio streamed out of the rasping car speakers with their loose hanging cords, and he leaned closer to the dashboard to turn it off, breathed slowly and deeply and closed his eyes until the flashing coloured spots inside his eyelids disappeared – finally, in all that stillness he could hear the warbling of birds from the edge of the woods, which picked up where the concrete wall of the prison left off.

08.22.

Thirty-eight minutes left. Not much in the old jalopy worked, but he could count on the clock.

And time, which otherwise pursued and vexed and muddled it all up, was absolutely key today. He had even decided to come in good time. Good time? What the fuck is that? Good time is 09.00 on the third of April. The most important point in time in many, many years.

The late winter sun was growing stronger every minute and it let loose its blaze against a solitary car forty kilometres north of Stockholm. The light struck scum on the unwashed glass and sliced through it. Ivan bent the sun visor down and glanced towards the outer barbed wire fence. The

Österåker correctional facility. The sort of prison where a highly dangerous individual with a long sentence does the last part of his time.

And the more he stared at it, the more obvious it became: it was truly an ugly wall. Grey along the endless sides, equally grey on the back, but painted flashy bright red on the front. As if that would make a visitor happier. He didn't give a damn about the colour. It was the gate and the steel door that meant everything. It was through that door that his eldest son would step out. And it's just then, when a locked-up human takes the first step into freedom, that he or she decides what they will be – not when the days are unfolding in there. It isn't possible to think clearly behind walls. As for himself, he had kept on drinking mush that tasted like mould and urine – orange juice blended with rotten apples and old bread that had stood and fermented behind a radiator. But, two years ago, when he had taken *his* first step into freedom, he had decided: not a drop more. And he had succeeded. Without foolish meetings and miracle methods, without sitting in a circle and holding hands and singing in chorus.

They had locked up Ivan Dûvnjac but not what was inside him. And if a father can change, a son can change. That was what was about to happen. A father might fail when his son is young. But it can turn out well to meet again as adults.

Engine noises from the banked, winding side road.

The car was so quiet, it hardly drowned out the warbling, but rather was blended with it. Some little Japanese model. Not entirely modern, but entirely blue and entirely washed clean. A windscreen that could be looked through without getting stinging eyes. It stopped at the other end of the car park. He stretched and caught sight of a woman and a man in the front seats, other visitors who were also waiting for some longed-for person who would be released. They usually released them at this time of day. Not a single bloody person was waiting for him the last two turns, not even the mother of his three sons.

The woman was sitting in the passenger seat, and was wearing a blue and white dotted scarf over her hair and dark sunglasses. And a coat, it looked like. The man in the driver's seat seemed dark and had a haircut that needed trimming, a little too long, just like a lot of people seemed to wear it these days.

The clock on the dashboard read 08.33. Twenty-seven minutes to go.

In *very* good time.

24

Ivan drew his hand through his hair, spreading his fingers out to make a rough comb and glancing at the rear-view mirror – not that he necessarily wanted to look smart, but what had begun on the inside ought to be possible to discern on the outside.

Then a door of the other car opened. The woman. She walked towards the wall, stood there and waited, relaxing with arms crossed and with her weight equally distributed on her legs, and her gaze turned to the gate, steady, resolute.

And suddenly he knew.

She didn't have to take off those sunglasses. He knew exactly who she was. Who she was waiting for.

Eighteen years. It didn't matter to him about the time that had passed. Eighteen years and her legs were just as steady, her gaze just as steady. It was just like that that she had stood and looked at him when he opened the door to her home and passed by their children, when he began to hit her in the kitchen, intending to kill her.

Britt-Marie.

Feelings don't disappear. Hate sleeps under the surface like an evil virus and – when you least expect it – it expands and explodes between two thoughts.

He had stood in the stairwell with a finger on the doorbell's black plastic button and had a choice. He had chosen *not* to turn back, *not* to walk back down the stairs. But he would have acted differently today, and he wondered if she would have done so, too.

Ivan stretched forward a little more, rubbed at the layer of shit to scrape away at least the part that was sticking on the inside. He could see a little better and it hit him between the lungs, the hate that had to be controlled. He hadn't felt it for a long time, not so forcibly as now, when his whole body was preparing to charge towards Britt-Marie, towards the man who was still sitting in the car, thinking that he was waiting for *Ivan's* son. He wanted to see the bastard's face, to understand Britt-Marie, who she had become. The choice of partner revealed a person.

The rear-view mirror again and his splayed hand through his hair. The collar on his suit jacket must be folded down. The black shirt must be tucked into his trousers.

Whatever had happened so far, whatever might still happen, they belonged together.

Bound together.

That's what you are for ever if you have children.

Responsibility, inward. Trust, inward. Against the world, outward.

He climbed out of the car and started to walk. If she was standing there, then her son's own father should also stand nearer to the prison gate than the new man in a spotless Japanese car. New man? Why is she dragging him along here? What the fuck does he know about how a prison gets to you? How many times has he signed a receipt to get his personal belongings from the bottom of a cardboard box in order to step out into a changed reality?

He knows nothing. A coward who hides in the car.

Ivan was heading for the wall and gate but was soon forced to measure out the length of his steps – to walk more confidently. What was hurrying on the inside must not hurry on the outside. He must not walk too quickly, too aggressively, must pause at each placement of the foot.

He wanted to turn his head a little and look into the car, but she must not see how much he cared about it. The long-haired man would maybe toddle off when her ex-husband began to talk to her. She had certainly told him everything about who he was – or who she *believed* he was.

Britt-Marie.

So steady there by the steel gate, which would swing open and let their son out. Ivan walked nearer but not too close, not yet. He stopped at the gate's other end, wanting first to see how she reacted.

Not a word.

Not a look.

She stood there like a wax doll, silent, and looked away from him.

'I . . . have changed, Britt-Marie.'

It was as if he weren't there. As if all the years of silence weren't enough.

'And you weren't there, Britt-Marie, in the cabin when we were arrested.'

A furious snowstorm. A getaway car helpless in the ditch. A summer cabin surrounded by the police task-force.

'But I was there. When it happened. Do you hear that, Britt-Marie? If I hadn't . . . For the first time in my life, Britt-Marie, I was at the wrong place at the wrong time but did the right thing.'

And I delayed. I delayed.

'Leo would never have surrendered. You know that. Our eldest son would not have survived. Do you hear that, Britt-Marie?'

'Ivan?'

She spoke to him. He existed, again.

'Is it . . . but please, is *that* what you go around imagining? So you can

26

live with yourself? Ivan – you didn't prevent anything at all! If you hadn't been the way you were when they were growing up . . . good God, Leo would never have robbed any banks! Or ended up in a derelict summer cabin surrounded by elite police – with you!' She kept her sunglasses on but he was certain she was observing him. 'And Felix and Vincent wouldn't have done time, either.'

Then he walked closer until only one half of the giant gate separated them. Between the steel bars of the grating, he glimpsed the central guard and the way in, the way out.

'What happened then, Ivan, the first years when the boys were little, it was . . . the *circumstances* that formed them. All your bloody clan-building!'

He walked even closer while she was talking, a couple of metres between them, not more. She showed no fear, only determination.

'But you didn't give up! You had to keep going, to follow me, force your way into my new life. And it was then, right then, Ivan, when you tried to beat me to death in front of the eyes of your own sons, that the circumstances became *the genesis*.'

'The genesis? What a fucking word. You talk like that nowadays?'

'You drove him there, Ivan!'

'Come on – we wouldn't be fucking standing here in front of a prison waiting for our eldest son if *you* hadn't split up the family.'

It was hard to see whether she was still beautiful, whether she had aged well. The scarf covered her forehead and the sunglasses covered most of her cheeks. She still had thin lips, at least, which she pursed so damn tight when she was angry or frustrated.

'So . . . you've brought your new man here with you?'

He looked at the spotless car, since he was a little closer now. It didn't help much. The head lacked clear contours and most of him stayed pale blue behind the tinted windows. Long hair and a beardless chin. You couldn't even judge his age in the glittering light.

'Is it even fair to him, Britt-Marie? Does Leo know that someone else is waiting for him too?'

A weak bloody smile. A sneer. She does it all with her lips. She likes it, he thought to himself, she's even enjoying that I mind about the coward in the driver's seat.

He tried, again, to see who it was. Impossible. But it was obvious that the eyes behind the spotless windscreen were watching him, pursuing him. And then – a body turning, an arm raised.

27

Her companion had decided to open the door and dare to come out.
'Is there a problem?'

A young man's voice. What the fuck? He hadn't even considered that.

Same height as him. Dark in the same way he was himself. Broad shoulders like his own. Damn it, she's just picked a younger copy. So fucking . . . unimaginative.

'Mamma, is everything OK?'

Ivan didn't take it in at first.

'Mamma?'

That meant . . . It must be . . . Was it really him?

'Hey, Mamma – is everything OK?'

A body that moved like Ivan's own, forearms clearly swinging to and fro with wide gestures and motions that became gentle and demanded space without exertion. Felix. On his way to the gate to position himself between them; a large, empty car park and soon they would all be in the same small spot, contained within a strange force field.

'Felix? Is that you? It was so . . .'

Now he saw clearly – his second oldest son wasn't the same height at all, he was taller. And even broader.

'. . . can't we get together sometime . . . you and I, Felix?'

So many years, the same as with her, if you didn't count one late evening and a couple of minutes in a hallway when both Felix and Vincent knocked on Leo's door and tried to convince him not to commit that last bank robbery. When they opened the door, the robber who was going to replace them – the two brothers who had dropped out – was standing right there: their father.

'Get together?'

'It would be . . . nice to find out how things are with you, you know. How you are.'

'It's not any of your business how I am.'

He had already known before he asked the question that past events were still lingering, were in the way. He could see that in Felix's face.

'But, look, that was long ago.'

'What I'd like to talk to you about, Ivan, I won't talk to you about here.'

His face hissed *Pappa, you should not have been there robbing that bank, it cost Vincent and me several years inside those fucking walls.*

Ivan looked at the clock, this time a ticking watch. Perhaps to avoid facing the contempt. Perhaps time, which he hadn't grasped, finally meant something.

That it was eighteen minutes until his eldest son was a free man.

That two years had passed without his drinking a drop.

That if he could change, Leo could change.

HE WAS ESCORTED through a several-hundred-metre-long passage, a dead straight, windowless transportation route underneath the prison's dusty gravel courtyard. The stiff fabric of the shirt and trousers chafed the skin, but today he didn't feel it. The click of the guards' heels ricocheted off the concrete walls, but today he didn't hear it.

The passage was divided by equidistant locked metal doors. At the next one, for those who remained, the stairs climbed up to C building's divisions. But he kept going straight ahead, and both guards glanced up at the ceiling and the humming surveillance cameras; a wait of a few seconds, then there was a click as the lock was opened from the central guard.

At the same time, above them, the facility's other inmates were on their way to the day's scheduled work. Some to the workshop, others to the small factory to assemble green- and red-coloured blocks or sort screws into different sizes.

That was what he had done. Day after day, week after week – the first five years alternating between Kumla and Hall, Sweden's only high-security prisons, the last year at Österåker. Together with murderers, assassins, drug smugglers and other bank robbers, he had sorted blocks on an assembly line. Until the evening came, the hours after being locked in the cell. Then he read. First the entire police investigation that was presented against him at the trial – separate preliminary investigations for each bank robbery and security van robbery and the one for the bomb at Stockholm's Central Station and the one classified as *blackmail against the police force*. Six thousand pages of stilted police text, until he had memorised interrogations and arguments, and then he'd gone over to reading books. For him, the reading and sorting blocks were really the same thing, an attempt to stop, to prevent the brain from doing what he always otherwise did – think of time. He had of course always known how much. Exactly. The clock was ticking inside him. But behind bars, and for the first time without days and seasons, not one single bastard had got to him.

The next metal door.

More glances towards the surveillance camera, towards the humming and the click.

And they continued to walk in an underground passage that culminated in freedom, to that part of the world where time moved forward.

Now he would make use of it again. Become a part of it. Feel seconds and breaths. He knew what he would do when he had passed through the wrought-iron gate in the wall.

Take back.

Take back what doesn't exist.

One more door in the passage, but this one was located directly in the concrete wall, and led neither further up to the division stairs nor was it controlled from the central guard. It was the door to the equipment room, containing jute sacks – which lay all over the place and smelled like a mud cellar – for those with shorter sentences, and cardboard boxes with hand-written name tags for lifers without a home other than Österåker correctional facility.

'Dûvnjac?'

'Yes?'

'Your belongings – at the back if you follow the wall to the left.'

The symbolic prison release. To find his box among a few hundred other ones and unpack the past, all the way back to the day he was arrested. There. 0338 Dûvnjac. He ripped off the silver tape and folded out the flaps.

On the top was the watch he had worn then, stopped at a quarter past four, its battery having died long ago. He fastened it onto his wrist. Then the wallet, a couple of crumpled hundred kronor notes in one fold and the expired driving licence in the other. That was how the escape from the last bank robbery was planned – a normal family out driving the day before Christmas Eve, the car filled with gifts for celebrating Christmas with relatives – when a snowstorm and a ditch intervened. That – and a cop named John Broncks.

In the middle of the piles of clothes were his jeans. Still dirty and smelling of mud from the pond he had fallen into when the ice broke during the snowstorm.

The smell of failure.

'You can throw that shit out. There should be something new.'

He put the trousers back in the bottom of the box, over the pile with equally reeking T-shirt, underwear, socks and boots, and waited while one

31

of the guards dug around in another pile in the middle of the basement storage room.

'Here.'

The plastic bag sailed in a wide curve through the room and he caught it and emptied it out. The clothes Mamma had left at her last visit. He tore off the ugly, loose-hanging correctional facility outfit and let six years fall to the floor.

'I saw that the whole family is gathered outside,' said the guard who threw the plastic bag of clothes to him, one of the few that it was possible to exchange a proper word with when no one was looking.

'That's how it is between brothers. Especially mine.'

'They . . . haven't they been out for a while?'

'A couple of years. Now they are nearly as old as I am. We don't age in here.'

'Then they've made it through the worst of it. Two out of three. Do you get it? Two out of three are standing there knocking at the gate again after only a couple of months. Recidivism, you know. It'd be bloody nice to keep you out of that statistic.'

New jeans, socks, underwear. Clean shirt. The light windproof jacket and the black Reebok trainers. Each article of clothing in the same size as when he was locked up.

A flight of stairs led up to the central guard and the very last door. Leo looked into the glass booth at a uniformed woman who swivelled slightly in her office chair, framed by small, square monitors piled from floor to ceiling – black-and-white pictures collected from sixty-four cameras.

The prisoner named Leo Dûvnjac was no longer an object to be watched on any of them.

A few metres left.

To the ugly, grey, seven-metre-high concrete wall. To those who were standing on the other side, waiting. To an embrace that he could already feel in his body. Big, warm hugs. They had always greeted each other like that, his brothers, Felix and Vincent.

Six years in this world.

The twenty steps took him across the asphalt area to a wrought-iron gate that slowly opened out. The air was pleasant to breathe; the dusty, incarcerated, restricted world entirely gone. He stopped to take another breath, drawing it in and becoming dizzy. Then he saw them: the three he expected and hoped would be there, who he'd missed every day, many times every day. Mamma, Felix, Vincent.

He walked closer. And there was something that didn't feel right.

Felix was there in the middle, like a border guard between two islands. They hadn't seen each other for many years but it *was* him – that dark hair, the broad shoulders. And on one side of him, to the left – the strawberry blonde hair a shade greyer, the slightly stooping posture – was Mamma in a coat that looked like all her other ones. But on Felix's other side, to the right, dressed up, the grey suit even pressed . . . Father? What the fuck was he doing here? And Vincent – why was he *not* here?

The gate's slight creaking stopped when it was wide open, and as it began to swing shut again, he took his first step out, his back turned to a world he would leave and never return to again.

Mamma got the first hug. She was so small, she could easily fit in his arms.

'Thanks for the clothes, dear Mamma.'

'I'm so happy, Leo, so insanely happy that you are out.'

They held each other. To do that in freedom was very different. She wasn't the only one holding tightly; he was too.

Then Felix.

'Wonderful to see you.'

A bear hug. Like always.

'Likewise, little brother.'

Then . . . Leo spun around once, and again, searching the car park.

'Where the hell is Vincent?'

'He's . . . working. Couldn't get away.'

'Six years, Felix – and he "couldn't get away"?'

'A customer causing trouble. You know how it is.'

One left. Pappa. He stood there with both arms outstretched. A man who never ever hugged had clearly seen how the others acted.

'Leo, my son.'

'You? I really didn't think that . . . that you'd come here.'

The arms remained outstretched as Ivan took the final step and embraced him.

'If I can change, Leo, you can change.'

A forced hug. And his father whispered again, louder.

'If I can change, you can change.'

'Pappa, what the hell are you talking about?'

33

The two outstretched arms became two raised fingers.

'Two years, my son.'

'Two years, what?'

'I've been out for two years. And not a goddamn drop.'

The hug. And Pappa hadn't smelled at all. The weak scent of red wine, which always swirled around him, was gone.

'And, Leo, listen, now we should—'

'Later.'

'Later?'

'I don't have time, Pappa.'

'But you're released now!'

'Yeah. A whole lot to arrange.'

His father didn't move.

'Look, Leo, how the fuck would I know that Felix and . . . *she* would come. I've reserved a table, but only for us, for you and me, a welcome home lunch, we really need to talk, we—'

'This evening.'

Not a drop?

Leo examined his father, uncertain whether it had made him a whole lot calmer. Last time they saw each other he hadn't drunk anything either because that had been Leo's demand – that Ivan should stay sober the days before the robbery.

Everything had gone to hell anyway.

For the moment he needed to keep his father at a distance without alienating him. Without stirring that paternal instinct that occasionally showed itself.

'Did you say this evening?'

'Yes. We can get together for a bit. I have . . . a little to do before that. OK?'

Leo avoided a disappointed look and passed by the shitty little Saab his Pappa pointed to and offered a ride in, and continued away from the wall and the prison gate and all those days locked up. He was already on the way somewhere else.

To a motorway a couple of dozen kilometres south-west of Stockholm.

And a completely ordinary rest area.

To dig up the past, and then, to take back what didn't exist.

HE SHOULD FEEL HAPPY, through and through. Free. Free to drive wherever the fuck he wanted, to stop to piss exactly where and when he wanted. But he hadn't counted on the combination outside the gate. Three people, sure. Mamma. Felix. That was as expected. But the third should not have been Pappa. *A customer causing trouble.* After all these years, Vincent couldn't come and meet his big brother?

Leo travelled south, through a Stockholm he hadn't seen for a long time. Past the suburban exits to Västertorp, Fruängen and Bredäng, and when he later reached the stretch where the old motorway ran parallel with the new, he couldn't resist turning in his seat for a glimpse of the woodland tract he had lain in evening after evening, on a carpet of moss and among the humming mosquitoes, in order to scout and map out the military control unit. Back then, when he was faceless and had no criminal record; when he lacked criminal contacts both outside and inside the walls; when he had emptied a military weapons caisson of two hundred and twenty-one automatic weapons without being noticed.

Now they knew who he was.

Now he must think and plan in a new way.

The slow journey took him through a landscape that seemed to never end, not limited by cell doors and concrete crowned with double-toothed, razor-blade-sharp barbed wire. He passed Salem and Rönninge and waved at the exit to Hall – Sweden's most oppressive prison, together with Kumla, and a place he had resided in three times when he was doing his time. The prison system operated like this – unannounced disciplinary removals in the early dawn – because an inmate should never know how the next day would look, shouldn't have time to build up relationships, networks. He was a risk factor, classified as highly dangerous, and if you can break into weapons caissons, you can bust out of prison cells later on.

Södertälje Bridge – he had forgotten that something as simple as a motorway bridge and a view of a canal below could be so beautiful. The abrupt right turn onto the E20, the motorway that ends somewhere at Sweden's coast, straight out to a sea towards the rest of the world. He

35

wouldn't drive that far, not yet, and he put on the brakes for the first time near a motorway sign giving the distance to Örebro and Strängnäs. He braked again at the next sign – a smaller blue and black one with an illustration of a bench beside a spruce tree next to the number 3. That meant a rest area and the first stage of his goal.

A long-distance lorry with Polish registration plates. Two toilets. A group of benches surrounded by rubbish bins.

That was all – no kiosk, no petrol station, the sort of place that looks the same after a long time in prison.

That was why he had picked out this site; it was here he had buried his cache.

He turned off the hire car's engine and stepped out into the streaming sun, which enticed him to yawn and stretch. He looked around. Just one person here. Balding, untended beard, an unfiltered cigarette in one corner of his mouth. A driver who spent his life behind the lorry's padded steering wheel.

Leo nodded to him, got a nod back and turned away. Vehicle after vehicle passed at high speed nearby while he looked around in the other direction, into the woodland – mostly pines and an occasional birch with heavy, hanging branches, here and there white patches of snow.

Sometime between bank robberies seven and eight he had stood exactly here and identified a tall, nearly round rock thirty-two paces away from the edge of the ditch. The first landmark. It had been autumn and early morning and it had smelled of compost. Now it smelled of meltwater, yellow grass and exhaust.

He moved to the car's boot and observed, before he opened it, how the lorry driver was still occupied in lighting cigarettes and blowing out smoke in old-fashioned rings. And when he opened the boot lid and looked down, everything was in place. The hire car, which had been prepaid and was waiting with a full tank at the service station in Västberga, had been stocked according to his instructions – the sports kitbag and the plastic tub and the folding spade to the left, the box with waterproof boots, compass and two preprogrammed mobile phones to the right.

He changed shoes, folded the jacket and waited out the lorry driver. Not until the driver had disappeared into the inside lane of the busy road and he was entirely convinced that no other living creature was approaching did Leo jump over the gravel-filled ditch with the kitbag on his shoulder and go into the spruce forest. His boots sank deep into the wet grass and heavy snow but he felt light, strong. During the last six months of his sentence he had filled much of his time with building up his muscles. Not bulk, like the others. Strength training – push-ups, lat pull-downs, lunges, sit-ups – fine-tuning a body that would never get in the way of its own movements. If he ended up in that situation once again – hunted by twenty-five elite police officers – he would move quicker and for a longer time than his pursuers.

He didn't remember the rock being so big; he felt over the rough surface with his hand at chest height until his fingertips discovered the narrow crevice. Cold, heavy snow came loose and fell down, but it was here he should stand, with his back against the crevice, to identify landmark number two.

The split tree.

One half was gone, decomposed for a long time, while the other half was reaching towards a crisp spring sky – he had already guessed the last time that it had been a lightning strike.

Correctly positioned, he turned his back to the remaining tree trunk and held the transparent compass against the glossy paper of the map. He twisted the compass housing until the meridian lines lay parallel with the lines on the map. The north arrow pointed to the north, the orienting arrow on the compass slanted to the left, and he began to walk the last ninety-two paces of the final stretch.

They had been everything to one another that day they were locked up in three different prisons – now one of them didn't even show up when they were to be reunited.

The irritation gnawed, chafed, didn't let go.

Fourteen paces.

All this time separated and his youngest little brother, whose nappies he had changed, who he'd prepared breakfast for, hadn't even been there!

Twenty-two paces.

Two mobile phones in his breast pocket: the one with the encryption program built in which he'd use later, and the ordinary one, pay as you go, without a registered subscriber, to contact one of the numbers that had been preprogrammed. He waited while the signal searched for purchase. One ring, another, another. No answer.

Twenty-seven paces.

He rang again. Several rings.

Or . . . twenty-eight?

Still no fucking answer.

Maybe twenty-nine?

Leo stopped, breathed deeply. That didn't help. He had totally lost count. The irritation was gliding across his skin and pricked everywhere like a needle, in, out, in, out.

He went back. Landmark two. The split tree, his back to the healthy trunk and the compass on the glossy paper of the map. And he began to walk and count again, at the same time as he rang the number for the third time.

Long rings. Then the voice he wanted.

'Hello . . . ?'

It had been a teenager's voice then, and now belonged to someone halfway between twenty and thirty.

'Hello yourself, little brother.'

Who was the same age he had been himself at the time of the arrest.

'Leo?'

'Yeah.'

'Is that you . . . Shit, I didn't recognise the number.'

'You weren't there today.'

'I . . .'

Fifteen paces.

'. . . shit, Leo, I'm sorry . . .'

It was easier to count now.

'. . . the job, you know, a customer who couldn't decide what fucking tile she wanted above the cooker.'

Leo's irritation began to fade slowly.

'The job? Mamma mentioned that. Vincent – so you have your own business!'

'Mmm.'

Six conversations from a telephone in a grubby prison corridor. One a year. That had been all the contact, and now – with the sound of someone opening a paint tin in the background – it became very clear. His little brother was actually at a construction site, living an adult life with a well-ordered workday.

'So when can we see each other?'

'See each other?'

'Yeah, Vincent. Meet. Naturally I want to see my youngest brother.'

'There's, well, a lot going on right now . . . Shit, I don't really know. I—'

'Tomorrow maybe? Or will you have a *customer* causing trouble then too?'

'Yes . . . maybe, I'll . . .'

'Are you trying to get out of seeing me, Vincent?'

'No. No, dammit. You know that. I just—'

'Well, then. Tomorrow at Mamma's. OK?'

'Sure. See you tomorrow.'

Thirty-two paces. The forest was so still, the sun piercing through the tight lattice of branches, the persistent rays heating up as they did in April. *Forty-four paces.* He avoided stepping into a muddy puddle, looked around and checked the compass one last time. *Fifty-seven paces.* The red arrow quavered under the plastic base plate and pointed towards the magnetic north pole, while the other arrow, the one in the compass housing, pointed towards his future.

Thirty-five paces left.

————————

Vincent held the phone for a long time, cradling it in his hand. The whole conversation was still there. Words he didn't want to utter again, to trot out again, as usual when you're ashamed.

If he turned off the ringtone, if he laid the phone on the tin of filler's lid with the display turned downward, then if it rang again, then with no sound, no light, he would not have to know. Not need to answer.

He was kneeling in a bathroom that was covered with standard white tiles, apart from a thin row of yellow-speckled mosaic tiles around a heart-shaped mirror, colour that seemed to ooze out of the wall and become a pus-filled sore.

He tried to smile at the image in the mirror.

It didn't work. The lips formed an uncertain straight line instead.

Are you trying to get out of seeing me?

If his voice had sounded as guilty as the eyes that were staring back at him now, then Leo had understood. A lie. From one brother to another.

Only the grouting left to do, the sticky, white paste that would make the tile wall come together. Out of the kitchen came the slapping sound of a wet roller as it applied paint onto a ceiling. One more day and this flat would be finished and the new owners could move in.

He tried to think away the anxiety.

Whatever, all thoughts were allowed, the more twisted the better, as

39

long as they kick-started his brain and drove away the hellish anxiety that had climbed into his chest in earnest a couple of weeks earlier and from there had crept upward – from the moment he had suddenly realised that his brother would be let out, that he was getting ready for his release.

He walked out into the hall, his steps echoing in empty rooms, and he looked around at what was his job now, his life. He had started the business half a year after his own release; no more foremen who asked about his past. Everything got going quickly and one job led to another, one satisfied customer becoming the next satisfied customer.

Employment that was enough, just: income that made the workday go round, but nothing more. But dammit, he had employed a worker part-time – those wet roller strokes that were painting the ceiling in the kitchen. From never having had any contact, they painted and nailed and tiled side by side now. But he hadn't told anyone yet, neither Felix nor Mamma. How could he when he couldn't explain *why* even to himself? Why he had offered employment to an additional pair of hands when his own were enough. Why a one-time case of stepping-in for a single paint job had turned into another and another.

'When you're done in here, there are a few small spots on the bathroom ceiling too.'

He had stopped at the doorway to the kitchen, following the painter's practised movements.

'In a minute. But here, have you seen this? The idiots want to have matt paint – not glossy. Who the fuck's that brainless – matt on a kitchen ceiling? And by the way, Vincent, who was that? Who were you talking to?'

He knew.

Vincent felt himself slipping closer. Closer to hazy memories.

He is seven years old when his father comes back and forces his way in through the front door and hall – furious and sober and with clenched fists that methodically smash Mamma.

That's why. Why he'd employed him. But, in spite of a couple of months among tins of paint and tile cutters, he hadn't come any closer to understanding those memories.

'Vincent?'

'Yes?'

'Who *was* that?'

The newly employed painter looked at him. It was a small flat, not more than a couple of metres between bathroom and kitchen, and sound easily carried through empty rooms. He had heard the whole conversation and gathered who had called.

'What do you mean, who?'

'The person you were talking to.'

'Nobody.'

Vincent swallowed down what was stuck in his throat. He had called Leo *nobody*.

'Nobody, Vincent? Who the fuck is that? Or do you sit there on the toilet and talk to the tiles?'

'You know who.'

Nobody.

'Leo. It was Leo. My big brother. Your oldest son.'

Nobody.

Vincent was ashamed, like before, when he looked into the kitchen and met his father's eyes, *their* father's eyes. The roller in the rough hand was lowered from the ceiling and wayward paint drops fell onto the hard protective lining paper.

'I was there, Vincent. This morning.'

Paint drops on lining paper. The kind of spill that he otherwise hated, which quickly stiffened on the surface so that, when you walked on it, it cracked like a soft-boiled egg and the sticky goo in the middle would get tracked onto other floors.

'When the gates were opened. When he came out.'

It was difficult to get bothered about paint on the heels of shoes when the rest of the world might collapse.

'You were . . . there?'

'Yes.'

'Without saying anything to me?'

His father placed the roller in the pan and leaned the long, grooved shaft against the wall and sat comfortably on a paint tin.

'Yes. It seemed best that way.'

'Best . . . that way?'

'Since you don't seem to want to talk about him.'

Ivan relaxed against the imaginary backrest of the paint tin, fished out a packet of rolling tobacco and the smaller, red-coloured one of Rizla rolling paper, and spread the light brown tobacco on one of the thin, dry sheets.

41

'Or am I wrong? Every time I try to talk about your brother, about Leo, you keep on . . . sanding or filling or whatever the fuck you're doing instead of answering.'

Ivan stood up, opened the window wide and took out his lighter in the wide window bay and drew in the first drag.

'You are my sons, you belong together. Dammit, I've taught you that and now it's more important than ever – you need to be able to keep together without robbing banks.'

'So you were there? At the wall?'

'Yes.'

'You were standing there, with Mamma and Felix?'

'Yes.'

Vincent moved around nervously, one foot very near the paint drops.

'Did you talk, did you say anything about . . . your working with me?'

'No. I don't want to meddle. You're all adults now.'

Ivan spat out small tobacco flecks into the spring air.

'So. The telephone call just now. Why were *you* not there?'

'I didn't have time.'

'Of course you had time, Vincent.'

His father looked at him, through him, with his head lowered and his chin jutting out and his gaze razor sharp, exactly the way Leo and Felix said he used to scrutinise them – he had been too young to register it back then and remember now.

'Don't push him away. He needs you. Don't you get it, Vincent? Leo can change. Like I did. Like you did. You are all still brothers, in spite of what happened.'

'I'm not pushing him away.'

Vincent took a step closer to his father. They were the same height and had bushy hair that made its way forward over two crowns in identical waves.

'It's not about that – I just couldn't stand there and wait. Not in front of those bloody walls, again. I don't ever want to see a prison again! Do you understand, Pappa? I was seventeen when we started. Seventeen! And behind those fucking bars of Mariestad prison I got it. That it was me, then. That it was me, who at the age of seventeen, jumped over checkout desks with a machine gun over my shoulder. And that fucking isn't me now. *Never again.*'

He let the anger subside. He had learned to do that. It would be hissed

42

out in small doses, like fiery fumes. If you let too much ooze out all at once, it didn't ebb away. Quite the opposite, it grew and demanded more space.

'I *will* see him. Tomorrow. We're having lunch.'

'You and Leo?'

'Me and Leo and Felix . . . and Mamma.'

'Her too?'

Shit. He hadn't planned to mention Mamma, who wanted to gather her sons together at her house. It was unnecessary. Maybe even unkind.

'Yeah, it was her idea to . . . you know, at her place.'

An indifferent look. His father tried to glance at him nonchalantly before he grabbed the long, grooved pole to roll more paint onto the roller. But he wasn't indifferent. Not on the inside. Vincent was sure of that. Every time he tried to get close – which was the whole idea, to get close to a different father, having entirely missed the earlier one – the words had frozen inside the heavy body, encapsulated and unformed. The only thing he had learned was that his father never let him in by talking about himself.

And that nothing would come out now either. So while Ivan was spreading the matt paint on the roller onto the other half of the kitchen ceiling, Vincent turned towards the sink and tap and he filled the pail with water and mixed the grout. *Leo can change.* Wide, gentle arm motions, kneeling on the hard floor filling in the spaces between the tiles. *Like you. Like me.* Just a few days ago the bathroom had been framed by chocolate-brown, very glossy tiles halfway up and then yellow and orange flowery wallpaper that took over for the rest of the wall up to the ceiling. Now everything was chalky white. The change was simple and beautiful on the outside. But in the world Leo had just left, you wake up every morning, face the daily routine and know all that shit is just a thin veil covering the violence on the ladder that everyone clings to. And you participate because you have to and you hold on tight as you struggle to be free, as the kicks hit the snitch, who won't be able to stand, sit or piss afterwards. What he himself experienced, Leo of course had also experienced. His big brother, whom he loved so much and who once was everything to him, had served a longer time behind the concrete, in even worse prisons. That meant there were more clinging to the very top of the ladder of violence.

Yeah. He had lied just now on the telephone. Not because he was avoiding him – because he was afraid. Afraid that when Leo was outside

43

those walls, he would continue to plan crimes that required his brothers' involvement.

———————

Twelve paces remaining. And he recognised it – the expanse of grass and moss enclosed by a metre-high stone, a single beautiful fir tree and two low-growing birches.

Leo's breathing was calm and he felt at ease. To stand here like this, thirty-two paces plus thirty-seven paces plus ninety-two paces in a forest away from a rest area in northern Södermanland, somewhere between Södertälje and Strängnäs, it was as if no time at all had passed. He remembered everything so well.

He whisked away tufts of grass, moss and brown leaves. The folding spade's edge was sharp and cut through meandering roots in the black soil. Thirty centimetres down. No deeper. There he bumped against it – the cover under protective plastic that could be torn away; an end cap that had been carefully protected with insulation tape and then gaffer tape. In about a minute the spade edge had carved its way through every layer. The cover itself could be screwed off. The inside was rounded, made of smooth, hard grey plastic. An ordinary PVC pipe, or soil pipe as it was called when it had sprung a leak at someone's house and the stench wafted out into the house. There was no smell of sewage, shit or marsh here. It smelled of motor oil.

Next to the pipe was another one just like it. Plastic, sleeve cover, tape. He had buried two of them vertically in the ground.

His own 'safe house'. If everything went to hell, he would always have a way out. And it had gone that way. A failed robbery and then a policeman named John Broncks.

Leo lay down on his stomach and stuck his right arm down into one of the grey pipes, which pointed upwards. He felt the black rubbish bag and the thick motor oil. And then, a piece of metal. It too was rounded.

He pulled up the black rubbish bags, one assault rifle out of each pipe, greased and wrapped up in layer after layer of plastic wrap. And as he reached deeper down, his hand felt around under them. First he reached the packets of ammunition, twenty bullets in each, vacuum-packed to protect them against fluctuations between hot and cold, as well as condensation that would have made them useless. Then, under them in turn, were the packets of banknotes, warm clothes, safety razors, scissors and hair

44

dye. He counted the money, kept half and put the other half back, together with the clothes and supplies for changing his appearance. These were intended for escape. Then he carried soil and grass and leaves and moss to the hole and raked over the whole area with a branch to wipe away footprints.

A quick look at his watch. Four hours and twenty-three minutes left. He was in a hurry.

That cop's brother was likely wondering where the hell he was.

BACK THROUGH THE FOREST barely woken by spring, the kitbag full and a little heavier on the axle with ten kilos of assault rifles, ammunition and money. He crept carefully forward the last bit to the rest area – not to be seen, never to leave tracks. Two new long-distance lorries had stopped there while he was hiking and digging. Now they were close to the busy European road, parked temporarily in front of the car he'd hired for the day. Leo crept closer, hidden by two rather small fir trees. The transport vehicles had Lithuanian registration. Two youngish drivers were smoking, chatting and laughing. He waited them out, just as he had done before with the Polish driver, until they had had time to drive a good distance away in the inner lane and no one else was on the way in. Then he hurried to the car, opened the boot and lowered the plastic bags with the weapons down into the empty plastic tub.

Not far to the next medium-sized town, Strängnäs, which had a large enough population to have a do-it-yourself car wash. The woman behind the checkout at the petrol station had a beautiful smile and a friendly voice. She explained that behind the station there were three large washing bays of the same size with solid walls between them, that one of them would be available soon and that the shortest possible booking time was an hour. He paid for it and for a degreasing agent. He was on his way out when he turned back.

'I'd also like a tin of lube oil. Regular 5-56 would be fine.'

'Something that jams?'

'More to be on the safe side. So that something *won't* jam.'

'Yeah, it works for most things, I use it myself to fix my cycle chain and—'

'Thanks.'

Three identical cubed structures about the size of typical garages. Through the window in the folding door to the left he caught a glimpse of a local taxi. It was probably the taxi owner himself who was wiping the dark blue car roof. To the right, an older car with extra lights, foglights, dual exhausts and a bumper sticker that said 'Volvo Top Dog' was being carefully pressure-washed by a very young man with a gold cap turned backwards. So the cube in the middle was available and Leo backed the hire car in, with the boot turned away from view. It had real walls on each side, exactly as the woman at the cash register had promised, not the flimsy kind of hanging walls that exposed more than they hid.

He began by washing the car, not especially carefully, but it needed to have a slightly wet, nicely clean shine when he drove out again in a little while. He verified again that the car blocked the view in one direction and that the three walls took care of the rest. He opened the boot, took out the plastic tub holding the black rubbish bags and spilled them out on the floor of the car wash. Two AK4s. Before he'd buried them, he'd thoroughly greased the metal and then smeared on thick motor oil, as much as possible, both rifles bathed in it, and finally encased them in plastic. Not so that the oil would stay there – so that water wouldn't get in. With grease and oil they never rusted. Encase them properly and drop them down into the pipe and they could stay there for ever. As long as the accompanying ammunition was properly vacuum-packed, the depth of the hole didn't mean a thing.

Now all that had to go.

Leo unwound the plastic wrap, layer by layer. He drowned the weapons in both petroleum and alkaline degreasing agents, let it work awhile and flushed all the surfaces with the high pressure hose like the guy in the gold cap with his Volvo in the next garage – but on full force. Weapons are not as fragile as car engines. He blew them clean and dry with compressed air. Last he dried them off with one of the rags that were hanging on the hooks over the hose and sprayed them with lubricant.

He left the petrol station and headed for route 55 north, via Strängnäs Bridge with its fantastic view of Lake Mälaren's still, glittering water and with two ready-to-fire automatic weapons in the boot. Twenty-one kilometres according to Sam's directions, from the beautiful bridge to the ferry landing to the car ferry that left once an hour, a car trip through the original Sweden. In these woods the runestones were jostling with Bronze Age graves, and on the edge of the road were signs for bed-and-breakfasts and flea markets. He was supposed to turn right then at the country store and drive a little slower the last bit on a winding, badly repaired, godforsaken road.

Sam.

A friend.

Someone he even trusted.

He who never trusted anyone outside the family circle, and yet he had learned to do exactly that. In spite of the rage, the hate he'd felt the first time they spoke to each other.

———————

A sleepy morning, yet another shift with the wood blocks and screws. Leo had stood up, stretched and seen, through the window, a car parked outside the prison gate. And then, when a man about forty years old climbed out of the driver's seat, something in him snapped, exploded and became waves pushed up to his throat in a yell. Blind fury felt like this. That fucking cop! Broncks even looked like he had on the last day of the trial. Shit, if he wasn't even wearing the same clothes – jeans, leather jacket, ordinary shoes. A moment later the yell came back, stronger.

The prisoner on the other side of the corridor in the middle, cell 7, was called Sam Larsen. He was serving a life sentence – the prison guards had come and got him for an unannounced visit. Just that cop and Larsen together in a narrow visitors' room! Broncks must be there to receive information. Broncks, who had carried out the investigation, framed him and split apart three brothers and their father but lacked both the weapons cache and evidence for most of the bank robberies the prosecutor was aiming for. And now he was visiting Sam Larsen, head of the prison council, with access to all the fucking gossip.

That afternoon Leo set foot uninvited into a fellow prisoner's cell for the first time.

Confronted him.

Spoke of rules of conduct, the prison's age-old rules, the sex offenders on the bottom just like the snitches, the phony ethics he hadn't cared about – a sort of hierarchy for those who chose being locked up as a lifestyle and who didn't interest him. He wasn't a criminal in that sense. He asked his questions only on his own account and was only interested in protecting himself and his brothers.

Sam stared and waited him out.

'Are you done?'

'No.'

And then he came closer.

'Then see to it that you are – if you want to leave my cell without broken bones.'

48

'A little snitch? Threatening? It's usually the other way round, isn't it? Especially if everyone here knows before long.'

So close that everything was blurred.

'Will you listen?'

'Yeah?'

'That fucking cop you're talking about . . . he came here to let me know my mother died. So show a little respect and get out of my cell. Let me grieve in peace.'

No more threats. No raised voice.

There had been no need.

The prisoner who had forced his way into cell 7 felt stupid and ashamed and he left.

It was of course later, after being locked in the cell in the evening with a long night ahead, that Leo thought a lot about why a police officer, a detective in the investigation squad, had a job description that included informing prisoners if their mothers had passed away. He'd come to the conclusion that a detective wouldn't be likely to. That Sam Larsen hadn't told the whole truth. That tomorrow morning he'd have to make another visit to that cell, and that he wouldn't leave until everything was said.

———

The winding, narrow, bumpy road ultimately did have an end. Having arrived, after the sharp bend and the clearing two deer fled into, Leo faced beautiful blue water and a bright yellow cable ferry. Arnö was visible on the other side of the sound. It was always difficult to judge distance across lakes and seas but he guessed it was just about a kilometre. He looked at the display on his mobile phone. It was almost one o'clock and in a minute the ferryman would come out of the red wooden house, fold up the boom gate and turn on the engine for a short, five-minute trip between the mainland and one of Lake Mälaren's islands, five minutes that divided silence from still more silence. Twelve year-round residents and not that many holidaymakers, that was how Sam described the island. Thus it was the perfect place to be able to prepare and to be able to dismantle everything undisturbed. He drove on board, answered the ferryman's wave and, when they had left the land, he got out of the car to breathe the fresh air, look down into the water and follow the white swirls that played about the boat's hull.

———

He had done it, made a second visit, forced his way into cell number 7 where Sam Larsen was standing with his back towards the door making his bed. The unwritten, the forbidden. Despite the agreed signal – the red string that Sam had wound around the door handle and which, in that cellblock, meant stay the hell away, don't bother me – he went in uninvited. It gave the advantage. The man in the cell wasn't prepared. Leo had opened the door carefully and examined the broad shoulders, aware that the inmate in front of him was clearly bigger than he was himself, and stronger. He had been transforming frustration into musculature in the prison gym for a period of twenty years. A single blow was all he'd have if Sam decided to lunge, to act. If dialogue were replaced by violence, Leo would go for the larynx. And after a perfect punch right there, the snitch wouldn't be able to talk with that fucking cop again either.

'You were lying yesterday.'

Sam turned around quickly. But didn't attack. After a moment, he answered, not even raising his voice. The unreasonable aggression between them, the unexpressed, impending threat, the mutual hate and hostility that filled every breath in the seven-square-metre room, was obvious nevertheless.

'Excuse me?'

'How much did you squeal? You're running around out there in the cellblock with your big ears, snatching up everything, and then pissing all over me by trying to hide the shit behind an incredibly stupid explanation – that a cop would come here just to say a mother is dead.'

'Kindly back off. Out. Now.'

'Yesterday. That Broncks cop. And you – together in a fucking visitors' room. What did he want to learn from his own little prison rat? Where the guns are? How he should search for the booty from the bank robberies he couldn't get us for?'

Put any of the other prisoners in this section, in the entire facility, in the same situation, in the same cell, and there'd be blood flowing out of the walls.

'Hey, you listen!'

'What?'

'I think it is . . . well, rather unfortunate that you don't respect the string and come into my cell without knocking. I had thought better of you. You fooled him, that Broncks cop, for quite a long time. A couple of years. And I liked that.'

It was as if it was already at that point of some sort of extraordinary meeting. In the middle of hate, of threats, they somehow belonged together.

'You know, his mother died also.'

'What?'

'You heard me.'

Leo heard, but hadn't understood at first.

'He is your . . . brother?'

'Yes.'

'The cop who came to visit – the one we're talking about? Broncks?'

'Yes.'

'Broncks – your brother? You have different last names, but you are the BROTHER of the fucking cop who got me?'

'Yeah. Police officer. But also my brother. Police officer, brother. You know how it can be with brothers, Leo, if anyone does. Our mother was the link we still had. The only one. Now that she's dead, John and I never need to speak to each other again.'

There and then, with that conversation, began to grow something which over time would slowly become friendship, then deep trust. They certainly had a lot in common.

They both hated the cop named Broncks.

They were both locked up in a high-security prison.

They both had grown up as the oldest brother in worlds built around the same structure – a mother who held the family together, a father who broke it apart.

––––––––––

Three winding kilometres, even more beautiful if that was possible, even more of a country idyll. He drove through thick forest, open fields, past the thirteenth-century church and the manor house and the fort from the 700s and turned – as Sam had instructed him – at the curve by the old school which at another time had been full of noisy, playing children but was now empty, echoing. Leo slowed down when he glimpsed the water again and then the red fence. He made his way across the whole island to a little, similarly red house, which hid behind five spreading, unkempt apple trees.

And there he was. Just as big, a goddamn heavyweight, crossing with powerful steps over the lawn to the car. They hugged each other just as everybody did in prisons, sort of a habit that stayed. Two and a half months. They hadn't seen each other since Sam's release. After, Leo realised how much he valued it, had taken it for granted, and how much and how deeply you could miss a true friend behind walls and locked doors. Then, after twenty-three years, Sam had had his life sentence commuted, the time was set and he was released.

A few deep breaths. Forest air. It had a stronger taste. A fly, buzzing insistently, criss-crossed his face. Birds of prey, a pair, circled high above. Otherwise, calm. Not a single human.

'And completely cop-proof?'

Sam smiled. They both knew who he was referring to.

'The most cop-proof place in the country. My brother hates this house. You can figure out why, of course, since you know a lot about me. About us.'

He slung his trunk over the shoulder and they walked over the grass towards the wildly growing apple trees and the wooden cabin, which seemed even smaller now that he came close to it. The door was ajar and Sam showed him in to a bedroom, then another. They'd clearly come in from the back.

'The loo's in there. There's the tiny sitting room. And there's the kitchen. Forty-seven square metres.'

Sam pointed to the two bedrooms.

'It's cramped, like two cells. Mamma and Pappa in that room, John and me in a bunk bed in there. Every summer until I was eighteen, when I switched to another cell. Then the summers had a little less sun and swimming.'

Leo lingered a little, his eyes on what had been the parents' bedroom, on the unmade double bed.

'You sleep there?'

Hesitation. As if Leo had nothing to do with that.

'There aren't any more beds here.'

'You should be the one to hate this house, for God's sake, not your cop brother.'

'I thought I did when I first came here after being released, but instead I felt . . . enormous peace. Understand?'

'No. Not at all. I would never go back to *my* childhood.'

The sitting room was small – armchair, table from the sixties, TV – the sort of room a visitor just passes through on the way to the kitchen with its slanted cabinets, Windsor-style chairs and black woodstove. And the kitchen table – which had been laid with one year's worth of robbery planning: the rolled-up map in A3 format; the moving box with masks, boots, bulletproof vests; the driving licence, with a photo of Sam but someone else's name, John Martin Erik Lundberg; the two work overalls, one blue, one black.

And on the sofa in the kitchen, there was something that would be used in a couple of days, on the final job: the first half of the police identifications with photos of himself – with a shaved head, taken on leave from prison nearly a year ago – and of Sam. Next to these stood the 3D printer for metal alloys, ordered in Shanghai and slipped through to Sweden via customs in Leipzig, the prerequisite for being able to produce the other halves of the identifications.

'And the milk lorry?'

'Jari is parking it behind the unloading bay right now.'

'And we trust him? Still?'

'Look, someone who gets things like these, he's taking it seriously.' Sam fished out the driving licence and held it out to Leo who slid his thumb over the plastic surface.

'Yeah. Genuine. Even the embossed S. And the UV. That's exactly what they'll do, Sam, when the milk lorry needs to go through the roadblocks. The police do it unconsciously, running their thumbs over the driving licence. And with the lorry ready to go and already in place . . . whatever happens, even if they block off the entire shopping centre, *it will be able to drive off*. After the transformation, the magic, the camouflage. When the cops start screening the idiots who are desperately trying to get out, if the guy sitting in the front seat isn't wearing a mask any more and doesn't fit the description, then a milk lorry will sail right through. Especially with a cargo space that's easily checked since it contains only . . . milk.'

Leo had put the trunk down on the kitchen floor. Now he opened it. Inside were two thoroughly cleaned and newly greased AK4s and enough ammunition should the robbers be forced to shoot their way out. He handed one to Sam and kept the other for himself.

'We have time to check two points on our list at most.'

'I don't understand why we have to be in such a hurry. We've been planning this for a year, Leo, in detail. And now we don't even have the time to go through the *entire* first robbery.'

One year. All the meetings taking place in Sam's cell, with the red string clearly wound around the door handle. That was how a prison worked, the surfaces of contact were multiplied and the only thing they all had in common was crime – a greenhouse for criminality with the meeting's participants already in place, locked up together. They had met almost daily, sitting on the bed and the single chair in Sam's cell. They drilled each part into their heads. They had ticked off times, guard routines, escape routes, vehicles. But after Sam's release, they had spoken not a word of it because of the risk of being bugged. So it had become Sam's mission to complete alone the part that could only be prepared out in the world.

'I get what's going on here, Sam. You have been in jail a fucking lot of years and been classified as a high-risk prisoner, but you've never robbed a bank. You're nervous. Trying to put it off.'

Leo reached for the rolled-up map, pushed off the rubber band and unfurled the picture of the place that would be visited soon.

'Right? But you know why we've been in a hurry. And that robberies work if I plan them. And that if we don't do it now, it will be too late, for good.'

Sam didn't answer, he didn't need to – Leo knew of course that he got it.

Their joint plan: four stages over four days.

The first, which they had given the name *the milking stool* during the course of planning, would be in just a few hours. The second, *the house call*, tomorrow. The third, *the test*, in two days and the fourth, *the police station*, as the conclusion. It was then, at 14.00, that the transport departed. On the last Thursday of every month, normally carrying small sums. But this time was unique. It would take several years before the next time when it would carry anything even approaching this volume.

Take back what didn't exist. In the greatest heist ever. And at the same time, bring down the fucking cop that locked him and his brothers up. Then vanish for ever.

'Here. The first point to go over.'

Leo had placed a glass on each corner of the map to hold down paper that stubbornly tried to roll itself up again.

'We are still expecting six cash cassettes with banknotes. Only five hundreds. Around five or six million kronor – exactly as much as we need.'

He pointed to a cross in a square inside a bigger square at about the centre of the map. Then he held up his gun, aimed at something and patted the gun barrel lightly.

54

'Our very own master key. The moment the ATMs signal *temporarily out of order*, that means the guards have opened them on the inside and it's time to use it, Sam: the fat master key. To open the security door while they are standing there with their trousers down and the safe, with its alarm disabled, wide open. They're most on their guard when they're carrying the money in. When they close the door, they feel safe. That's when we start shooting for the first time. You in blue overalls – the Blue Robber. But we shouldn't shoot straight in, the bullets would wound or, in the worst case, kill someone. So it's best to shoot away the lock at an angle. Then the bullet won't ricochet; it will get stuck in the concrete wall. That's why we're using Swedish army ammunition – it has a thicker and harder casing. That's why we are using Swedish army guns, to avoid shooting straight like you have to with a Russian AK47, and then there's just a bloody mess on the inside.'

The unfurled map also hid two green rings among all the crosses and arrows. Leo pointed to them now, his fingertips fitting precisely inside the circles.

'Next point. The moment when everything is decided. The vehicle exchange – the transformation when the robbers cease to exist. This is what amateurs don't plan – the moment you have to own if you don't want to give the cops the upper hand.'

That's what the green rings meant: vehicles 1 and 2.

'A vehicle change that happens right before their eyes.'

He had talked about that in particular so many times. Yet it was just what Sam wanted and needed to hear. All they had rehearsed and memorised was no longer a distant plan – it was reality.

'Once before a bank robbery I parked two identical cars, one at each exit of a small town, same colour and model and number plates. The tips came flooding in to the cops from two different directions and that forced your goddamn cop brother to set up two search routes while we got away. Another time, I changed the first getaway car just a couple of hundred metres from the bank we had just robbed while people were walking by eating hot dogs, and your brother didn't get that we had parked the car next to one like it, already there – two delivery vans pointing in different directions – and that we were able to go from one vehicle to the next without it being seen from the outside. But, Sam, I've never been in on this before, switching the getaway car at the very scene of the crime, *while* the cops are watching. And nobody else has done it either.'

His voice sounded just as pleased and certain as he felt – aiming to calm the other man, who in a couple of hours was going to shoot automatic weapons at other people for the first time, and to get him to understand that, if a robber of security vans acts during that gap that violence creates, he freezes time for both those who are lying down to take cover on the floor and for those who are radioing a message through that robbers are shooting wildly. A free zone. Time for the robber to act without hindrance.

'And it's you, Sam, who'll sit behind the wheel at the crucial moment – when the car approaches the police roadblock. It's *you* they'll look at. If *you* are calm, the cops will be calm. They're going to be looking for robbers, not milk cartons. They're going to be looking for black and blue overalls and automatic weapons, and if the driver and his assistant are wearing green-and-white uniforms and have proper driving licences and don't act nervous . . . then when the cops run their fucking thumbs over the identification information, they'll be relieved and state that *the vehicle seems OK, a regular milk lorry, drive through, we have more interesting vehicles to inspect.*'

On the floor next to the woodstove was a rusty metal box filled with birch wood, carefully cut and chopped firewood in white birch bark with a bit of moss on it. Leo picked up two logs and then felt around with his fingers at the bottom of the metal box, looking for kindling to start the fire with until he found three straggling, sharp birch chips.

'Does it work properly?'

He opened the cast iron doors of the woodstove, which made a low creaking sound.

'Yes. Perfectly. It helps me avoid those electric heaters, and it gives off a nice warmth from the chimney that's enough for the whole house on any winter day.'

The firewood was thrown into the square stove opening, the thin sticks beneath and between them. It took a while before the flames settled down and fell together. The familiar crackling of dry wood accompanied the conversation.

'OK then, Leo.'

He saw Sam take one of the bottles down from the shelf over the cooker. Aquavit. At least he guessed that's what it was. The bottle had no label. Sam took two small glasses from the dish drainer and poured some.

'I got this from the fellow who runs the ferry. He makes it himself.

Always spiced only with plants that grow wild on the island. This run has elderflowers and something else that I haven't been able to figure out.'

'No, thanks, not now, not before the first robbery.'

'You got to talk to make me calm. Now it's my turn to make you calm.'

'I said no thanks, Sam.'

'And I heard you. But it's not about drinking or not drinking a few centilitres of alcohol. It's about us being free now. And we can do whatever the fuck we want.'

Leo took the glass hanging there in the air in Sam's hand, and brought it towards his mouth. It smelled of elderflowers. And juniper berries, Leo was sure of it, maybe even tormentil. But he didn't take a drink.

'No. We aren't free, yet. When we are sitting on the boat on the way to Riga and St Petersburg and Sberbank Rossii, *then*, in the suite, we'll drink. Fuck it, we'll bring in a case of champagne. *Then* we'll be free, Sam.'

In one motion he gestured a toast in the thin air, lowered the glass down to the sink and poured out the drink that smelled of elderflowers and juniper berries. Then he reached for the unfurled map, with a last glance at the cross in a square inside a still bigger square next to numerous other squares in Sweden's largest trade area, before he opened the cast iron door to the fire and stuffed the map in. The paper went up in flames, smoked a little and broke down to grey ash.

NONE OF THE AFTERNOON customers knew that a human being would be lying lifeless in his own blood on the asphalt in the middle of the car park in four and a half minutes. At this very moment they were just getting out of their cars and going into the shops in the huge mall.

Nor could any of the hundreds of eager customers know as they waited patiently in the business complex's countless queues, getting ready to pay for their items and then walk out through the automatic doors with heavy bags in their hands.

Nor did a single one of the guards in the security van, rolling slowly over the asphalt wet with April rain.

This lack of awareness of impending death also encompassed the two masked men, one in blue overalls, one in black overalls, who were sitting in the front seat of the black Audi RS 7, the current year's model, parked right outside the shopping centre's main entrance, a vehicle the police would wrongly identify as a classic getaway car when they arrived.

16:14:10

The car doors burst open simultaneously. One guard's back was so broad that it was pulling apart the seams of his brownish-black uniform jacket when he climbed out in front of a square in a still bigger square next to plenty of other squares – building supplies shops linked to electronics retailers, supermarkets, furniture dealers and a lot of other sorts of shops. And here and there in the cubist pattern they'd been placed strategically in blue and white shells – the ATMs, the cash machines, the prerequisite for commerce. The other guard, a woman who was wearing her work uniform more casually, held the security case in a steady grip. And despite the fact that it wouldn't actually be a particularly big problem for a potential robber to break into the silver-grey case's outer shell with a blowtorch, she knew it was impossible to get to the paint capsules inside the casing. They would be triggered if a robbery took place during the short walk between the vehicle and the security room.

58

The glass doors slid open gently and the guards went into the warm shopping centre to two of the cash machines that were built into the wall. The display on the screens read *insert your card*.

Soon, when the guards had reached the security room and started switching the cash cassettes, the message would change to *out of order*. Not just a signal for young shoppers to wait for a while, but also a signal for two armed robbers to begin.

Instead of continuing straight ahead and into the aisles with stacks of products, the guards veered towards the café and betting shop. Leaning over benches attached to the wall, a couple of young women in quilted jackets were filling in the week's betting slips, and a taxi driver and two fathers with prams drank coffee in plastic cups at colourful corrugated cardboard tables. The two watchmen helped move a walking frame that was blocking the security room's door. They took out a bunch of keys, unlocked the door and cast a methodical look back before they went in.

16:14:40

Outside the café's elongated windows, no one noticed what was happening inside an illegally parked black Audi. The tinted car windows made it hard to perceive that the Blue Robber, who was sitting in the passenger seat, held up binoculars pointed at the ATM screens.

16:15:05

The security room was cramped – room for just a wooden chair and a wobbly plastic table beside the back of the ATMs, which in fact consisted of the doors to the safe. The key and magnetic card reader were required to open it. The male guard pulled the nearly empty cash cassettes out of the ATMs while his female co-worker lifted the lid of the security case and revealed the six replacement cassettes with unfolded banknotes. And it was when she was placing the third cassette into the ATM to the right that the little room exploded.

Eight blasts spread a ferocious cloud of coarse-grained dust, while thousands of splinters struck the walls and ceiling, and cut their faces and hands like pieces of glass.

Silence, a few seconds.

Then five shots as bullets penetrated the bolt and flew at an angle into the wall, which hissed back and spat out more chips, forcing the guards, their hearts beating, to press themselves down against the floor.

The next impression was not sound. Vibrations. From rough soles stepping on the fragments of concrete, crunching under the grooved rubber surfaces.

One of the robbers, in black overalls, aimed at the female guard who was trying to turn her gaze towards the steps. Her eyes were bloodshot from the dust and, when she blinked, tears squeezed out and became a grey mass that settled below and above her eyelashes, glue that dried between each blink. So she couldn't see that the robbers' faces were covered with black masks, that the blue overalls were identical to the black, or that one of them was carrying a large nylon bag over his shoulder.

Neither could she see the automatic weapons, or the hand that pressed her head very hard against the floor.

She couldn't even scream.

A short, low moan was all that was left in her, drowned out by the loudspeaker outside announcing the week's special offers to customers who still hadn't realised that they were in the middle of a violent robbery.

16:15:45

Sharp, thin plastic was tightened around the guards' wrists and ankles.

Tape strips were pressed firmly over their lips.

Earplugs were pushed into their ear canals.

Dark pillowcases were pulled down over their heads.

They were now completely isolated from impressions of the outside world.

16:16:10

The Black Robber passed the shattered security door and aimed his weapon into a department store, which quickly emptied out. The customers who hadn't managed to escape took cover behind pillars, shelving and checkout counters. He continued towards the entrance and car park and the panicked people throwing themselves down on the asphalt. Then he fired, above them. He emptied the magazine, changed it and emptied the next one.

Everyone was to be frightened away, not to be confused with those who were on the way.

He was then careful to walk back and forth in front of the department store entrance so that the door opened and closed every time he set off the detector. He held the gun in two hands, aiming it upwards. Those who would arrive soon would see his powerful weapon just as clearly as they would the getaway car parked next to him.

16:16:40

The picture was easy to take in.

Deserted. A robber keeping watch. Doors of the getaway car open, the engine idling.

It was then that the first police car stormed into the car park. The distance wasn't more than fifty metres between a not-yet-fired round and the front of the police car.

Between control and chaos.

16:17:00

The Blue Robber was prepared – that was of course part of the plan. Nonetheless he flinched at the shots, heard almost as clearly in the security room as out there in the car park. They knew that the nearest police station was only a couple of kilometres away and so had expected that the first patrol car would arrive promptly. It was the Black Robber's job to shoot, wildly. To frighten. The police would understand that the robbers had guns as powerful as the ones they were equipped with themselves and that they couldn't hide behind their cars – projectiles from an AK4 cut up protective sheet metal as if it were paper.

While the shooting continued outside, the Blue Robber assured himself that the two guards remained lying on their stomachs with their hands and feet restrained and heads covered with cloth.

It was absolutely crucial that they couldn't see what he would do now.

The nylon bag he had carried over his shoulder was on the floor in front of him, with its contents revealed – six green-and-white milk cartons, all in the one-and-a-half-litre size. He picked up one of them, holding it by the top and bottom, and in the one motion pulled it apart. It was completely drained of liquid. And in two parts, held together by an inner glued edge.

He put one of the banknote cassettes in the lower portion and pressed on the upper. The joint was virtually invisible. The first prepared milk carton, transformed into a storage place before the robbery, now contained nine hundred thousand kronor. He placed it in the bag and repeated the procedure five times – the remaining five cash cassettes. At the same time he heard the shooting escalate out in the car park. What had begun with single blasts had developed into fierce, turbulent drumming.

The Blue Robber sensed the smell even before he saw the light yellow spreading out and darkening the stone floor. With a powerful jerk, he lifted the bag up to keep the male guard's body fluids from soaking it.

He threw the strap of the bag over his head so that it hung on his left shoulder and rested on his right hip. Then he ran to the entrance to signal to the Black Robber that the first phase was completed.

Each new step left a successively drier shoeprint of urine behind.

16:18:05

The two police cars that arrived first were shot to pieces. But they were parked where they would block the exit effectively. The black-clad robber's bullets had forced the four police officers to seek shelter on the ground. And, not at first realising just how a military-grade automatic weapon damages vehicles, they could smell it now, burnt rubber from the interior as the shooter's bullets penetrated the sheet metal body of the car.

16:18:15

Six full cash cassettes in milk cartons, which in turn lay in a nylon bag, hung over the shoulder of the robber in blue overalls. From his position just inside the entrance he yelled *done* to the robber in black overalls.

They would now turn back in again. That was how they planned the robbery in cell 7 on block H. The police, who were waiting for reinforcements while they pressed down against the ground behind the vehicles perforated by bullets, would believe that the robbers were cut off from their getaway car and therefore taking shelter in the shopping centre.

What the robbers hadn't expected, however, was that the reinforcements would get there so quickly. That there, somewhere in the row of parked cars, eight police officers from the swat team had already moved forward, metre by metre, taken their positions and were ready for action.

Nor had they expected that the police would be prepared to meet violence with violence on a whole new level than they had done during the series of robberies several years earlier.

16:18:25

The right leg buckled first. The fabric fluttered around the entrance wound, like when the nozzle on a balloon releases air. Then the leg's muscles stopped cooperating.

When the robber in black overalls fell backwards, he aimed the gun barrel in the direction that he gathered the return fire came from, and let loose a new, brief series of shots.

He tried to get up again and sensed another person's hand reaching out and taking his, support that replaced a leg that did not bear his weight. A hand that held and dragged him towards the doors of the entrance.

It was then that he felt the three hard thuds at stomach height before the fifth bullet found its way into the area where the bulletproof vest wasn't closed tightly.

That was his last conscious thought . . .

. . . since the sixth bullet hit the back of his head and exited through his forehead.

16:18:40

Sam was holding a dead hand.

He felt it, just as he felt that it was bone fragments and blood that hit him exactly where the cut-out holes on the robber's mask bared his own skin.

He let a lifeless body fall to the ground, ran back to the entrance and waited for the next bullet that would bore its way into blue overalls, into *his* body. He had to get out of the line of fire. That was the only thing he could think of.

Into the shopping centre.

He must get himself to getaway vehicle 2 and carry out the rest of the plan alone.

Sam heard the glass in the entrance doors shatter behind him. The

63

bullets had missed. He was in. He ran to the part of the building where food was sold and followed the sketch that they had carefully drawn together.

He hopped over a chrome fence and landed between baskets of cherry tomatoes and boxes of lemons gleaming under the hissing mist. He knocked over a pile of cucumbers when he veered off to the left and rushed through the aisle where various forms of pasta were crowded in with Italian sauces in jars. Next he would force open the swinging doors of the stockroom. He was on his way there with the bag over his shoulder and the gun he was holding tightly onto.

All of a sudden he stopped. Not for long, just for a couple of breaths – while he realised what was happening.

People were running away from him.

No one came into the area he had control of. He was the one who didn't belong, who frightened and drove people away. And if he concentrated, really listened, he could hear their breathing too – the customers who were hiding behind the freezer cabinets; someone crying, someone else mumbling incoherently. The only thing that seemed normal was the voice from the loudspeaker that continued to entice customers with the week's offers.

Three shots.

The swinging doors crackled, started to open up and he ran into the stockroom to the rolled-up gateway that led him to the loading dock.

16:19:25

The lorry – which had large pictures of milk on its side – was there exactly where Jari had parked it in advance before the robbery. Across from waste management and cold storage for goods that had passed their expiration date. A good location, inconspicuous but without seeming hidden.

The traffic, a short distance away, seemed to be still flowing normally. If he was lucky, it meant that the police hadn't had time to put up roadblocks.

And it was at that moment, when he jumped down from the loading dock and ran to the milk lorry, that he realised he was shaking. His whole body was vibrating as in an aftershock. He was forced to hold his hands together hard until the knuckles whitened before he had the strength to open the back doors to the space filled with milk pallets.

64

Each pallet had room for eight crates, each holding sixteen milk cartons. But in the upper one, which Sam lifted down, six cartons were missing. There, in that hole, he placed the six specially prepared ones, which now contained cassettes filled with five-hundred-kronor notes.

He pulled off the blue overalls and the robber's mask, put them in the shoulder bag and shoved it in the middle of the next milk crate – just like in the crate before it where six cartons were removed. So the bag was surrounded and covered.

The automatic weapon also had its prepared place. Under the pallet's base, between the wheels, they had attached metal loops that the barrel and stock could rest on without knocking and clattering during the drive.

He jumped out, took a step back and inspected.

And he thought he heard Leo's voice.

When the cops start screening the idiots who are desperately trying to get out, then a milk lorry will sail right through. Especially with a cargo space that's easily checked since it contains only . . . milk.

Sam closed the rear doors.

Their plan had been based on the fact that it would be the two of them sitting there together, and they would help each other if they were stopped.

That was no longer the case. Now it was only he who could talk his way through.

Since he was now alone.

He noticed it as soon as he swung out from the back of the shopping centre: the traffic was moving slowly over there, and that could be due to only one thing. The police had put up their roadblock.

Further along he glimpsed the cars. Blue and white, with flashing blue lights.

Sam looked at his hands. They weren't shaking any more. The police were looking for a robber who stole a new black Audi. Not for a milk lorry. His fingertips dived down into the green and white jacket's breast pocket. There. The driving licence. With a relief in the shape of the country of Sweden in the plastic.

And it's you, Sam, who'll sit behind the wheel at the crucial moment

– when the car approaches the police roadblock. It's you they'll look at. If you are calm, the cops will be calm.

He was close.

Three cars between the milk lorry and the police patrol that was checking every vehicle.

And when he glanced at the rear-view mirror, he couldn't see, in the dim light, the small drops of blood that had dried on his skin.

IT WAS THE LARGEST TV he had ever seen. High up on the wall, actually the *whole* wall, from one corner of the service counter to the oblong cart that carried deep bowls of green salad and cabbage drenched in oil.

Ivan leaned heavily forward with his elbows against the worn restaurant table placed in the second row by the window. He often sat here with a cup of black coffee and a pile of betting slips for the day's broadcast of the Keno draw. He had tried various tables, and it was from this table that the view was the best, no supporting pillars in the way, no backs of guests who were queuing for the toilets or got the idea they would pay at the checkout. A picture in gigantic size. Something had happened to TV equipment during the years he was on the inside. It was as if the manufacturers had retained the same volume and the same weight and then just flattened out their products with a steamroller.

He was in a local restaurant a short stroll from Skanstull. It was in the neighbourhood he kept to nowadays, in a one-room flat leased under a secondary contract in downtown Stockholm. How the hell did he end up here?

It was called Dráva, the restaurant. And Dacso, he was the one who had eyebrows stragglier than a porcupine's bristles and darted between convection ovens in the kitchen. He owned the restaurant together with Szilvia, his wife – very pretty but in an instant could become so cold that the beauty turned into ugliness. They knew who he was. What he had done. The Pappa Robber who no longer drank alcohol. And they were always nice, on the verge of fawning. They sent their employees a little too often to refill his coffee cup. Perhaps it had something to do with the fact that at some particular point during his first visit he had let it be known that if Ivan Dûvnjac hadn't been at the hideout after the last bank robbery, the son he was about to meet here would have been dead. Between parents, that sort of thing that sometimes makes all the difference. And it brought a kind of respect that it was easy to like and rely on. But right now it was just annoying, the curious, searching glances from the simple bar and marble pizza counter feeling bothersome.

It had begun so well. An evening he would spend in the company of family, not with Keno betting slips and bad tips. He had felt so happy and been talkative – Leo, his son who was a free man as of today, was going to eat dinner with him here, at Dacso and Szilvia's. But then, after the news report on the goddamn gigantic TV, Dacso had walked over to whisper something to his wife instead of saying it out loud. Their attempts to be discreet had been equally idiotic and impossible when the images from a robbery of a security van filled the wide screen and the Pappa Robber was waiting for the Son Robber two tables away.

Now they were whispering in front of the pizza oven again, and not even discreetly. They had switched to another channel and the next news report. Several pictures from an armed robbery somewhere south of the city, new pictures that hadn't been shown earlier.

It was about then that the unpleasantness began to be irritating – what took root deep inside him every time and, if it grew too large, lay there and lured him. If he didn't watch out, he could slip, slide down and then in a moment fall headlong.

Several years ago he had sat on his own sofa watching television just like this. On that very evening the programme *Wanted* had broadcast a one-hour special on the group of robbers that the media dubbed the Military League because of their method of hitting banks – violent and precise like military operations – and because of the record-breaking stunt against the military armoury. He had come all too quickly to the realisation he knew them. Something he recognised on the screen as they strode into the bank with their weapons at the ready. A movement. The gait, angle of the foot, a hand pointing with the wrist slightly bent. And then when he continued to watch the short video from a surveillance camera, he recognised something else, what connected all those movements – a personality. And then it didn't matter that on the television they had black masks pulled down over their faces, because the tracks they left on the screen were movements they had in common – movements that had been there all their lives.

He hadn't felt ill at ease then. Only a sense of belonging. And when it wasn't possible to persuade Leo, to stop him, his father changed course, and asked instead to be allowed to be a part of their lives, to rob the next bank side by side with his own sons.

The discomfort now was related to the contents of the news report. The difference. These robbers had encountered the police already on the scene. In a firefight one of them had been hit by a fatal bullet.

'Your lad? Isn't he a bit late? You've even reserved a table, though we're never full.'

Dacso, so curious that he didn't even send a minion. The restaurant owner himself stood there with the coffee pot in his hand, offering a refill.

'Leo's on the way.'

Hot black coffee fell into the half-full cup.

'You asked me to arrange something special, Ivan. For you and your son. And I bought the best I could find.'

Then he didn't leave the table even though the cup had been refilled. He turned towards the television and saw what his customer saw. The new pictures, taken on a mobile phone camera from a distance, yet clear all the same. A lifeless body in black overalls, a mask over the face and an assault rifle fallen a short distance from the right arm.

'It cost a lot. The meat, I mean.'

And blood smeared on the ground, which the robber, according to the voice of the reporter, slipped in while he was trying to get up, when he was hit by a bullet that wedged in under the bulletproof vest. Before the next one – in the head.

'And if something's happened, you know, if your son isn't coming, I mean, if . . .'

Ivan hadn't drunk a drop for two years. During that time he had also controlled his temper, hadn't assaulted or struck anyone. But now he was so close to grabbing hold of Dacso's bristly eyebrows. To ripping them off and shoving them down his throat to silence him.

'What the fuck are you saying?'

'Today. He was released. And I mean—'

'Leo is never going to do a robbery again. He'll be here in a minute. Go and fix your expensive fucking meat.'

'Fillet of beef. Dry-aged from Argentina.'

'Whatever you want. I don't eat for the taste. If I did, I would certainly never come here to you and your lovely wife.'

That got him to leave. But not to stop whispering, and Ivan was sure that what the restaurant owner was blowing into his wife's ear was more insinuations – that it can't be a coincidence that a spectacular, violent robbery had been carried out the same day the Pappa Robber's son was released.

He had indeed felt something that morning, there at the gate. Something that couldn't be put into words but that a father senses. Lack of approachability. Leo was cut off, only existing inside himself.

69

He had thought then, had hoped, that it was the freedom. He had experienced that himself every time he was released from prison – years of longing and joy that were broken apart the moment the gate was opened and they turned into uncertainty and confusion. But . . . the fucking blood on the television screen. Was it his? Was that why he was late? Only ten minutes, so far. Leo could be a whole lot later and damn well not have managed to carry out a robbery in a Stockholm suburb, go through the roadblock, escape the police, hide the booty, change his clothes and a bit later sit in a Hungarian restaurant in the city centre with his Pappa.

'Dacso?'

'Yeah?'

'Go ahead and cook your Argentinian beef.'

'But if he doesn't come, Ivan, if—'

'Just cook it!'

The wall. The gate. Even Felix and *she* had been there.

If you hadn't been the way you were when they were growing up . . . good God, Leo would never have robbed any banks!

Britt-Marie broke the family. So he broke her.

And Felix and Vincent wouldn't have done time either.

But now he would fix it, renovate it like a house in decline. The mistakes lay behind them. A better future was before them.

If I can change, you can change.

'Are you cooking it?'

'In a minute.'

'Because he's coming now!'

Those footsteps.

Ivan leaned towards the cold windowpane in order to see better.

Each step so bloody blatant, that was how he always had walked. Those very steps were on the way to the door now.

And Ivan hugged his son for the second time that day.

'Dacso . . . goddamn it! We want to eat now. Get the hell going.'

'No food for me, Dad.'

Ivan stopped hugging his son and took him aside, away from curious ears.

'Leo, aren't you hungry? Let's sit down now. What do you want to drink?'

'I don't have time. I just wanted to come by and tell you that. Something's come up.'

70

The voices from the giant television floated down from the wall and settled between them, a thin, temporary veil around their conversation – an expert was talking about increased violence between police and criminals, a researcher assessed AK4s as unusual weapons for a robbery, and finally a spokeswoman for the police authority who explained that there was still no trace of the surviving robber.

'Listen, we'll be in touch, I'll call you.'

Leo had only got as far as half of the red carpet in the entrance before he turned and was on the way out again.

'But the dinner? The meat? Ivan, I have prepared everything for you and your lad.'

Dacso lifted the frying pan and held it up as if for evidence. At the same moment Leo pulled a wad of cash out of his back pocket, mostly five-hundred-kronor notes, and held out four.

'Is that enough?'

Dacso shook both his hands and head.

'It's way too much.'

'Keep them. I'll come back and eat with my father some other time.'

And so he left, his steps as certain as the ones that recently brought him there, and Ivan followed. He did not have time to fetch his coat, even though the tentative heat that crept up during the day had slipped away. It was raw, like autumn. As he used to think it felt in Yugoslavia, the country he left for Sweden in the sixties and whose border with Hungary consisted of a river named Dráva. Now he was running to catch up with his eldest son outside a restaurant bearing the same name.

'Hey, Leo . . . stop.'

'Sorry, Dad. I really don't have time. I have a meeting.'

'But that's a lot of money you have.'

That got him to stop.

'Do you have a problem with that, Dad?'

'Yes, just a few hours after your release. I thought . . .'

Ivan fell silent and Leo understood why. Two men in their fifties came along, crouching slightly and with their hands in their jacket pockets. Both of them nodded at Ivan as if they knew him, and he nodded back. People often tried to keep on good terms with him, without even being aware of it.

'. . . that you burned everything up in that woodstove before the police arrested us?'

71

'I found them in the forest today. If you look in the right place, they are growing in the soil more or less everywhere.'

A quick glance at the restaurant Dráva's window. Dacso and his ice-cold wife were standing there in full view, staring out, had stopped pretending.

'So . . . so that was the reason, Dad?'

'What?'

'So is that why it was so damn important to invite me to dinner? To check up on me? To interrogate me a little about my plans for the future?'

And behind the pair of curious restaurant owners the giant television's bluish glow continued to give off light. More images from the manhunt after the robbery.

'I get it. You've been looking at that. You don't have to worry. I have nothing to do with that shit.'

He looked around, mostly to avoid meeting his father's eyes, which were perhaps likely to see more.

It was the beginning of the evening in a capital city, yet so oddly deserted, silent.

'Dad – I was released today. Do you think I'd commit a robbery the same day? Not even the cops think that. No one's watching me.'

'You were late. And now you don't have time. Today, at the gate, it felt like . . . like when I tried to persuade you the time before not to do it. And it ended up with you surviving.'

A father who was convinced he had saved his son's life.

A son who was convinced once he had saved his mother's life.

'Look, Dad, don't go mixing our rugs up.'

His father winced.

'What the hell are you talking about, Leo?'

'Don't you remember, Dad? When I visited you in jail?'

They both remembered. Nonetheless the older of the two shook his head.

'No.'

'No?'

'Nothing about any rugs.'

'Don't you remember how it can be when someone believes that he saved a life – and then how someone else can so easily take it away from him?'

The giant TV set inside the restaurant window. The newscast had moved on to the rest of the world. A feature on the big UN building in New York, mixed with quick clips of some war somewhere.

At about that moment Leo smiled for the first time.

'Listen, don't worry so damned much. If it had been me there today, that never would have happened. It doesn't end like that when I'm part of it. The people I rob with don't end up dying.'

'You can never do it again, Leo! Next time the sentence won't ever end!'

'I wasn't there. I'm here, right?'

'Never again – got that? You all were damn lucky last time. You stole two hundred and twenty-one automatic weapons, robbed a shitload of security vans and banks, and then, then you blew up a bomb in the middle of Stockholm. But, Leo, you were convicted of two bank robberies, and Felix and Vincent of one! The same amount as I got and I was just along for one. You've had so goddamn much luck. Or it was a lousy job by the prosecutor. In any case, one thing I've understood – nothing is barred by statute because you served a few years in various prisons. Mountains of papers from solid investigations are waiting out there. If you, or all of you, do it one more time, you are risking getting sent down for *everything* next time. And then you'll be middle-aged, as old as I am, when they let you out again.'

Another glance at the window. They had stopped spying now. Dacso was drying glasses and his wife was moving salt cellars around.

'Look at me, Leo.'

Ivan sought his son's eyes, waiting until he was sure they had made eye contact.

'You can change. Like I changed.'

'Oh – so I'm not good enough as I am?'

'You don't have to copy . . . me, Leo. Everyone can change. Even me! If you just use your will. Wills collide, remember? Just like I showed you when you were little. When I taught you to dance with the bear.'

'Dad – I robbed banks, I didn't drink. Bank robberies are something you *choose* to do, and if you plan them well, if you minimise all the risks . . . Drinking is what people like you do who can't handle reality.'

A dinner in a nice warm place, a good cut of meat, a conversation . . . but it had ended up like this, on a damp pavement in a neighbourhood at dusk, as far apart from each other as when they began.

'Nothing, Leo, of all that crap that went on before, none of it is left any more. We have everything before us. That's what matters.'

'It was nice to see you, Ivan.'

The car was parked facing out in the closest parking space. It had gone quickly, and he'd had no intention of staying. A hire car, as it said on the sticker in the rear window. They didn't say anything else to each other. They didn't look at each other. Leo opened the car door, got behind the wheel and started the engine, which barely made a sound as the car rolled away.

Ivan.

It had always been like this when the distance grew. *Dad* disappeared and he became *Ivan* to his son.

And that didn't feel good. The discomfort from the morning was carving out an even bigger hole now. His eldest son was truly cutting himself off, as he always did when he was on his way somewhere and it was no longer possible to reach him.

DARKNESS TO DROWN IN.

So incredibly black.

And so darkness that conceals.

Leo parked in a curve intended as a passing place on the narrow forest road's final stretch. Turned off the car engine. Turned off the headlights. Vanished into the blackness.

Breathing slowly. In, out, in, out, while his heart seemed to speed up even faster. When everything around him was completely quiet, it became so apparent how hard it was beating in his chest.

It was the cold of late winter, and there was quite a lot more snow remaining on the ground here than there had been at the rest area where he dug up the weapons. He hadn't thought about it when he drove here the first time, to the ferry at 13.00, but a little further inland it always got colder, and what had melted during the day froze slowly to a thin, fine crust of ice that cracked and gave way when he began to walk towards the light.

Over there, the road's absolute end, at the waters of Lake Mälaren – four hundred metres according to the map – three streetlights were blazing, piercing the darkness and casting their light proudly around the ferry landing.

He was walking too fast. His heart rate, which was galloping, must be kept under control. Without his knowing it, unease whipped his steps forward among the trees, but he should not be moving too fast. He was the one who should catch sight of them – not the other way round. If they were there, he must be able to turn around and go back without having been seen.

It was different here. A capital city had its enormous globe of light, an artificial glow that lay over the buildings like an enormous soft cap, stronger closer to where visitors came. Here there were just the stars, and three simple streetlights became everything then, the beckoning signal that led him on the right path. It was precisely at this point that the relief should come, the calm – his reward for having broken through the police search net. Not now. This time, he had not been able to control the course of events at the scene or during the flight afterwards. That was why he was late for the meeting with Dad. He must know! First there was the evening news at quarter to five. He had stopped by the side of the road, listening on the car radio to live reporting of an armed robbery of a security van that ended in gunfire, and the neutral voice of the news saying

. . . some information suggests that one of the robbers was shot.

Shot?

One of the robbers?

Who?

The dark was all around him, like the bottomless hole he used to so often dream about, a dark as if falling for ever or like when he used to swim further and further down to the lake's bottom as a child and wondered how it would be to stay there.

Something was moving in the bushes to the right. Then came the sharp odour that always meant living creatures, many of them, a herd of elk or wild boar resting for the night so close to his step. And in the midst of the pitch black, in the midst of the smell of animals, suddenly his phone rang, a soundless humming in his breast pocket. Sam! He groped for it, pulled it out, in a moment Sam's voice. Wrong. The wrong fucking phone! Not the encrypted one, the other one. An 08 number. Stockholm. What did it mean? Sam, but from another number? Sam, who was stuck somewhere? He should answer. Not here. Not so close to those who might be waiting for him. Or . . . was it Jari? No. Neither Sam nor Jari would contact him on the unencrypted phone. And if it *were* either of them he couldn't take the risk of answering almost halfway. The sound always travelled quickly and without resistance through such silence.

He turned slightly, headed for the road again, made his way along the edge of the ditch and tried to discern the ferry landing. He was attempting to make out whether a car stood in front of the boom gate waiting to be ferried across and if anyone was sneaking around on the circular asphalt area and was looking, watching.

He had been about to turn the car around then and there, in the middle of the evening news, to drive directly here and find out what had happened. But he had continued, just managed to get to the restaurant at the right time and be seen just as long as he needed to be so that he would be definitely remembered. And not just by his father – he had insisted on paying for the food they didn't eat, a couple of five-hundred-kronor notes too much. The owner wouldn't forget that. If, or rather when, the police came to the kitchen of the restaurant to ask their routine questions, Leo Dûvnjac had a solid alibi, and from outside the family – timing that made it theoretically impossible to carry out the robbery of the security van in one of Stockholm's southern suburbs, clean up, and then close the door to a Hungarian eating-house in the city centre.

It had been unbearable to stand there on the pavement outside the shitty restaurant glancing in at the television screen as the excited, chattering voices were reporting about a robbery he had planned himself.

Four days. That was all they had. He was the only one who couldn't be involved in the bankrolling robbery because he was the one, out of the three of them, who risked a routine check afterwards. He was the bank robber in this new constellation, as well as the well-known, newly released bank robber. The other two, Sam and Jari, had done time in cellblock H for different crimes. And if you didn't have time for unnecessary questioning and wanted to have time for the final heist and take back what didn't exist, you also had to ensure a watertight alibi.

What he saw through the steamed-up restaurant window were moving images from a shaking mobile that a witness had filmed. Mobile phones exploded in scope during the time he was in prison and had become a new part of the human body. In the first run of bank robberies they only had to concern themselves with registered surveillance cameras – shoot them apart as soon as they entered a bank, ending every possibility for an investigator to map out a pattern. Then only the confused testimony of witnesses survived, fragmentary and distorted pictures painted in different ways because people in shock see what they think they see, a collection of experiences that it would take the police a long time to piece together. These days the instant pictures from mobile phones provided a supplement, which he couldn't plan away from the hands of a public that couldn't be controlled. And the shaky amateur pictures confirmed that the worst might have happened, that it was Sam who lay there bathed in his own blood.

He approached the three lights of the small house where the ferryman spent his time between departures. The bright yellow car ferry could be made out faintly at the water's edge, unmoving in the pitch-black water. And right then, the humming again – the phone in his breast pocket, the same 08 number. He let the vibrations subside and continued walking.

77

With its motor off, a single car was waiting to drive on board. Waiting for him? A police car? And if so, was someone outside it hiding in the dark? He drew closer. He had no choice; he had to know. Sam was irreplaceable. Together they had done all the planning month after month in Sam's cell. Jari, the hitman who was doing time for manslaughter and aggravated blackmail, had been brought in late. The first meeting with Jari consisted of pure salary negotiation – compromises on both sides in order to meet halfway at an agreed price tag that included a quick robbery of a security van and an active role in the final heist's getaway plan. Jari had been relatively easy to reason with, just like everyone who knows what they're good at and what they contribute – he never wanted to know too much, always did what he was supposed to and was known for keeping quiet during interrogation. Fifteen million kronor – that's what he'd cost, and both sides were happy with the arrangement. With final booty expected to be so large, it was a reasonable sum in a criminal world for keeping your mouth shut for ever, corresponding to written contracts and clauses about confidential information in the other world.

So, *if* Sam was dead or arrested then everything crashed, because this plan was restricted by time. Never had there been so short a time for so many events. Before he was sent down, and became known to the police, Leo had been able to plan and conduct the next bank robbery right after the one before it. He had been faceless. He refined and committed one robbery after another that would bankroll him all the way to the grand finale. That wouldn't work any more. He was one of the most familiar faces in the police's criminal register, clearly etched in every cop's consciousness. One of the few they knew with the capacity to carry out a heist of that magnitude. That meant he got only one chance. The risk would be greater than ever, a risk he was willing to take because the profit would also be greater. A chance that would never come again.

The seven o'clock news, on the way here, hadn't given any more details. The identity of the man who had been shot was not provided; and not a word about the other robber either, whether he'd been arrested or was still on the run. The entire newscast had revolved around the gunfire and the dead man. The only new thing flowing out of the car speakers was the voices of witnesses from the car park and shopping centre, confused words about how shots tore metal bits off cars and they all took cover by throwing themselves on the ground. The chatter of terror. But nothing about the second robber.

78

The ferryman's little cottage had four windows, one on each side, the light gently flowing out. Leo crept towards the one overlooking the forest. From that direction he was hidden by the unruly shrubbery. He inched forward to the wood panelling, pressed up against it and looked in. A lone man, with a full cup of coffee and an open newspaper in front of him on the table. The same ferryman as in the afternoon.

No one else. He was sure of it.

The clock on the wall behind the older man hung there, white and too large. It reminded him of a school clock, the long hands on the clock face pointing to a quarter to eight. Fifteen minutes until departure.

He took the same way back, into the dense shrubbery, then a U-turn to be able to approach the stationary, waiting car from behind.

A man in the driver's seat, a woman in the passenger's seat.

As he came closer, he also saw that it was a rather old car, red, without antennas or dual rear-view mirrors. Not a painted car, nor a civilian police car either. They were listening to the radio, and a jingle was clearly audible, singing out from the station called Radio Uppland. And as he had crept up so close that he could have put his hand on the car, he saw that the woman was wearing a hat and a coat with a high collar, that the man was balding and had a cap and quilted jacket. The police probably weren't here. Not yet.

Leo returned to the station house, one last time. The ferryman seemed just as peaceful, and the contents of the coffee cup had sunk down to half of what it had been. The school clock said eleven minutes to eight. He was the only person with a full view of everyone who travelled to and from the little island, and on a weekday evening, very few crossed over. He sat there in his luminous yellow vest as if nothing beyond the expected had happened. If it had done so, he would have been more wary, attentive, walking around out there, standing in the wheelhouse and looking out over the asphalt area – not slurping coffee and reading the sports section.

Leo breathed in the humid lake air. Everything it was possible to confirm was now checked. He would cross the waterway with the ferry at 20.00 because that was what he had to do. He didn't need to run to the car to get there in time and drive the last stretch to the boom gate, but he probably should increase the length of his stride somewhat.

————

It felt so wrong.

He sat at the same table at the Dráva restaurant that he always did. The same regular guests around the other tables. The same Dacso, with his white cloth hat and pizza shovel, leaning over the oven. Nevertheless, there it was, the fucking discomfort that pressed so damn hard on his chest. He had not understood that it could spread so quickly, divide and attack, like restless cancer cells.

The dinner didn't happen. Nothing happened. Leo had been focused, extremely and disagreeably focused, exactly as he had been then, before the last robbery, when they were arrested together.

Nastily unapproachable.

Ivan had stood there on Ring Street for a while and watched the hire car drive away and disappear in the direction of Gullmarsplan, before he returned to the restaurant in the company of growing uneasiness and, despite the protests of the regular tramps, turned up the volume on the goddamn television with all its goddamn newscasts and all the goddamn pictures from a goddamn robbery of a security van. He had glanced at the restaurant owner and his wife, who were crouched behind the counter, just as interested in the stream of news as he was himself. Two hyenas who thought they knew who his son was.

And above the hyenas' heads the bottles stood there in a row.

Red wine.

For the first time in a long while he felt it, like an itchy amputated arm, the room-temperature wine dancing inside even though he hadn't swallowed it: phantom thirst. The safe, numb feeling that finds its way into one's head.

No, thought Ivan. No way in hell. Not weak. Not now. Only I can get him to change and lead him away from wherever the hell he's on his way to.

Ivan got up from the uncomfortable plastic stool and for the third time he borrowed the restaurant's phone, floury from Dacso's pizza hands. For the third time he got an alternating tone for an answer. He compared the number he had entered with the one handwritten on a slip of paper that he had badgered Vincent into giving him and that Leo had called from earlier in the day. Number by number, correct. One more time, the last, the same number – and he wasn't at all ready when someone answered.

'Yes?'

Leo's voice. Right?

'It's . . . Ivan.'

It went totally quiet. He tried to listen for where the other voice might have gone but heard nothing. Too quiet.

'And what do you want?'

'I . . . Listen, you know I care about you. You understand that, don't you?'

'Well?'

'Think about it. That I'm here. If you need help.'

'Where are you calling from?'

'The restaurant.'

'And my number?'

'From your brother.'

Silence again.

'Hey, Ivan?'

'Yeah?'

'In the future you call me only from numbers I've approved.'

A different sort of silence. Leo had hung up.

Ivan was confused. A moment ago, he was full of uneasiness, discomfort, worry. And now, anger.

He had been dismissed for the third time that day. First the wall, then the dinner and now again, he thought. Approve? I call from whatever fucking number I want to.

'Did you get hold of him?'

Dacso, the hyena, calling from the pizza oven. The hyena with his hyena wife. They were looking at him, laughing at him. Their hyena laugh.

'What does my phone call have to do with you? Mind your own business.'

'But surely that was your lad? It sounded like it anyway.'

'So hyenas eavesdrop as well?'

'What?'

'Bake your fucking pizza. And don't listen to what you shouldn't be listening to.'

He recognised that music on the television. It warbled and sang out every time before a new newscast. He turned the volume up more, not giving a shit about the tramps who were protesting again. One of them even stood up to register his complaint more physically until he saw who it was sitting there. Then he regretted it and turned away towards the

81

serving trolley, pretending to look for napkins or see if there was a salt cellar.

The first news item was presented by a male newsreader. He had taken care with his hair and make-up, but it didn't help. It was entirely clear that the gestures were the rehearsed mannerisms of someone *imitating* seriousness. Above the newsreader's shoulder, there was a still picture, an assault rifle swimming in a sea of blood.

Ivan shot out of his chair so that he could see better when the report began to roll. So far the same information as in earlier news broadcasts. More blood. A dead robber. Shocked guards on stretchers. A few minutes into the story Ivan was about to turn it off when suddenly new pictures pushed the old ones out of the way. A spokeswoman in police uniform in front of a police car. She hadn't been on before. She was being interviewed at the crime scene, which was clearly illuminated like a temporary backdrop in a scene from a film, as if she had had arranged and placed herself in the scenery, just as planned out as the newsreader's manner had been. Even her voice was just as artificially serious when she explained that police investigators confirmed that two masked men had carried out the attack, that the robber shot in the firefight had now been identified, that the other robber was still at large with the proceeds and that he was heavily armed, under stress and therefore highly dangerous.

Ivan reached for the glass of water – coffee and water while the wine waved attractively at him. He leaned back a little proudly and emptied it without releasing the spokeswoman from his gaze.

Now she was ducking questions. She explained that, in consideration of the sensitive state of the investigation, it was too early to talk about this and that. That was what she said – but he saw that she was lying. Cops always knew about more than they said. Probably they had already fucking sussed out who it was. With one robber identified, it never took long to home in on the others. He and his three sons, if anyone, had a lot of experience with that.

It *couldn't* be Leo. He knew that too. His visit to the restaurant made it impossible.

But still, he couldn't quite put it all together.

Why did his son behave in such a peculiar way towards him on his first day of freedom? And where was he now, instead of being at the dinner table with his father as they had agreed?

A five-minute crossing by ferry and a five-minute drive from one side of the island to the other took him the same way as a few hours ago, but the journey was edged with hellish worry. Everything was possibly over now, before it had even begun. Then came the last section, with dimmed headlights. He put on the brakes and stopped. There, a way off in the dense blackness, the lights switched off, was the house that couldn't be seen but that right now meant everything.

If Sam was there.

If Sam wasn't there.

Leo lingered in the car and rolled down the window. Cold air. Wide awake. To stay sitting here was the same as not knowing – and not knowing was the same as Sam still being alive and the swag still his.

His mobile had rung a third and fourth time. Persistently, pleadingly – it could have been the Blue Robber. He broke, jerked it out of his breast pocket, pressed the button and answered. Dad, from a fucking restaurant telephone. With other people around him, for a conversation that could be overheard, tracked.

He rolled the window up again. It was raw and cold outside but the warmth inside the car hung on.

Before, there was always a solution, a way out. But this time . . . maybe there wasn't one – not if the police were waiting in the dark house, if they had come over on the earlier ferry in an unmarked car and not alerted the ferryman, if they were also bedded down in the same darkness that hid him. If at that very moment they were watching him, following his body heat with night-vision goggles when it shone in greenish, shimmering light.

He opened the car door, feeling around for firm footing, and started to walk towards the fence and gate. He stopped and listened. Nothing. Not even the wind.

They had been two who became three. The bank robber, the murderer, the muscle. Now one of them was dead. They were two again – but which two?

Spreading out, the lawn formed a gently ascending slope. The lightly frozen ground was therefore deceptively slippery and the hard soles of his shoes sometimes slid against his will. Here somewhere, close to the stone wall, Sam's car had been parked during his visit in the afternoon. The parking space was empty now. It might mean the worst – or that he had deliberately hidden it somewhere else.

Leo remembered that the door to the house had a small angular window in it at about face height, the kind you couldn't see through. And there was too large a risk of detection to look into the kitchen through the ordinary window, or the one at the back of the house.

The door handle was made of light metal and gleamed a little when he touched it and carefully pulled it. Unlocked. He stepped into the small, dark hall, over the threshold and into the kitchen, past the wood stove they had burnt up the map in.

Breathing.

Or was he imagining it?

The two kitchen chairs were waiting as empty as the sofa in the kitchen.

He continued into the small sitting room. And . . . yes, there. Maybe. In the armchair. It seemed as if someone was sitting in it, slightly hunched forward.

Like the shadow of someone.

'It could have just as easily been me.'

Sam.

And Leo did not know if it was joy he felt now or relief, or even some sort of disguised rage. The only thing he knew for certain was that he felt so much more than he had time for.

He reached for the kitchen chair and pulled it closer to the shadow.

'But it wasn't, Sam. It wasn't you.'

'Damn, I saw . . . how he staggered. And grabbed himself . . . here.'

Sam's shadowy arm fluttered and pointed to his side, between the hip and the shoulder blade.

'And I ran out. Got hold of him, tried . . . I didn't understand that he got a bullet in the head too. That it hit, there. But I felt Jari die then – felt it in his hand, you know, when the muscles stop functioning. And I understand now – it could have just as easily been me.'

Leo had probably never touched Sam much, apart from the ritual hugs that they, and so many others on cellblock H, greeted each other with. But now he reached for Sam's shadowy hand and put his own hand on it.

'But *you* are alive. I feel it in *your* hand.'

It was strange considering the crime he had been convicted of, but in Sam, Leo was sitting in front of a man who really did not know how violence could be used. A man who used violence once, twenty-five years ago, and then never went back to it or sought it out.

Leo pressed the shadowy hand lightly but got no reaction, no push in return. Leo pressed the hand again a bit harder, still nothing in return, nothing signalling contact.

So he got up and in one motion drew down the blinds, covering both windows of the room. He groped along the floor with his fingers, searching for the cord to the only floor lamp. He switched it on, a weak filament, but good enough to see and read someone.

Sam's light hair was flat and dishevelled as it got when one has been wearing a black balaclava for a long time and sweated into it. His eyes looked inward, not outward, and still lingered at a car park outside a shopping centre, repeating the same sequence. And barely visible were small drops of dried blood that had hit the only exposed parts of his skin – around his left eye and left corner of his mouth – drops of blood ending where the cloth edge had begun.

'The thumb. The cop at the roadblock. It was just like you said.'

The first words other than *it could have just as easily been me*, and they squeaked. As if the vocal cords didn't want to release them.

'He rubbed it back and forth, unconsciously. Over the embossing. Over the UV image. Rubbed his thumb and looked more at it than at me.'

The squeaking slowly slackened off as he leaned in closer.

'The hood, overalls, boots – I burned all of it, exactly as we said.'

'And what you were wearing at the roadblock? The milk uniform?'

'That, too.'

Leo saw so strongly how Sam's eyes dared to leave that car park for a second time to come here.

'And the milk lorry. It burned up at the same time.'

The eyes of a shocked robber of a security van became an asset when the preoccupied gaze was taken for the calm of a professional driver who has just delivered today's dairy products.

'And the gun, my gun – I dropped it along with the empty cassettes into twenty-five metres of water, two minutes out by rowing boat down there by the pier.'

They looked at each other, and it was as if the friendship, the trust, grew right there, right then. In spite of the shock, Sam had acted exactly as they had agreed upon – transformed himself from robber to private individual and made it through the roadblock, burned his clothes and the first getaway vehicle, switched to the next getaway vehicle, his personal car, and continued to the island where he'd got rid of the gun and the last traces. And only when he had reached the darkness and solitude of the house had he allowed himself to fall apart.

Leo smiled faintly, perhaps proud he had chosen the right partner. He stood up and went into the kitchen, opened the pantry and began to turn a metal cap that sat in the wall between the second and third shelf – the air intake.

'It's in here, right?'

Sam nodded and Leo spun the metal disc until the gap widened enough to stick his hand in and pull out an oblong package wrapped in protective plastic.

'Do you have a ruler? A folding ruler?'

'I think my mother had an old tape measure here somewhere.'

Sam pulled out a workbench drawer, rooted around in it and soon handed over a small coil that shone, changing between red and green and yellow. Leo released it, a metre-long tape measure, and placed the soft, slack strip along the bundle of banknotes encased in plastic.

'Twenty centimetres. If each centimetre corresponds to fifty thousand – one million. And six bundles of equal length, that's six million. That's enough for conducting *the house call* and having a little pocket money.'

He stuffed the bundle of banknotes into the hole in the wall, between and above those already in there, screwed on the cap and closed the pantry door.

'And the other gun?'

'It was left lying there on the asphalt a few metres from his body. No way I could have had time to pick it up.'

Never, ever leave traces.

The only traces left are the ones I choose to place there.

They looked at each other in silence, in the midst of some sort of calm. And even though the gentle glow of the floor lamp from the sitting room was too faint to distinguish facial features, Leo was certain that Sam's eyes were back. The only reminders of death on his face were the spots of blood near his left eye and the left corner of his mouth.

'Tomorrow, Sam, we have to think a little. If I know cops right, the gun left behind means that I'll be spending a couple of hours in a room I wasn't planning to spend any more time in.'

The gun was now lying on a forensic technician's table. Leo was aware what that meant, to have left that kind of trace. They could bring him in and interview him, but only for gathering information until they checked whether he had a solid alibi. They didn't have a damn thing that could be linked directly to him – only tired old suspicions, which hadn't worked to connect together a credible chain of evidence before.

'And when I'm done sitting with your cop brother, I'll need a few more hours – to find a replacement for Jari.'

To be able to accomplish the very last stage – *the police station* – with someone he trusted. But he didn't have time to build such relationships, so there were only two to choose from.

Felix and Vincent.

'So, Sam – I want you to contact the Albanians, and move *the house call* to the evening.'

Maybe Felix – who'd already said no, and was the most stubborn person he knew?

Or Vincent – who also said no, and seemed to be avoiding him?

'You're alive, Sam. And the loot is entirely intact and sitting here in your pantry. We'll be a few hours late tomorrow because of . . . well, what happened today. But we'll have time. Our plan holds – and we'll finish it in three days.'

PANIC.

That was what she felt, without understanding where it came from.

Britt-Marie rolled over again in bed, sweaty from her neck to her lower back. The alarm clock on the night table shouted angular numbers at her – 23.47.

She had gone to bed early, an hour and a half ago, hoping to find sleep somewhere in the dark – to avoid knowing when and in what condition he came home. She would wake up the next morning and he would just be lying there in her guest room, snoring lightly, wrapped up in the sheet as he had been as a child.

Strange feelings jostled and fought with each other and she tried to understand if they were abnormal during those first sleepless hours, or whether she was simply a mother who loved and worried about her son, in spite of the fact that he had been released that morning after a long prison sentence and was probably just out celebrating.

They *were* normal, she had decided. It was love she felt – but also, in the midst of it, something else. Panic. A feeling so strong, so familiar, that every time she had been close to falling asleep and gliding into a dreamlike state, an image of the prison cell would appear right at that very moment, jolting her wide awake. Her panic was connected to her visits to musty, barren rooms at various prisons. Once every fortnight, year after year, in spite of the long journeys, she continued to visit her three sons who were doing time behind bars in different parts of the country.

She looked around the small and rather simple house.

It had been built in a different era, about five kilometres south of Stockholm in an area called Tallkrogen, which consisted of cramped but cosy homes for ordinary wage earners to create their own living space in. She was happy here, in spite of the busy Nynäs motorway stretching along just outside one of her windows. It formed a backdrop of sound she never heard during the day because she'd built it into her own daily fabric long ago. But now, when night came and the vehicles came one by one, she could hear them clearly, and even felt the tremors from the heavy lorries as perceptible vibrations in the wooden façade, wooden floor and wooden bed. She had moved here in the time between her sons' arrests and the first day of the trial. Partly to get away from all the talk in the small city of Falun – whispers out of the daily newspaper headlines sneaked behind her back both in the city and in the corridors of the nursing home where she worked – but also to be closer to her sons when they would be spread out in Sweden's high-security prisons.

Two visits per month to each of them, and they had been so different. When she visited Vincent for the first time, she already felt that he had grown up, repented and would never commit a crime again. *That's the last time, Mamma.* He had put it just like that, word for word. *The last time.* Felix remained silent during interrogation, and then spoke not a single word referring to the crimes he was convicted of, not even when he was alone with her – she still didn't know. But she hoped . . . With Leo, as with Vincent, one visit was enough to understand – but with him, that he would never stop. That he had stepped into a criminal world that he did not want to leave. That he would never change.

She turned over in bed, her forehead and temples also sweating now. The brightly shining clock was soundless, but nevertheless was ticking too loudly.

The panic didn't subside. Rather it spread out with her here in the bed. It jostled and shoved from beside her.

She should be pleased, happy even, that they were all free. When was the last time they saw each other, all of them together? She should think about tomorrow, when they would all be here for lunch. She should be ready to cry out *you see, my beloved boys, this is the beginning of the continuation of our family.* But she knew, deep inside, that it wasn't so. On the contrary, it was perhaps the beginning of the end.

From somewhere the panic rose up again, and she understood, finally, what it was connected with: the twisted, pathetic, sick bonds Ivan had created. He had stood there this morning by the gate, and had reminded her of them, and all she had built up, all the years of distance, had meant nothing. He had made his way back in, like before.

And now, again, the fucking bonds would be able to destroy the determination of her younger sons.

Could Vincent and Felix stand up to Leo? Was their will strong enough for that?

That was exactly where the panic stemmed from – that Leo would start to pull on the bonds again, pulling his brothers *with* him once again, pulling them *down* once again. He would use the bonds as Ivan used them. He would act like the man she had been forced to leave in order to survive. And she did not want to be forced to leave her own son.

She heard a car, just as clear as the others, but not from the motorway.

This engine noise came through the kitchen window facing the other direction, towards the neighbours' houses and the narrow, crescent-shaped street that divided the housing estate. The car drove closer, the brakes were applied and it stopped outside her house. Then came steps, she recognised them perhaps, forceful but gentle at the same time – if he still walked that way – and the door to the house opened.

She never heard the latch bolt click, but the hall floor creaked as usual.

And now she knew that it was his step and that she wanted to see her eldest son – to see how he was, and try to figure out where he had been.

She straightened her nightgown before she opened the bedroom door.

Leo was standing in the middle of the glow streaming out of the fridge. Since neither the overhead light nor any of the kitchen cabinet lights were on, his skin, pale from prison, was almost white.

'Mamma? Aren't you sleeping?'

Dead. That was what she thought – her son would look just like that if the blood wasn't pumped through his thirty-one-year-old body any longer.

'Not yet. It's only twelve o'clock.'

He took the Herrgård cheese and the smoked pork and put both the plates on the stovetop.

'Where do you keep the bread?'

Britt-Marie fetched a wicker basket with triangular knäckebröd.

'Where have you . . . Have you been out?'

'And celebrated, you mean?'

She nodded. And he shrugged his shoulders.

'No, Mother. I haven't been celebrating.'

'So what did you do then?'

'Nothing special.'

The cheese slicer was blunt, and the slices were small crumpled heaps that he divided up, one in each corner of the triangular bread.

'Mostly drove around. Enjoying being able to do it.'

He cut thick slices of the pork and put them on the next piece of bread.

'So don't worry, Mamma.'

She looked at his white skin again; now it was almost blue. She tried

90

not to worry, but what he had just said didn't give her any relief. So she lingered there in front of him, in her nightgown, with her hair in some sort of ponytail so that it wouldn't get tangled during the night, with her bare feet on the cold floor.

She might have seemed small but she was steady and well balanced on her feet nevertheless.

'Whatever you do, Leo,' she stood as she had the times she had gone against Ivan, '*don't* get your brothers involved.'

She reached out, up, and the back of her hand caressed an unshaven cheek.

Leo listened to the sound of her bare feet until it ebbed in the darkness of the hall.

His mother's touch had always been there. She was soft, physical. But now, the back of her hand against his cheek had felt almost unpleasant.

He took the two knäckebröd sandwiches and two glasses of orange juice to the guest room.

The sofa bed was folded out and had fresh sheets. She had placed a reading lamp on one of the kitchen chairs, and next to it had laid a new toothbrush, new underwear and a new pair of socks.

This would be his home for the first week following his release from prison. Then he would be offered a place in a halfway house called The Maple, a ten-square-metre room in a corridor among others who had been released from prison and treatment centres.

He wouldn't stay there.

He was on his way somewhere. And so he must do exactly what she'd just asked him *not* to do.

I have no choice, Mamma, thought Leo. Jari has to be replaced by either Felix or Vincent. And then, Mamma, I'm going to worry you even more. Because the gun Jari held is now in the hands of the police. And tomorrow that fucking cop Broncks will be informed of the fact. And at lunchtime, or preferably after, he's coming here to your home and he's going to bring me in.

91

ELISA SQUINTED CAUTIOUSLY, one eye, two eyes. The edge of a table. Further away, a cooker, a cabinet and a wall painted white.

She was certain she was lying down.

And she had slept. How had that happened?

A gap of skin was showing between the edge of her jersey and her trousers, and was glued as if permanently to the surface. An angry red vinyl upholstered sofa had bitten into her back.

The light from the window facing the police station courtyard was hitting her through the glass pane. That was what woke her up. Or, maybe it was the feeling of not sleeping at home, of feeling naked even though you're dressed.

The watch on her left wrist read seven twenty-five. *In the morning, right?* Her back was really stiff when she got up from the hard sofa, just as her neck had become from the temporary pillow – her rolled-up white quilted jacket. She was in a kitchenette in the investigation division's corridor at the city police station, in the middle of the police building that linked all the other police units in the area on Kungsholmen in Stockholm constituting the core of the operations of the Swedish police. She had sworn to never do this – live out the cliché of sleeping overnight at the workplace with a cup of black cop coffee and two pastries for breakfast.

The loo shared the space with the kitchenette; she rinsed out her mouth, washed her face with unperfumed soap from an economy pack, wet her hand and ran it through her dark hair, wet her index finger and straightened the hairs of her equally dark eyebrows. As one of the youngest detectives at the age of thirty-four, she had managed to lead several major investigations and every time kept her promise to herself to never wake up as a police cliché. Never sleep over, never end the evening with shit food, and perhaps most importantly, never, ever make reference to gut feelings – a police investigation was a puzzle, every piece of which served a function. Sometimes she had to leave the puzzle behind, look at the pieces with fresh eyes to be able to join them together – but never guess.

92

And never make allowances. Whoever it was about, whatever consequences a new piece had for others, or for herself, it must be put in place.

Gut feelings were disastrous.

Gut feelings rarely agreed with the final results.

Gut feelings never held up in court and never got anyone convicted.

Last night she broke two of her three rules. She had fallen asleep and eaten shit food. Last night at ten o'clock – four and a half hours after being called to a car park at a shopping centre and a pool of blood with a dead robber – when she suddenly held a document connected with a forty-one-page, seven-year-old report from a theft and realised that this was so much more than a robbery of a security van, she couldn't go home. An entire evening became an entire night and just past five in the morning she had the thought to just lie down on the sofa in the kitchenette and stretch out for a little while.

She yawned as she headed out into the still silent corridor. Breaking a promise always had consequences. She was standing now for the first time ever at the vending machine. Number 41 – machine latte. Number 12 – two slices of hard bread cemented together with a thick layer of soft herb cheese. Number 23 – vanilla yoghurt with a compartment of round biscuit crumbs and plastic spoon under the lid. Her bag with damp exercise clothes was on the desk where she had left it after the alarm during yesterday's workout. And here in her office, the clichés stopped. They didn't come in here, not even this morning. There was no whiteboard with notes and arrows and blurry photos that would be linked together during the course of the investigation, no baskets overflowing with papers, no rows of plastic mugs that had been drunk out of.

Her own system was in command in here. Each current investigation was reduced to three piles of papers on her desk, a photograph on the top of each one, photos that functioned like a poster for a film; if you have seen the film and then look at the poster, you can also fill in the story, placing the scenes in order underneath the photo.

Three piles. Three key moments.

She was still trying to wake up, yawned again and distractedly picked up the picture lying on top of the pile to the left, the one she always called *You struck first, you bastard*. The moment of the deed, when a thought becomes a crime, this time represented by a reasonably sharp photo of a shot-up security door. Behind it, the loot, the robbers' target, was exposed. And they had struck at the exact moment when the guards felt most secure.

She called the pile in the middle *You fucked up*. When crimes become clues. This pile was always the thinnest at the start of the investigation but grew the most in the end. This time it already contained a strong card at the beginning. The photo on top depicted a dead robber, but it wasn't the robber's identity that formed the you-fucked-up goad. Nor the blood he was lying in, or the fact that he was dead. But the gun – a military-grade assault rifle, AK4, about a metre from his body – that was the link to the forty-one-page-long report of a theft that had transformed her evening and night and morning. At the far right was the third pile – *You can't fucking think you'll get away*. When the clues become the perpetrator. On top there was a photo of a man who was stepping onto a loading dock with his back to the camera, wearing a cap and bulky jacket, a grainy black-and-white image from a surveillance camera.

She drank some of the coffee and it was bitter, even acidic, without containing an ounce of taste. It entirely lacked roundness. The vending machine needed to be decalcified and she made a note to call the provider and request a servicing. A tasteless, warm drink, bread and soft cheese – baby gruel for adults.

Three piles that were just beginning. Large pieces of the facts, witness testimony and evidence were lacking. But even though she had just scratched the surface, she would soon hand over the investigation. In ordinary cases it would have seemed damned hopeless, but given the gun and the document she was drawing out now from pile number two along with the photo on top and considering *who* she would hand it over to, it was an obvious step forwards.

She went out into the corridor again and stopped by the shop, open round the clock, for the second time that morning – a number 41, machine coffee and one that lacked a number, a cup of hot water. Hot water with milk: silver tea. She knew that he was usually early, and that was his preferred drink. If she walked quickly and held the photo and document under her arm and kept her fingers high up on the slightly thicker edges of the paper cups, she would manage to get there without burning herself.

'Knock, knock.'

The door was open and she raised the cups slightly higher up by way of an explanation for the verbal knocking. He looked up from his desk chair, nodded, and she walked in.

'Thought we should celebrate a little, Broncks. A cup for you and a cup for me.'

She sat down in front of a man who somehow always looked the same, no matter what clothes he was wearing. Today – blue jeans, grey pullover, black shoes next to pale skin. The only difference in him from how he looked when they first met as colleagues was his hairline, the bays above his temples having become deeper, pulled backwards. In a year or so he would start to shave the entire top of his head. They usually did that, balding men of his age. In addition he looked exactly like his room, pared down, impersonal, with institutional furniture and nothing on the slightly damaged walls. Not a thought about covering the traces of the previous inhabitant. Just bundles of papers for investigations that broke off – unlike her piles they lay spread out over the entire floor. They were all old and some, at least for him, represented unsolved cases. The bundles, she knew, were permeated with aggravated violence, up and down the pages. She had always thought it odd that they did not reappear in his blank face, that he could keep the violence away – it was present in all her other colleagues. It was possible to trace in their eyes and its colour wore off in their voice and gestures. It was as if he had decided it would not affect him, and so then it didn't. She had always thought that didn't seem entirely healthy. He was not someone she would like to wake up next to the following morning.

'Thanks, Elisa . . . but most likely it's been celebrated enough by now, as far as I'm concerned. It's a finished investigation, since the sentence has been confirmed.'

He nodded knowingly towards the window, or rather towards the large building, the roof of which was providing shade there outside the old courthouse, where the trials began for what was dubbed the Robbery of the Century in the media, the biggest heist in Scandinavian history. One hundred and three million kronor. A case that consumed all his waking hours the year before and now had been pounded through questioning, district court and court of appeals. And two weeks ago when the Supreme Court chose not to take it up, it was finally over.

There was a binding judgement now. The perpetrators' sentences could be enforced. John Broncks was praised internally as the hero, as the man behind the prosecution, and the loot from the robbery was still entirely intact. None of them had spent a single krona, having been careful not to change their habits.

'But thanks for the cup of tea. Which, if you excuse me, Elisa, I would rather drink alone – with all that, there's been a little too much running around lately.'

He smiled, drank the warm water and let his gaze linger on the town hall roof.

It had been dubbed the Robbery of the Century, in most newspapers, the CIT of CITs in others. Money that was to be transported from the federal bank's main branch by the Mall in the middle of downtown Stockholm, and out to security companies, which in turn would fill all the ATMs in the central area of the city before the big sales after Christmas – it was the time of year when commerce was at its greatest and the amounts of money at their highest. A female security guard had been attacked and forced at gunpoint to relinquish the whole security van. She had been a victim in the eyes of the media and the rest of the police station – until Broncks saw something else. Broncks saw a woman who'd had an intimate relationship with one of the robbers, who had applied for the job as a guard a couple of years earlier, and had slowly worked her way up in the organisation with just one goal in mind – to gain enough trust to be allowed to drive that particular vehicle on that particular day.

'I'm sorry, John, I know what you're thinking, but that's not what I wanted to celebrate. I think just like you – that it's simply our job. That it's not so sodding worthy of note that we do what we're paid for.'

He blushed. She saw it, although he was pretending to fumble with his cup in front of his face, embarrassed that he'd assumed she was yet another impressed admirer.

'This, on the other hand . . .'

The two documents had been lying upside down on her knee. Now she picked one of them up and placed it on the desk next to the cup.

'This is what I want to celebrate.'

John Broncks glanced at the document. A photograph. He recognised it. He had seen it several times on the news yesterday evening. A man's body lying on asphalt.

'Jari Ojala. Hitman, enforcer. Does anything for the right price. Responsible for the occasional shot-up kneecap. But – according to previous convictions and the register of suspects – never involved in an armed robbery before.'

'So we should celebrate this instead – that he's stone dead?'

Wounded pride. But at least he wasn't blushing any more.

'No. Ojala is not interesting. However, the weapon lying there . . .'

She leaned forward, pointing at the photo.

'. . . we should celebrate. You've been waiting for it for a long time.

With this, you should be able to throw out at least this gigantic pile of papers.'

She was pointing now at one of the unfinished investigations lying on his floor, the most comprehensive – a six-thousand-page investigation.

'Because that gun, John, is going to link the guilty parties to all the crimes they've committed – not just the few they were convicted of.'

Then she laid the other document on his desk.

A copy of one of the six thousand pages. An excerpt from the report of a weapons heist that started a unique series of bank robberies.

```
Item: Rifle     Item: Rifle     Item: Rifle     Item: Rifle     Item: Rifle
Model: AK4      Model: AK4      Model: AK4      Model: AK4      Model: AK4
No: 11237       No: 10042       No: 11534       No: 12621       No: 10668
```

Column after column, up and down the pages – two hundred and twenty-one automatic weapons had been stolen from a secret military ammunition depot and then transported away. The investigator named John Broncks had been entirely unaware of where to.

'The gun in the photo, John, is one of those that disappeared without a trace, and you have been looking for them ever since. The serial number is correct. The stamp with Three Crowns is correct. It's one of the guns in the large collection that you were sure Leo Dûvnjac and his family controlled and used in ten bank robberies. And now on the same day Dûvnjac is released, it shows up. At another robbery.'

She picked up her cup and raised it as if for a toast – the celebration she'd intended – and drank the coffee that didn't taste like anything this time either.

'Here's your chance, John. If you follow that gun, you will find the rest.'

John Broncks didn't toast. He had heard what she said, he really had, but he hadn't really taken it in.

Dûvnjac?

The weapons heist?

He left his chair and sank down to a squatting position and began to browse in the giant pile. He knew it by heart, knew the exact pages. There. The photos of a tunnel dug under the security door underneath the bunker, the floor blown up and the guns handed out one at a time. A heist that wasn't discovered until half a year later even though the weapons depot was checked daily – but only from the outside.

'You're right. The serial number matches the one in the report. It could have something to do with Leo Dûvnjac. But it could just as easily be the case that he sold them, which he threatened to do when he tried to commit blackmail against us and exchange them for twenty-five million kronor.'

'John, you don't believe that yourself.'

'The entire collection could have leaked out onto the market already then. The gun in the picture might be in the hands of any criminal organisation whatsoever.'

'You don't believe that – six years have gone by. The AK4 was a common weapon used during bank robberies back then, and it's never used today. Think about it, John. When's the last time you heard of one? It's only been Kalashnikovs since then. That's part of what I was doing last night. I didn't give a shit about gut feelings and verified the facts. Not a single robbery has been carried out with AK4s.'

He looked at her, at a slight angle from below, stayed there and sat down on the pile of papers as if it were a wobbly stool.

'Leo Dûvnjac. I know him if anyone does. Shooting people at the scene of the robbery, that's not his modus operandi. He shoots at surveillance cameras, walls, protective glass, ceilings, whatever the fuck – but to terrify, to force the surroundings to become passive. It worked every time. Even we, the police, backed off. He had just as heavy weapons and demonstrated that he could use them. Dûvnjac gave some thought to violence. Each shot was like a new . . . word. Violence was his language. To start shooting like a fool without any motive, that's not like him at all.'

Elisa, on the other hand, looked at him, at a slight angle from above.

'John?'

And it didn't feel entirely comfortable.

'You hate violence, that's what makes you tick. Piecing facts together, that's what makes me tick. Do you understand?'

So she pulled slightly on the lever that raised and lowered the chair and sank down.

'You went around, then, with a few years of gut instinct. You *knew* that Leo Dûvnjac committed ten bank robberies and set off a bomb and was behind northern Europe's largest weapons heist, but managed to get him convicted on only two counts. Because you didn't have enough evidence. Gut feelings are shit, John. Gut feelings trick good police officers into not going all the way. And then when they have to change course, the gut feelings lie there like a dead weight and point in the wrong direction – the same direction as at the beginning.'

She wasn't sure he was listening, or if he was only looking at her, past her.

'And a police officer, who followed gut feelings at first, and then slowly realised that he or she is wrong, must of course change that. And to what, do you think? Don't answer humility, because that's wrong, John. Prestige. An investigation can never be driven by prestige. Listen to me – to facts. *If* you follow the gun, you will find the rest.'

She grew silent. If he had listened, it was now he must reflect, react.

He was doing that.

'Elisa, this is actually my *second* cup today.'

He reached for a sip of the hot drink, and then leaned back so much that it moved the stool made of papers. He rubbed his eyes.

'The first, you see, I made myself in the kitchenette, as I usually do when I arrive in the morning. And, by the way, you seemed to be sleeping very soundly then.'

He smiled at her, and she realised that, that morning, she had done what she had thought she would never do. She'd woken up with him. It wasn't the light from the courtyard that woke her. It was the sound of someone moving around in the same room she was sleeping in.

He looked so pleased, as if he'd just taken back what he'd lost by the embarrassment over what should be celebrated.

But, hell no, she wouldn't blush, as he had done.

'OK, John. If you don't think that the gun is enough as a link – then we'll take a look at the getaway, which happened when we thought robber number two in blue overalls was still in the security room behind the ATMs.'

She took her mobile phone out of her jacket pocket, pressed the arrow symbol in the middle of the display screen and handed it to Broncks. It played a silent video clip from a surveillance camera. It was far from perfect resolution – good enough for a general idea, insufficient for identification. John Broncks lowered the phone to avoid the daylight reflecting on the small screen.

A loading dock. A man steps out onto it, with his back to the camera, a bag over his shoulder. As usual, the chain of events is jerky, since a couple of frames are missing for each step, but it is clear that he jumps down from the loading dock and is running at the edge of the picture to a parked lorry. He opens the back doors and jumps in. Twenty-one seconds later he jumps out again and moves quickly to the cab.

Broncks looked up briefly and met Elisa's gaze.

They were thinking the same thing.

Who's missing? What was the dead man's role in the getaway? Was he supposed to have driven the milk lorry, the getaway car, or was he supposed to have loaded the bag with the stolen goods?

'The escape plan's various parts – what you've always said was Dûvnjac's hallmark – hook together in a ridiculously simple way. And, John, that impresses me – against my will.'

She reached out her hand and he put the phone in it.

'They knew that the armoured transport company was still using the system called generation two – that the case was protected but not the cassettes. They knew that there would most likely be patrol cars nearby. That we would get there and see both the getaway car with the engine running and the robber standing watch with his gun. And they knew that we knew that in one hundred cases out of one hundred the robbers leave the scene in the same car they arrived in.'

She pressed the display arrow again and every movement of the man dressed in blue was shown in slow motion. They were on edge even then and it was clear that he was also working for someone who would soon be left at the car park.

'They got us to look at *one* car, while they would be vanishing in another vehicle that would blend in with a million others, and that had been placed there long before the execution of the robbery. I found out that a lorry was stolen the night before last from Arla Dairy's distribution terminal in Västerås and that the registration plates went missing from another vehicle at Arla Dairy's distribution centre in Kallhäll a few hours later.'

That really *was* a milk lorry. Broncks saw it now, the logo on the side of the lorry when it was driving away so much slower in the video sequence.

'They went from being violent robbers to being a natural part of the surroundings, and even the stolen goods became a natural part of the surroundings. They got through the roadblock without us seeing them. And tricks of that sort, John, of such a high calibre, can really only be the work of one bank robber you've investigated in the last few years.'

John Broncks remained seated on his temporary stool. It was almost pleasant. The constantly wobbling stack of papers forced his back to move, to compensate for small shifts, forcing it to relax.

She was probably right.

It most likely was Dûvnjac.

Unique inventiveness in the exchange of escape vehicles and a robber who vanished without a trace: he certainly recognised that. Brilliant escape plans with the kind of targets that were attractive – always small, out-of-the-way banks, with many alternative escape routes and with decent money in their vaults.

'OK, Elisa. I agree with you. There are three patterns, all of which point in the same direction. The gun. The getaway. And the fact that he was released the same day.'

'Four.'

'Four?'

Another paper. This one was in the other pocket of her jacket. A page from the correctional system's register.

'The dead robber was released from his latest prison term five months ago. And do you know from which prison?'

'No. But I guess that you do.'

'Österåker. Cellblock H.'

'Is that so?'

'The same cellblock that Leo Dûvnjac was released from yesterday.'

When he suddenly got up, his makeshift chair collapsed and spread out across the floor. The doubts he had tried to construct were gone. It was no longer probably Dûvnjac – it *was* Dûvnjac. And John Broncks felt almost . . . dizzy. As if all the energy and strength he had ever carried and burned now filled him again.

'Son of a bitch.'

'Yeah. Son of a bitch. That's what I was thinking last night.'

'And . . . so you want to hand it over to me?'

'Yes. There are three piles started on my desk.'

Energy shot him through the room and he walked restlessly back and forth between the door and the window, the desk and the extra chair she was sitting in. He almost spat out the words when he spoke.

'Elisa?'

'Yeah?'

'You can forget that. I don't want your damn piles of paper.'

'Sorry?'

'I want you to work with me. So that we send down that bastard together.'

He stopped in the middle of his eager pacing and looked at her, waiting for a reaction, perhaps even with a smile.

She didn't smile at all. She just sat there as if she hadn't understood what he said.

'Well, I mean, Elisa, I would like you to work with me and—'

'I heard what you said.'

She got up from the chair.

'But I'm not sure I want to.'

What he had interpreted as not being there was actually the opposite, presence.

Her way of speaking, moving. She was completely present.

'Have I understood you right – you aren't sure you want to work on the case?'

'You misunderstand me – I'm not sure I want to work with you.'

She kept her gaze on him. She meant every word.

He ought to be offended but instead he was curious.

'What exactly are you saying?'

'What you just tried to say – that was the second time. And that is one time too many.'

'The second time? The second time – what?'

'You used the oldest trick just now, pulling the rug out – *I don't want your damn piles of paper* – so that I'll submit and gratefully accept what you have to offer when I'm down – *I want you to work with me*. And a little while ago, when I presented those facts I came up with, and you didn't agree, trying to marginalise me by talking about the fact that you stood watching me as I slept. *You seemed to be sleeping very soundly.* That's what psychopaths do. And I don't like it.'

Broncks began walking through the room again, even though it was not his choice. The energy demanded it.

He should have been offended, earlier.

But he wasn't.

He should have been insulted, now.

But he wasn't this time either.

'Before you go, Elisa, and leave the investigation, I want to ask you something.'

She had managed to get halfway to the door – she stopped now.

'Yes?'

'That you bring him in – for me. Interview him for me. If I sit down

102

across from Leo Dûvnjac at this point, it won't accomplish shit. I tried for almost six months of investigation back then, and now it's total stalemate. Plus, I don't want him to gather that I have the investigation on my desk. Not yet.'

'Bring him in, for what? As I see it, we have nothing – and can hold him for at most a couple of hours.'

'Yeah. And he knows it. But if we *don't* bring him in – when he also knows that we have one of the guns he stole, and with time can link the robbery to the day he was released – we'll make him anxious and he'll be on his guard. I want him to stay confident so he'll continue with what I'm certain was just a robbery for bankrolling, the first stop on the way to something bigger. I want to be able to grab him when he commits *that* crime. And, at the same time, find the rest of the guns.'

She didn't respond and just started walking to the door again while he kept talking.

'And, by the way, Elisa, you sat up the whole night, in this hellish building. Until you were so tired that you dropped off in the kitchenette. Can you honestly say to me that you aren't a little curious about him?'

IN THE MIDDLE of his chest.

John Broncks had not felt it right there in such a long time.

Yet he remembered the feeling exactly – how the energy pushed up inside him, seeking its way in an arc from the stomach to the point called the solar plexus. That is where it always settled first, burning, hot and fiery. The next place was in the throat. As if all the joy and anger and fear melted together in the flames. As if breathing got caught there.

Half an hour. Then it burned less, each time he moved the cursor along the timeline on his computer, following the robber on the video sequence she had copied and sent. A large man in bulky clothing jumping down from a loading dock and driving away in a lorry transporting milk.

The first trace after all these years.

The fire in his chest so often scared him as a child, pushing out when every muscle in his stomach tightened inwards, not outwards. When violence was near, it could strike at any time.

Now, as an adult, he had learned to keep the fire under control, carrying the flame with him like an early cave dweller, protecting it so that it never went out and letting it flare up only when he wanted.

Broncks moved the cursor along the timeline again, watching the man carrying a shoulder bag. The description fitted, to a degree. But it was difficult to decide if it was Dûvnjac. This man looked . . . bigger. Which actually wasn't strange. Inmates always increased in muscle mass inside the prison walls. And the gym wasn't only an area for training and the exchange of anabolic steroids. Just like everywhere else in a prison, it was a meeting place for contacts to be established and for ideas to grow and take shape.

He leaned in closer to the rather blurry, jerking picture.

If the man he was studying was Leo Dûvnjac, why was it that someone named Jari Ojala was lying there, dead, and not one of Dûvnjac's two brothers?

Broncks had sensed the rift between the brothers when he interviewed each one of them, not that any of them spoke about it. And he thought

104

he understood how the rift had begun – the two younger brothers had quit while the oldest brother continued robbing banks with their father, and was sent down. And for that reason the younger brothers were also sent down. Fourteen days after a snowstorm and a crashed getaway car, Felix and Vincent Dûvnjac were also arrested in a flat in Göteborg without drama, as if they were waiting for it. Then everyone involved was silent throughout the investigation, and the two younger brothers thought they would get off entirely. But with the publicity and the media attention – which grew further after all their arrests – tips flooded in from the general public. One of them was so good that Broncks was able to locate the destroyed weapons used for one of the robberies. A private individual had stated that he had seen the vehicle that appeared in some of the photos shown on television, a company car that the brothers drove around in. Their robbers' façade. The tipster had seen the car drive into a wooded area and unload 'something heavy' there which they then dumped in a small lake. Divers found the heavy objects – boxes with gun parts, infused with concrete. DNA and fingerprints linked Leo as well as Felix and Vincent Dûvnjac to one of the bank robberies.

John Broncks followed the man dressed in overalls to the lorry one last time.

If you had succeeded in involving your brothers, you would have been equally unwilling as you were then to allow one of them to die. You have assembled a new constellation – and one of them is already dead.

If it is you driving away in the milk truck, maybe you're the only one left.

If it isn't you, you have at least one partner who's alive.

You, or your partner, are acting totally calm. You, or your partner, are walking around as if nothing happened. One of you was shot, and you, or your partner, simply continue.

And I haven't felt this good in six years.

Because, you see, what's burning in my chest is happiness.

I just got a second chance to bust you, to make your life the same hell you emerged from yesterday, although for a whole lot longer this time.

THE BLACK CAR was too new, too expensive, too shiny. It glided past her kitchen window for the third time now and slowed down at the driveway without stopping completely.

Britt-Marie could see the two men in the front seat clearly, an older, grey-haired one and a younger one with short-cropped hair, the same men every time.

It was a car that didn't belong here.

The windows on one side of the house faced the wide, humming Nynäs motorway, groaning with constant traffic from dawn to dusk, with just a sparse hedge between. From the window on the other side, where the narrow road formed a U, or was it a V, binding together fourteen semi-detached houses, the only other thing she saw was the neighbours' cars. But the black, shiny car, with its stealth and streamlined bonnet, made her think of a predator's drawn-back shoulders.

The first time she observed it must have been around nine o'clock. She had just woken up on her day off from the nursing home and was sitting with a cup of coffee. Through the window she saw it glide past like a shark, at a time when usually no one ever passed by. It became so empty in a residential area where everyone was still working and could afford to drive alone to work. She noticed the car the most then, thinking that it didn't seem to know where it was going. Then she forgot about it, and started preparing the lunch instead. The pot with potatoes and water would stand ready on the hob, and she'd simply have to turn the knob. The side of salmon was on the cutting board in front of her, glossy and pink, much like raspberry gumdrops. She had pulled out the salmon's small, transparent bones, like plucking eyebrows, except the salmon bones were harder to remove, having become entrenched like rebar even though they were delicate, and put it in an oblong ovenproof dish on the top shelf in the fridge. She would simply have to put it in the oven for twenty minutes when all three of her sons had arrived. Salt and pepper, pile on the full-fat cream and dill, let it sit an additional ten minutes. It was Vincent's favourite dish – he had managed to visit her several times since *his* release – but she was a bit uncertain whether Leo liked salmon these days, it was so long ago. Together.

She shivered, involuntarily, quite moved, which she seldom was but it was also seldom that she saw them all at the same time.

The second time she saw the black predator car slink by was about half an hour later. She felt strong discomfort without knowing why. Suddenly she thought of – him. Of Ivan. What did he have to do with predator cars? Showing up at the wall and buzzing about like a foul-smelling bluebottle. What was he really doing there? Was he going to start meddling again? The same going-on about changing and that he had made new decisions and would start over and that it included other people who didn't want it?

Change – it was hardened in concrete. It could no longer be changed. Could never be undone.

She had chosen not to think about him for six years – actually eighteen. But six years ago she was forced to think about him again in connection with the bank robbery, trial and sentence. How in heaven's name can a father be made in such a way that he gets involved in a bank robbery together with his own son? And believes that it is a good way to get to know the sons he lost because of violence and blows; that he can receive, as well as give, closeness? And then has the gall to stand in front of the wrought-iron gate at the wall and maintain that if he hadn't been there, Leo would have died. With his infernal ideas about creating conflicts, building a clan united against the whole world! The bloody holy family! And now – would these bonds continue to entangle her sons? The bonds Ivan tied so tight during their childhood, at a time when her sons were finally heading in different directions?

She leaned further forward to see better, resting one cheek against the windowpane. That was the third time the predator car had slowed down then slipped past. She didn't take her eyes off it, moving from room to room and window to window, until it turned off towards Nynäs motorway and the rumbling traffic. Gone. She'd imagined it. And she knew why. Her panic from the night, over the bonds held together that could pull down. She'd let Ivan, like the predator, sneak into her head, churning, going around and around and watching her, making her overinterpret what she saw.

A rippling, hearty laugh.

She heard Leo and Felix's voices from the dining room, Felix laughing though he didn't often laugh these days. He seemed pleased, almost happy about sitting there again with his big brother. Felix's laugh answered Leo's silly, disguised voice imitating someone as he used to do, when the two were together, the jargon they'd always had between them. Leo had always been the one who could most easily break through Felix's blunt opposition.

Britt-Marie shook off the unpleasant feelings brought on by the predator car. Now they were going to have a lovely time, and celebrate being together again as a family, *her* image of a family.

She had been waiting and longing for it.

This lunch – reuniting, all her sons around the table. The image had become the goal she thought about before each new prison visit, which made her able to carry on.

The telephone attached to the wall above the work desk didn't ring especially often these days – most phone calls had stopped at the time of her sons' arrests. Shame works like that and she had had her own share of silence. Shame isolates and makes the ashamed withdraw.

But now it rang. Repeated, penetrating rings.

'Hello, Mamma.'

'Vincent! So good that you called.'

She walked towards the fridge with the telephone cord stretched out and pulled out the prepared oven dish.

'When are you getting here? Should I put the salmon in now? It needs some time, you know, for the cream to thicken, which you like so much.'

'I can't come, Mamma.'

She stood in the middle of the kitchen floor, the telephone receiver in one hand and the oven dish in the other, balanced, perfectly still.

'Has something . . . happened?'

'I just can't make it. The flat, I have the inspection tomorrow, and two large floor tiles have cracked. Expensive Italian crap that's always breaking in old bathrooms. I told the owners right from the start.'

She listened to a son who never usually talked so much, nor was so specific. Too much and too detailed, as when a person is lying.

'Is that really true, Vincent? Is it?'

'Mamma?'

'Yes?'

'I can't cope with it. Not right now.'

She should have felt betrayed, disappointed. Her goal, the image of them all together, would now be missing one of the three. But she felt the opposite, she felt relieved. She thought she understood what it was that he couldn't cope with. It was the bonds – the same bonds she herself had broken loose from. Vincent didn't show up at the prison yesterday either. And somehow she was glad that her youngest son seemed aware that bonds can ensnare – because only then is it possible to face them. Even if it includes lying to Mamma.

'I'll save you some. Put it in the fridge. Come by when you're hungry.'

She balanced the glass dish, opened the oven door and placed it roughly in the centre. She turned on the potatoes and took out the pitcher of iced water. Lemon wedges were crowded in with ice cubes, which rattled when they hit the glass. She walked towards the infectious laughter and the consciously idiotic voice: Felix and Leo, as they were back then. With the pitcher on the table the ice cubes weren't rattling any more. Then she took away one of the four plates that had been set on the table.

'The food will be ready soon. But there'll just be three of us. Vincent isn't coming.'

It was as if she was hurrying to turn back, and had managed to get to the kitchen doorway when Leo's question caught up with her.

'Mamma?'

'Yes?'

'Why?'

'It was something about . . . Italian tiles cracking. And an inspection.'

'What the fuck? The job again.'

She heard in Leo's voice that he had heard a lie, that he understood. His mother was participating in the lie, not just conveying it. He realised that his little brother was avoiding him. And when she stepped into the kitchen, the laughter and merriment, which had been so heartwarming, stopped.

'Mamma?'

They looked at each other from separate rooms.

'If Vincent calls again – tell him that I've worked quite a lot in construction also, tiled a few bathrooms, and have a pretty good idea of what an inspector is looking for when he wants to expose scams in the building trade.'

Felix had sat passively until then but when his mother disappeared behind the kitchen wall he leaned forward, whispering.

'Leave him alone, Leo. He'll be in touch with you when he's ready.'

Leo didn't answer, and instead reached for the door to the dining room, pulled it gently shut and invited in the sort of blank silence that enters when an oven and kitchen fan's monotonous hum is suddenly abated.

'Now we have a moment to ourselves.'

'To ourselves? What the fuck are you up to, Leo?'

'More or less the same thing as when we were little and Mamma called from the balcony that dinner would be ready soon.'

The ice cubes clinked like before when he filled their glasses.

Closed doors, water, two parties.

Like at a negotiation.

'Felix?'

'Yeah?'

'How do you want to live? I mean, really *live?*'

'Stop it.'

'Do you want to continue to live on student grants? Hounded for debts to the crime victims' authority? Not able to take out even a shit loan at the bank? Turned down for jobs because you're on the crime register? Or . . . do you maybe want instead to have unlimited money, move away from this hellish country and start over?'

Felix leaned back, as they do in negotiations to announce that they dislike the question.

'It's almost time for lunch, big brother, so what the fuck do you want?'

'I need your help.'

'Help? What does that mean?'

'A replacement.'

A sip of water and a piece of ice was stuck between chewing surfaces on the right side of Felix's jaw and it crunched loudly when it was bitten in two.

'Replacement? Oh, yeah, there was evidently a lot of shooting yesterday. I have a television too.'

Leo waited for the damn crunching to subside.

'Help with a one-time deal. No armed robbery, nothing like what we were doing before. A job.'

'A one-time deal, Leo? A job? That was exactly how it sounded all those bloody years ago. Do you remember? Before the ICA shop. Before the thirty thousand in the leather bag, *one time and then we don't need any more.* Or what was it you called it . . . a heist? Heist, brother!'

'That's exactly what it is. A heist. A supercool robbery. We walk right

110

in, take out a hundred million and no one is going to see it. I would never do it, or get you involved, if it was about, say . . . twenty million. That wouldn't be enough, when it's full speed ahead and all the damn costs to disappear and the loot's gone in two years. But now, my brother, a hundred million. And they won't even know we're doing it.'

Leo put his hand lightly on Felix's forearm, and it was as if Felix jumped, so familiar that both of them rather regretted it – Leo for putting his hand there, Felix for reacting to it.

'And look, by the way, we didn't do anything else. At least not for ten years.'

'But I knew the whole time. That you would continue. At some point. That's . . . you. What you became, then. When Pappa beat Mamma. When you took over.'

'Amateur psychologists. I got my fill of them inside.'

'Call it whatever the fuck you want. But it was never about the money – about snatching a bank money bag and making off with thirty thousand. It was about . . . the fact that you could. Plan. Get away. Control the circumstances. Just as ten banks were never about the money either, not for you, Leo. Whatever you say about it, it was the same thing – because you could. A robbery would become a double robbery would become a triple robbery. And who the fuck knows what it would have become if someone hadn't stopped you then.'

'This time.'

'What?'

'What I'm trying to get you to understand. That you should be a part of it. That we will finish what someone interrupted. The largest Swedish hold-up ever.'

'Because you can.'

'Keep calling it whatever you want, brother, if it makes you feel good. I'm going to do it. Are you in or are you not?'

Felix glanced at the closed door and whispered again.

'Burst blood.'

'What?'

'It's a hell of a lot better than black gaps.'

'Brother, are you OK?'

'I'm fine, Leo. The question is – are you? Do you know what you really want? And where you're actually heading? I know where I'm heading. And I will choose burst blood every time.'

'Felix . . . what in fuck's name are you talking about?'

'When we were little – how old were you? Nine? Ten? – you and Pappa and that bloody Bear Dance. It was just you and him, Leo. Your fucking . . . philosophy. Your philosophy of violence that he taught you so that you could lash back if someone went after us. I am sure you remember that – but I remember something else. When Pappa beat Mamma's eyes red, on the outside, and at the same time beat in black gaps on the inside. I remember that the red disappeared but the gaps remained.'

He didn't have to whisper. The door was closed – she couldn't hear. But that wasn't the reason. It was as if the words weren't allowed to become too large and imagine they would get to stay.

'Do you get it, big brother? It is simple, but it's my philosophy of violence – burst blood is better than black gaps.'

Leo smiled a scornful smile.

'Now I get it! You *have* gone to the prison psychologist and harped on about a whole load of shit—'

'Why?'

'—about how everyone feels bad on the fucking childhood potty, Felix—'

'Why?'

'—and sat there and thought backwards while I thought forwards and then—'

'Leo – listen for fuck's sake! *Why are you doing this?*'

Felix had stood up and he wasn't whispering any more.

'Because it's my only chance.'

'No. We've had our chances.'

'In two days we are going to do something the police won't understand. That cop bastard Broncks won't see it – not before we disappear.'

'Disappear?'

'For ever. You can't stay around after a heist like this. That's why we're talking with each other now. I don't want to disappear without you, without Vincent.'

It would have been easier to be dealing with a big brother who was teasing, almost excessive. But he was serious now. What he was saying was absolutely in earnest and required an even clearer response.

'I don't want to have your stolen money, Leo. I decided that long before you were sent down – and you know it.'

A glance towards the closed dining room door – it sounded like a

112

doorbell out there, two high tones turning into two low tones and then two high tones again.

'So there'll be no heist with me along. You said it then, a one-time thing. Exactly as you are saying now. But it will keep on, keep on, keep on. I know it and you know it, Leo. And that isn't my life, not any more.'

The doorbell, again. They were both sure of it. Then the footsteps, Mamma's footsteps, and the humming from the kitchen fan came rushing in when she opened the dining room door.

'Leo, you have visitors.'

The kitchen fan was accompanied by the smell of oily fish in dill, which would be ready soon, but she didn't look so pleased when she looked in. All the recent expectations were gone.

'Police. And they want to speak to you.'

The door was ajar. It was possible to see into the kitchen. Two men and a woman. Outdoor clothing on, shoes on. But obviously police, despite the civilian clothes. Leo vaguely recognised both the men – he had seen them in the morning when they were gliding by in a black unmarked car, the older one with a grey moustache and the younger one, fit from working out and sunburned. He had understood that they constituted the vanguard sent out to confirm that Leo Dûvnjac was currently here.

Since a robber had been shot to death and his weapon had fallen to the ground, he had foreseen that Broncks would come but he hadn't known *when*. He also guessed right about how the cop bastard would reason – bring him in when he was at his mother's house because the probability of violence was low.

Lunchtime. Still a long way until evening.

They would have plenty of time to implement stage two of the plan – *the house call* – afterwards, albeit somewhat modified. Now that one of the weapons lay in Broncks's hands, the house call must be made more comprehensive, taking up more time than he had imagined. But an altered plan didn't have to mean a worse plan. New conditions can always, should always, be changed to an advantage. He would use the afternoon's interview to provoke the bastard, to lead Broncks in the wrong direction so that, when the final stunt was carried out two days from now, he would find himself in an entirely different place – tricked twice.

Leo shrugged his shoulders and stood up, while Felix leaned forward and hissed 'You will never speak to me about that again.' He passed his mother, smiled at her and caressed her cheek as she had done his yesterday

113

evening and whispered 'It will be all right, Mamma', and continued into the kitchen. He looked around and out through the window. There were two cars in the drive and in one an additional cop waiting for him.

But not Broncks. Where the hell was he?

He turned to the grey-haired one.

'And you want?'

He got an answer, but not from the person he'd posed the question to – from the woman. She was not very much older than he was himself.

'My name is Elisa Cuesta. And I'd like you to come with us. For an interview. For information.'

He examined her, tall and slim, with a steady gaze, seemingly unconcerned. The same eyes that Mamma looked at him with now, neither reproachful nor sad. Joy and expectation had been replaced by the hardened armour she wore sometimes when they were little – that which was nothing – and therefore so much worse. He nodded silently. It hadn't mattered what he tried to say to her just now, and he walked towards the front door and the two police cars on her drive.

'We are taking your son in for an interview – but we'll also conduct a search of the premises since he provided your address as his current one.'

Britt-Marie looked at the young policewoman. Search? Here? In her home? Her new security? She'd moved here herself and built it up when she left the shame, the constant whispering about a criminal family.

'I don't understand.'

And now strangers would be rooting around in this new security as the new neighbours looked on?

'If so, I'd like to see the warrant.'

Even back then they hadn't rooted around in her home. Had something even worse happened now? Had Leo done something even worse? He came home late yesterday. *Mostly drove around.*

She was just about to repeat her question to the woman who seemed to be in charge of the small group of police, when she felt a pair of steady hands around her shoulders. Someone was holding her, from behind.

'They don't need one, Mamma.'

Arms that turned her around and hugged her. Felix.

'In this country they can walk right in and turn your house upside down without a warrant. It's enough if the prosecutor on duty is having a bad day.'

'You're Felix, I presume.'

114

Elisa looked at the young man who was a little taller than his older brother and rougher in some way, and as dark as his brother was fair.

'Yes.'

She pulled out a paper from the outside pocket of her jacket.

'In that case I would like you to confirm that this . . .'

She pointed to the lines of text at the bottom.

'. . . is a correct home address.'

He nodded.

'Yes. That's right.'

'And the one under that, can you verify that it is the correct home address for your younger brother?'

'Yeah.'

'Thank you. Then I would appreciate it if you would write down at the very bottom the addresses where you can be reached during the day.'

She handed him a pen and at the same time Britt-Marie opened the oven door and took out the salmon. The cream was a little burnt. She put it down hard on the hob. A muted clunk.

'Now I demand to know what this is about! You take one of my sons and then gather information about my two other sons – even though they have served their sentences, been free for two years and during that time have not done a single thing to gain your interest!'

The policewoman did not seem affected in the least by a woman shouting at her.

'I am sorry, but it's a routine procedure, which – and certainly we both are hoping this – will be able to show that none of your sons needs to be investigated further.'

Britt-Marie was looking at her but didn't really hear what she was saying. She heard something entirely different. A wardrobe squeaking in her bedroom and clothes hangers clattering when they were thrown onto her bed. And now, now she heard someone pulling the drawers that contained her underwear out from her chest of drawers. She hurried to the room. And she got there in time to see them empty them out onto the floor, do the same with the drawer of her night table and tear her towels and bedding out of the corner cabinet. She was about to step in through the doorway to protest when the policewoman caught up with her.

'If you leave, Britt-Marie, I will see to it that it is done a bit more carefully.'

Elisa waited as the house owner walked to the kitchen.

'Stop.'

The two colleagues looked at her and kept on searching through the pants and pillowcases with their hands.

'I said *stop*.'

Then they did. They stopped.

'From now on conduct this in a dignified manner. We aren't in a hurry. All you're doing right now is destroying trust and room for collaboration – and perhaps we'll need her help later.'

Elisa stayed long enough to establish that they'd both listened to her. Then she returned to the woman who was standing by the cooker, her back towards her as she scraped away the burnt layer of salmon in the ovenproof dish.

'I apologise, Britt-Marie. I know how it feels. It's like witnessing a burglary at your own home.'

Britt-Marie didn't respond even though the young police officer made an effort to sound pleasant. She didn't even turn around – she quite simply lacked the strength. She used a fork to poke away the burnt surface of the cream, dropping what couldn't be eaten into the rubbish bag. She pulled out a piece of aluminium foil long enough to cover the entire dish. All the while she heard the two men continue to root around, but more calmly, with less clattering, and then the female detective open and close the front door on her way out to the drive and the car with Leo in the back seat.

And it was then that she realised that what she had just tried, to bring them together, would never succeed. Because this was how division looked, bonds loosened and torn apart.

A STERILE ROOM. Cramped, like a large wardrobe. A simple table with a monitor, 16-inch, in the middle of it. That was all. Nothing on the walls. Not much in the way of lighting.

But a cup of silver tea.

John Broncks grabbed the hot cup, took a first sip and swallowed it.

Silver tea. It would have been unthinkable in a previous life. Until the police authority's doctor explained five years ago that at the age of thirty-five he had consumed a lifetime's supply of coffee. It seemed so strangely empty. Not the emptiness without twelve cups of caffeine – *that* withdrawal stopped after a couple of weeks: the fatigue, headache, shaky hands – it was the absence of the *habit,* the regularity becoming abstinence that preyed on him. Not stirring a spoon around in a hot cup, holding onto the heat of the liquid and feeling it fill his chest. Then he remembered his grandfather, a white-haired man, as wise and friendly as he was old, who began every morning with a cup of what he called silver tea: regular, heated water. Once, he'd jazzed it up, hot water with a teaspoon of cream. When Broncks arrived early at the station the next day and felt the infernal loss, he went into the kitchenette, turned on the electric kettle and made his own first cup of silver tea. The missing habit was replaced by a new one. Still the hot cup to hold on to, and the warmth spreading in his chest.

He put the cup down by the monitor and with his right hand adjusted the microphone, which formed a gentle arc from his ear to mouth, and fine-tuned it until it didn't slide with the movements of his head.

'Elisa?'

No answer.

'Elisa, can you hear me?'

It crackled in his ear, and then she did as he had done, adjusted the microphone and earpiece.

'Now I hear you, John. Perfectly.'

'Right then. Before you go in I'll go over what we agreed on. Under

117

no circumstances does he get to know that I am overseeing the interview. Because it is only the beginning of something much bigger. And when he leaves here, he has to feel so calm that he will continue with his plans. Good luck.'

Broncks turned one of the monitor's few knobs. It was working and he peered into a room just like the one he was sitting in. Bare walls, a drab table as the focal point with the monitor replaced by a smaller camera. But it was neither the table nor what was on it that interested him. It was the man who sat at it, leaning on his elbows. Someone he knew so incredibly well, yet not at all. The fair hair, blue eyes and stiff, thin lips.

They had sat in the interview room John Broncks was looking into now, across from each other, during a period of six months. Days filled with a family – interviews switching from oldest brother to middle brother to youngest brother to father and back to oldest brother. And not a word out of place from any of them. They were fully synchronised in their rehearsed reactions – the superior silence, the provocative stare at the floor. The smile accompanying 'no comment', which became a new smile along with 'I've never heard of that' and 'I don't know him, have never met him – what did you say his name was?'

Twenty-nine hours in freedom. And that bastard was sitting there again, waiting for the door to open, for the other chair to be pulled out and the questions that would not bring forth answers.

Broncks leaned closer to the screen.

Leo Dûvnjac seemed calm, not like someone who had robbed a security van the day before and seen his fellow robber shot to death. Nonetheless – the gun, the robber holding it, the getaway, the timing – all in all it made John certain that Elisa's piecing together of the facts was correct.

I am looking at you.

Do you know that?

Dûvnjac seemed not only calm but also focused, almost pleased. When he examined the ugly institutional table, he was trying to sink down into it. Broncks had already realised in the last round that they were similar in that way, both being fascinated by the interview's built-in theatrical art. Leo Dûvnjac studied the tabletop and ran his palm slowly over it and soon after performed the same motion with just his middle finger.

Gently, almost sensually.

As if he were rectifying an invisible board, waiting for the pieces that would be moved, one at a time.

But not by me, you bastard, not this time.

John Broncks had not even managed to finish his thought when the man he was watching also leaned forward, aiming his gaze straight at the camera, his eyes full of intensity. As if he was not just observing a camera lens, but rather a person. So he smiled, as if at a mirror, and Broncks was close to smiling back.

Now. The clicking sound of a door handle being pushed down and of light footsteps he had come to recognise – after a few years in the corridor of the criminal investigation division – as Elisa's. Finally, the sound of a chair scraping against the floor as it was dragged by someone not seen in the picture but who sat down. On the left edge of the picture, the camera showed a trace of shoulder and a cheek and short, dark hair at the back of a neck.

'You made me wait. Was that deliberate? To make me stressed? If so, you should know that it didn't work. You've tried that trick before.'

Leo Dûvnjac's voice was composed, as always during interviews. He had been the only one who had sometimes engaged in real conversation between all the silence and 'no comments' without giving away too much. Dûvnjac, an intelligent man, had shown himself to be surprisingly well read, with a sense of humour that stemmed from the kind of thoughts that range freely, albeit through forced conversation.

'And, listen, policewoman? This is an interrogation room. I have seen enough of them to know that. And back at my mother's house I thought that it sounded as though it was going to be an interview to get some information, not that you were going to interrogate me.'

Elisa didn't answer. It wasn't a question.

'Do you mind if I turn on the camera?'

'Yes.'

'Yes? And why would you—'

'I think it would be rather strange. Even a bit peculiar and not amusing. To turn it on, I mean. Since it already *is* on.'

He looked into it again and smiled at Broncks, who remembered how it felt. To realise that the man he was interrogating, and who he was certain had committed ten bank robberies, had an adult child's brain – impossible to predict – and that he had wished so strongly that he could penetrate and understand it.

Elisa's chair scraped but not like before. Now the plastic tips of the chair legs cut into the plastic carpet and she approached the camera's microphone, looking for the red light. She checked and saw that it *was* on. And her voice was ironic when she admitted it.

'Yes, you're right – it *is* on. The *technician* should have let me know when he turned it on.'

The technician.

She had looked directly into the camera when she said that. At him.

And she was certainly right. He should of course have informed her. But he had been so eager, almost looking forward to it as if he was seeing an old friend again. Wondering if the face had changed. If the wisdom in the eyes was different. If the smile had become stiff. If the man who was sitting there, filling the monitor, had altered. If the time in prison had given any insight, or if daily life among Sweden's worst criminals, with the status a successful bank robber has, had, on the contrary, strengthened his criminal identity. It was like meeting an old friend, but with one essential difference – he hoped that time *hadn't* changed him for the better.

Elisa disappeared out of the picture and when she was visible again it was just a bit of her neck and shoulder and cheek, as before.

INTERVIEWING OFFICER ELISA CUESTA (IO): Information-gathering interview with Leo Ivan Dûvnjac beginning 14.17 at the City Police Department, Kronoberg.

She held a folder in her hands, and she hit it hard against the wooden surface, as if to straighten what was in it. That wasn't the reason at all, Broncks was certain of that. She thumped it again, a powerful blow amplified by the bare room. It found its way into the camera's microphone and drilled into his earpiece. She knew precisely where the blow would land. He supposed she had finished her demonstration, but he lowered the volume for incoming sound to be on the safe side.

Then she put the folder down, opened it and pushed the document on top towards the man being interviewed.

A photograph of a man lying on the ground at a car park.

IO: Do you know who this is?
LEO DÛVNJAC (LD): No. There's a balaclava in the way.

No unintended look. No unintended gesture.

Not the fleeting finger on the tip of the nose, the temple or point of the chin – touching the face to feel security in an insecure situation. Not the second of hesitation when the eye steers its gaze upwards off to the right for constructing a lie, instead of off to the left for searching among existing memories.

Even though he was forced to look at a dead man he might have had a relationship with.

On the contrary.

Leo Dûvnjac ran one hand over the surface of the table, adjusted something that wasn't there and moved pieces on the invisible board game.

> IO: In that case . . . perhaps you know now. Who it is. Since this is the same person – without a mask.

No reaction. Even though the photograph, which they had agreed should be number two in the sequence, showed a head lying on a steel frame on a shiny metal autopsy table. The eyes lifeless. The mouth almost disappointed, sullen, frozen at the moment of death. The forehead with an opening that resembled red, upturned, glossy petals, which had just burst out of the exit hole and now were covered with fragments of the skull, skin and tufts of hair.

> LD: No.
> IO: No . . . what?
> LD: I don't recognise him.

The third and final photo from the folder.

> IO: Let's try again. The same person. When he was alive. A photo from the criminal register you're in yourself.

She pushed it forward, careful so that it would reach all the way to his side of the table.

> IO: Do you know who he is?
> LD: Yes.
> IO: Can you expand on that?
> LD: Yes, I know who it is.
> IO: OK. You want to have it that way. Then we'll try this. *Who* is it?

LD: Jari Ojala.

IO: How do you know Jari Ojala?

LD: We were in the same cellblock at Österåker. But surely you knew that already?

IO: How well did you know him?

LD: And how well do you know *him*? The man who's sitting looking at the monitor on the other side of the camera? People who spend their time in the same corridor, a few locked doors away, don't always know each other so well, right?

Broncks had heard – and he knew exactly what it meant.

The man who's sitting looking at the monitor on the other side of the camera.

Leo Dûvnjac assumed that John Broncks was leading the investigation. But they had made him uncertain and he was looking for confirmation.

IO: You can keep looking at me. I am the one conducting this interview and I want to know if you had any contact since his release.

LD: No.

IO: In that case did you have any contact since your release?

LD: No.

IO: No contact at all?

LD: Hey, policewoman, Broncks's puppet?

Broncks's puppet.

An additional gamble.

LD: If it is as you are saying – that it is the same person in all the photos – I don't really understand how it would have come about. It is difficult to have contact with the dead.

The same facial expressions and restricted patterns of motion. Whether he replied yes or no, whether he admitted he recognised him or not.

Broncks saw Elisa gather up the three photographs and put them back in the folder. A planned break before the next question.

IO: I want to know where you were yesterday at 4.30 p.m.

LD: In a car.

IO: Where?

LD: On the way to dinner with my father. The Dráva restaurant, near Skanstull. There are several witnesses who can confirm that. My father, the owner and his wife, who were well paid for the food, and other patrons who sat drinking beer. But I don't understand why that would be of interest – am I suspected of something?

IO: I am the one who asks the questions of you.

LD: No, it's . . .

Leo reached across the table and suddenly hit the lens of the camera with his fingertips, knocking it hard.

LD: . . . him sitting in there.

And he stared straight into the camera. Challenging. Provoking. Broncks managed to think that it was good that he had placed himself in a different room and let Elisa sit there – because it was working. He *felt* the challenge, *became* provoked and actually wanted to get up and shout that.

LD: In there!

Leo hit the lens again and his gaze penetrated the camera and into the room Broncks was sitting in. And it remained there. Pure hatred of the cop who once locked him up.

IO: On the way to a restaurant, you say. Then I would like to know where you were before that. Before 4.30.

Disappointment.

Broncks was certain of it. That was what he caught a glimpse of in the face of the man being interviewed.

Leo Dûvnjac hadn't got the reaction he expected.

No matter how she was attacked or disturbed, Elisa had not taken the bait and acknowledged what he'd hoped.

IO: Perhaps you did not understand what I said? So I'll take it one more time. Slowly. Where were you before 4.30 p.m.?
LD: I was in prison. For six years.

Broncks realised that Elisa had just given Dûvnjac the same look he'd received himself not long ago, the ice-cold look hurled at anyone trying to marginalise her.

IO: A third time. Even clearer. According to the correctional system's personnel at Österåker, you were released at 09.00. Eleven minutes later, according to the surveillance cameras, you disappeared from the area in a car delivered by a younger man, identified as your brother, and a middle-aged woman, identified as your mother. I would like to know what you did between 09.11 and 4.30.
LD: And why does Broncks's puppet want to know that?
IO: I want to know that because yesterday an AK4 with the serial number 10663 was used at the robbery of a security van. Because it comes from a cache of guns stolen nearly eight years ago and you were a suspect. *That is why I'm asking that question.*

It happened so quickly then. Dûvnjac grabbed hold of the camera's microphone and the picture went dark, his chest covering the light.

IO: May I ask you to stay seated!

Deep breaths. His mouth close to the microphone.

LD: Broncks?

And then he hit the palm of his hand against the microphone several times, dull blows that grew to cracks of a whip in a cramped room.

LD: Broncks – your little puppet and I have just been talking about how well people know their neighbours in a corridor. That they don't always, that secrets are hidden behind the next door. Just like you're trying to hide yourself from me right now. But you should know something – we get to know each other there, in the

124

prison corridors. We have plenty of time, sitting together – bank robbers, drug kings, even the occasional . . . patricide.

The face out of focus.

But Broncks didn't see it. Now there was only the sound of Leo's voice, in an interview during which control had slowly dissolved and lost its planned form.

LD: Broncks – you *get* trust if you earn it. And I got the trust of many in there.

A plan that was based on the idea of Leo Dûvnjac leaving here feeling calm.

LD: For example, there was a prisoner, can you imagine, who told me about how he stabbed his father to death in a summer cabin.

But he would never do that now, unless the person he was trying to flush out now, John Broncks, made himself known.

LD: Twenty-seven fucking cuts in his own father's chest.

No one beyond the police investigation team knew about the twenty-seven stab wounds in John Broncks's own father.

LD: Broncks? You hear? I even know the details.

John Broncks was not aware that he'd got up, hurried to the door and opened it.

It was several years since he'd had regular contact with Sam. That was when his brother was at Kumla. But prisoners were moved around between prisons, and he remembered Sam was at Österåker when he came with the news of their mother's death.

Did those two get to know each other? Sam – and this bastard?

LD: Listen, Broncks, a fucking fishing knife, evidently. Cut after cut. Do you want to hear even more?

Broncks had left his seat in front of the monitor, and when he no longer heard Leo Dûvnjac's voice filtered through a microphone, when he met Elisa's warning look, he first realised that he had entered the interview room.

'I think we'll . . . stop now.'

'Stop?'

Elisa's gaze demanded he look at her but he turned away towards the interview chair.

'And I'll follow you out to the exit.'

Now.

Now he was aware.

Of every step he took. That *they* took.

Side by side, in silence, through the first of Kronoberg police station's corridors, down the stairs, through still more corridors.

Aware of how long it took for a stride on average. Of how powerful the forward motion of the foot was and how it began in the hip, not in the ball of the foot or heel, as he'd always thought. Of how the sound from the heels of the shoes stole over the stone floor before it struck the wall of the corridor and became entangled with the next step. Of how everything around him had to be larger to make what was breaking inside him smaller.

My corridors. My world.

I was supposed to see through him, penetrate his brain. Whereas he saw through me and has already forced his way into my brain.

As Broncks put his hand on the cold, grooved handle of the heavy iron door that would lead them out into the afternoon light of Berg Street he stopped staring down at the floor and could bear to look at him again. It was then that he realised it.

That bastard knows my brother better than I do.

My history.

I have avoided it, even broke off an interview to dodge it – it came in uninvited. And on his face, that is not a superior sneer, that is years of accumulated hate.

'Hey, Broncks?'

They had just parted company and Dûvnjac had gone down the last of the stone steps that ended at the pavement when he began to speak, attacking again.

'Black thread, Broncks.'

126

Broncks grabbed the heavy iron door to stop it from closing again and responded to Dûvnjac's hateful sneer in a low voice.

'I don't understand what you're talking about. But it doesn't matter – you and I are finished for today.'

Dûvnjac continued to walk away, while Broncks stood there, wanting to be sure that he was actually leaving. Dûvnjac walked ten steps before he stopped again, and began moving his arms against his upper body like a rower, or gymnast. Broncks couldn't put the gestures into a context.

Then Dûvnjac raised his voice, and repeated the incomprehensible phrase.

'Today, John Broncks, was a truly black fucking thread for you.'

LEO TURNED AROUND one last time and watched the bastard cop go in before the heavy door to the police station slid shut.

He set off on a walk along Hantverkar Street in the slightly cold weather. He passed a clock on the wall of a café which pointed to a quarter past three and continued to walk for a couple more blocks, this time in the shade with the wind biting his cheeks, just enough to feel pleasant. The afternoon rush hour had just started and at this time of day walking or riding the bus took the same amount of time, so he decided to continue walking the whole way to Skanstull.

Somewhere around the heights of City Hall he slowly started to understand what had made him suddenly shout out *black thread* at the cop bastard. It had felt so familiar – like when he was little and had left a different police station with the same light steps. The feeling now with Broncks was similar to a feeling then with Pappa – a feeling of having turned a situation to his advantage, having won and gained strength from it. It was always a dizzying feeling.

An information-gathering interview? Then I'm going to gather information from you, you bastard Broncks.

And now he would use both of them, linking the antagonist then with the antagonist now, Broncks and Pappa, who were in some way responsible for himself and his brothers being arrested and split up. As a present to his pappa, he would see to it that none of them was in the way when he walked into the police station that he had just left – to carry out the final job.

He walked across the bridge along the railway tracks, and around Riddarholmen on the outer edge, enjoying watching the remains of chipped ice formations drift with the current. He could see the houseboats at the quay at Söder Mälarstrand with their lights, and a bit higher up the other light shooting from the cliffs of Södermalm, a dome of artificial glow that he had missed in the compact darkness on Sam's island. He passed Slussen and Götgatsbacken, which these days was a pedestrian street, and continued down Göt Street past the rebuilt and completely commercialised 'Tax

128

Scraper', towards Ring Road, unfurling like a runway from the southern footing of Johanneshovs Bridge and the Dráva restaurant.

But he wasn't intending to go there yet. For the moment, he turned to enter Ring Galleria and the sort of telephone shop he didn't normally frequent. Telephones that needed to be secure and properly encrypted were bought in another way – the one in his pocket, called Quasar X, came from Japan. It had been chosen as the world's best terrorist phone in product tests. The one he was here to buy needed to be the opposite – to operate like the world's worst terrorist phone, completely without encryption programs and guaranteed to be easily tracked.

When he came out of the shop twenty minutes later with the present in his pocket, he crossed Ring Road and walked back past Åhléns department store at Skanstull with the blue clock hanging on the façade, still five minutes off. He approached the restaurant his father had chosen as his regular hangout. It was strange, if you thought about it, that he spent a large number of his waking hours at a bar *after* having decided to never drink alcohol again. It was as if he wanted to show the world that will is stronger than desire.

Through an illuminated window, with D-R-Á-V-A written in letters divided into three colours horizontally, green, white and red, he could see it was nearly empty inside, apart from a pair of day drinkers – the sort who managed to keep up a routine of steady drinking, but would never sink below the surface and be mistaken for outcasts. Then he saw his father, staring at the beer taps. Was he going to buy a pint and surrender? Maybe it was already standing there, a glittering gold tankard hidden by his body?

It had sounded different yesterday.

Not a drop in two years.

He went in and tapped on his father's somewhat drooping but still broad shoulder.

'Dad.'

His father barely turned his head.

'Today I'm evidently Dad – yesterday I was *Ivan*.'

Ivan's gaze wandered back to the beer taps, which stood in a row and smelled sour and sweet at the same time. That was probably the reason two black flies hovered there. He'd noticed them when he came in looking for Dacso, hankering like hell for coffee.

'Dad, listen, it was stupid of me to sound so cross when you called yesterday.'

129

The flies had caught his interest straight away, two black dots equipped with wings, defying gravity. He had increasingly failing vision, and that he could still see a fly that was not making a sound put him in high spirits, even though he knew very well that the smell attracting them was a sign that Dacso wasn't keeping his bar clean.

'I had no reason to, Dad, when . . . Well, you tried.'

'No reason?'

Ivan turned around, the irritation pressing against his neck. He knew his eldest son was lying. Lies always lay there, right below the back of the skull, scratching and foreboding, like the edge of an axe that would separate his head from his body.

'There is always a reason, Leo. I am old enough to know that. I even know that if you suddenly have to run to the toilet, it's not because of what you ate but because of all the shit you've filled yourself with.'

'The toilet? It's been many years since I got to go there without permission.'

Leo took the object from his jacket pocket, and put it down on the bar but it wasn't covered with his hand.

'And not a telephone call during all that time in prison that wasn't scheduled. I don't know how it was for you, Dad, when you got out, but I get tense as hell when the phone rings and I don't recognise the number.'

Leo shot the object along the bar towards Ivan: a black mobile phone with a wide, shiny screen.

'With that you can give me a ring whenever you want. Look at it as the direct line between you and me. We'll even register it in your name. You just have to sign a paper and send it in so that it's your own contract, which I'll pay the bills for. If you are worried or just want to talk, then use it.'

Ivan picked up the shiny black phone that was lying on the transfer agreement document and balanced it between his thumb and his index finger. It was narrow and light, a couple hundred grams at most, and not longer than ten or eleven centimetres.

'So damn little. The fucking thing will disappear in my pockets. I'm never going to find it when you call.'

'Just a second. You can try out how it feels.'

Leo pressed a shortcut key on his own phone and Ivan at once felt how the slender black object vibrated like a small drill in his hand, giving off a signal that sounded like a trumpet.

'Not even you can mistake where it is.'

Ivan rubbed his neck. The pain was beginning to lessen. The conversation was starting to resemble what he had imagined it would be during yesterday's cancelled dinner.

'When you ring my phone I know that it can only be you, Dad, and when I ring yours you'll know it is me and no one else.'

Ivan turned all the way around to face his son for the first time, and it felt good again.

'What do you say – do you want a cup of coffee?'

'Which of my brothers gave you the number yesterday, Dad?'

'So you don't want a cup of coffee?'

'Tomorrow, when we meet again, I promise we'll drink a cup.'

Ivan was certain his son's words weren't constructing a lie. Leo would call.

'Vincent. He gave me the number. Who the hell else would it be?'

Leo nodded. He understood. Their father had no contact with Felix. It would take years – perhaps they would never speak to each other again.

'Where can I find him – Vincent? Where does he live?'

'I have no idea. But I know where he's working. And he's there late today.'

'How do you know?'

'I help him sometimes during the day.'

Ivan saw the surprise in Leo's face, and felt a little pleased.

'So you are . . . working together?'

'Mmm.'

'And how long have you . . . ?'

'A couple of months. We aren't all that strict. I help out with a bit of painting.'

Leo folded a napkin from Dacso's serving trolley and took a pen from the bowl by the till.

'Write down the address. Where he is now, that is.'

Ivan did so, even remembering what was on the door plaque, and handed the napkin to Leo. At the same time Dacso finally rattled out of the kitchen with a blue plastic crate in his arms, heavy with steaming white cups right out of the dishwasher. He was smiling when he filled one of them with black coffee and placed it on the bar.

'And you? Leo – that's your name, right? Do you want to have some too? Or are you going to eat the dinner you've already paid for?'

'Some other day.'

'You are welcome here, whenever you want.'

Leo laid his hand lightly on his father's shoulder.

'I'll call you, Dad.'

'On my new telephone?'

'I promise. We'll get together tomorrow, for a little longer.'

As Leo left, Dacso fetched a bowl, filled it with lumps of sugar, the brown kind, and placed it next to Ivan's steaming cup.

'Yesterday, Ivan, I didn't see it. Your lad is fair and you're dark. I thought, damn, has the mailman delivered the wrong post again?'

Dacso dropped in two lumps and stirred the cup with a teaspoon. He knew how Ivan liked it.

'But today I saw it right away, in his eyes. It's the look that shows it – end of story. A spark! You both have a spark in the eye.'

Ivan tasted his coffee, the same dishwater as usual, and then nodded at Dacso's wife who came out from the kitchen through the swinging doors.

'I was wrong. You aren't hyenas.'

'What?'

'You and your wife.'

'Yes, well, that sounds good. No one wants to be a hyena.'

'You and your wife are like tinder. Tinder that is never going to catch fire. There is no spark at all between you!'

Ivan looked at the restaurant owner, who seemed to be unsure whether he had understood correctly. He took his cup of coffee and moved to the window. The evening was already beginning to close in around his eldest son. It had been light outside when Leo came, and now was almost dusk.

Ivan caught himself waiting for Leo to turn around and wave, like when he was little.

He was even more convinced that Leo was heading in a direction that would lead him back to the cell. It was as clear as the small black flies.

Now he was on the way to Vincent, taking with him the influence he had as Vincent's stand-in father – influence that he, Vincent's real father, had never had.

And right then, far off in the twilight, Leo turned around and waved.

LEO FELT HE was being watched. When he realised he was, he turned around and waved. Pappa was standing between the letters Á and V in the Dráva Restaurant's window with a coffee cup in his hand. He looked smaller than he used to, with slouched shoulders, a bit sad.

One and a half cigarettes in the bus shelter on Ring Road later, the number 4 blue articulated bus had swung in, and seventeen minutes later let him off at St Eriksplan. From there it was a couple of hundred metres' walk to the stairs on Rörstrand Street. Leo checked the napkin with Pappa's straggly handwriting: number 12, entry code 7543, third floor, STENBERG on the door.

He rang the doorbell, and in spite of its being the old original bell, a clear electronic signal reverberated. That meant that a plastic box was fixed above the inside of the door, and that Vincent had unscrewed the cover when he'd painted the wall.

He listened with his ear pressed against the front door's wooden panel as the signal faded out, and could just hear the advertising jingles from a scratchy radio that formed part of the background noise of every construction site. When he flipped up the letterbox's flap the music became louder and he was blinded by a cold, sharp beam from the shadeless builder's light.

He rang again. Twice he had expected to be greeted by his youngest brother – first outside the prison gate and then at the lunch. Now it was the other way around – Vincent wouldn't expect his older brother to be here.

A third ring. And then he heard the volume of the radio lower and steps approaching.

'Hello, little brother.'

Vincent looked at him in silence.

'Aren't you happy to see me?'

Yesterday when they had spoken on the telephone – when Leo had rung from the forest – he had heard the change, a teenager who had become an adult. Now he could see it. But he could also *feel* the change – which was not only about the growth in his body, and how his face had resolved

133

as to the features that would settle there. It was about something altogether different, about how his adult body related to him in distance, even though they stood close to each other.

'Leo?'

'Are you going to let me in?'

'What the hell are you doing here?'

'Do you really want to talk about it in the stairwell?'

Leo walked from room to room in the beautiful flat, accompanied by the hollow echo that comes when nothing stops a sound playing freely between bare walls. Newly sanded parquet floors, plaster with lustre and high, glistening skirting board made of wood. He guessed it was about a hundred flawlessly renovated square metres.

'Hey, Vincent?'

'What?'

Even in the bathroom.

'This isn't Italian tile.'

'What?'

As Leo walked around, Vincent remained by the front door with his hand still on the door handle.

'This isn't Italian tile that has cracked.'

Leo turned and went out into the long, narrow hall, empty apart from the corner with paint tins, tile cutters and two toolboxes.

'As you said to Mamma.'

He ran his hand along the white woodwork that framed one of the doors, an even, shiny, well-painted surface.

'And the inspection? How did it go, by the way?'

They looked at each other as two brothers do when both know that a white lie only works as long as it isn't visible.

'Vincent?'

Leo pulled out the toolboxes, which were as long as trunks and as high as pallets.

'Let go of the handle and sit down. We need to talk.'

'Why?'

'Because I want to know if you know what the largest ever robbery in Sweden was. In Scandinavia.'

The only thing that hadn't changed between them was the natural way Leo could talk about criminal plans.

'Come on, Vincent. The largest robbery?'

It would have sounded absurd in other company but sounded natural with his brothers.

'OK, that must be . . . the terminal robbery.'

'And you call yourself a former bank robber? The terminal robbery was only a lousy forty-five million.'

'What about Bromma?'

'Yes. That's still the highest. A lousy fifty million.'

'We forgot the Robbery of the Century.'

'No.'

'But that was so much bigger.'

'They went to prison. *With* all the loot. So it doesn't count.'

Leo moved his toolbox a little so they would be closer to each other.

'Are you OK sitting there, little brother?'

'Say what you came to say.'

'You're OK sitting there? So you can listen to this – think of the loot from Bromma. Then think of a robbery where you double that. More than double it.'

'Well?'

'I plan to pull it off. On Thursday. But I have a small problem. There were going to be three of us. Now there are only two. So I need one more person.'

Vincent got up from his temporary chair, walked around and around in the empty flat, and even though he was wearing soft shoes so as not to scratch the parquet, his steps pounded.

'Vincent, come and sit down again.'

And to silence his footsteps, silence his big brother, silence all the fucking shit ruining everything, he struck his right fist in misery against the beautiful bedroom door, and watched the paint come loose at the dent.

'Sit down, dammit – I just want to talk with you!'

Vincent struck the door again with the same fist and this time cracked not just the paint but the wood of the door panel, too.

'Don't you understand?' The freshly painted door was red with blood, as were his knuckles. 'It's just this fucking shit that I was afraid of. I knew it! That was why I didn't want to see you! I knew you'd come out of there with some ridiculous idea of continuing!'

He went into the bathroom and the blood was dropping onto the floor. He turned on the tap above the washbasin, waited until the water became ice cold and rinsed his knuckles, wrist and forearm.

135

'Leo, I was in prison for four years. I was released with five hundred kronor and a train ticket. Do you understand how hard it is to get back into society without fighting every bit of your way there? I've tried like hell. I've paid off the crime victims' reparation. And still, it becomes fucking complicated when a girl gets to know what I did, that I did time. When her parents and brothers and sisters and friends get to know and try to get her to end it. I'm never going to commit a crime again. Understand that!'

Vincent undid the toilet paper roll and wrapped up his hand in several layers of paper until the blood stopped seeping through. Then he went back to the toolbox and sat down opposite Leo, holding the paper in place with his other hand.

'Are you finished now?'

'I don't understand how you can stand it, Leo – can't you just stop?'

'The biggest ever robbery. And at the same time, little brother, we take away from Broncks all that pride and cred that he's running around with right now. We become insanely rich and he becomes nothing at all.'

The paper around Vincent's injured hand loosened a little as he desperately struck it again, this time against his chest.

'I have made a promise to never commit crimes again. A promise to myself, in here.'

'Break it.'

'What?'

'The promise. You'll gain something from it. I'll take the risks but I need one more person to minimise them.'

His hand was bleeding again. The blow to his chest had hit harder than he intended.

'Leo? Can't you just let it go, all of it? Live a normal life. Get a job.'

'A normal life? What the hell is that – is it running around being afraid? Like you? Vincent, it's not about you being afraid to go to prison again. It's because he got to you, that cop bastard. When he arrested you. When he interrogated you. Don't you understand that that was exactly what he wanted to achieve – to divide us?'

'You know what I mean.'

'No.'

'Pappa believes in you.'

'Does he?'

'If I can change, Leo can change. He often says that.'

'Well, you work together now so you have time to chat a good deal.'

Vincent looked down and away, perhaps having hoped to tell Leo about that himself.

'And after? What the hell are you planning to do then? After the fucking idiocy?'

'Then, little brother, I disappear. That's why I'm pestering you – I want to have you with me. I love you, little brother, you know that.'

'And I love you. But it's not about that.'

'We'll disappear. I want you to disappear with me. It's us against the world, right?'

There was a balcony leading out from the sitting room. Leo had noticed it when he'd arrived. So as Vincent was weighing the question that lay on the floor between the two toolboxes one last time, Leo opened the doors to it and went out in the cold, pleasant air. The cold that nibbled his cheeks on the way to Pappa was now biting into his bare skin. He leaned on the railing and thought about his little brother who was seriously trying to become ordinary. There were no secret rooms under the floor in his life. He took a couple of deep breaths and was just about to turn to go back in when he caught sight of the coffee tin with cigarette butts in it. Vincent didn't smoke – but he recognised these. Hand-rolled. Rizla paper and rolling tobacco. Pappa.

'Leo?'

Vincent was still sitting on the toolbox, leaning forward as he had been a little while ago.

'No.'

'No?'

'Not a single time more.'

Leo looked at him. He was not going to change.

'In that case, little brother . . . we'll never see each other again. This is where our paths part. There is no alternative for me. I can't break my promise to myself, Vincent, exactly like you can't break yours.'

After a few minutes, maybe more, Vincent stood up.

'I would never have robbed any banks if it hadn't been for the fact that you exist.'

He looked at his big brother and his gaze was calm, steady.

'All the blokes in their twenties, the ones I know, have at one time or another sat with a case of beer and fantasised about the big heist. But there was a difference for me, and for Felix. You were there, Leo. You are the sort of person who says OK – we'll do it. And gets others to follow you.'

Adult, independent eyes.

'And today, Leo? After having waited so long to have lunch together, how the hell do you think it felt for Mamma? First, I didn't come. And then the cops pick you up and turn everything upside down. Everything you do has consequences for us. It doesn't matter that we aren't part of it – we are still somehow involved.'

'OK, little brother. So it's decided. I'll put a million in your bank account.'

'I prefer to earn my own money.'

Then Vincent took a step forward, stretched out his arms and didn't stop hugging until it was completely over. He stood there a long time in the empty hall and laid his cheek carefully on his swollen knuckles, which had begun to ache, a pulse throbbing in time with his heart.

It felt unreal, and if it weren't for the pain in his hand, he would not have been certain that he had just met his big brother for the first time in six years – and the last time in his life.

DARK. COLD. The roads were well and truly slippery, as always when the temperature danced around the zero mark.

'We leave the main road at the crossing in about five hundred metres.'

Leo pointed and Sam put on the brakes a little, hand on the gearstick, ready. The trip through the suburb called Tumba, the residential area, was so familiar. It was here they had lived back then, the base for all the plans during the couple of crazy years of bank robberies – a house among other houses, a neighbour among other neighbours.

'Up there, by the blue building, we go to the right. And then, after just fifty metres, right again.'

They were to stop at the gate in the three-metre-high chain-link fence, crowned with coiled barbed wire. He had probably not thought of it then, how much the enclosure resembled the perimeter security around a prison.

They parked by a black BMW, this year's model. The rest of the meeting's participants were already in place.

'The 3D printer, Leo, is in a box back there, just like you wanted. Don't forget it. Getting another through customs . . . we don't have enough time.'

Sam nodded towards the small lorry's otherwise empty cargo space where it lay – the key that would take them to *the test* and *the police station* – to the final heist.

'Constable Dûvnjac thanks you very much.'

With the lorry's lights off, the dark was even darker. No one lived on this plot of land, in this house. They walked across the asphalt, which was as uneven as he remembered. The pools of water that had formed in depressions in the surface were encapsulated under a thin layer of ice. They passed the big garage that, when he bought the place, had functioned as a showroom for a small car dealership, but that they'd transformed into a training place. It was there they had made scale models of bank premises, with the cash desks built out of chipboard and mannequins as cashiers. There had been plenty of room for drilling the movements until they were perfect – all within the one hundred and eighty seconds which every bank robbery had to take. Each of them had a role and everything was rehearsed.

After the giant garage, the house awaited. It was his and Anneli's jointly owned home and was the centre for every new plan for a robbery. It looked the same. 'Compact' was surely the word that best described it. Ninety square metres – officially, he had extended it somewhat – divided between two floors.

Leo took a short break before going in, taking deep drags on his cigarette. He peered through the fence into the neighbouring plot – the beautiful wooden house that Anneli had admired so much, her picture of their next shared home. Separate cells – that was how it actually happened.

It was hardly possible to see through the fence now. The neighbour's planted bushes had transformed into small trees. He made out the light in one of the windows, the room he remembered as the kitchen, with the same neighbouring family lighting a candle, gathered around the dinner table. Without knowing, they had been the neighbours of Sweden's most dangerous bank robber, and they were sitting there again now, without the slightest clue that in the same neighbours' house a transaction would soon be completed between that very bank robber and two representatives of the Albanian mafia.

Leo put out his cigarette with the heel of his shoe, nodded at Sam and walked to the door of the house, which so obviously had once been his. The sign on the wall to the left still read Dûvnjac on a white, handwritten note under the doorbell's plastic cover. And in the diamond-shaped window a crack was still finding its way along like a crystal worm, from the fight with Felix before the last robbery.

He pushed the handle down and opened the door.

On the inside of the house, the signs of time having stood still had a different character. Here there was a strong odour from waste pipes and floor drains which hadn't been cleaned and dried out, and closed-in, scratchy dry air tearing into his throat.

The two Albanians had placed themselves in the room immediately to the left; previously the guest room. The older one, who stood leaning on the window sill, matched the description – suit and balding and a notice-ably caved-in nasal bone, having been exposed to external violence one or more times without having lost the certainty of his eyes. The other one corresponded to the archetype of someone there to protect, if what shouldn't happen happened after all. He was tall, broadly built without having had to train himself to it, with a shaved head and wearing baggy grey tracksuit bottoms worn for a long time without being washed – and probably armed under the puffy hooded jacket. Repeated scarring, identical cuts all the way from the wrist to the crook of the arm on his exposed forearms, showed he was a man who wasn't just dangerous to his surroundings.

'Well, I'll be damned – here comes the home owner himself, and wouldn't you know that he . . .'

It was only now – when the one in the suit was talking – that Leo understood *how* far his nasal bone was caved in. It was even in the way of his words, nasal and drawling each time he exhaled.

'. . . is here in the company of his little keeper?'

Sam was wise and said nothing. An entire adult life in prison fosters an individual's impulse control. And Leo also, even if he had considered for a moment throwing back a sarcastic remark, decided they didn't have time to reprimand small bosses who ran errands for big bosses. He was here to complete an almost year-long business deal, and to do it as smoothly as possible.

'Jahmir? Is that your name? I have what you would need – do you have what I want?'

Leo looked around the room, and especially at the floor, while he waited for an answer. Everything seemed untouched. He had succeeded in keeping the house locked up for five years, but then the money for the mortgage and interest ran out with a final year to pay and no more possessions to sell off. The bank had foreclosed and the house was about to be lost, so he had taken action in the only possible way, reaching an agreement with the contacts he'd made inside the walls.

The sort of contacts you would rather not be in debt to – but he'd had no choice.

'I have your title deed, purchase contract and house keys. Do you have our money?'

Two and a half million kronor. That's how much it cost the contact's organisation to acquire the house at the executive auction and make Sam the official owner. And for interest of an additional two and a half million kronor they promised to wait a year for the debt to be paid off.

'Exactly one hundred centimetres of five hundred kronor banknotes, in a plastic bag from the shopping centre at Kungens kurva. We usually shop there.'

When the man with the caved-in nose ran a thumbnail over the plastic, the banknotes gave off a sound like a deck of cards being shuffled. He nodded, seemed content and handed over the documents and keys.

141

'And of course you wanted a very special computer too?'

The man in the suit's nod to his partner in the baggy tracksuit bottoms meant that the bright red Adidas bag on the floor should be opened, revealing a single item at the bottom of the bag – a seemingly simple laptop.

'Exactly the special kind you ordered. It costs two centimetres of your five hundred kronor notes. It might be nice to have a password also? That costs a centimetre extra.'

After, Leo waited until the visitors had left the house and were across the asphalt. When he saw the BMW's rear lights disappear out through the exit, he went back to the guest room.

'Help me with the sofa.'

He took one end of the guest-room sofa and Sam took the other. They carried it through the hall and into the kitchen so that it wouldn't be in the way. There were four loose tiles he had once placed in the centre of the guest room. That way, when he wedged one of the door keys into the joint between two of them and wiggled one of them up, it was easy to lift up the other three as well. A concrete block the same size as the removed tiles with two metal handles was waiting there. He grabbed the handles, lifted it and put it aside. And there, under the concrete block, lowered and embedded in the floor, was a safe. It lay horizontally, with its back downwards. He entered the numbers, turned the combination lock and opened it. The inside was still covered with black velvet, and that was as far as the police would have reached if they had ever discovered it. A forensic technician would have been able to vacuum every millimetre and yet barely find what lay there now – a couple of crumpled thousand kronor notes, a pile of papers that seemed important and some rifle cartridges for fruit-less test firing.

'Sam?'

'Yeah?'

'Go over to the window, about where the suit was leaning against the wall. See the electrical box up there? Open the protective cover and hold the bare electric cables together.'

Leo picked up the banknotes, documents and cartridges and remained squatting by the now opened safe as Sam connected the wires and closed the electrical circuit – he wanted to be close by, to listen and be certain that everything still worked.

It did.

The metallic humming and buzzing played in time with the bottom of the safe sinking down. The black velvet slot slowly widened between the wall and floor and joined up with an even darker blackness under the floor.

It appeared to be exactly as he remembered it.

No matter how many times he saw the back of the safe be lowered or sensed the smell of oil hitting him, he felt profound happiness.

'A room under the floor. A cellar where there shouldn't be one, since the entire residential area is built on an old lake bottom.'

Sam looked over his shoulder down into the square opening. Leo was leaning down into the hole and reaching for a loose hanging flex. He grabbed it, pulled it up and stuck it in one of the guest-room's wall sockets.

An angry, naked light revealed a secret underground room.

'Do you know how many cubic metres of clay and mud we shovelled out of here?'

The aluminium ladder stood leaning against the only wall of the hidden room. He pulled it to the hole, climbed down and waited for Sam to join him, looking silently around.

'How many wheelbarrows of gravel we poured down to get control of the water level when the fucking lake tried to come back in? Or what a hellish job it was to frame a safe in rebar and embed it in the floor? And then bring down everything here, an item at a time, and place it neatly on the shelves?'

Leo spun all the way around in the room he and his brothers had dug out, shovelful after shovelful. He didn't need to count them. Eighty-two AK4s. One hundred and thirteen submachine guns. Four machine guns. Tightly, tightly packed in neat rows in the country's largest private weapons cache.

'If you climb up, Sam, I'll hand them up to you.'

Kneeling down, Sam grabbed the first gun when Leo stuck it up through the opening, and then the second, third, fourth and fifth. That was all they needed and he stood up and stretched, ignoring the sixth that appeared.

'Five. That's enough.'

'We should bring them all up.'

'Five. Two for the uniforms and three for our little heist. That was what we agreed.'

'All of them have to be brought up and put in the hire car.'

'Five. Because we have a joint plan.'

143

'That *was* the plan, Sam. Until Jari dropped his gun and your brother got hold of it. And thought he could use it to get me. He was even looking at me on a monitor, imagining he was in control and that the gun had given him an advantage that he'd get me with.'

Leo was still holding the barrel and pointing the stock of the rifle straight up in the air.

'And yeah – he'll get them. The whole lot. My entire collection of weapons. Your brother will be proud and think he has succeeded.'

He was interrupted by a gurgling from the cement pipe in the floor of the hidden room, a well with a drainage pump mounted on the inside of the pipe, announcing that it was still working perfectly and had decided to begin pumping since the water level had reached the upper limit.

'But when he is standing there, your fucking brother, glowing away, then we'll take from him what he thinks doesn't exist. Because it's the exact opposite – I'm the one in control.'

'Huh?'

'Well?'

'Now I don't understand. How many are going to have guns? Are there more people involved that I don't know about? You and I, Leo, have taken the decisions together so far. And we should continue doing that if I'm going to be a part of this.'

'Sam, I'm sorry but Jari fucked up and I've been interviewed by the police. You're right, that wasn't the plan, but now it is. Trust me – I'll tell you everything in the car when we drive away, OK? Pulling off major robberies works like that. New circumstances come up and you have to adjust to them. Otherwise everything goes to hell and we end up where we just were – in the slammer. And you don't simply adjust, you turn it around. I should have told you all this, but there hasn't been a chance, a time and place.'

Sam stood there for a while, just staring at the butt of the rifle, the sixth gun hanging in the air between them. Then, his decision made, he grabbed it and laid it next to the five others. And before he even had time to turn back again, the next one was held up, and the next one. In twenty-four minutes the entire collection, a couple of hundred automatic weapons, filled up the guest-room floor.

'Hello, Pappa.'

While he was climbing up, Leo had pressed the button for the direct number to the newly purchased, definitely traceable mobile.

'Leo?'

And now, leaning against the same window the small-time Albanian boss had about half an hour earlier, he began a conversation, which Sam could hear clearly.

'I just wanted to hear your voice, Dad.'

'My voice? You wanted . . .'

His Swedish was still accented in spite of so many years in the country, and it was clear that he was almost proud of being called by his eldest son.

'. . . to hear my voice, Leo? Just a few hours after we saw each other? Do you understand how happy that makes me?'

A tone that collided with the last image Leo had, the man waving in the window of the Dráva Restaurant, hunched over and sad.

'Yes, and I'm sorry I vanished so quickly again. Talk to you tomorrow.'

Sam had caught every word of the short, odd conversation.

'Well?'

'Yeah?'

'Leo, what the hell was that? Are you serious? When we're handling hot weapons that the police are looking for? A nonsense call to your own father, from the house you lived in and that the cops would trace as easily as hell if they decided to work on it?'

The electrical box up on the wall was open as Sam had left it and Leo stuck his thumb and index finger in and put together the two loose cables a second time. He listened to the humming sound as the metal cylinders that were attached to the base of the safe slowly pulled up the secret trapdoor.

'Yes. Exactly. They *should* be able to trace it, as easily as possible. That's why we're going to leave the floor tiles loose. That's why I'm not going to close up the electrical box all the way and I'm leaving the cover open at a slight angle. And why I'm about to set up the first web camera hidden on the shelf in the entrance. Since my weapon collection guarantees that we won't be disturbed when we strike for the very last time – and then disappear.'

Burst Blood

SOMEONE IS PULLING on his right arm.

Large jaws are dragging him through an untamed, entangled forest. Over a hard, sharp-edged mountain. Until he falls headlong through the hidden, bottomless gap.

'Felix, wake up.'

And even though there is no end, he lands. In a second pair of jaws. Then they are fighting over him, tearing and tugging at both of his arms, from opposite directions.

'Hey, Felix?'

'What . . . ?'

It is always pitch black in the bottomless pit.

'Rise and shine, brother.'

The jaws are above him. Bright contours in eternal darkness.

'Who . . . ? Let go! Let go of me!'

'Felix? It's me – Leo. You have to get up.'

The light gets clearer. Leo's hair. Leo's face. It *is* him.

'But . . . it's really dark.'

'Shhh. Not so loud. Don't wake Vincent.'

'Has something happened?'

'No. Nothing's happened. Yet.'

His big brother is dressed, even wearing a jacket and gym shoes.

Felix sits up and is completely still on the edge of the bed.

Outdoor clothes inside? In the middle of the night?

His legs and arms aren't working. He thinks that he is going to move them but it doesn't work. Everything is stuck.

Then he feels one of his feet wiggle a little and that someone is putting it into a shoe and tying it. Then the other foot. Then his arms are raised at his sides and a warmish jacket is slipped over them. Leo disappears out into the kitchen and the tap can be heard running a while before he returns with what looks like a glass full of blood.

'Drink it down.'

It isn't blood, but a red mixed-fruit drink, the glass full right up to the brim.

'Drink up now. So you'll be more alert.'

'More alert? For what?'

'You'll see.'

Somewhere in the middle of the hallway, when they are on the way to the front door, Leo sneaks into Vincent's room to peer at his bandaged body and listen to his regular breathing.

'We can't leave him, Leo, can we?'

'We'll be right back. Half an hour at most.'

Leo wiggles the blinds and closes them, shutting out the shining from the full moon, and from one of the streetlights, which has broken glass and glares angrily.

'But what if he wakes up? And is all alone?'

'He won't wake up. When Vincent sleeps, he really sleeps. And no one should ever wake up mummies against their will. Then a curse is unleashed. Don't you know that, Felix?'

They carry out a last check around his mouth, and widen the opening in the bandages. It's important that the air flows freely. Then they leave the flat. But Felix thinks it's a bit strange that Leo is carrying his schoolbag over his shoulder. Surely school is not open in the middle of the night?

There are no traces left in the stairwell of Mamma's escape – Leo finally succeeded in wiping away the last spots and it's as if it had never happened. They creep past Agnetha's door on the second floor. She offered to sleep at their flat the first few nights their mother was in hospital but Leo convinced her that they would be fine on their own and promised to let her know if they needed help and to make sure they all went to bed early.

Outside, there is only darkness and the long row of streetlights. And at a distance, music and cars accelerating quickly and putting on the brakes abruptly. Friday night in Falun. In the other direction, into the city, it's lively. But here, along an asphalt walkway to the school, it's quiet and still.

Leo breathes in deeply. It is a lot hotter than he thought. Or else he himself is hot on the inside, with the tension trying to make its way out.

It's September and there are several piles of leaves on the ground, which are fun to kick around in. They are now about one month into the autumn term. He is in the eighth year and Felix in the fifth. Even Vincent, their big little brother, has started in the first class and so they are now all going to the same school together.

He knows exactly what he needs for their caper.

He knows where wigs are sold, one hundred and twenty-five kronor for the long ones he has picked out. And the big grey cloth jacket with a hood is at H&M for ninety-nine kronor and fifty öre – it's going to be made greenish and dirty with textile paint from the shop that sells fabric and sewing machines. Then the body will need to look different, with shoulder pads and extra stomach, which he could easily sculpt out of padding from the same fabric shop with the paint. Finally, he'll need the cigarettes. He has to smoke, unfiltered cigarettes, the strongest – John Silver.

The kind boozers smoke.

When the heat from his inside has evened out, it's pleasant to walk around outside in the middle of the night. Only a small city can feel like this – a connection but empty all the same. The first sign that there are also people out this way is the cyclist behind them. They hear the dynamo pressing against the front wheel and how she comes closer, passes and disappears.

Druggie-Lasse. A good name. That's what he has dubbed his character.

It's Druggie-Lasse who is going to snatch the ICA lady's bag.

But a Druggie-Lasse costs money to create, which is why Leo had to wake his brother up a little while ago and force him to get up at two in the morning.

'I borrowed a book today. At the school library.'

'Oh. Is that why we're here?'

It's a lot longer to school in Falun than it was in Skogås just outside Stockholm. Leo remembers how their father used to stand on the balcony, at the top of the block of flats, following their backs as they crossed the car park and went through the bushes.

Four years ago. Another life.

'No. But I had to borrow something to make the plan work.'

'Leo – I don't get it.'

'You'll understand. And that damn book, it was almost good. About the US and things that happened there. A lot about prohibition of booze and a bloke called Al Capone.'

'I've heard that name.'

'And I thought about Pappa.'

'Did they write about him? About Pappa?'

'Of course not. But I thought that Pappa would probably act like Al Capone. If it was against the law to drink booze in Sweden, I mean.'

151

'What do you mean, act?'

'Like Al Capone, who sold alcohol anyway. Pissed on the rules.'

They are approaching a meadow with occasional trees spreading thin against the night sky. On the other side of the meadow, partially lit by another cycle path, is the school.

'No, Leo. I don't think so.'

'What?'

'That Pappa would act like him, Capone. Pappa doesn't like selling things, does he? He would drink up all the booze himself. And then beat people up.'

They have reached Leo's part of the school – the secondary school. Felix has hardly ever been there. He's still in primary school and they are like two different worlds with a guarded border crossing that you don't pass through willingly since you know that there will be fights waiting on the other side with those who are much more powerful than you. When they moved here, he was in the first year and started in a new class in the middle of term. Completely new – that's what he was. Most kids hate to change schools and classmates but he liked it. Not like Jonna, he remembered her clearly, Jonna who always wore her hair in a yellow clasp and cried so much before her move that the teacher had to interrupt the music lesson. She didn't want change – while he was the opposite. Moving was perfect. No one in his new class had any idea about what happened, how his father was in prison for a firebomb.

He was so sure that all the terrible stuff would stop when his father vanished, and his mother and *those* social service ladies decided that a move of two hundred and twenty kilometres was for the best. They would be normal. He would stop feeling the scraping and burning against his ribs, sometimes right up to his throat.

Now the fire in his chest has begun again.

They have come all the way to the schoolyard and are squatting, concealed, behind an electrical cabinet, remaining still and silent as another cyclist approaches and passes.

The Skogås school was made with white limestone bricks, whereas this one was made with light yellow plaster and was formed of two buildings linked together by a glassed-in middle section where students could stay during the breaks.

'Your job is to keep watch.'

'Watch?'

'You'll understand. It has to go quickly now. No one can see us.'

Suddenly Leo starts to run. Felix wants to ask *where* but it is too late and he decides to follow after him, over the asphalt, which is damp, steam coming out of their mouths when they breathe. They sneak the last bit to the assembly room, the middle wing. All of its large windows have a smaller window above for ventilation.

'Leo – what do you mean by watch?'

'If someone else comes on the cycle path, your job is to knock on the window ledge. With this.'

Leo holds up a coin. One krona. It gleams in the shine from the street-light.

'And then you have to hide.'

'Hide? And you?' Felix is still breathing heavily from the run and every word is clipped when he pushes it out. 'What the hell will *you* do?'

His big brother doesn't answer, just smiles and sticks his hand into the schoolbag and fishes out what looks like a Phillips screwdriver. Then he jumps up on the lower window's narrow ledge and balances as he stretches on his toes towards the smaller oblong window above.

Felix is watching everything from a strange angle, crooked and from below, and what he's taking part in is for that reason hard to interpret. But if it is happening as it seems to be, Leo is pushing his hands halfway into the vent window and is removing the screw that holds the metal frame in place with his screwdriver as if by magic. The frame is to prevent anyone from opening the window entirely. It takes awhile and the position for doing the work is far from ideal so he is sliding slowly downwards on the slippery ledge.

Meanwhile Felix keeps watch, his face flushed red, his cheeks burning with everything but excitement – he just wants to go home.

Leo is also hot, even hotter than before. Even more tension is trying to make its way out. He has planned everything – and it will work. Inside the window there is the assembly room with the oblong tables where he and the others in class 8B play cards or just hang out between the classes. The cafeteria opens at two o'clock every afternoon, and then a disgusting day of food – cinnamon buns, chocolate balls, pastries and cheese sandwiches and juices in small square packs with straws in plastic wrap – is served and purchased. For today's lunch it was some kind of white fish and the cafeteria sales were enormous as a result.

The money is kept in a white cash box that is emptied daily at twenty

153

past four. According to the rules, only a small amount of change should be left. But every other Friday that's not the case. If he has understood correctly, it has to do with Leisure-time Lena's schedule. She is replaced by the gym teacher who comes in and takes care of the sales once a fortnight. Then the box is locked up over the weekend in one of the kitchen cabinets, without being emptied, until Monday, the next time Leisure-time Lena is on duty.

That's why he stayed longer today, in spite of his gnawing worry about Vincent, who still refused to take off the bandage. After his last class he strolled – instead of hurrying home as he should have – into the school library and pretended to be borrowing books. After a while he even started reading one of them a little, the one about Capone and prohibition. Because if you sit in the right place, in line with the back bookshelves, from there you can watch the assembly room. He was doing that when he looked up from the page of the book and noticed the gym teacher selling another chocolate ball and another bun. Until it was twenty past four, and she placed the cash box in the cabinet behind the café's counter.

He was also watching the school caretaker from his vantage point, who was on his regular Friday rounds. He checked that everything was as it should be, went around and tried every window, pushed chairs and tables back to the right place and then just as planned, went to the library. As quick as lightning, Leo moved two reading tables away – a table the caretaker would place him at later if anyone asked, a place that you *couldn't* see into the assembly room from.

You have to go home, he explained, *the school is closing*, and Leo pretended to obey and packed up his bag as the caretaker watched. Then, when the last zip was fastened, he remembered his maths homework, which he had forgotten, in cabinet 442. He promised to run the entire way there – if the caretaker would only keep an eye on his bag.

He ran, but not to the cabinet. Instead he ran to the place that it wasn't possible to peer in to. The assembly room. He placed a chair against the wall there and turned the two handles of the upper vent window.

The same window they are now standing outside.

Leo heaves himself up, slides in easily through the opening, lands softly on the assembly room's floor and sneaks up to the counter in the café.

He realises how different it feels, being in the school in the middle of the night. In still and abandoned rooms, which are slowly being filled with his own movement.

And suddenly it comes back, the eager, alive, tense, joyful feeling.

When he cleaned up the blood and saved his mamma's life, the same feeling had made him light and happy on the inside and stronger than ever on the outside. He wasn't even afraid that his father might come back and start hitting again.

The cabinet is equipped with a padlock. That's why he packed more items in his bag: a chisel as well as a hammer. He won't tackle the padlock itself; that would be too much. He'll go for the small, fragile hinges.

Two blows are enough – they fall to the floor and he can bend the cabinet door outward.

The white tin box is standing on the lower shelf.

He looks around the dark assembly room filled with movements that are only his – and moves the box into his bag.

He is about to leave when his gaze fastens on the large door at the end of the cabinet. From behind the door comes the smell of chocolate and coconut flakes, something he and every student can recognise almost immediately.

As I am here anyway . . .

It's an ordinary wooden door. If he presses the hinge exactly at the locked bolt, he should also be able to prise it up with a little force and separate it from the doorframe without it making a sound.

––––––––

The deserted cycle path slumbers on – not a single person has passed Felix during the time he's stood watch. Now and then he has glimpsed Leo through the window. It seems that first he broke into a cabinet and then the door to another room.

Leo had said he was getting a box. That's what he was going to do in there. Hasn't he found it yet?

Now. *There*. Finally.

Felix sees his big brother approach in the dark carting a black rubbish bag, before he throws something out through the vent window.

'Felix?'

It is a similar rubbish bag – but an empty one.

'Fill it.'

Then he throws something else. A carton. It lands in the wet grass, chocolate balls. There's a picture of them on the side.

The next carton has a different picture. Coconut balls. Fluffy. It says so on the carton.

155

'This is not a fucking box, Leo. A box – that's what you were going to take. That's what you said. That's why you woke me up.'

Leo meets his gaze without replying. Then he is gone again. Felix hears him running back to the room behind the café counter and wooden door.

One full turn. And another. Felix spins when he looks around, searching, but cannot see a soul. His hands are shaking anyway as they unfold the empty rubbish bag and drop the cartons in.

If someone comes.

Two more cartons. They almost land on his foot. Pear juice. Mazarin tarts.

I can hide myself. But I have to leave this fucking bag.

He catches them and lets them be enveloped by the black plastic.

And then the next cyclist comes passing by and maybe sees and stops, understanding what's going on.

More juice packs. More cartons. Hard drops that thump when they hit the ground.

'Leo! Come out now, dammit!'

'In a minute.'

Leo smiles quickly before he returns to the darkness of the schoolhouse. And now Felix feels just as he does before beginning to cry. Shit. He's so fucking scared, but the worst part is that Leo doesn't listen. That's happened before, Leo vanishing into himself.

Never, ever, ever am I going to help him again.

Then the final cartons fly out.

When Leo jumps back out, anxiety is matched by anger in Felix's chest. But Leo, on the other hand, is calmer and happier than ever.

'Little brother – what is it?'

'Nothing.'

'The whole sack full, Felix, you know. Vincent is going to—'

'If you eat too much, you get tired. Doesn't matter how good it is.'

'Felix? It's good to have it. If something happens, I mean.'

'Happens?'

'You never know.'

'What would happen? Tell me! Leo – what the hell is going to happen?'

They walk back the same way through the same silent night. But everything has changed. They have done something they've never done before. For that reason, Leo thinks the sack is light when he is carrying it. For that reason, Felix thinks it's heavy when it's his turn. The boxes of sweets scrape against his back, but hell if he's going to cry. Or whinge. Not a chance. He's not going to say a word on the way home.

The windows in the block of flats are dimmed, all except the watchman's, who is always awake. A luminous nose in the grey façade's face. And inside, in the stairwell, every door is sleeping. The ceiling light on the second floor switches on, the German shepherd on the third floor snarls, otherwise everything waits for tomorrow.

They enter their equally silent flat.

The two peek into Vincent's room and he does what the neighbours do; he snorts and breathes slowly.

'I said so.' Leo winks at Felix.

'Mummies always sleep long and soundly. Something about the bandages, I think.'

Leo thinks the tin box ought to sit in the middle of the table. He chooses the same spot where Mamma put down the hot oven dish just before . . . before.

'Felix – fetch the kitchen towels.'

'Why?'

He is going to attack it exactly as Mamma does when she hits the pork schnitzel with a wooden mallet.

'Just do it.'

Felix vanishes out into the hall, returns right away and Leo stares at the single towel in his outstretched hand.

'One?'

'Yeah?'

'All of them, Felix, all there are.'

Felix slinks through the hallway to Mamma's bedroom and one of the wardrobes there. A whole pile of white towels in his arms, each with three letters embroidered with red thread in one corner. BMA. Britt-Marie Axelsson. Mamma's name when she was little.

'Satisfied?'

Leo counts six, puts them under the cash box, takes the tools out of the rucksack and wraps the seventh towel around the head of the chisel. Then he takes a step backwards and decides to turn the box upside down. It's easier to access that way.

'Hold it.'

'The cash box?'

'With your hands. One on each side.'

157

'Are you going to open it up?'

'Yes.'

'Then I'm not holding it.'

'Felix?'

'What if you miss?'

'Trust me. A single blow. That's what it takes.'

Leo balances the chisel in his hand, letting its rather sharp edge rest against the narrow gap of a few millimetres running parallel to the lock mechanism. He sneaks a quick glance at Felix who has his eyes closed, but holds it as he is told. Leo aims and strikes. A good hit – but just when the hammer meets the chisel and the force should transfer from one tool to the next, Felix releases his grip. And without resistance the lock manages to fend off an external force trying to push its way in.

They both watch the tin box slide across the tabletop until it reaches the edge, tips over and falls to the floor. An angry thump goes through the kitchen walls out into the hall, towards Vincent and towards the front door.

'What the hell are you doing? You're supposed to hold it!'

'You might hit me. Instead of the box.'

Leo rubs his hand over the now wrinkled towels, flattens them out, picks up the box and puts it in the same place as before.

'Felix – Vincent is going to wake up next time. Or the neighbours. Hold it right this time.'

Felix grasps the tin's ice-cold sides, squeezes his eyes shut, and holds it tight while Leo aims, and strikes again in the middle of the lock mechanism.

And this time he succeeds. A minimal opening gets slightly wider. The chisel's edge in exactly the right place. The whole weight of his body over the kitchen table and he prises and prises until they both perceive an almost infinitesimal click.

The lock gives in.

He is careful to press together the top and bottom of the tin when he turns it the right way up again. This kind of cash box has a loose plastic shelf for coins and everything would fall out higgledy-piggledy.

He opens it rather grandly. The shelf with its compartments lies exactly as it should lie. Each one is nearly full.

He empties out the coins on the towels, chasing and pushing together those that are about to roll away.

'Felix – start sorting. Fifty-öre pieces, one krona, five kronor. All of them need to be separated.'

He has deliberately refrained from trying to see how much is hiding under the plastic shelf. But he knows roughly how much he *wants* it to be – enough for everything. Now he takes a peek. And there are notes there, exactly as there should be. Five-kronor notes. But not the amount he needs, he is rather certain of that. He picks them up and counts.

Twenty-seven five-kronor notes.

One hundred and thirty-five kronor.

Not enough. Can the coins be enough to make up the rest?

His eager hands collide with Felix's slower hands as they help each other with the sorting. Three stacks. Different heights. He counts silently to forty-seven kronor and fifty öre.

A total of one hundred and eighty-two kronor and fifty öre.

He rushes to his room to get the slip of paper lying on a speaker that he built himself and which is as tall as Vincent. After a deep breath he unfolds the paper. Jacket 99.50. Wig 125. Cigarettes 14. Textile paint 28.50. Padding 20. Everything that he can't swipe from somewhere. Well, he could, but a good plan exposes the perpetrator to the risk of getting caught only once, at the main hit. The bicycle, the getaway vehicle, is the only thing he can take without risk, if he does it the night before.

'We're missing one hundred and four kronor and fifty öre.'

'Missing?'

'Yeah. I need two hundred and eighty-seven kronor.'

'For what?'

'For Druggie-Lasse. And I know where the rest is.'

HE MEASURES four hundred and fifty millilitres of milk, a little more than in the original recipe. Semolina, four tablespoons, for which he is usually more careful. Finally, salt, not much, a pinch between his index finger and thumb. He stirs the mixture in wide circles with a wooden spoon. He does it constantly, stirs and stirs the saucepan. The porridge can't burn – if it does neither Felix nor Vincent will eat it.

Meanwhile, Felix sets the table. Plates, spoons, napkins, glasses. Pulling one of the chairs to the sink and kitchen cupboards, he gets down the sugar and the glass jar of cinnamon. Now they're alone, they have as much as they want.

'Felix – wake Vincent up.'

'I looked in on him a while ago. How long is he going to be like that? Wrapped in gauze? His whole life?'

'No, he won't be. I'll lure him out.'

Then Felix goes, not to Vincent's room, but to the laundry basket in the corner by the front door, the brown plastic one that is a little smaller than the one in the bathroom, which Mamma can manage to carry down to the laundry room. He whips his arm around among the dirty underwear and socks and T-shirts and fishes out a pair of jeans too small for himself.

'Felix?'

Leo leaves the cooker for a moment and the saucepan he should be stirring. He sees a pair of jeans that he is certain belongs to Vincent go by in the hallway.

'What are you doing?'

'I was thinking, when we visit Mamma . . . now, Leo. We can do what you said now – lure him out of the mummy.'

Felix continues on to Vincent's room and Leo grabs a leg of his trousers.

'No.'

'Why not?'

'Because we aren't going to, not yet.'

'I'm thinking of asking anyway.'

They both pull the trousers, Leo holding on tight until his little brother

160

lets go of them but manages to also break free from Leo's tight grip around his wrist.

'If we . . . shit, Leo, if we get him to come with us, he'll have to take off that fucking gauze bandage! Don't you get it?'

'And how do you think Mamma looks?'

Suddenly Felix stops mid-step.

'How? What do you mean . . . ?'

'Her face. She bled like a pig, right? How many bandages do you think *she* has? I don't want Vincent to see her. Do you?'

Felix realises what his older brother is actually saying. He hardly saw the blows and doesn't remember them, or any of what happened while his father was beating her. It's as if the blows struck big black gaps into his memory.

'Leo?'

'Yes?'

'How does she look, do you think?'

Felix glances at his older brother, as if that's all he dares to do, as if the answer will be smaller then.

Leo saw the blows and even cleaned up Mamma's blood.

'We'll get to know soon, little brother.'

———————

It smells as if something's burning.

The semolina porridge. The fucking milk. Leo jerks the pan away from the hob, fills it with cold water, digs with the spoon and throws the brown clump in the rubbish. He scrubs and scrapes the bottom of the pan but it's only when he finds the box with steel wool that the burned coating goes away.

He measures grain and milk and salt like before and begins to stir around and around when he hears the door open, by someone who has a key.

'Good morning.'

A woman's voice.

Agnetha.

She must have got the key from Mamma or the social services lady.

Leo runs to the window and opens it wide. She musn't think he can't make fucking porridge.

'So you are already eating?'

She stands in the doorway and peers in at someone stirring a pan and the table already set.

'Not yet. Felix was supposed to cook the porridge but he can't. You have to stir it all the time.'

'And I've brought . . . well, now you have breakfast for tomorrow also. And in the other bag there's lunch and dinner.'

She opens the fridge, unpacks the bag and puts some items in and the rest in the pantry.

'Tomorrow morning you don't need to come up here. I'll fix it. I have made breakfast for those two since . . . well, for ever.'

Light knocks on the kitchen door's frame and they automatically turn in that direction.

Felix.

'He doesn't want it. The mummy doesn't want to have any.'

'Let him be, Felix. He can eat later.'

The first bag is emptied and Agnetha is about to start on the next when she stops.

'So . . . he still has that on him?'

'Yeah. And I don't think he should have it on. But Leo thinks so.'

'That's not at all what I said, Felix. I said that we shouldn't force him. Not to take it off and not to come with us to visit Mamma.'

Strong, divided opinions. Agnetha sees what's going on and turns to them alternately.

'I agree with Leo on this. Bandages can't be taken off you until you are ready yourself. Before you have, well, healed. I'll stay with him when you visit her.'

Now the porridge is perfect and Leo pours it into two of the three bowls on the table.

'But there's another thing I want to talk to you about.'

She waits until Leo has rinsed out the pan and sat down, even until the cheese is spread on the first knäckebröd sandwich.

'I woke up last night because of someone running in the stairwell. Or I think that's what woke me. It sounded as if the person doing it passed by my door, all the way up to this floor. Then, just as I fell back asleep, I woke up again. Because of loud thumps. At least twice. Maybe three times. As if someone hit the wall. Then I didn't hear anything else. Or I fell asleep again.'

162

The boys began to chew, crumbly knäckebröd with cheese.

But neither that nor the porridge covered with an extra layer of cinnamon and sugar tasted as it usually did.

'The running. The thumping. Was it you?'

Leo stares at Felix and Felix stares at Leo.

'No. And I didn't hear anything. Did you, Felix?'

Felix hesitates, which Leo catches, but not Agnetha – he hesitates and speaks quietly.

'No. Not me either. I didn't hear a single sound.'

It's not very far to Falu Hospital. But it takes a long time to walk there. Felix is dragging his feet, more slowly every metre, and Leo knows what it is about.

'Hurry up now.'

Anxiety, over an image neither of them wants to see.

'Why? Are we in a rush?'

'Mamma will look how she looks.'

Leo has already decided not to think about it. So he thinks about the ICA shop instead, and about the square and the guard who might ruin the job. He *must* convince Felix. Without him it will be difficult. It might work – but the odds of failure change. Felix's job is to divert Click-with-the-baton. And Click is the single greatest odds reducer.

They glimpse Falu Hospital on the other side of the park, the buildings sticking up beyond the planted trees. When they are a few minutes away, Felix's steps become even shorter, even more sluggish.

'Little brother?'

'Yeah?'

'If you want to. Only if you want to, that is.'

'What?'

'I can look first. If Mamma appears too bashed up, I can tell you, so you don't need to look too.'

The three buildings that make up the Falu Hospital are situated together even though they are so different. A bright building fourteen storeys high, a darker one with eleven storeys and one wedged between them, seven storeys if you count the windowless bottom part. Different buildings in different colours. Exactly like three brothers.

They stop at the hospital kiosk. Cut flowers are too expensive, but raspberry gumdrops, the kind Mamma likes, don't cost much. Leo pays with the fifty öringar that was recently in the coin compartment of the tin box, and then the right front pocket of his trousers.

Corridors. Lift. Hospital smell.

There are people in white clothes – some wearing name badges, who are here to heal, others in robes, here to be healed.

They enter a ward with three beds. Two empty, one with Mamma in it.

She is lying on the side that Pappa didn't beat, her face turned away.

'It's us, Mamma.'

She is startled. Maybe she was sleeping.

'Vincent will come some other day.'

Leo is hesitating at the door to the ward, and in the square between his right shoulder and the doorframe Felix can see in. It is not an especially big square, but it is protecting him, should Mamma turn around. It's like a television, and what you see on the screen isn't quite real.

'Hello, Leo.'

Mamma turns around and Leo moves quickly to the right, standing tightly against the doorframe so that the TV screen is gone. That means Mamma's face doesn't look at all good.

'Come in, my boys.'

Mamma's voice is weak, but still Mamma's.

Leo turns around to Felix.

'Do you want to?'

'No.'

Leo shakes his head in response to their mother and she raises her weak voice as much as possible, almost calling out.

'Felix, I want you to come in also.'

'No.'

'I want . . . I just want to hold your hand.'

Felix clears his throat and remains behind the back that is blocking his view.

'Are you in pain, Mamma?'

'Of course she's in pain, Felix. You don't need to ask that.'

'I *am* in pain.'

Mamma moans when she tries to raise her upper body a little, perhaps so she can see better.

'But you can have pain in various places. Sometimes it is invisible.'

164

Then she gives up. It hurts too much and she slides back down the small distance she has struggled to move herself up.

'But how do you look?'

'It is not how I look now that is important. In a few weeks, maybe a month, it will all be gone.'

Then Leo moves back, revealing the square TV screen between his shoulder and the frame, and Felix sees her face.

She has a thick bandage around her forehead, and medical tape over large parts of her face – a strip down over the bridge of her nose, another from cheek to cheek, a white cross that covers her purplish skin.

'Here, Mamma. Your favourite.'

Leo goes in first and is about to put the bag of gumdrops on her stomach, then changes his mind and chooses the empty space next to her, the wrinkled sheet. But she moves it to the table jutting out next to the bed, which is part of the rolling cabinet and is the place where food is served.

Then Felix makes up his mind and follows his brother. They sit, one on each side of the bed, while Mamma adjusts her position, grimacing strongly. She wants to be able to see them both equally – grimacing and smiling at the same time.

'How sweet of you. Raspberry gumdrops. I'll eat them later.'

It is sometimes hard to hear because she is speaking so quietly. Her mouth is hardly moving and Felix thinks of a ventriloquist he saw on television, who also spoke without it being seen, just a little at one corner of his mouth every time the puppet was pretending to talk.

Her right eye is the worst. Swollen shut.

Felix longs for Leo's shoulder and the television screen. If he looks too long at her eye, maybe Mamma will go blind and there will be no eye left under the swelling, only a black gap. He still doesn't remember what happened, but maybe the hole works like one of the black gaps in his memory. The ones beaten into his head when Pappa beat up Mamma.

'And Vincent, is he well?'

She turns to Leo since he is the oldest.

'Absolutely. Agnetha is with him while we're here.'

'Is he eating OK?'

'Like usual. I'm taking care of everything.'

The other eye is clearer, but tired. And in it, where it should normally be white, it is very red – like burst blood. Felix decides to just look into this eye, not the other one, when it is his turn to talk to her.

Burst blood is better than black gaps.

'Yes, Vincent is fine. He can eat all the coconut balls he wants.'

What happens then is exactly what Felix knew would happen. Leo's gaze drills into his cheek, through it, but he takes no notice. You have to say what you have to say.

'Because we have who knows how many under the bed.'

For the first time Mamma's voice is more than just a whisper. And her tired eye, with the burst blood vessel, looks at him in the way only she sometimes does.

'What . . . Felix, listen to me, what are you talking about?'

And then the tip of Leo's gym shoe kicks hard against his ankle.

'Nothing, Mamma. Felix is just prattling on.'

Too late. She is their mother. She knows them. She knows why one says something and the other one does not want to talk more about it. And even though she didn't see the kick on the leg, she perceived it somehow anyway.

'Leo? Felix? What have you done?'

The two brothers sit there silently as they meet their mother's swollen, bloodshot eyes. Leo doesn't want to talk about it. And Felix doesn't know why he said what he said. It sort of slipped out of him. Like when you vomit – first you can't help it and then you can't swallow it.

'There's a whole lot of cartons of different sweets, and almost one hundred drink packs with straws. All under Vincent's bed.'

Now the words slipped out of him again. It was easier to say it than to hold it in or swallow.

'Leo and Felix – look at me. Talk to me, really. What's under Vincent's bed – did you take it from somewhere? Steal it?'

'No.'

'Yes.'

They answered at the same time. Rather, Leo got it out a little bit before. In any case, Mamma tries to make eye contact with him. Her eye, the one Felix wasn't able to see moments ago, somehow looks out of the swollen, blue eyelid.

'Leo? You do not steal from other people. You know that. You are fourteen, not a child any more.'

Her voice is no longer weak. It is distinct and clear and when anger forces her to raise it a little, Felix realises that she is missing a tooth on the right side. That's why she didn't eat any of the gumdrops, which are as chewy as rubber. It hurts to chew.

'Coconut balls and fruit drinks? *Where* did you take them from, Leo?'

Her eldest son meets her gaze. He does not try to avoid it because he has made up his mind not to do so.

'I promise. I will return everything under Vincent's bed.'

'How?'

'I'll leave it just outside. The place I took it from, I mean. So they'll find it.'

He didn't think it was possible. But Mamma looked sadder now than when they came.

'That's not enough, Leo, do you hear me? You also have to apologise.'

'Mamma, the door was open and I went in. It was just lying there. And I thought . . . Vincent would be happy.'

Felix hasn't spoken for a while. He said enough already. But he knows his brother is lying and it feels strange because his mother's body seems to shrink at the same time. It becomes as small as her voice, which barely comes out of her at all.

'Leo, you're the oldest. That's how it is. It means you have responsibilities at home as long as I am lying here. But that doesn't mean you can solve problems that way. Do you hear me? I can't bear it if you *also* do that . . .'

She regrets it, in the middle of the sentence. But it is too late – Felix knows what she was thinking, who it is that she meant Leo is solving problems like. Leo knows it too – Felix sees it in his lips, which become narrow when he is angry.

'I can't apologise. Mamma? If I did . . . don't you get it? Everyone would talk about it. It's better as it is. Now no one knows. Can't it just stay like that?'

'No. You *must* do it. That's what it means to be the eldest.'

Fourteen years old. That is what he is. Surely that's not so damn old? Really?

He would like to leave now. Disappear, to somewhere away from Mamma who doesn't understand. But he promised Pappa he'd take over.

'Listen, Mamma? The social services lady – what will she say, for example?'

So it seems he's challenging Mamma, threatening her. He doesn't really mean to do it but that's how it sounds.

He tries to explain one more time.

'I just wanted Vincent and Felix to . . . I'm sorry. It won't ever happen again.'

167

'Really?'

'Really.'

And suddenly Mamma looks terribly tired again. The eye sinks back into the swelling, as it was when they first arrived.

'We'll talk about this again later. When I come home.'

Felix hugs Mamma tightly before they go. She kisses him lightly on the cheek and whispers that she loves him. Leo doesn't hug her, he can't. He just mumbles goodbye. Then they don't say a word to each other on the way through the bright hospital corridor and in the lift Felix stands on one side and Leo on the other. It feels like there are many kilometres between them.

'What a big lift. About as far as I can jump in the long jump.'

Leo doesn't meet Felix's gaze when he answers.

'It's so you can bring in stretchers with sick people on them. And dead people.'

'Dead people?'

'People die in hospital. Corpses – lying on stretchers. On the way to the morgue.'

'The . . . morgue?'

'It's just a freezing cold room in the hospital's cellar for all the dead people. Loads of corpses that are cut up to find out why they died.'

The lift doors open and Leo hurries out with big steps. Felix has a hard time keeping up. He can't let go of the freezing cold room with cut-up bodies. People are supposed to get well here, not die.

'But, Leo . . . Mamma?'

'Yeah?'

'She won't die, will she?'

Leo stops halfway across the park and Felix is half a step behind. The park? Felix spins around. He never before understood how far you could walk without thinking what you're doing. The hospital is several hundred metres away.

'No, little brother. Mamma isn't dying.'

It should be nice to hear that. But Leo seems to hesitate and that doesn't feel good at all. He's welcome to hesitate about stealing the ICA shop money but not about whether or not Mamma is going to die.

'She won't die as long as you do what I say.'

168

Leo puts his hand on Felix's shoulder as he often does.

'Felix – you can't talk to Mamma about what we are doing. Or anyone else.'

'I can talk if I want to.'

'We never talk about something that's within the family. That's what Pappa taught us.'

'Sorry, but I'll do it if I want to.'

'Listen – you can never talk with anyone about this again! Or about the ICA shop and the leather bag! No one can know. Don't you get what will happen if you do? The social services lady will report us and you'll end up somewhere up in Norrland, Vincent down in Skåne and I'll be in the middle in some fucking youth detention facility. Is that what you want?'

'No.'

'And Mamma will get even worse than she is now. Is that what you want?'

'No.'

'So why don't you keep your mouth shut then! So why are you blabbing about me!'

'Because Click will catch up with you!'

Leo takes his hand from Felix's shoulder. Instead both arms hold him now in a giant hug, the hug Mamma couldn't get.

'Little brother, shit, is that what you're going around imagining? I told you – I'm going to trick that Click. If you help me. If we keep together.'

And then he smiles broadly, as he does when he knows that Felix has nothing more to say in opposition.

'I'm going to be away a short while. Two hours, tops. Look after Vincent in the meantime. Move that shit away from his mouth when he drinks. It is important for the blood sugar.'

'And where are you going?'

'Just go home to Vincent. I'll cook later.'

It takes a while – then his brother begins to walk slowly home. Leo, on the other hand, goes in the opposite direction, the way to the bus station and to what he needs for Druggie-Lasse. He feels quite pleased. He did the right thing. In spite of the disappointment when Felix blabbed, he held the anger in. He has to convince Felix, to get him to change his mind. He needs him. What he understands – what Felix *doesn't* understand – is that no mother or police or social services lady in the whole world

169

knows shit about what's going to happen tomorrow. Everything can collapse in a second. It has done so before.

But he won't do it the way Pappa did – Mamma is wrong about that. Pappa is never prepared.

That's why his oldest son is taking a detour now to check the car park, stretched out between low blocks of flats and the sort of thick shrubbery you can hide in. Parking meters stand at attention, in a long row in front of each parking space, straight-backed and silent. The remaining part of what he needs.

He will return when it is dark. When no one can see him and it is full of cars.

It goes smoothly at the bus station – the right bus is standing there and he pays for a return ticket to Borlänge with coins from the cash box that he has already counted out and laid in a special plastic bag, only fifty-öre coins. It's thirty-eight minutes to the next town, a monotonous journey, mostly conifers and the odd empty picnic place. When he arrives, he starts with the shop that sells perfume and make-up, with shelves of wigs, an anonymous collection of plastic heads with eyeholes. He takes a liking to one that looks just like the bloke who came into the pizzeria in Skogås, whose hair Pappa cut. Shoulder length and brunette – darker than his own blond hair and on sale for one hundred and twenty-five kronor. Then he goes to the tobacco shop. It's better to avoid curious questions and buy cigarettes twenty kilometres or so away than at home in Falun. A small pack of John Silver, the same name as the one-legged pirate in *Treasure Island*. He pays again with the cash box money. The bank notes don't require much space but the coins create a bulging bubble in one jacket pocket – almost all of it is spent. More than ever he needs the parking meters, if he is to complete Druggie-Lasse.

FULL MOON.

A powerful light outside their window, a glare mixed with the streetlights forcing its way through the rolled-down blinds. It's half an hour to midnight. He has waited for the darkness, and for Felix and Vincent's snores.

Gumdrops, bus ticket, wig, cigs. Twenty-four kronor left, not enough. He still needs one hundred and twenty-four to be able to buy the rest.

He is going to fix that now.

The chisel and the hammer in his rucksack can be used for most things.

From the hall he peers into Vincent's room. The snores have turned into regular breathing and his youngest little brother is not even dreaming. He is sleeping the dreamless sleep, which clearly is the best. The loops of the bandages hanging around his mouth are light brown, like after a lot of chocolate balls.

Leo moves through the dark, illuminated by the full moon, to the shrubbery that surrounds the car park. He creeps into it and watches, hidden by the leafy branches, until he is certain he is alone. When he creeps out it is just as it was during the night at school – only his movements are heard, the soft soles of his gym shoes against the asphalt.

He has wrapped the chisel with insulation tape. The hammer has to hit the top of it several times with force. Each meter serves two parking spaces and branches into two metal heads, each with a slot for coins. Ten posts means twenty possible containers to break into.

He wonders sometimes about these kinds of devices. Sweets vending machines and drinks machines and the small red ones that contain plastic balls with meaningless toys. Devices that give you something back if you swap money for it. Each time he puts a coin in a vending machine he wonders how he can get it back again, imagining the cover off and trying to see the mechanical play that one krona or a fifty-öre coin sets in motion. But there's no automatic device that people put more money into than a parking meter. And what do they get for it? Time. A lousy hour per krona.

He examines one of a parking meter's metal heads – the green plastic teardrop that turns red when the time is up, the narrow cracks that serve as coin slots and the very small door that is opened with a key for emptying. This door distinguishes parking meters from other automatic devices. The rivets that hold it in place are small and brittle.

They hold the most money, and are the easiest to break into.

Chisel tight in one hand, the hammer in the other, he breathes in, takes aim and strikes.

A single blow and the flat head is separated from the body of the rivet.

He pushes the door to one side and sticks in his right hand. Coins. A lot of them. Two fistfuls. He counts them, only one krona coins, twenty-two of them.

The parking space's second meter contains twenty-eight and the third, seventeen.

Focused – that's what he is, alone in a world of accessible cash tills. That's why he doesn't react to the light that precedes the sound. The car's headlights light up the entire car park, followed by the car engine cutting off when the car parks just two spaces away.

He throws himself down on the asphalt.

Too late?

He holds his breath, counts to ten, and then crawls into the shrubbery.

He lies down, one cheek against the bare ground, and he sees the driver's foot step out. Black boots. A man closes the car door and searches in his pocket for coins. Three coins. Leo hears them landing in the newly emptied parking meter's interior.

His heart is beating against the ground. His upper body rises and sinks in rhythm.

Because the man is lingering, seems to have seen something. Then he finally decides to go, but not to the building – to the bushes. Towards the person lying there.

The black boots come nearer, and stop about a metre away.

Hell.

It would be enough if the man happens to see the rucksack, or the chisel and hammer.

Leo closes his eyes. Holds his breath.

Until suddenly he almost laughs.

A stream. Liquid with a clear, acrid odour meeting the leafy branches.

So fucking close.

The fourth parking meter contains eight kronor, the next twenty-nine, the next twenty.

It is enough to buy the last items. The jacket, the pads, the paint. Then his disguise is complete.

A LIGHT SHINES brightly in his eyes. The moon is hanging outside his window. He forgot to lower the blinds and the round ball glows, directing its light towards the Earth. But that wasn't what woke him. It was the smell. He recognises it so well.

Felix sits up in his bed.

Cigarette smoke. It smells like Pappa.

He tests the floor with a naked foot. It is cold but there's no sound. He creeps towards the other light, the light from the kitchen. That's where Pappa used to smoke. They figured out how long he would sleep the next day based on how long he stayed up drinking black wine. Every decapitated cigarette butt in the ashtray meant peace and quiet a little while longer.

The smell, so strong.

He breathes in and out three times and then leans into the kitchen.

It *is* cigarettes – five of them, and they are lying next to each other on one of Mamma's blue-flowered saucers. They are lit and forming a combined cloud of smoke rising up to the ceiling.

Felix leans further in.

Someone is sitting there. He sees a back, a neck.

But it isn't Pappa. It is someone he has never seen.

His legs are being pulled in opposite directions. He wants to go into the kitchen but doesn't dare. He wants to go back to his room and his bed but he is fastened to the spot.

He can't see the face, not even a glimpse of the visitor's profile. Only the weak light on the kitchen fan is on and doesn't reach the kitchen table. Half of the body stays hidden in the shadows.

Felix tries to stay still but it is difficult when the blood is pumping around between his arms and legs, in spite of light breathing that goes unnoticed.

It is a man, a very tall man. His hair hangs down to his shoulders.

Then all of a sudden he turns around, and they look at each other before Felix runs. He dashes through the hall, to the bathroom. He hears the man running after him but he makes it just in time and locks the door behind him.

174

'Felix?'

The man with long hair pulls hard on the door. The handle jiggles up and down, up and down.

'Felix? Hear me?'

The man with the long hair even knows his name.

'It's just me. Leo.'

And now he claims that his name is Leo.

'Come out. It *is* me.'

'What have you done with your hair?'

'Open up and you'll see.'

One. Two. Three. Then he does it. He opens the door, and it really is Leo. With long brown hair.

'Come here, into the kitchen. I'll show you.'

A table with five glowing cigarette butts. And next to them – Felix hadn't seen it before – a pile of coins. A new pile, he is sure of it. It consists only of one krona coins and there are clearly more than what was in the cash box.

'Felix – imagine this on my head.'

His big brother points at the hair that isn't his, a bloody ugly wig. It's obvious now that he is closer.

'And a big, dirty jacket with a hood. And then, these.'

The burning cigarettes, that's what Leo is referring to.

'You've started smoking?'

'False leads.'

'False leads? I don't understand.'

'Druggie-Lasse. I am going to throw them on the ground when I am standing and waiting a little way away from the ICA shop. The police will discover them.'

'What police?'

'False leads to trick the cops. Suppose I am standing there in the square and someone walks by and sees . . .'

He picks up a cigarette that is giving off its last bit of smoke and puts it in his mouth. He lets it sit in one corner, just like in all the films. He lowers his forehead and slouches. The straggling hair dangles like vines in front of his eyes. And his voice is rough.

'Hey, matey, they call me Druggie-Lasse.'

Felix hears in Leo's voice that he thinks it's funny, that *he* is funny. But he isn't.

'And watta bout you, you're Light-Fingered Johnny, yeah? Watcha think, you wanna do this, a little B and E, you 'n' me?'

Stupid wig. Stupid voice. Stupid dialect.

'Leo – the police. They're going to search for you.'

Leo straightens out his upper body and his voice sounds normal.

'No, little brother. They are going to look for Druggie-Lasse. We'll trick them. We're smarter. A fourteen-year-old and an eleven-year-old. No one will imagine we did it.'

He puts his arms around Felix.

'Well? Druggie-Lasse needs his mate. He needs Light-Fingered Johnny to make it work. To pull it off.'

But Felix moves away.

'Last night you woke me up for a damn rubbish bag and a damn cash box. And this fucking money, one krona coins, where did *they* come from? And now do you seriously think that we are going to snatch a bag with thousands? Why are you doing this?'

You have the responsibility from now on.

Facing each other. That was how he and his father were standing after the beating, after Mamma's escape, about the same place the largest bloodstain spread out. The house smelled like the food Mamma was serving and that they did not get to eat, spaghetti and meat sauce, and the food blended with the smell of Mamma's blood.

Leo had stopped him from beating Mamma to death and they were looking at each other.

You understand, right, Leonard? That you have the responsibility?

'He said that to me. But you didn't hear it because you ran and hid.'

'Did he say that we should swipe money? No, he sure as hell didn't. And I heard something too – what Mamma said. But maybe you didn't.'

'He said that I should take over. And I've done that.'

The wig doesn't fit right. It is easy to take off and Leo puts it on the table and puts out the cigarettes one by one. It is easier to argue with him when he's himself again. Felix feels it, how the words pour out of him quickly and take hold of his older brother.

'OK – Vincent is a damn mummy. And Mamma's in hospital. And Pappa's in custody. And now are you also going to get arrested and disappear?'

'I won't get arrested.'

'Everything was fine for four years. Everything was normal. Then they released Pappa, and he came straight here and beat up Mamma. And now everything is bad again.'

Then when the words run out, the tears come. He sobs all the more explosively. Felix never cries, not even when Pappa was beating Mamma up, not once since it all began.

Now all the tears are coming out at once.

'I'm not doing it. Do you hear that? I refuse.'

'Felix, you know Light-Fingered Johnny always helps Druggie-Lasse.'

'I am not going to do it because . . . it's not good. It is that simple.'

He turns towards the kitchen table and remembers another one in another flat. When he lay on the floor, hidden at the doorway, and peered in without having been invited. There was a different collection of odd things on *that* kitchen table. Petrol, torn pillowcases, empty wine bottles. Pappa taught Leo how to make Molotov cocktails, the firebombs that burnt down their grandparents' house. Now a wig is lying on the tabletop between a huge pile of one krona coins and a saucer with five cigarettes.

'Strange things on a kitchen table. I don't care if it was four years ago – I know you remember it, Leo, as well as I do. I know you think you are deciding but Mamma said it, you don't need to do the same thing.'

He keeps on crying. The tears come from deep down and they are nearly as big as his cheeks. Until his big brother gathers up the things on the table, fetches an empty plastic bag with the Konsum shop logo and buries both the wig and the packs of cigarettes.

'What are you doing?'

Leo pulls hard on the bag's handles, ties a knot and pulls again, then puts it next to the bucket under the kitchen sink.

'You're right.'

Felix dries his tears with the palms of his hands.

'What, Leo?'

'Let's forget it.'

Leo holds his brother, a firm grip around his shoulders.

'Druggie-Lasse doesn't exist any more.'

'Do you promise?'

And then he hugs him.

'Yeah, I promise.'

'If you get my brother involved, I'll
get your brother involved.'

THE SHOVEL IS HEAVY in his hand. Perhaps that's why it sinks so easily and so deeply into the ground. Or perhaps it is the lack of tangled roots and angular stone. When the steel tip hits the wooden lid, it encounters a porous surface – as happens when time passes and a coffin has been buried a long time.

He knows exactly what is in it.

Pappa.

He wiggles the coffin lid and opens it slowly.

It doesn't smell like anything. Shouldn't it, though? And Pappa is lying exactly as he did at the wake in one of the hospital's prayer rooms. Fine suit. Hair combed back. Ashen complexion.

John Broncks unbuttons his pappa's pinstriped suit jacket and white shirt. He keeps the tie knotted but pushes it to one side so it won't be in the way. When he bends forward he happens to bump his shoulder against the wall of the hole. The soil falls on his pappa's exposed stomach and chest. He pushes it away with his hand and feels the edges of the wounds with his palms and begins to count. Twenty-six holes. It said twenty-seven in the medical examiner's report.

'You should look higher up.'

It sounds like Pappa's voice.

'The rib directly under the left arm. The last cut was there.'

And when he grabs hold of his pappa's arm and turns it to be able to see the twenty-seventh hole better, he hears his father's heart beating, hard. Thump, thump. Thump, thump. As if his father is fighting back.

Thump, thump.

Broncks sat up in bed.

Thump, thump.

A dream – so bizarre. But the part that had felt so real, standing there in the middle of a grave, had not been real at all.

He felt relieved.

But then the thump came again, from the front door.

181

His mobile phone was lying on the floor – 05.57. He hadn't even slept two hours.

Thump, thump.

Who the hell was banging on the door at this hour?

He padded softly through the hallway of his two-room flat, sockless feet on the cold pine floor. There was a peephole above the door handle and lock. He leaned forward.

Her?

'What are *you* doing here?'

'Leo Dûvnjac.'

'Well?'

'We have to talk about him.'

'I thought you were clear when you explained that you didn't want to work on that investigation – or was it that you didn't want to work with me.'

'Listen, Broncks?'

'Yeah?'

'I *want* to keep working on it. I don't care if you are a psychopath. He sat in the interview chair yesterday and he is even worse.'

People don't look sensible when they are smiling through a peephole that distorts lines and perspective. Elisa didn't either. Her smile was crooked and round at the same time, and too big. Or perhaps that was what she looked like? He probably had not seen her smile especially often before. And now she was holding up something black, gesturing with it at the peephole. It was an investigation folder, at least he thought so.

'Wait a minute.'

He went back to the bedroom, ignored the unmade bed and pulled on his jeans, which were lying on the floor, and a T-shirt hanging on the armchair. Then he opened the front door. As she came in and hung her jacket on the hook on top of his jacket, it felt as if she was examining him, taking in his dishevelled hair and bare feet.

'Yes, you are seeing correctly – you woke me up. Would you like something? Water? Coffee?'

'No, thanks.'

'Then I'll just get some for myself.'

Broncks went into the kitchen and Elisa followed him.

'You broke off the interview, John.'

He filled the kettle and turned on the hob.

182

'You showed Dûvnjac out. And you didn't come back.'

Hot water. Silver tea.

'Since then I've tried to call you.'

'And I thought you came here to talk about the job. Not about how I spend my time.'

'I said that I came here to talk about Leo Dûvnjac.'

He poured his steaming water into a large cup. From her seat she could take in the whole flat with a glance. Single. She was certain of that. Not gay, although he had never looked at her in the way heterosexual men sometimes did. A home that could have been clipped out of any page of an Ikea catalogue, entirely without personal effects. No photographs. Nothing on the walls that he was proud of. Nice but not distinctive. A hotel room. Anyone at all could stay here a couple of nights and then move on.

'I checked Dûvnjac's alibi. It holds, John. He was at the restaurant he named and met his father at the time he stated. It was confirmed by the couple that run the place and by a slightly drunk regular. And our house search at his mother's gave us nothing either, as we anticipated.'

'But from what I have heard, it gave you something else – enemies. Because correcting colleagues, as you evidently did when they turned her bedroom upside down, is the best way to make yourself uncomfortable in the building where we work.'

'I have no problem with that if I know I'm right. I didn't become a police officer because I was lonely – I already have friends.'

She looked at him. That look that only she had.

'You, on the other hand, don't seem to have too many friends there – so what have *you* said?'

He drank the warm water, so pleasant when it spread through his chest.

'Alibi, no result. House search, no result. So you came here and woke me entirely unnecessarily? If so, you can go home now. And I can go back to sleep.'

She made no attempt at all to go, but instead pulled out one of the pine chairs and sat down at the kitchen table.

'John, when I don't find what I'm looking for, I keep looking. Until I find it.'

She opened the folder she had waved in front of the peephole and the first paper she picked up seemed – at least from what he could see upside down – to be a page from the correctional system's register.

'We knew that Jari Ojala, the dead robber, served the last six months of his sentence at Österåker prison. In cell 2, cellblock H – the same prison and same cellblock as Leo Dûvnjac. That they knew each other, and that Dûvnjac could certainly have planned, and led, exactly as before, but without being at the scene of the crime.'

The next paper also had the correctional system's logo in the upper corner.

'Now we know that an additional fourteen were in cellblock H during the time both Dûvnjac and Ojala were there. Ten of them are still locked up and no one had temporary leave right then. So we can eliminate them.'

'Well?'

'That leaves four. This one . . . We can call him A. Joaquín Sánchez. Twelve years for serious drug offences. Belongs to a Bolivian cartel. If you are prepared to cross a border with a suitcase full of clothes impregnated with cocaine, you would probably be ready to carry out a robbery of a security van.'

Four bundles of paper, each held together with a paper clip.

'And this one, the one with the ruddy complexion, in the next bundle, we'll call B.'

She laid them out on the table in front of her, careful to make sure they formed a semicircle.

'Thor Bernard. Eight years for kidnapping when he was advancing from probationer to regular member in a motorcycle club. Ready to do anything to gain the leader's appreciation. Next, this bundle, John, we'll call C. Sam Larsen. Life sentence for murder, now released. Even though he was not convicted for anything like robbery, he was inside long enough to be totally damaged by the slammer. And the last, that bundle, which we'll call D. Semir Mhamdi. Six years for manslaughter. Member of a Moroccan criminal network, or rather North African. It extends over the border to Algeria. Exhibits extreme contempt for the police and is known for keeping his mouth shut during interrogation, just like the dead man Ojala.'

The water in the kettle was still hot. Broncks turned around and filled his cup again, even though he did not intend to drink more.

Sam.

You – again.

We have only seen each other four times in twelve years, most recently when I told you in the visitors' room that our mother was dead – and you did not even want to touch me. Then suddenly you were there again in the interview. Then last night when I couldn't sleep. And now, as one of the names on a list that will be investigated further. I know you. You are not a robber. At the same time I don't know you at all.

'So if you finish dressing now, John, we'll start to deal with them. One after another.'

And you, Sam.

If we are going to see each other again now, under these circumstances, an investigation to eliminate you from our inquiries, I do not want to do it in the company of someone who runs around calling me a psychopath.

'Elisa – let's divide them up instead.'

Someone who still doesn't know about our background, and won't afterwards.

'You take the first two and I'll take the last two.'

'I don't understand – when you invited me in, John, you said you wanted to work side by side.'

Because there have been enough outsiders digging in our family grave for now.

'It's better like this. It's about time, Elisa – if Dûvnjac decides to strike on his first day of freedom, then he's working to a deadline. Don't you think?'

He pulled two of the bundles towards him.

'I'll take, yeah, these ones, C and D. And you take A and B. OK?'

He sat down across from her to do what she was doing – browsing through the small piles of personal details and criminal records and photographs. But while Elisa flipped pages methodically forwards, John Broncks was already stuck on the first photo of a then very young inmate. Sam Larsen.

Broncks had forgotten how he once looked.

It was as if every childhood memory of his big brother was replaced with a different Sam he met in the visitors' room – muscles and bad prison tattoos and eyes that repel. The Sam who looked at him now from a black-and-white photograph – eighteen years old, narrow neck, fringe a bit too long and tousled, and eyes staring straight into the camera – well knew that the twenty-seventh and last stab with a serrated fishing knife was stuck in their father's left side, high up under his arm.

185

PEOPLE'S CALVES LOOK so incredibly different.

He had not thought about it before. But now, as he saw them passing by out there on Hallands Street through two long, narrow and rather dirty windows which were placed immediately under the cellar's ceiling, it was clear how the rest of the body might be imagined – age, status, even inner well-being – from twenty centimetres of feet and calves.

'Leo?'

He glanced in the room Fredrik Sullo Söderberg called his office – sixty square metres of basement in a building by Rosenlunds Park in central Stockholm.

'Leo, hello?'

'Yeah?'

'I shouldn't ask, but . . . you have everything with you?'

Leo let the bag's strap slide down from his shoulder.

'Two kinds of payment. Paper and metal, just as we agreed.'

'I trust you, Leo, but I have to check for the seller's sake, you know?'

Sullo's voice always sounded nice, even seconds before a broken jaw. It had gone so quickly that time that the prison guards didn't notice the blow. Leo had verified Sullo's story – that the Russian rapist dropped a barbell on himself while bench-pressing in the prison gym. This was how trust between two inmates strengthened.

'And you – have you arranged what *you* are supposed to?'

The ceiling was painted in lime green and the grey concrete floor was covered with worn Persian-style rugs, a way to keep the heat in on a freezing spring day. Based on Sullo's own description, Leo had likely imagined the office to be a little more organised. An improvised shelving system had grown on the walls all the way to the ceiling at the same pace as the business, which was expanding, uncontrolled, and a little too fast. Cartons and cardboard boxes and plastic bags with not yet unpacked mobile telephones, surround systems, projectors and computers. Below the shelves was the rather large packaging for television sets and screens and the odd hard drive.

'Over here, Leo, are a few gadgets for you.'

Sullo pointed to the room's far corner and the items waiting there. Leo was one of the few invited into the heart of the business. This was not as a consequence of his official qualifications. Sullo had been clear on that point. Anyone could rob a bank and get sent to prison. It had to do with the eight armed robberies that the police still suspected Leo Dûvnjac for. Someone with that particular qualification did not talk to the police about his fellow workers.

'The trousers and jackets you ordered came knocking on the door last night.'

'My wish list was longer than that.'

'Everything is here. There were several deliveries.'

They passed two clothes racks with Armani, Givenchy, Prada and Hugo Boss packed in tightly together, suits packaged in thin plastic that *happened* to fall out of some long-distance lorry on the E4 between Malmö and Stockholm. The large room was a halfway station where the products were stored for a while on their way between new sellers and new buyers. And Sullo was the station manager who guaranteed a secure stop-over in his waiting hall, where everyone involved got a fair share of a shady transaction.

He presented himself in this manner at Kumla prison four years ago: the safe middleman when sellers and buyers did not want to meet and learn each other's names and descriptions.

'Here – your *entire* wish list.'

Sullo stopped at the only clean tabletop and picked up a moving box with a brown tube sticking up in the middle like a chimney out of a house.

'But the bloody shield . . .'

He folded the carton's flaps aside and picked up the little metal shield that made up half of every police officer's identification. Blue, red and gold. District and number imprinted on the brass plate that went with it.

'. . . it was not easy – just as difficult to obtain as I tried to explain to you. There was only one little bastard out there in the market who was the real deal. So it cost. Shit – not even the best pickpocket can pick the pockets of cops any more.'

Leo held it on the palm of his hand. Light metal. Not more than thirty grams.

'One is enough. I'm arranging the other one myself. I'm already prepared.'

Sullo looked at Leo curiously. That didn't happen often since he was the one who arranged things.

'How's that?'

'The miracle of technology. Can I see the rest now?'

Sullo picked up two folded dark blue jackets and two equally dark blue trousers.

'The police authority's current uniform, standard model.'

Leo took the jacket and let it unfold – he felt the shoulder flaps that extended the thick collar, checked the zip inside the Velcro and inspected the labels with the specifications.

'Trousers? Shirt? Leather gloves? Boots? Do you want to examine them also?'

'No. No need. But I want to see the belt.'

Sullo fished out the nylon belt with an expandable baton, handcuffs, pepper spray, extra magazines, radio, walkie-talkie and gun holster. All told, four kilos to be carried around the waist. Leo weighed the single heaviest item in his hand, the gun, the model that was the Swedish police's service weapon, the Sig Sauer P226.

'OK, Leo. If you are satisfied, you know what it costs.'

Leo opened the sports bag and pulled out two assault rifles.

'Paper and metal. We'll start with the metal.'

Sullo took them and put them on the shipping table without examining them more closely.

'One more thing. A little consumer information. Just so you know, Leo, the uniforms, with the belts attached, are going to be missing tomorrow or – if you're lucky – at the latest the day after that.'

'Missing where?'

'From the police authority in Örebro.'

'The essential thing is that no one is going to miss them in Stockholm. Örebro, it's going to take at least a couple of days for the news to reach here. And then I will already have changed clothes for ever.'

The drawing tube sticking up like a chimney was capped at one end with a plastic lid. Sullo opened it and pulled out a piece of hand-drawn A3 paper.

'Directly from the cleaning company.'

Leo interpreted the sharp black marker lines that summarised a building that had both already had and would acquire great meaning in his life

– corridors and stairs and central rooms marked off on the different floors.

'And here – the accompanying access card. The entrance to the underground passage from the courthouse. We've both been there a few times, right – in shackles. But the seized property room. Do you hear that, Leo? You can't move freely down there. Otherwise all hell will break loose. To the property room and back. Because if someone finds this piece of plastic and figures out where it comes from, then . . .'

'No need to worry. I don't plan to go anywhere else. When I get what I want, I'll get out of there clean.'

Sullo held out the access card, not much bigger than an ordinary Visa card, but did not let go when Leo slipped his hand around it.

'I got the metal. Now I want the paper. Your order costs, exactly as we agreed, seven centimetres of five-hundred-kronor notes, in addition to the two AK4s.'

The envelope Leo put on the table contained the five-hundred-kronor notes, seven hundred of them, and it was bulging precariously.

On top of it was another envelope, a slightly thinner one.

'And this, Sullo, is for the information about transport times to Tumba paper mill.'

'That was on the house. It was the first test sample. Satisfied customers come back.'

'No, you should have them. You decided to trust me even though I couldn't pay then. Now I just need the flat.'

Sullo rummaged around in the moving carton and it took a while to find the bunch of keys.

'Gamla Sickla, 25 Atlas Road, fourth floor. Close to the diesel workshop.'

'I'm staying two nights max. I'll put the key in the letterbox when I leave. OK?'

Leo packed the whole wish list in a few minutes and left the extraordinary office located in an ordinary basement. Soon he too would pass by the long, narrow, dirty window on Hallands Street where only people's lower legs could be seen. And in his case, on the basis of twenty centimetres of feet and calves, it would just be possible to imagine one shape – the other one lay in the bag hanging from a strap over his shoulder.

THE BOOM GATE was red and white and was gliding upwards a little at a time, as if it had to stop regularly and get ready so that it could manage to go the whole way. John Broncks rolled on board the small car ferry and the gate was lowered behind him. His was the only car on that particular crossing, so it seemed like a normal day. Five minutes from the mainland to the island in the middle of Lake Mälaren. He turned in the driver's seat and waved to the ferryman up in the control room as Pappa always did when he and Sam were little. Everyone on Arnö had a habit of waving – it separated the tourists from the homeowners. He drove up to the ramp that would open soon and represented never coming back. That is how it was every time they left the mainland for a weekend or the summer holidays – as if they were surrendering to another world isolated by violence. That was why Sam always whispered 'Welcome to Alcatraz' when the car lurched over the bump between the ramp and the land.

Broncks felt – as he had done then – the hellish nausea. Deep down in his stomach. The kind that he usually felt in his chest as an adult, taking the form of a large black ball that got in the way of breathing. But now – just like then – it sank to his stomach and settled there as if he had eaten anxiety.

I am an adult now, for fuck's sake.

That didn't help – not with how he thought or what he thought about. It stayed there in the pit of his stomach, weighed him down and entered into him.

The children he had met earlier in the morning had been the complete opposite. Noisy, inquisitive, full of self-confidence, constantly in motion. He had stepped into a flat in Fruängen and at the same time into something so entirely different from what he had expected because of prejudice. D on the list – Semir Mhamdi – had found his way back to his wife and children with his newly found religious beliefs and an entirely new life. He was someone who was truly trying. Broncks had ended up in the middle of a school drop-off and walked there together with the family. Without being aware of it, the daughters had given their father the alibi that the

190

policeman was there to investigate. *Both yesterday and the day before, yeah, right after school when Pappa took us to the swimming pool, then, can you believe it, he made a giant bomb in the middle of the pool, and it splashed far, really, really, really far.*

So very different from how he grew up himself.

On the way from the boat he waved to the ferryman's control room again, just as a real islander would do. He did it automatically even though he had never been here as an adult.

He had searched for the registration in the census without having a clue where his own brother was living after his release. He knew that Sam inherited the summer house – Mamma had wanted that in her will. His immediate feeling of jealousy had later transformed in his thoughts to a feeling of indifference. If Sam wanted the fucking house, he was welcome to do whatever the fuck he wanted with it. But John Broncks never could have imagined that his brother would choose to live in it.

He passed the thirteenth-century church. Its white plaster was considerably discoloured, and the lawn and gravel paths seemed no longer as well tended. It was there they met most recently, without saying a word to each other either before or after their mother's burial. In spite of that, from a little distance, it could have made an ordinary picture of an ordinary family at an ordinary funeral – if it hadn't been for the two prison guards standing on either side of Sam during the entire ceremony, and even they were in black suits.

The road's asphalt gave way to coarse-grained gravel and the farmland was replaced by dense forest. It seemed just as beautiful as when they were children. He turned off the engine at the end of the hillside and rolled silently along the final stretch to the red wooden fence.

He remained in the car.

A summer house on an early spring day always suggested lack of occupancy.

Are you living here?

How can a person voluntarily move into the house of his darkest memories?

He opened the car door and perceived the sound very clearly – an axe meeting logs that were breaking apart and landing on either side of a chopping block.

And it was then – when he was going to take the very first step – that the nausea increased, as if eating anxiety had turned into force-fed anxiety.

191

If he could have vomited out his memories, he would have done so here and now.

He moved slowly over the frozen, nearly snowless lawn towards a light that was increasing in strength. He heard the wooden fibres moaning as they were torn apart. But it wasn't until he walked around the lilac arbour with its thick branches that he saw him. His back, the axe over his head, the concentrated force when the sharp edge was thrown forward. Broncks waited for the pieces to settle in their piles.

'Hello.'

Sam wasn't startled and didn't spin around – as if he had heard someone standing there behind him without caring about it. One more birch log, the axe in the air, the crack when it hit exactly where it was aimed.

'I said . . . hello.'

Then he turned around, and their eyes met briefly before Sam bent down and gathered up an armful of firewood. The moment passed quickly, but it was long enough for Broncks to catch his face, which had aged since Mamma died. Broncks calculated, forty-two. That was how old his big brother was.

'I thought you would have sold this shit.'

Sam was silent and gathered the pile of firewood on the other side of the block as well. He carried it across to a stack against the wall of the firewood shed.

'Surely it must be worth about a million?'

Sam placed firewood on top of firewood in a stack that would not collapse, then closed the door to the shed and fastened the padlock.

'Seriously, John – do you imagine that it would be possible to sell it? The murder house? That is what they still call it after all these fucking years.'

It was just a few steps to the house. Sam went inside, leaving the door wide open behind him.

'On a lousy little island the gossip never moves on. It sort of travels around and around along the shoreline. Shit, they barely look at me, whispering that the murderer is back. That is what they say when they think I don't hear them.'

Broncks looked beyond the open door into the little hall and kitchen but his feet refused to move. They did not want to enter the place where violence infused the walls.

'The ferryman, he's the only damn one of them who isn't prejudiced.

Do you remember him, John? I think he even almost likes me. Not so strange, maybe? He was certainly the only one who saw through our father.'

Broncks stood where he was and listened to Sam's voice coming to him from a distance, entirely devoid of feelings, exactly as if they were in any visitors' cell.

'You're letting the heat out.'

Broncks watched Sam laying the firewood in the rusty tin box that had always stood there by the right side of the woodstove.

'I have to close it now – either come in or stay out there.'

The hall.

He hadn't even been an adult yet the last time he'd stood there.

Now, when he stepped in, it seemed so incredibly small, same as the kitchen where Sam was putting a piece of firewood in through the wood-burning stove's door and then stirring the red coals with the poker. He saw Sam's face clearly. So many more wrinkles under the eyes than last time. Exactly like their father. He had never thought in that vein before; that their father had been in his forties when he was murdered, about the same age his two sons were now.

'Well? Are you here to give me good wishes and welcome me back?'

Sam smiled a mocking smile.

'In that case, brother, you are a few months late.'

'No. You don't want to have anything to do with me in private life – so I am here as a police officer.'

John Broncks took a photograph out of his coat pocket and laid it down on the kitchen table at the place that had once been his own.

'Do you know him?'

Sam didn't even look at the photo from the correctional system's register.

'I still don't rat on people.'

'Sam, you're not in the slammer any more.'

'But, John, you are just as much a policeman.'

Broncks pushed the photo closer to Sam.

'I *know* that you knew him – you were at Österåker at the same time. Jari Ojala was shot to death last night during a robbery of a security van. We believe that his accomplice, who got away, also did time at Österåker. You are one of them, Sam. I have come here to eliminate you from our inquiries. When I have done so, you can do what you want – we won't see each other again.'

'So do that. Eliminate me.'

'When you have told me what you were doing on Monday between four and five.'

'You're a police officer – find out for yourself.'

Broncks laid another photo on top of the first one. The second one covered it exactly, as if the register had a standard size.

'You did time with him also. Leo Dûvnjac.'

'And?'

'Listen, Sam, fuck . . . We should be able to take care of this quickly and then both of us can get to where we want to be – you want to be left in peace and I want to get away from here. If you just talk to me.'

Sam threw a new log into the flames, though it wasn't necessary.

'OK. Then talk.'

Broncks saw thick, dark smoke streaming up from the edges of a broken stove plate. It was getting harder to breathe.

'You and Dûvnjac did time together for more than a year, according to the correctional facility's notes. Which inmate or inmates were close to him during that time?'

'How the hell should I know?'

You talked to each other, Sam.

'Was there anyone he spent a lot of time with?'

'One socialises as one socialises in a cellblock.'

You were talking about us, Sam.

'A prison corridor isn't all that fucking big – you ran into each other all the time. You must have seen who he associated with.'

You knew each other well, Sam.

'No one knows anyone when everyone is longing to get out.'

It was quiet in the little house, as quiet as it was outside. And the logs, which earlier were moaning weakly, crackled loudly now.

'The smoke is coming out of the stove there, you see that, don't you? You need to replace the plate. I remember Mamma replaced the other one when we were little.'

The grey smoke formed beautiful veils above the stove. Broncks relaxed in it as it slowly made its way to the ceiling. Then he went to the kitchen table and gathered up the photos. He would not get any detailed answers, no matter how many times he repeated and varied the same questions.

He opened the front door and the smoke followed, playing awkwardly.

But he stopped outside on the small stone step, turned and went in again.

194

'Have you told anyone about us, Sam?'

'What?'

'About what happened here?'

'Is it still the cop who's asking?'

'Interpret it as you want.'

Sam smiled mockingly, like before.

'Whether I've told?'

And he went into the sitting room and pointed to the two small bedrooms.

'You mean about what happened in there? Come in, John, and I'll *tell* you what happened. Come in!'

'I know what happened.'

'The hell you do!'

Sam vanished out of sight, a few steps further in towards the bedrooms and Broncks was forced to do the same to be able to see him.

'I decided not to feel any more – but you didn't. Because one can do that, John, decide not to feel pain. One can think, *I don't feel* and then you damn well don't. I remember the last time, how I just looked at him, and said that – hit me, go ahead and hit me, I don't even feel it – and the old man turned red in the face and beat me and beat me and I didn't feel at all. That was the last time. He did not go for me any more, and he knew it. We knew it, both of us. So he started to beat you, John. And you, you felt it.'

Sam nodded at the green wall telephone still hanging there.

'That was why you called me that night, crying, and asked me to come here.'

There was only the firewood crackling.

And the cast-iron stove radiating heat, dry and pleasant.

And the nausea that couldn't be vomited out, with someone who decided to live among his memories, in the same fucking house.

And it was as if Sam was enjoying that it was the first time in so many years that he had the upper hand. He was free. Not locked in a cell. He was safe here, unlike his visitor.

'Come on in! John, dammit, come and try out the bed he slept in. If you want to investigate so bloody much.'

On the small shelf for trinkets there was something that looked like a knife on a crocheted cloth among the photographs and glass bowls. Sam reached for it, picked it up and waved it in front of himself.

It was *that* knife. Serrated blade, the very end of the point broken.

195

'I requested it. Dammit, it was left as an old piece of evidence in a fucking archive box. You see the dried blood, John, and without the steel at the tip that came off and stayed in his sternum.'

Broncks left for the second time. For the last time. Down the sloping lawn, towards the fence and the car by the edge of the gravel road. He didn't think much on the way back to the ferry, not while he waited for it nor when he got out of the car during the short crossing to let the wind play in his face and to be able to see the gulls chasing the foaming water.

He knew that the nausea would accompany him until he saw the contour of Stockholm in the distance again.

But he hadn't counted on the doubt that was following him back. He had gone there to eliminate his brother but that was no longer possible. And it wasn't about the blows within those walls. They had echoed precisely as much and as loudly as he knew they would. It was the questions concerning Leo Dûvnjac. When he'd broached the subject of how well they knew each other, Sam responded with arrogance, evaded, attacked with counter questions and was vague. But at least he answered. However, when John Broncks turned at the door and posed the question that had been bothering him since yesterday's interview, whether Sam had told someone about their shared history, what happened in the house – the kind of thing you tell only someone very close – instead of answering, Sam had gone on the attack, launching a shitload of guilt.

He had known that would knock his little brother off balance.

Broncks wandered aimlessly on the empty ferry – from rail to rail, inside the warm passenger lounge and out again. He tapped the lifeboat lightly as if to assure himself it would hold and he fiddled with the timetables on the metal rack. When he was looking up at the control room and ferryman for a while, he saw it.

The surveillance camera.

Perhaps they were there – the answers that Sam didn't want to give.

Broncks rolled off the ferry but got out of his car right past the gate. He waited for the ferryman at the entrance to the little house.

'Excuse me.'

He held out his identification and the ferryman looked at it without it registering.

'I am a police officer – and I would like to take a look at your surveillance footage from the last couple of days.'

'Surveillance footage?'

'From the camera by the control room on the ferry.'

'It has been there all these years without anyone ever actually asking to see what is recorded on it.'

'Then it's about time. The last forty-eight hours.'

The ferryman went into the house and Broncks followed him to the computer.

'I think it's easier if you look yourself. I have never . . . I don't even know if I could get any life out of that bloody machine.'

John Broncks sat down and found the icon for the surveillance camera on the screen, clicked on it and then clicked on today's date.

'And what is it you're looking for?'

'I don't really know. It's more that I'm looking for something that should *not* be there.'

'Now I really don't understand.'

'And I must ask you not to tell anyone I was here.'

The quality was like that of all images from surveillance cameras. Jerky, grainy and lacking both colour and sound. There was a timeline at the bottom and he caught Monday with the computer mouse and dragged the cursor forward.

Sixty-four crossings. More vehicles than average. It was made clear by a tally in the right margin of the picture.

He was looking for what he didn't want to find – Sam leaving the island that day. So he almost missed the vehicle that arrived on the crossing at 13.00. A smallish passenger car, probably a Toyota, which seemed reasonably new, with a driver who couldn't be seen through the slightly tinted windows. Before the ferry was halfway across, two and a half minutes into the journey, the door on the driver's side opened. A male stepped out, walked to the rail and stared down into the water.

It was then Broncks saw it.

Him.

Leo Dûvnjac. And he was just standing there, on his way to John Broncks's childhood home.

The nausea had never been so strong, settled so deep and drilled so sharply in. He tried to embrace reasonable explanations that it was not at all particularly strange that two old cellmates who spent a long time together found each other and built a friendship of the sort that forced confinement made possible; that it wasn't at all odd if they wanted to meet the first day they both were now free.

'Excuse me?'

The ferryman tapped him on the shoulder and studied him intensely.

'I recognise you.'

'Yeah? Well, I made the crossing. An hour ago.'

'No. Not that. I *recognise you*. You were just a boy then. But you are Sam's brother. Little brother. John, isn't it?'

'John.'

'I read about you. But wasn't certain if it was you. The Robbery of the Century. One hundred and three million.'

'Mmm.'

'And *you* got them?'

'Yes.'

'So you never changed your surname?'

'No.'

'Larsen, what sort of name is that actually?'

'You ask too many questions.'

'Otherwise you don't find anything out.'

'It was Mamma's. Before she married. He took it the day he came of age.'

'I remember how it was for all of you. It was fucked up.'

Broncks continued to move the cursor forward. To the crossing at 14.00 back to the mainland. When he saw the car again, it was parked, pointing in the other direction, in the middle of the ferry. Leo Dûvnjac was seen clearly through the windscreen.

After that no one was on the 14.30 ferry, not to the island and not on the way back.

But then what he didn't want to see. Sam. He left on the 15.00 ferry.

John Broncks got up and rushed out of the house, into the rising wind. The seagulls were screeching even louder.

He leaned against the lowered gate and looked away towards the island, as afraid as he was angry.

He vomited down into the water.

That is how the memories were.

'Are you OK?'

The ferryman stood in the doorway and Broncks nodded weakly. He breathed in and out slowly a couple of times and went back to looking at the images. According to the numbers in the right margin an additional thirty-four vehicles were transported before the final crossing in the evening.

'So you became a police officer?'

The ferryman moved closer to him as if he were concerned and would like assurance that his guest didn't need to run out again.

'You really went separate ways. One locked up. And one who locks people up for a living.'

Fear, anger – actually the same feeling. It came three more times.

19.00 Sam returned to the island.

20.00 Leo returned to the island.

22.00 Leo left the island on the next to last crossing.

By the time he thanked the ferryman for his help, John Broncks had watched parts of an entire day in the lives of two men. They were completely synchronised with a very serious crime committed an hour of travel time away.

He knew now.

He still had no evidence that both men had shared a prison corridor with a recently killed robber, and that they had ample time to be able to prepare and complete a robbery of a security van by travelling back and forth by ferry. It would not hold up in court.

But he knew all the same it was true. The gut feeling that Elisa despised so much was enough for him.

Dammit, Sam, what have you done?

And with him?

LEO COUNTED TWENTY-SEVEN advertising brochures and three weeks' worth of free newspapers spread out over the hall floor. The window envelope lying in the middle of the unsorted pile of post looked like it contained a rental bill addressed to Fredrik Söderberg c/o Larsson. One of the flats included in Sullo's operation – temporary housing for individuals who needed to lie low for a few days.

He put the sports bags down on the hall rug. The Puma bag containing the newly fulfilled wish list and the bright red Adidas bag handed over a day earlier by the Albanian bruiser in baggy tracksuit bottoms. The laptop costing one hundred thousand kronor was still at the bottom of the bag. He put it up on the kitchen counter and typed in the letters that cost an additional forty thousand kronor. Ten thousand per letter. The policeman who once owned the computer had either been a clown or a crossword fanatic. The password spelled out S-T-A-R backwards – R-A-T-S.

The document he needed first took seven and a half minutes to locate among the submenus and folders and links – the template for requisitions. He made a copy of the form and started to look for the two files that held what he needed to be able to fill it in correctly – the roster of duty officers and the register of relevant seized property from ongoing investigations.

THE DOOR AT the police station's exit to Kungsholms Street was caught by a sudden wind, and Elisa Cuesta held on to it hard so that it wouldn't fly open and hit the wall. She put on her leather gloves and began to walk. It should only take ten minutes to get there. Fleming Street. St Eriks Street. She slipped forwards on the poorly maintained pavement, a layer of ice lingering stubbornly on the asphalt. She passed the avenue with red plastic signs warning of sharp icicles, which were clinging to the drainpipe despite the approaching spring and were ready to fall like deadly spears at any moment.

Investigating and eliminating the two names on the short task list had been quick to do. A and B. Sánchez and Bernard. According to the police authority in Bolivia, Joaquín Sánchez had moved to the land of his birth after serving his sentence and now a few months later was at El penal de San Pedro prison awaiting trial, suspected for a drug-related triple murder. Thor Bernard's alibi checked out. Several witnesses had unanimously confirmed that at the time of interest he was on board a ferry between Gdánsk and Nynäshamn. Now she was waiting to hear from Broncks about C and D. He had looked so miserable standing by the gas cooker in the cramped kitchen of his flat, squeezing the bundles of paper hard that he himself had so stubbornly insisted they divide between them. Perhaps she shouldn't have woken him after only two hours of sleep. Perhaps she shouldn't have called him a psychopath again, either – the first time had been a label, the second time a joke that could have been perceived as harassment. Maybe he'd understood the joke as little as he had understood the admonishment earlier. And for a moment, just before he stepped out of the hallway, she had even considered giving him a hug. But if she had done so, she would probably have regretted it too.

St Eriks Bridge and Rörstrands Street. She stopped short before the door to the building, looking up to be sure that the icicles would stay up there a while longer. Then she opened the door to the block of flats that Leo Dûvnjac's middle brother had given as the current work address of the youngest brother.

201

In the hall was a beautiful staircase with light, peaceful walls, wide stairs of stone worn down by time and footsteps, and flowers in pots in the round windows, looking out over a well-maintained courtyard. They were flats with a price per square metre surely matching those of exclusive districts in London and Paris. Insanely expensive.

She stopped at the door on the third floor. It stood open a little and had empty paint tins on both sides, sharp-edged flakes of paint all over the landing. She rang the bell and through the gap heard how the signal drowned in a radio's pop music moving freely through the bare rooms. When no one seemed to have noticed her, she opened it all the way and went into a hall framed by toolboxes and tool bags along the newly painted white walls. The flat was under complete renovation, a building site that reminded her of her own plumbing renovation – four weeks of dust morning, noon and night.

'Hello?'

Like the music, her voice danced around the empty rooms and settled unheard at her feet. She kept on going into what she assumed was the sitting room. It was cold, as if all the heating elements were turned off. And the room seemed basically finished. This wouldn't be his workplace much longer.

Then she saw him. Rather, she saw two people, out on the balcony. Because of that the heat was blowing out of the room. They had their backs to her, cigarettes in their hands. As soon as she knocked on the open door of the balcony, they turned around. A young man about twenty-five, a middle-aged man about fifty-five. The younger man was dressed in blue carpenters' overalls and the older man in white painters' trousers. She recognised them both. The father and youngest son in the Dûvnjac family.

'My name is Elisa Cuesta and I'm from the investigation division, city police. And I have some questions for you, Vincent – you're Vincent, right?'

The younger one in overalls nodded, put his cigarette out and stepped into the sitting room.

'First I would like to know where you were on Monday between four and five p.m.'

'Here. Right now it's round-the-clock work if I'm going to finish in time.'

'Can anyone confirm that?'

'I – he was here!'

The older one in painters' trousers shouted from the balcony and then he came in.

'We were working here, both of us.'

She looked at him, long enough for it to become uncomfortable.

'Ivan, that's right, yeah? What you're saying sounds, to be frank, strange. Since the couple running a restaurant called Dráva, where you're a regular, say you were there then in the company of your *eldest* son. That, conveniently enough, gave both you and him an alibi for the time I'm asking about.'

'Yes, I said that. I left here, when the hell was it, Vincent, 4.10, maybe 4.15 – so I can give alibis to *both* of my sons!'

'They also said that you were there that day by 3.30. You were evidently planning to have dinner with your eldest son. So what you are saying can't be right.'

She turned again to the younger man.

'So is there anyone else, Vincent, who can confirm that you were here?'

'I *was* here. That's how it goes when you get this sort of job. Deadline. Working like hell. Ready for the moving-in day. Good money – a lot of demands.'

'And who can back that up?'

'I don't know. My father was obviously done for the day. The pizza shop, maybe. I don't remember exactly when I picked it up, a capricciosa. I always get one of those. Maybe the old lady next door? She was here sometime in the afternoon, complaining as usual that I bang too much. And yourself, where were you, by the way? Would you be able to answer that? And if so, do you remember whether anyone saw you?'

'So no alibi. And Leo, your big brother – how and where and when have you met him since his release?'

'What the fuck is all this?'

The older man raised his voice again even though he was standing close to her. Then he came even closer. He stuck out his chin and bottom lip while he lowered his forehead and stared at her through his eyebrows in a way that was most likely intended to make her afraid, or at least uncertain.

'What do you have to do with this? You say yourself that I can give Leo an alibi – so why are you going on about him? You can leave now, police lady, and leave my family in peace.'

She was neither afraid nor uncertain. She was furious. That's what she was.

'Family? If we're going to talk about family, Ivan, I met your ex-wife yesterday. And *she* was very cooperative.'

203

'She usually is. When it comes to talking too much to cops.'

'Too much? Well, yeah, maybe that depends on whose perspective. I've been looking at your record. Including the assaults.'

'I've changed now.'

Elisa didn't close the door when she went – she let the front door stand half open as it was when she came. *Changed.* When Ivan had repeated that for a third time in response to each new question, she realised she wouldn't get any further and that the visit to the nearly finished flat was over.

She went back down the beautiful staircase, pushed open the heavy door and stepped into Rörstrands Street and the same wind she had just felt from the balcony.

No.

You are not changed.

On the other hand, Ivan's youngest son might very well be. He has no alibi, but no facts at this point show that the picture your ex-wife gave of him at the house search is wrong – that he'll never commit a crime again.

She walked in the other direction, back to the police station.

Icicles hung above her and fallen ice crunched beneath her feet. It was a season that seemed as lost and unpredictable as the people she was investigating.

Yesterday she had met two brothers and their mother in a house smelling of salmon in the oven. She thought that outwardly they could be perceived as members of any family at all. Now, when she met the third brother and their pappa, she felt something else. The father was the broken hub of the Dûvnjac family. The father set the pace by defiance. Even the eldest son, whom she'd interviewed, was sublime by comparison.

She came to the crossing at the intersection of St Eriks Street and Fleming Street. The blinking green light unexpectedly turned red and she stopped mid-step, waiting for the signal's slow ticking to speed up again.

Ivan Dûvnjac had forced his way into the conversation when she addressed her questions to Vincent Dûvnjac. He tried to protect his son but it had the opposite effect. She noticed that Vincent, like a child ashamed at an embarrassing parent, backed away and looked down every time Ivan interrupted. As if he still didn't know his father essentially, didn't know what to expect and became vulnerable, unsure of how he would act.

The green light again – she crossed the busy street and, as she sometimes did when she had a little extra time, turned left on St Görans Street and through Kronobergs Park and by the playground with noisy children and their mothers, all about her age. Whenever she tried to see herself there, it just didn't work. She wasn't interested. It simply was not her, at least not yet, and she wondered if it ever would be.

Vincent and his father had performed like an out-of-tune band that had never rehearsed and it was not until they stepped out onto the stage and greeted their audience – her – that they realised their notes clashed – a discord.

She decided to go in the Polhems Street entrance and continued through the whole police complex to reach the investigation division and John Broncks's office located at one end of it.

Discord.

A fitting word also when you don't understand someone you share a corridor with, never talk with, and are suddenly going to work with.

She went into Broncks's office without knocking.

A surveillance film. He sat engrossed in front of the computer screen. In the gap between his shoulder and the point of his chin, she could see that it was the same images they had looked at the day before. The surveillance camera at the back of the shopping centre, a loading dock and a milk lorry and the back of a fleeing robber.

She waited for him to finish, the whole sequence, frame by frame, while studying him. He had looked miserable when they parted earlier, and now he was, as usual, unreachable. The contact surface that had been exposed was hidden again. But he smiled at her, something he never used to do. The smile was also discordant.

'That back.'

She pointed at the screen and the man in overalls who jumped from the loading dock.

'It is exactly that piece of information that rules him out.'

Then the back ran to the lorry cab.

'Because of that Vincent Dûvnjac is the fourth possible suspect I am eliminating today. A and B – Sánchez and Bernard – have solid alibis, just like the middle brother, Felix Dûvnjac. The youngest brother, Vincent, lacks an alibi – but all the other facts clear him. He is the one in the brotherhood who has most clearly left criminality and has paid off his penalty to the crime victims' authority. He has a functioning company with a turnover that has increased each quarter and according to the prison personnel was the only one of the family who *didn't* meet the big brother at the gate, as if he disapproved. He plainly lacks a motive, and, in addition, about thirty kilos of muscles, if you compare him with the back there – he doesn't match the description.'

She waited for Broncks to begin telling her how things had gone for him. But he didn't seem ready so she continued.

'And then, well, if I go outside the collected facts for a moment, the youngest brother also seems to have a . . . well, vulnerability, which I haven't seen in the others.'

'Vulnerability?'

'Yes. He's open. Possible to reach. If we need to.'

She waited for him again.

'John? Now is when you explain to me – how it went for you today.'

In vain, again.

'With C. And D.'

He was taking notes. She noticed that now and realised that there seemed to be a whole lot in the corner of an A4 piece of paper. He must have been writing them when he was watching the film on the computer screen.

That was why he wasn't answering. He had discovered something.

She came closer.

He was doodling.

That was what he was doing – he was running the ballpoint pen aimlessly over the paper in some sort of pattern of broken lines, maybe a flower, possibly a star.

'Sam Larsen. Semir Mhamdi. John – how did it go?'

Then he put down the pen. He had been drawing a man, a face, she saw it now. He stopped the sequence of images and froze the man's back just as he jumped into the lorry cab.

And John looked at her.

'Alibis.'

With that bloody discordant smile.

'Both of them, unfortunately.'

THE STRANDS LANDED in uneven balls in the white sink and were so unlike the mental picture he went around with. He had grown up as the one out of three brothers who inherited Mamma's hair colour. He had always been the blond. And then it had sort of become a fixed idea and he continued to think of himself as fair. It was only now, when his hair was coming off his head and he was confronted with memories, that the adult Leo Dûvnjac's colour became clear. It was considerably darker.

The electric shaver was set to zero millimetres and left bare skin behind. Stroke after stroke after stroke over the top of his head until the image in the mirror could have belonged to someone else, if it hadn't been for his eyes with clear blue irises. They were still his own.

The new ones lay in a grey plastic container and were brown, even dark brown. He placed the two lenses on his fingertips and carefully tipped them in, one at a time, over each cornea. After that he avoided the mirror, not wanting to take away from the first impression of the whole image, when he would be looking at a completely changed person.

Leo left the bathroom and went into the hall, heading for the only room. A nearly unfurnished one-room flat with a kitchen at the top of the building, in the section of the city called Gamla Sickla, commonly sought after for its beautiful view of both Nacka and downtown Stockholm. But this particular temporary tenant preferred to have all the blinds pulled down.

A single bed was the room's remaining piece of furniture and the glow from the makeshift ceiling light settled softly by the uniform and belt lying stretched out on the blanket. A pair of boots stood on the floor in the shadows below the bed.

He got dressed.

Just before going back to the mirror, he grabbed hold of the doorframe and closed his eyes. He groped his way forward the last step and stopped when his hip bumped into the sink. The contact lenses rubbed and tickled at the same time. In a moment he would open his eyes and look, but first he felt for the high doorsill with his left heel and stepped up on it. The right distance was important. His upper body should be visible.

He stretched and let his eyelids glide up.

The policeman in front of him smiled. The crown of his head gleamed and his eyes were as dark as they were friendly. But it was the uniform that carried the illusion, creating a balance between the head and body.

He was more than satisfied with his new image in the mirror.

Now all that was missing was property reference number 2017-0310-BG4743 – a pair of sunglasses.

HE HAD LIED TO HER.

John Broncks crouched a little further down behind the computer screen, staring into it as the image's edges dissolved and became blurry. He hoped that Elisa wouldn't see him when she passed by in the corridor. Just as he hoped she had not understood from the outside what was going on inside.

Alibis. For both of them.

That his attempt to pretend everything was as usual had worked.

He had been forced to do it, after a day of all-seeing surveillance cameras, images which revealed what only *he* so far could see – that his own brother was involved.

He straightened up and leaned back, and the blur became comprehensible – a frozen image of the back belonging to the robber in the black mask. He couldn't escape it. He'd stood and watched it in real life just a few hours ago – the axe above Sam's head and its sharp edge on the chopping block.

Broncks zoomed in to get even closer to the fleeing robber – not so close that identification became possible, the resolution was too bad for that, but good enough to get part of the movement pattern – that which could not be masked or altered. At least not in a situation like this one, flight, when instinct becomes the movement that binds the personality together.

He saw what he already knew.

Sam.

While the silent sequence of images was moving in front of him, John Broncks could also faintly perceive a sound. The coffee beans were being ground in the machine next to the vending machine in the corridor and the hot liquid was running down into the paper cup. Then he saw Elisa go by in the other direction, heading back to her office. The first time he had actively invited someone to join an investigation, to share it and work side by side – when conditions changed direction completely – had become the first time he really had to work alone.

I lied, Sam, and will continue to do so.

The moment it comes out that you are my brother, I will be taken off the case.

I will catch Leo Dûvnjac. *I will* lock him up for everything.

And to be able to do that, I also have to catch you, Sam. You are connected. I'll sacrifice you. You understand, I am finished – my fucking debt to you does not exist any longer.

You stood there again, trying to lay it on me, to make it stick. Even next to our father's bed! So that I'd do what I always do – act on the basis of that.

I don't owe you shit.

It was not my fault he decided to attack.

It was not my fault you decided to kill him.

No bastard is ever going to poke around in our shared history again, dig into it, dig up the guilt.

I will work alone from now on.

I will catch you both by myself.

THE PARCEL HAD been confiscated on four occasions – each time getting stuck in customs at Arlanda even though they used different consignees – until they realised the problem was the method of delivery, as well as the choice of supplier. A parcel commissioned in Shanghai and posted to Stockholm via UPS – the American delivery company – had to be registered at the Swedish airport's reception centre to be assessed for customs duty. So when they ordered the same 3D printer for the fifth time but chose the German company DHL, the parcel glided through bureaucracy via a different sorting system in Leipzeig – and everything worked perfectly.

Leo stretched as the strange machine continued to work on the table in front of him. He unconsciously drew his hand through his hair that wasn't there. He still hadn't become used to the fact that the gesture, which had been with him all his life, was superfluous, that there was no longer a fringe to adjust.

The hair.

The lenses.

The uniforms.

The requisitions.

The property reference number.

The duty roster.

Only one detail remained before the third stage could be carried out, *the test*. He was taking care of that now: police identification. That's why he needed the 3D printer.

He looked at his watch. The machine required half an hour, according to the instructions, then the new police ID would be complete.

The rest of the prerequisite for a successful identification check lay already finished on the kitchen counter. A black leather case contained both identification cards with photographs, on which a blond Sam meets a dark-haired one. He smiled at the camera with a shaved head and brown eyes. Both have new names and personal identification numbers below the word *POLICE* in large red capitals and *Police Authority in Stockholm County* in smaller letters. Before the act that became his last job, Jari had

211

been just as reliable and careful in the production of the identification cards for two policemen as he was for the driving licences for two milkmen.

There was also the one police shield – the only copy Sullo was able to obtain, and which therefore was now having its clone manufactured by a machine that hadn't even been invented the day Leo had been sent to prison.

So much had happened in a few years.

Leo went closer to the square-shaped pot occasionally hissing a little, puffing and murmuring tentatively.

He had scanned in Sullo's authentic shield and let the printer's 3D reader analyse the form and size and identify colour codes. The correct red, blue and gold shades. That was all. The machine solved the rest itself. *Liquid metal printing* – it also spat out the metal alloy in the right direction as it built up a perfect copy. It was fascinating how it even painted the fucking thing. An hour and a half, and now they had an additional authentic police shield at their disposal. The round black disc, the golden crown, the blue bottom, even the brass-coloured plate with STOCKHOLM 4321.

He picked up the leather case, poked the service card into the plastic sleeve to the left, the shield with the police department's coat of arms into the plastic sleeve to the right and pushed it down into the uniform jacket's inner pocket. He now carried identification that was exactly the same, and could open as many doors as that of everyone else in the police headquarters in Kronoberg.

THE ROLL OF brown lining paper grew with each new turn of the roll, laying bare new parts of the sitting room's beautiful herringbone parquet. In spite of the intense pain in his hand, Vincent pushed the roll down into a rubbish bag of rugged plastic, carried it into the hall, through the front door and placed it in the stairwell. When he came back to roll up the paper in the other part of the sitting room as well, he passed the bedroom where Ivan was putting the final touches on the shiny white paint of the window trim with his small, fine paintbrush. They glanced at each other but said nothing. The quiet left behind by the policewoman became a tense, maintained silence. His father made several attempts to get a conversation going while just as many times Vincent avoided it – anything to prevent more talk that could lead to his father realising what his eldest son was up to.

'Uh, Vincent?'

His persistent voice echoed again, took off inside the bedroom and ricocheted dangerously between them.

'I like you too.'

And this time it caught hold.

'What? What'd you say?'

'I know what you're doing, Vincent, why you go around and talk as little as my paint tins do.'

'Exactly what are you saying?'

'First, I don't say that I was there at the wall. Then I don't say that I met him again the same evening. And now I'm even going to confess another thing – Leo and I had time for a phone call also. You know, *how are you, I'm fine*, the sort of things sons and fathers do.'

Ivan smiled, his eyes sparkling.

'So I certainly understand if my youngest son is a little jealous.'

Vincent looked at him without answering. *If you only knew, Pappa. If you could only imagine how it looked when I came here at five in the morning. I filled and sanded and painted a door that I had broken apart for a second time because Leo was here.*

'But surely you know, Vincent, that I like you too?'

213

Then he patted his breast with the palm of his hand, just as pleased.

'Because all my sons have a place in here.'

'Listen, Pappa, we have worked for . . . what the hell is it now, two months, barely? It's not enough to become jealous. Leo is more pappa, has been more pappa, no matter how you figure it. If it's about how many hours we have been together, who protected me, taught me, was a male role model. No matter how, Pappa.'

'That doesn't mean that *I* wouldn't care about how everything is going for you all. For you.'

'You don't need to worry about me.'

The pain in his hand.

'Pappa?'

'Yeah?'

'Haven't you thought that he went there, to the restaurant, because he was using you? Saying *how are you, I'm fine* on the telephone because he's *using you*? Just as he is also using us?'

'What the hell do you mean? Why would he use me?'

'Maybe because he needed an alibi?'

'Come on, Vincent. Don't turn us against each other. What're you doing? Are you trying to create a conflict between us? Just like your fucking mother always did?'

The last roll of paper became thicker and Vincent had more to pick up and his hand hurt again when he stuffed it into the rubbish bag. But if he was working, he could stay turned away and they didn't have to look at each other.

'Listen, Pappa, when Leo was planning all the bank robberies we did, we used to sit in the garage. He had two blocks of wood and a sheet of plywood as a table. He would spread out a big map of the target on it.'

He couldn't stand to meet his father's scrutinising gaze any longer, the one which pursued them when they were little, always demanding truth and loyalty, and which would be able to see that his youngest son knew so very much more about his eldest son's plans than he wanted to show.

'And then he laid a ten kronor coin on the map, sometimes several, to symbolise the bank or banks, and every getaway car was a toy car that he placed out on the map's roads. And do you know how the fuck we were represented? Little green plastic soldiers, model warriors, 1:72 scale. Because that's what we were to him, and always will be. And you too, Pappa. Little toy pieces in his plan for the next job.'

FROM HERE THE courthouse resembled a palace. Broad wings, with a tiled roof, supported the large tower clad in green-coloured copper. One-hundred-year-old patina.

The car park at Kungsholms Square, a few minutes' walk away, was as close as he could get to this proud building without stepping out of the car in front of the police complex, thus limiting the time of exposure outside. Leo was seldom nervous; he didn't function that way. Worrying did not solve very many problems. But now he was nervous. He would soon take his first steps, as a policeman, inside the police station. He had the correct uniform. He had the correct identification and police shield. He had the correct requisition signed by the correct duty officer with the correct evidence number. He had modified his appearance. He knew where he should go and had memorised the route on the map. He had done everything properly for appearances, what would be seen. But he must also act correctly, completing the illusion by becoming the policeman he was dressed up as. He was by himself now. The original plan had been that Sam would be here beside him for enhanced credibility, but instead he was replacing a dead Jari. Thus a year of planning and his whole future would now be decided. Because if any of the three checkpoints he was on his way to should be unsuccessful, go wrong, then everything would come crashing down before tomorrow.

Three police cars and two prisoner transport vehicles stood in front of the courthouse's main entrance on Scheele Street. It was what he expected. Every day legal proceedings were taking place in there, which would set people free or impose sentences on them. Judges and prosecutors and lawyers and plaintiff's counsels and cops and guards and journalists all gathered together in various courtrooms to feed on the accused.

He opened the door, which was as heavy as it looked, and went into the building that seemed to sigh incessantly, with coarse, worn stone in dark corridors and stairs, a stern church resting on a foundation of law books. Each step echoed. Every breath slid down, dusty and without oxygen.

A voice over a loudspeaker called out the next hearing somewhere on the ground floor and he automatically looked towards the ceiling. It was a couple of floors up in the old high-security courtroom where he himself had sat in sessions during a trial several months long. And not on a single occasion had he arrived as he had just now, through the public entrance. At each new day of a trial he had come from there – the stairs ahead of him to the left that led up from the basement, always wearing handcuffs and escorted by four prison guards.

That was where he was going now – to the underground entrance.

To the door of the passage leading to and from the police station.

He glanced into the corridor in both directions, then at the administration office straight ahead and finally at the little sentry box for the guards and the short queue for the toilets. No one seemed to care about the lone policeman.

The stairs to the basement echoed exactly like the rest of the interior of the building, in spite of how gently he tried to put down the soles of his boots. The door to the passage looked how he remembered it. Back then, someone else would always open it with their access card. Now Leo took the card Sullo had sold him out of his breast pocket, pulled it through the card reader and waited for the mechanical click.

He pressed lightly on the door handle and the metal door yielded – it worked.

The first checkpoint was passed.

Two deep breaths of the dusty, oxygen-poor air.

Then he started the mobile's stopwatch and went in.

So different to move around here without a pair of guards in front and a pair of guards behind. With his arms free. Without a prison uniform.

It was about fifty metres until the first intersection in the path, where he was supposed to turn right, when he heard them: the heels of shoes, two or even three pairs.

When he veered off, he realised that there were more than that. He counted two prisoners who came towards him escorted by four prison guards and, furthest back – the one he would meet last – a uniformed policeman.

Don't go faster than normal. Or slower either. Don't look away. Don't make eye contact unnecessarily.

In just a moment, a couple of metres more, they would be side by side.

He nodded to the prisoners who did not nod back. And for a thousandth of a second it felt as if something was so damn wrong – until he realised that it was his own appearance, the uniform. No fucking way they would greet a cop. The prison guards nodded, not much, but politely. Now the cops. They would look at him as a colleague. They *must* look at him as a colleague.

A quick nod.

And a quick nod back.

It was all that was needed. Sometimes the difference between going on and giving up was no bigger than that.

That cop hesitated – or was it just him overinterpreting? – but the nod came.

A stiff fucking nod from someone who was not sure if he should recognise the colleague with the shaved head and brown eyes.

Maybe he even did – recognised something familiar without knowing what.

Then the moment was over.

Leo wanted to turn around to reassure himself that they were continuing – the one thing he shouldn't do. But he became increasingly confident – their steps were slowly going away.

Those who walked around here every day had bought into the illusion.

The country's infamous bank robber was not only dressed as a police officer in a police station – he *was* a police officer and was being treated like one.

The second checkpoint was passed.

Sixty metres later came the next crossroads. The passage was broken by a four-way crossing where he would change direction, turning left. The property room was halfway down the corridor – the third and last and absolutely critical checkpoint. Inside the steel door, his paperwork would be examined minutely, the sum of his preparation assessed and evaluated by the Swedish bureaucracy. The grand treasure chest was always buried at the end of the rainbow.

With his index finger on the doorbell and his identification towards the camera on the wall, he waited to be let in, glancing at his phone and the stopwatch's first interval. One minute and fifteen seconds from the courthouse to the property room. An additional ten seconds before someone decided to let him in, with the paper that was folded in half in his wide front pocket.

Here there was an even stronger smell of dust, if that was possible, and even less oxygen. He was in a basement flowing into a large room, surrounded by thousands of objects involved in ongoing investigations, or investigations that had been closed but were still not legally binding, or that were deemed necessary to move work forward or constituted direct evidence. Seizure after seizure in envelope after envelope, on shelf after shelf.

The man behind the wooden counter, probably the eyes that had observed him through the camera, was in his sixties and looked as Leo expected. Grey jacket and checked shirt, balding and sufficiently overweight that he would no longer be able to keep up with the thugs. This was the last stop for a police officer finished working in the field, soon to be shunted out into the civilian world. Exactly like the brown envelope his visitor was here to collect – and the envelopes he would come back and pick up tomorrow.

'A requisition for . . .'

Leo unfolded the paper on the counter.

'. . . property reference number 2017-0310-BG4743.'

The senior police officer had been wearing his reading glasses perched on his balding pate. Now he moved them to the bridge of his nose and studied the requisition Leo had filled in.

'Identification?'

The uniformed visitor held out his black leather case with the service card Jari had got manufactured and the shield he had made himself in an empty flat in Sickla.

'We haven't met before, have we?'

The leather case remained in the older man's hand as he alternately looked at the photo of someone named Peter Eriksson, according to the service card, and then at the same face in reality.

'I don't think so. I came straight from Örebro.'

'Örebro? Then maybe you know Zacke?'

'Zacke?'

'Yeah.'

Leo was weighing his answer to a question, which if asked in an interview room, would have had the aim of exposing a lie.

'Zacke's about your age, right?'

But here between two colleagues it was only about being friendly, passing the time between brown envelopes, distinguished only by different reference numbers.

'Yeah, we patrolled a lot together in the eighties.'

The police officer, who had moved down from patrolling streets and people and lives, to a concrete room in a basement without windows, disappeared into the aisles between the rows of shelves. Leo assumed it was also in that direction that the Rosengrens safes stood lined up against the wall, safes that held valuable seized property. One of them appeared less valuable; one that could only be picked up during a ten-minute time window the next day.

'Yeah, well, there isn't much in this.'

The old man turned the envelope up and down, his open hand like a fine-tuned scale, before he lay it down on the counter.

'And then your signature.'

He gestured to a form with fine lines in a grid. Date and property reference number to the left, rank and signature to the right. Leo quickly glanced at the lines above, of earlier retrievals signed by real police, to be certain he did the same. He handed the pen to the storage manager.

'If I run into Zacke again . . .'

'Yeah?'

What was friendly conversation to pass the time for some was friendly conversation to be remembered for others.

'. . . who should I say hello from?'

'Hell no, no greetings. I don't want him to know I ended up down here.'

'OK – who *shouldn't* I say hello from?'

The storage manager held out the brown envelope, light as a feather, with a bulge in the middle.

'Oscarsson.'

'Have a nice day, Oscarsson.'

According to the mobile telephone's stopwatch, it had taken four minutes and twenty seconds to pick up a confiscated article without anyone in a queue in front of him. Then it took a minute and ten seconds to move back down the corridor – this time with no encounters – to the underground entrance to the courthouse. And an additional two minutes and thirty-five seconds to walk along Scheele Street to Kungsholms Square and the parked hired truck.

There was a rubbish bin just outside the door to the driver's seat and there he opened the envelope and pulled out what was bulging in the middle – a pair of Versace sunglasses. He dropped them in the bin and they landed between a couple of beer cans and a banana peel. Evidence in an ongoing investigation he picked out at random on the computer from the Albanians, which only had value in connection with the last checkpoint.

Everything had worked.

Now he could begin the second stage of the plan – laying out false leads, steering Broncks far away from here, in order to collect the real seized property tomorrow afternoon at ten minutes to two.

TUMBA 1:21.

The results on the computer screen were as simple to read as they were difficult to interpret.

But that was all John Broncks found after searching for a couple of hours in both public and protected records.

He had visited Sam, who lied at first and then went on the attack using guilt. He had knocked on the ferryman's door and charted movements synchronised with an aggravated robbery that had had a fatal outcome. And – when he had decided that biological ties were subordinate to a police investigation – he assumed that Sam and Leo Dûvnjac's shared criminal journey must have already begun in prison. After Sam's release, one of them had been planning inside the walls while the other made preparations on the outside. Anyone preparing for such a long time out in the world leaves a trail sooner or later.

And there it was on the screen: the trail.

The document out of the land registry, that he was staring at without comprehending.

A plot in Tumba, about ten kilometres south of Stockholm, linked them.

He was aware that Sam owned a house on Arnö. But not that he owned *another* house. And this one, Tumba 1:21, he had acquired when he was in prison.

BUYER: Sam George Larsen. SELLER: the Swedish Enforcement Authority.

And if Broncks flipped back through the pages of the transaction:

PREVIOUS OWNER: Leo Ivan Dûvnjac.

It wasn't simply the home address for Dûvnjac during the series of bank robberies. The plot with the small house and the big garage had been the brains and heart of the entire operation, where the crimes were planned, behind the façade of the construction company.

The same small house with the same big garage that Broncks could see now if he leaned forward and looked out through the restaurant window. The reality corresponded with the downloaded land registry file on the computer screen. The coffee cup next to him was untouched. He didn't

221

sit down in Robban's Pizzeria in Tumba because he wanted a cup of coffee; he wanted to be reassured that no one was in the house right then. And forty-five minutes of reconnaissance from the opposite side of the main thoroughfare made him virtually certain – no movements in the dark inside the curtainless windows, no vehicles arriving at the property. Broncks folded up his laptop, put thirty kronor down on the table for an untouched cup of coffee that cost fifteen and walked out to the car park by the little shopping centre housed in a building made of blue sheet metal. He placed the computer under the front seat of the car – a police computer in the wrong hands was a more valuable weapon in the criminal world than a fully loaded gun – and waited for a short break in the heavy traffic long enough to be able to sprint across the road. A short walk past the beautiful turn-of-the-century home with green timber cladding and in through the barbed wire gate to the asphalt drive. It looked the same as it had many years before when he was there in connection with the arrest of the Dûvnjac family. The door of the giant garage was locked and when he jumped up on a pile of tyres to be able to look in through an oval window on the side, he saw a space large enough for five vehicles, empty and unlit. Exactly like every other room when he peered into the house, which was completely unfurnished except for an out-of-place sofa bed in front of a cooker in the kitchen. It was obvious – no bastard had been living there for quite some time.

So why are you listed as the owner, Sam?

The daylight gleamed in a long crack on the front door's diamond-shaped window. He aimed and hit it with a stone in his hand. Two more blows and he got rid of most of the sharp glass shards, could put his arm in and reach the door handle.

Surprisingly, the narrow hall showed traces of visitors.

The several prints from damp rubber soles seemed reasonably fresh. Patterns from at least two different pairs. The tracks led in one direction – the guest room immediately to the left off the hall.

Broncks switched on a bare bulb hanging from the ceiling on a knotted cord. He saw it before he went in. The gap. One of the floor tiles not quite in place.

He bent down, moved it and discovered that the one next to it was also loose. And the two across from them. He coaxed up all four – two white squares and two black.

Underneath were two metal loops stuck in the concrete. He grabbed

222

them and pulled upwards. He held a concrete block the size of the four tiles in his hands.

He looked down.

A door to a safe.

Someone had cemented a safe into the floor.

It had not been here the last time. Or had they simply not discovered it?

He felt the handle.

Unlocked.

He opened it. Empty.

He ran his fingertips over the flooring of the safe and the walls covered with black velvet. Then he heard a noise from below. A brief humming that seemed to be coming from a basement, although this was a house that didn't have a basement.

Broncks knocked the safe floor with his fist. His knocking became pounding but nothing happened. He pressed both outstretched arms downwards using the force of his upper body. Still nothing.

Until the humming started again.

It was a mechanical sound ending with a short, grating cough.

There *was* something down there.

The little house must be hiding a secret entrance somewhere. A door to a basement that shouldn't be there. And when Broncks headed towards the guest room to look for it, he saw in the corner of his eye two loose cables hanging out of the electrical box on the wall above the window. To avoid an electric shock, he was careful to hold the plastic as he moved them to the side and investigated whether there was anything to them.

No answer there either.

But when the bare copper wires of the two cables happened to touch, he heard a mechanical sound again. This was clearer: a buzzing more than a humming. A noise that stopped the second he separated the wires.

The buzzing had come from the safe.

Broncks hurried over there and observed that the bottom of the safe seemed a little lower. Seven, maybe eight centimetres. He stuck his hand in and felt empty space. So he went back to the electrical box and put the wires together again.

The buzzing came again, and the safe sank even further down into the darkness.

The first thing he thought about was the smell. Gun oil, he was sure of it.

He aimed the torchlight from his mobile phone towards the hole and caught a glimpse of an aluminium ladder. And at the top of it, something was hanging. Broncks stuck his hand in and caught it. A flex for a standard wall socket. He fished it out and dragged it to the socket in the guest room.

An angry light.

It guided him seven steps down to an underground floor where for a long time he just stood still and looked around.

The four walls were lined with wooden shelving all the way around. A bit above the shelf there were two strips divided by milled grooves repeated every three centimetres. Groove after groove, hundreds of them.

He slowly realised what he actually was looking at.

A gun rack.

They had stood here all along: AK4 next to AK4, leaning against the upper strip; automatic weapon next to automatic weapon, leaning against the lower strip, with their barrels in the grooves.

Under our feet as we searched.

John Broncks thought about the smell of fresh gun oil. And the equally fresh tracks of two pairs of rubber-soled shoes in the hall.

Here he was in a secret room that had recently been emptied of automatic weapons, enough to equip a small army.

What the hell are you going to do with them?

TERRACOTTA. A thousand-year-old shield of earth and clay protecting against heat and fire. Each brown – or maybe orange – tile had been placed side by side, row after row, to protect the lorry floor, side walls and back hatch. What lay *on* the tiles – the guns that at one time were the basis of the bank robberies he was indicted for – would melt in thermite's sizzling flames, but not the lorry's cargo space.

He would destroy the past, so that the past would not destroy his two brothers once he himself was gone.

No evidence would be left. That was why he needed the terracotta tiles. They not only constituted the shield that resisted extremely high temperatures but they also formed a vat for the hot thermite, at a temperature of three thousand degrees, to run down into. AK4s and machine guns and submachine guns were lying in the vat now. Nearly two hundred automatic rifles stacked in piles that filled the entire lorry floor.

Leo went around the lorry he had parked inside a barn that smelled of hay and something else that made him think, as he worked, of old gauze bandages.

His mobile phone lay on the folding chair next to a bench that served as his workbench. It had given off two short beeps a few minutes apart and he hoped to catch it this time. A person. Not the same fucking bird that triggered the sensitive camera during the night.

He examined the first sequence playing up on the little screen.

It *was* a person.

A lone policeman. John Broncks was peering in through the kitchen window of the little house in the moving pictures taken obliquely from above. The house where these very guns had been hidden in a secret room, until Leo moved them here. Broncks tried the front door and when it became apparent it was locked, he looked for a stone, broke the diamond-shaped window and reached in to unlock the bolt.

The next camera showed the cop inside the house, as he discovered the little clues left behind: the loose floor tiles revealing the safe, the electrical box on the wall that opened it.

Broncks had found the empty room exactly as he was supposed to.

They were there the whole time, you bastard, right under your feet.

Leo paused the picture to look around the barn instead.

Two cameras had been sufficient to cover the main angles at the old weapons cache. Two should be enough here at the new one also. One would be disguised and placed inside, above the barn's doors. The other would be set up somewhere at the entrance. If the house was the starting point for Broncks, the barn was definitely the endpoint.

In the middle of the lorry's floor, in the middle of the enormous pile of guns, was a grey and red package – grey tape wrapped around a shoebox fastening a red mobile to it. Leo leaned into the cargo space of the lorry as far as possible without actually climbing up in it and he checked the three cables – a yellowish green, a red and a blue one. They ran from the back of the telephone into the box where they were connected to a battery via a relay.

On the outside it looked like a home-made bomb but it was actually an adapter activated when someone rang the right number. Then the relay became connected and the current ran from the box to the container on the lorry's roof.

A couple of seconds, and a ball of heating filament would be heated up, setting fire to what was in the container – twenty-five kilos of a thermite mixture.

He had conducted a test to be certain it would work with just a half kilo of thermite – and the result was almost comical. He picked out two submachine guns and put them in the terracotta vat. Before he even managed to sit down, they had been transformed into a soft, bubbling mass of metal. When the heat spread, it was as if a huge sparkler had been lit. The white light dazzled momentarily without hurting anyone standing nearby.

He looked at the truck and the two hundred automatic weapons. The thermite powder would rain like liquid fire and force the forensic technicians to step into a nightmare of fused metal, completely free of fingerprints.

This wasn't a bomb that would explode and kill – it was a bomb that would be lived through.

AN UNDERGROUND ROOM.

John Broncks had sat down on one of the rungs of the aluminium ladder in the concealed space for almost an hour. Chilly, damp, stuffy. But he didn't notice. He tried to figure out how he would handle the realisation that Leo Dûvnjac had stored over two hundred automatic weapons down there for several years. The house had passed into his own brother's possession and they probably emptied the shelves together recently. When he decided after a while to avoid getting a formal preliminary investigation started – to be able to act on his own until he clarified what Sam's involvement looked like – he began to call his contacts at the largest phone companies.

I'd like you to triangulate the telephone I'm speaking on now. The third try yielded the answer he was looking for. *And when you have determined my position, I want to know if more calls have registered from the same place over the last couple of days.* He had got a hit – an outgoing call from the same exact point where he was now, a mobile without a service contract. In contrast, the recipient's phone had one. Someone who was, according to the register, named Ivan Dûvnjac. And according to the three towers his phone was connected up to, he had answered at a location that corresponded to the Hungarian restaurant in the neighbourhood around Skanstull.

Ivan Dûvnjac.

Leo Dûvnjac had rung his father – the man he robbed his last bank with – at the same time he was going around and emptying northern Europe's largest private guns cache.

It was no coincidence.

They had contact. They were linked. They were on their way somewhere, and Sam was on the way there with them.

John Broncks was certain – tap the father's phone. Through him, map out Leo's and Sam's movements concerning the weapons trail. He would continue like this for a time to avoid involving colleagues.

After three informal contacts at phone companies, he made yet another call. *I want you to do it like you did the time before, sign a warrant for the tapping, without stating the degree of suspicion and without stating the offence.* The prosecutor's office and the prosecutor, whom he had persuaded some years earlier to tap the telephone of a female security guard with responsibility for transports from the federal bank's main branch. *You did it then, you trusted me, and it yielded one hundred and three million and quite a few career pats on the back, right?*

Broncks got up from the aluminium ladder and stretched as best he could with his hands on the hidden room's ceiling while he waited for the prosecutor to call back.

And again it sounded as if someone was coughing audibly below him.

Now he understood it was the pump that was wheezing on the floor next to him – the prerequisite for keeping the room intact all these years, ensuring that the old lake couldn't get back in. It was an incredibly clever construction and in spite of his frustration, it was hard not to be impressed.

He climbed up and out of the hole that was the safe's back. He unplugged the lamp, dropped the cord down, closed the trapdoor with the help of the wires in the electrical box on the wall and put back both the concrete lid and the four black and white pieces of floor covering. No one would notice that he had been there. No one would be able to even begin to find out what he himself still didn't know.

'Broncks?'

The prosecutor had returned his call.

'Yeah?'

John Broncks walked to the hall and front door, waiting for the answer that would soon be mixed in with the rising wind.

'OK. I'll approve your request. Now you had damn well better deliver.'

'You'll get your bust. At least as good a boost to your career as last time.'

He continued walking over the uneven asphalt courtyard to the exit, which reminded him of a prison gate because of the barbed wire. He had obtained the prosecutor's decision, his right to tap the telephone.

It would be an entrance straight into the criminal mind of Leo Dûvnjac.

THE INSPECTOR AT the Intelligence Unit had alerted him almost immediately that the line was connected. John Broncks hurried through the police complex, from the city police's corridor to the federal police agency's building on Polhems Street and then nine floors up in the lift.

'Hi, Dad, it's me. Do you have time to go for a little ride?'

The rather old man with a stoop always sat in one of the telephone tapping rooms to analyse the incoming and outgoing conversations. A blinking red LED lit up on the electronic map in the district of Södermalm approximately at the northern footing of Johanneshovs Bridge.

'Time? I have time – I'm just sitting here with a cup of black coffee. As usual.'

Then he pressed one of the keys on the keyboard's top row, paused the recording and looked at Broncks.

'You wanted me to get in touch every time – this call, the first one, lasts forty-eight seconds.'

The stooped-over detective pointed at the computer screen and a black line running below the blinking LED.

'And the recipient is located here – in one of the last dives on Göt Street.'

'Did you hear that, Leo? Not a bloody drop of anything else.'

'Good. Good, Dad. I'll pick you up in a couple of hours.'

'And where are we going . . .'

'I'm going to show you something.'

'What?'

'Our future. Seven o'clock on the dot in front of the door.'

John Broncks nodded at the screen with the electronic map.
'Is he still there?'

'Who?'

'The recipient of the call. The one whose life we're investigating.'

The expert on telephone tapping, and on pitch and intonation, smiled.

'Your prosecutorial decision concerns the right to listen to his telephone conversations. Not to find out his whereabouts when he isn't talking on the telephone.'

'But you can see it?'

'Yes.'

'Where?'

'In another room. From there – if I'd like, and when I've received the proper sort of formal request – I can follow the movements all the time for this particular telephone's signal.'

Broncks smiled. They had a way of carrying on like this. The older man, whose age corresponded to his father's, had once been an excellent police officer out in the real world, which he now partook of via headphones, trapped in a small, windowless space. It was clear he longed to be back out there, but with a different back and younger legs.

'The room three doors down on the left. If, on the way out, you happen to look in there, on the computer screen in the middle, I won't see you, since I'm thinking of staying in here a little while longer.'

'I would never do that of course, as you know.'

John Broncks was already halfway into the corridor when the inspector's 'Good luck, Broncks' caught up with him. Just as he had hoped, following Ivan Dûvnjac's tracks had given him the insight into Leo Dûvnjac's criminal mind that he had sought for such a long time.

Those damned guns came even closer.

TEN MINUTES.

Eleven minutes.

Twelve minutes.

His father was late – in spite of the fact that both the place and time had been chosen especially to make it easy for him. *Seven o'clock in front of the entrance.* The lost time, which for someone not involved could seem negligible, was sufficiently important that the pressure, like a damn big black knot in the chest, was moving up towards his throat. And then the hellish itching on his scalp under the tightly fitting cap became fire moving over the top of his head.

Leo tried to peer into the Dráva restaurant's dimmed light through the hire car's fogged windscreen. The inquisitive owner was there, as well as his inquisitive wife. A young couple was sitting at the table near the window, both chewing pieces of meat. A little further in, an older man was leaning over the service counter as he waited for his two full beer glasses, which he would soon balance, bringing them to the table where he was sitting alone.

But his father was not there.

Thirteen hellish minutes he waited, with less than a day left before the moment he would take back what didn't exist.

Stress never came calling when it was his own affair, when he was the one in charge and in control.

That was what the black knot in his chest and the itching on his scalp was about – that he was dependent on factors beyond his complete control for drawing the plan to conclusion. Like his father.

He had connected their direct line twice now – once to establish false leads, once to activate false leads.

The first call – *establishing* – had been at the weapons cache, which, because of a dropped gun, he'd realised Broncks would soon locate, with a little standard police work, through Sam's ownership. From there he had rung the registered and identifiable phone, a call long enough to be sure that the signal could be traced. Then it had simply been a matter of waiting for the surveillance camera to alert him, to study how Broncks broke in through a window and once in was so pleased to discover the small but clear signs that had been arranged there.

The second call – *activating* – had been just a few hours ago. When it was reasonable to conclude that, through more standard police work, the telephone tapping would have been set up.

Leo glanced at the digital clock hanging a short distance away on one of the building façades. Fourteen minutes of waiting with the clock ticking, for someone totally unaware of the importance of completing the false lead.

Then the itching stopped all of a sudden.

The pressure in his chest eased.

His father had arrived. He strolled out of the restaurant's door as if resurrected out of nothing. His coat fluttering in the eager wind, embers between his lips.

Leo flashed the full beam headlights twice.

His father saw the strong lights and flicked his cigarette towards a manhole.

'You are fourteen and a half minutes late.'

'Coffee, my son. Don't you know? You must both pay for it and shit it out. I was in the gents. Then that damn Dacso wanted to count every penny into the till.'

Ivan sank heavily into the passenger seat. But he let the door point straight out over the pavement as if by not closing it he was indicating that he did not go around waiting for his eldest son to give him a ring.

'And fourteen and a half minutes? What does that mean? Are we in a hurry?'

'Close the door.'

'You want to see me, fine, that makes a father happy, but it would make him even happier to understand why the time is so damn important again.'

'What are you on about?'

'I am talking about the cop woman running about in the flat where your brother and I are working. And asking questions about you, Leo. About where you were at such and such a time, and with whom, and where. You surely know that Vincent becomes nervous about that sort of thing? And if one becomes nervous, one starts to interpret.'

232

Ivan placed his hand on the door handle, but still without pulling the door shut.

'And he who interprets, Leo, can misinterpret . . .'

'It's cold. Close the door.'

'. . . can believe things are not as they are. Even feeling, well, *used*. Do you understand?'

Leo leaned over his father, hip against his stomach, got hold of the window frame and pulled the passenger door shut himself.

'Let's go.'

'And cold, by the way? You have a goddamn cap. And inside! Didn't I teach you that a real man never goes about in shorts? And that he never has a fucking cap on indoors?'

Leo shrugged his shoulders, and then pulled off the grey wool cap, revealing his head.

'That's why. Satisfied? Can we stop bickering and set off? That is, if you still want to hang out with me?'

Ivan looked at him in silence for a long time.

'What have you . . . Leo, why the hell have you shaved off your hair? The men in our family, your grandfather in Croatia, and your grandfather's father, had a lot of hair, year after year. Genes, Leo! Good genes! Thick hair, we aren't baldies. Only radiation and propaganda make people lose their hair like that. So – are you ill or have you read *Mein Kampf*?'

Leo turned the car key a half turn to the right. The accelerator pedal down, first gear and a U-turn across the double line and they were headed south. Ivan sat silent across Johanneshovs Bridge, silent through the tunnel from Gullmarsplan. Not until the heights of Västberga, where they turned off towards the E4, did he stop staring at Leo's bald head.

'And where are we headed with your shaved head?'

Interpreting and misinterpreting.

Leo had clearly understood the question his father had asked, without asking it, when he failed to close the car door.

'I said that over the phone.'

And if you only knew how correctly you are thinking, Dad.

'I'm going to show you our future.'

But sometimes it's better not to know.

'And what the hell's that supposed to mean, Leo? That I'm also going to shave off my hair?'

233

You don't need to know your role in order to take part.

'The future, Dad. Something we are going to build up, together. You'll understand when we're there.'

Since your actual task in this car, and at the place we are on the way to, is to be the bait.

THE GRAVEL CRUNCHED under the tyres as the hire car rolled into the courtyard twelve minutes later. The last part they had travelled in darkness, which reminded him of what he had gone smack into when he visited Sam on the island. But well ahead, the house, which stood proudly with its two storeys, the considerably larger red-and-white painted barn next to it, bathed the surroundings in bright light that made it easy to orient themselves.

It was several hundred metres to the nearest neighbour, and overgrown forest on both sides of the road.

Leo had time to think the desolation and silence made the location perfect.

No one – when it was time – would have to get hurt.

'We're here.'

A quick glance at his father, who was staring through the windscreen without the slightest indication of wanting to get out.

'This is what I wanted you to look at, Dad.'

'A fucking . . . farm?'

'Yes, it is. If it's wooden planks, walls and roofs you choose to see. But if you follow me, I'll show you what it could actually become.'

A small grove spread out between the farmhouse and the barn. Dense branches pointing outwards from a lot of pear trees and a few plum trees here and there, which someone should have pruned a few years ago. Leo was followed by his own long shadow, mimicking his movements, as Ivan slowly got out of the passenger seat, stretching himself using the car roof for support.

He had felt his father's hesitancy during the whole trip, hanging there between them and vibrating like an electric barrier, dividing the two front seats. And now his slowness, stretching his back and shuffling over the courtyard, were his way of demonstrating a lack of interest in what his son explained he wanted to show.

'Come on, Dad, what do you think?'

His father didn't answer, except with eyes that seemed to be entirely

235

somewhere else, somewhere other than the property Leo was pointing at.

'You and me, Dad. Together. As you wanted. A renovation project – this is exactly what we need.'

He grew up like this. With a father who made a living as a carpenter, painter, whatever that meant, for – preferably – black money improving the local houses and flats. Then, before the final conflict, they had even had a construction company together for a few years. For someone whose only task right now was to act unconsciously as bait, this project should be the bait's perfect bait.

'Dad, dammit, this is exactly what you ran around going on about for years, long before that fucking robbery we should never have carried out together. A dad and his eldest son who build together, again. So now I've bought this little farm for our sake. I thought you'd be happy.'

Cautious silence. The one that always stopped when Ivan drank. But now, when he hadn't had alcohol in his body for over two years, it filled more space and meant something.

'You and me renovating together, just like back then. Then we sell the shit at a profit. And I already have a potential buyer who's going to want to meet us here to ensure that we can deliver. Don't you recognise a good business deal when you see it, Dad?'

And with the silence came the suspicion.

Leo looked at his father.

He hadn't counted on that – that the bait wouldn't accept his own bait. His father's sobriety had sharpened his senses to crystal clarity.

'Business deal? What are you up to, Leo?'

'What am I up to? Planning our future. You said it yourself – if you can change, I can change.'

The light fell sharply on the worn, once perfectly painted red barn, and his father took his time as he let his eyes wander from side to side, from roof to foundation.

'So you want to show me some damn house with a damn barn that we should spend months fixing up, Leo?'

As a child, he had learned to avoid the sometimes temporarily sober eyes, in order to wait and confront the drunken ones instead. He learned to play against that father. But this was a new version of his father that he had no experience of.

'In the middle of pitch-black nothing, Leo? Where no bastard would want to live? Is that what you're trying to sell me?'

His father drew the fingers of one of his hands across the house's rough wood façade and brittle red paint fell off with the motion. The wood panelling had received as little maintenance as the pear trees. Cupping his hands like a temporary cyclops, he leaned forward to one of the dwelling's filthy windows and looked in. There were no curtains to obscure it. His father looked straight into a house that lacked life.

'Come, Dad.'

Now the crunching was under their shoes, not under the tyres. They both walked towards the giant barn. Leo stayed the whole time in the strong light from the farm's four lamp-posts. It was important that they be seen, and occasionally he glanced out into the darkness as if he wondered whether someone lay there watching them. That was also why they needed to go in, to open the large barn's door and attract attention.

'Follow me in. I especially want to show you this.'

There was a key in his hand and it fitted the heavy padlock. The shiny silver shackle was turned and lifted out of the two halves of the steel hasp that held the wooden doors together. Three solid hinges on each one, old and rusty. The barn had been built much earlier than the main house.

'Then we'll renovate in here as well.'

Leo made a sweeping gesture to indicate the huge room.

'Two storeys, duplex, stairs, bedrooms upstairs, lounge downstairs.'

After just a few steps the sensation of generations of grain and dry hay hit them. The roof seemed considerably higher from the inside and made the lorry standing in the middle look much smaller than it was.

'A lorry, Leo? What the hell is it doing here?'

'Full of tools. We're going to need them.'

'So, you've already had time to buy tools and put them in here? With what money?? What if there's no deal?'

'Dad – if you're with me, there will be a deal. Maybe as soon as tomorrow.'

Ivan stopped abruptly and Leo felt the critical gaze on his back. As if his father didn't plan to go a single step nearer to the lorry or anything else in the empty shell of a building.

'In my hometown of Karlovac, Leo, every spring when I was growing up and the water rose in the river . . .'

And his father's gaze there on his back was accompanied by his father's voice.

'. . . then the catfish played. It was thick with slippery fish. And when

237

they had finished playing, *we* could play, all the children. The water became warm and we threw ourselves in from the willow trees that were growing out over the river.'

They stood for a long time – a son a few metres in front of his father in the giant wooden room. A son who couldn't explain the real motive for their visit, and a father who longed for reconciliation and at the same time fought against the whisper pecking at his head – *he is using you.*

'We dived down into the green water. And with every dive we were forced to turn up straight away when we went in, otherwise we hit the bottom. Down and immediately up. Like a U.'

Leo sensed that his father might have taken a step forwards and he caught in the corner of his eye a hand slowly gliding through the air, up, down, as if in a U.

'But there was also a policeman in my hometown. The sort who wore his trousers stuffed into a pair of dirty leather boots. His hat with the unpolished police badge was too large and his shirt was as wrinkled as a morel. He was strong, had the strength of two men but a very small man's willpower. So we children could trick him. We laughed at him. He chased us with his baton. He wanted to give us a beating but we were too quick. We ran and threw ourselves into the river like flying fish. He stood there waving his fucking baton . . . *Dive in, dive in*, we shouted from the water, *you don't dare to, just dive, dive from the tree, like us.*'

Another slight step forwards and his father came up alongside him.

'So, one day, Leo, he had enough. He took off his wrinkled uniform but kept his dirty leather boots on and then he climbed high up in the proudest tree and out onto the thickest branch and stretched out over the water like a giraffe's neck.'

His father extended his long arm, slanted upwards.

Him and his bloody stories. They were merely intended to mirror underlying truths. His father had always done that back when the three brothers were children, when he tried to get at the falsehood – wrap it up with what resembled fairy tales, allowing the remarkable images to confuse and peel away the resistance, and then drill deeply in and expose it.

'When the policeman had crawled all the way out on the branch, he became scared. We could see that. But we kept on shouting – swimming around in the water and shouting that he should dive in. We shouted that he didn't dare to, that he was just as cowardly as he was stupid.'

Ivan grew silent and looked at Leo, a look that was completely sober.

'Finally he dived in. Without bending, he hit the water. The lousy boots stood straight up in the river like two periscopes. He broke his neck like a small chicken even though he was so big and so strong. The idiot had no will. He listened to the children and didn't follow his own will – he followed the children's.'

Leo felt his mobile buzzing in his jacket pocket. For a moment his father's voice ebbed away out of his mind, pushed away by the eagerness to carefully sneak his phone out and check whether what he thought must have happened had actually happened.

'Leo – are you listening to me? *I* am not that policeman. Do you understand that?'

The app connected to both security cameras had signalled. Camera A. The one sitting on the fence at the start of the gravel road, about a kilometre away.

'Leo – *I* am not stupid.'

And there. Not particularly clear, and captured by a single lens, he saw on the mobile's display a car passing by with the front headlights dimmed.

Perfect.

They were all here.

'So when you tell me to dive in, you have another thought along with it. Don't you, Leo?'

His father's eyes pursued his own, but he couldn't meet them.

'Leo – are you using me?'

'What?'

A simple question – are you *using* me?'

His voice needed to be composed and directed to his father; that was all Leo was thinking of.

'Dad, it was *you* who came to *me*. It was you who said that if you could change, I could change. Now I'm trying to do that.'

Their eyes met now.

He needed to deliver the words.

Only that.

'Even Felix. Even Vincent. They're also in on it.'

His father's energy, so filled with doubt, stopped blazing forth so angrily for the first time since they had opened the barn door.

'What did you say? Felix too?'

'Yes.'

'And . . . Vincent?'

They were still looking at each other. Leo managed to direct his gaze. He managed to face his father with a lie.

'Yeah. I've asked them both – and both agreed.'

It was so much easier now. What he'd come here for was perhaps already partly achieved. The person he hoped would follow them probably had followed, and would soon see the father and son from the Dûvnjac family step out of a desolate and mysterious barn in the middle of nowhere. If his father said yes – swallowed the bait and became the bait that he was here to become – then the false lead would continue tomorrow.

'So that would mean . . . all four? Father and sons in the same construction company?'

'Yes.'

'Leo, I don't know. Do you mean what you're saying?'

Leo hesitated, but only briefly. Then he held both of his arms out and did what he was not sure he had ever done before – taken the initiative and embraced his father.

'Yeah. I mean what I'm saying.'

And the chest he touched felt so thin.

His father had become smaller during his prison term.

'You don't need to decide now, Dad. Think about it when we're driving home.'

Or was it the fucking lie that had diminished him?

If Dad seemed smaller, was he perhaps also easier to get to?

Leo looked at the man who had once taught him to dance around and defeat the bear, while he forced himself to swallow down what was in his throat.

FROM HIS POSITION in the wooded area, protected by trees and bushes and evening darkness, he watched the son and the father as they came out of the large barn standing next to the main house on the fair-sized court-yard. They had spoken in low voices. In confidence, without John Broncks catching any of the words before they got in the car and drove away.

A deserted farm visited by one of Sweden's most notorious bank robbers and his father – after a short, cryptic telephone conversation.

'I'm going to show you something.'
'What?'
'Our future.'

The man with the stoop at the Intelligence Unit had also continued to help after Broncks's visit to the ninth floor. In spite of the lack of a formal request, after a little persuasion, the detective with the friendly face had followed the movements from the telephone lying in Ivan Dûvnjac's pocket, all from his seat in front of the electronic map. Broncks was guided from the E4 exit at Norsborg past Botkyrka church and then onto unfamiliar roads. It seemed so strange to drive around in the genuine countryside among isolated estates only a little more than ten kilometres from Sweden's capital. This same detective had also investigated the farm's ownership and found out that it belonged to a convicted hitman who did his time at Österåker. That was how Dûvnjac had found his way here to a guaranteed uninhabited property.

When he was sure that the men he was tailing had really left, he exchanged his hiding place in the woods for his equally hidden car and made his way to the barn. In the back seat he had a bag packed for this time when the network of police technical skills he otherwise had access to was no longer an alternative.

It seemed strange, as if he was going behind his own back, unfaithful to his own professional role.

But he had no choice – he couldn't tell Elisa or other colleagues, not

241

yet. Not before he knew how his own brother was connected to Leo Dûvnjac.

He fished a torch out of the boot of his car, switched it on and lit up the barn's long side, towards the door sealed up with a padlock. Then the beam of light caught a piece of rusty rebar lying on the ground a couple of metres from the foundation.

It was easier than he imagined. With the rebar he broke the hasp that held the padlock and opened the door. Afterwards he would push it back into the wooden façade to mask his trespass.

A small truck. That's what he saw first, since that was about the only thing he saw. A giant room with a vehicle and a small workbench and a folding chair and nothing else.

The lorry's flatbed was covered with a thick plastic tarpaulin. He removed three rubber straps and lifted up the cover so he could see into the cargo space.

There they were.

Row after row, on top of each other, next to each other.

And in the middle of the pile of stolen automatic weapons was something that made him want to let go of the plastic and step back. But he stayed there. In spite of being quite aware of what the three cables connected to a red mobile telephone on a small box meant.

A bomb.

That would be triggered if and when Leo Dûvnjac decided.

John Broncks had seen this before in connection with business deals of considerable worth between hardened criminals – the seller's insurance forcing the buyer to pay for both the goods and for the password or code protecting it.

So that was what he was up to. He had a buyer. The guns would change hands.

Broncks pulled a pair of thin rubber gloves out of the bag.

He was standing before a unique opportunity. He would be able to arrest the bastard at the moment of the sale and tie him to both that deed and the original theft. And for this kind of extremely aggravated theft of weapons – if it could be interpreted as an act of terror according to the law – Leo Dûvnjac would be sentenced to life imprisonment, with a little luck. In other words, an even longer sentence than he would have received if they succeeded in getting him convicted of all the bank robberies. Broncks was nearly certain that a couple of hundred automatic weapons from the

Swedish government, which were to be sold at an arms market controlled by madmen, would most likely match formulations in the law book such as . . . *inspiring serious fear among the people.*

He propped the torch against the edge of the lorry's floor and carefully lifted the gun lying furthest out on the top – an AK4 – and laid it on the oblong bench behind the vehicle. Then he took a zephyr brush out of the bag and also a box of fine fingerprint powder blended with a little soot. He hit the brush several times on the edge of the bench. It was important that the fibres on the tip be separated before he dipped the delicate brush in the soot powder and rubbed it over the butt, stock and barrel of the rifle. Rings stood out clearly in the greyish black powder, not just from one finger, but from several. With the rubber glove flat, he pressed down pieces of plastic film. Fingerprints were duplicated now and in about an hour they would be compared at the forensic technician's lab with patterns from more than one hundred thousand fingerprints taken earlier from suspects in criminal investigations and registered in the A file.

He put the gun back in the exact place he had taken it from. He pulled down the plastic cover and fastened it to the lorry's floor and took a few steps backwards to memorise the registration plate's three letters and three numbers.

You don't have a clue, Dûvnjac, how close I am.

They drove from the small gravel road to a somewhat larger gravel road, to an even larger gravel road, wide enough so that it was not necessary to stop every time you met a car going the other way. And finally to the paved, four-lane European motorway, number 4, which would take them back to Stockholm.

They remained silent, side by side in the front seat of the car until Leo turned off at a lay-by that took them into a service area.

'Why are we stopping here?'

There were no people, but it was quite nice. Well lit, with a very small concrete building with public toilets, and a lot of benches and tables and rubbish bins right at the edge of the forest.

'The loo, Dad. I need to piss. Be right back.'

He managed to get halfway between the car and the building when Ivan rolled down the window and called after him.

'Leo?'

And he stopped, turning towards his father, who stuck his head out of the window to hear better.

'Yeah?'

'Did you mean what you said at that damn barn?'

'Dad, let's not talk about it any more. If you don't want to, you don't want to.'

'But I'd like to.'

Leo was standing too far away and it was too dark for his father to be able to see the satisfied look on his face right now.

'I knew you would, Dad.'

'Together, Leo. We'll renovate the goddamn farm. You and me. And Felix. And Vincent.'

His father's head was now more outside than inside the window. Eager, that's what he was.

'The whole family! I must admit – I feel happy. Happy, Leo!'

The odour in the abandoned toilets was heavy with the stench of misaimed urine. The walls were obscured in unadorned light. And there was a considerable draught from the small window in one corner of the concrete block.

Leo passed a filthy urinal with two standing places and went into the only stall that could be locked.

When they were in the barn, the display on his mobile had shown a car with its lights off passing Camera A – mounted on the fence at the start of the gravel road. And just a little earlier he'd heard a bleep, when his father was too close for him to check. That bleep meant that Camera B had switched on. It felt good. But what he saw now on a little screen in his hand, at a reeking rest area in no-man's-land along the motorway, exceeded his expectations. A trap that had been tripped again. From the camera mounted high up on one of the inner walls of the barn, which thus transmitted an image viewed from above, a torch was seen wandering around in the dark of the derelict property. A beam of light approached a vehicle – and was shining into it. And when the person holding the torch moved and met his own face for a moment, Leo looked straight into the two eyes of John Broncks.

And Leo heard himself chuckling.

How his laughter knocked against the narrow walls of the stall.

Broncks would not interfere with his planning any more. While he was dropping his father off at the Hungarian restaurant soon and then picking up Sam, the cop bastard would act like the police officer he was and prepare an operation. He'd place elite cops behind every bush around the badly painted farm buildings and wait for a crackdown on what he was convinced would be classified as the greatest Swedish illegal arms deal of our time.

But what he did not know was that the seller himself, Leo Dûvnjac, had directed him there deliberately.

The timing of the raid would be steered by a phone call to his phone-tapped father, who was convinced that the business they would talk about related to something entirely different.

At the same time the real hold-up would be carried out far away from there.

VÄSTBERGA EXIT STOOD completely still, a stubborn queue between the E4 and first roundabout. It was one of the few times when Broncks wished he had driven a marked police car and not the investigation division's more discreet vehicle. But he was chasing time and so he passed the frustrated row of cars on the inside – halfway down in the ditch – to a chorus of loud honking. The petrol station was the first building after the exit and he parked at one of the vacant pumps without filling up. He went in and headed directly to the checkout where there was yet another stubborn queue, but this one impossible to pass on the inside or outside. There were two customers in front of him, a young man who had just picked out a film and was now choosing at great length the right hot dog with the right relish. And an elderly woman with her arms full of food for her evening and for breakfast.

His heart was pounding with impatience. To endure it, he forced himself to try to think of something other than the queue or his haste. It didn't work. Each new thought was an old one circling around the fact that all these years he had been wandering about on false leads after the extensive weapons robbery. He had searched for a faceless shadow that turned out to be Leo Dûvnjac. The individual who Broncks was convinced was the brains behind the operation, not least because of the direct contact they had in connection with the contemplated resale – which was labelled in the court proceedings 'aggravated blackmail against the police force', from how Dûvnjac formulated the threat at the time. If the police didn't buy back the two hundred military automatic weapons he stole, he'd threatened he would sell them to or even donate them to Sweden's criminal organisations, thus multiplying the number of serious available guns on the market.

In the end it was a skinny one with chilli on it for the young man at the front of the queue, who was now chewing on his hot dog. When he asked for more mustard for the second time, Broncks lost his patience and requested that he let the next person make her purchases. The woman between them turned around gratefully and smiled. She set down butter

246

and cheese and bread and liver paste and napkins and candles and frozen cabbage rolls. It was interesting how petrol stations had changed into today's general stores.

After the trial, John Broncks had continued to search for clues about the stolen weapons, now and then returning to the comprehensive preliminary investigation lying on his office floor just a few metres away. But now he had found the entrance to the hiding place where they were probably kept all this time! It had smelled like gun oil and fresh footprints trampled on each other. And just now he had been standing in an abandoned barn – and seen them! Spread out on terracotta tiles in the cargo space of a hired lorry. He was finally catching up. And it felt . . . hopeless. All the longing, all the zeal replaced by a big, ugly, hellish anxiety over his older brother's involvement, over the consequences it could have for both of them. He knew now that Sam and Dûvnjac could be linked together. But not yet how extensive the connection was, how involved Sam was. That was why he stood here waiting for an elderly woman with bags of food to pay and say good evening and ask for help with the door until it was his turn.

'You filled up?'

'No. No petrol. I would—'

'No? But that was you standing out there at pump 4, right?'

'—just like to confirm that—'

'A hot dog then? Or a drink? We have a good price for coffee. You get a cinnamon bun for half the price.'

'—that a hire truck with the registration BGY 397 is one of your vehicles.'

'Now I'm confused. Do you want to hire a car?'

'I just want to know if the lorry is yours. If it was hired here.'

'I can't tell you.'

'According to the car registry it is.'

'You surely know that I can't . . .'

While he was talking, John Broncks searched for his identification in all his pockets – then he found it in one of his leather jacket's inner pockets and put it down on the counter.

'Now be so kind as to do what I say.'

The petrol station clerk sceptically picked up the leather case and opened it. He examined the identification card in the plastic pocket to the left and checked the police shield in the plastic pocket to the right. Then he held

247

it out to give it back. And he opened a small, grey metal key cabinet on the wall behind him. Hooks with keys on them, hooks without keys. And above every hook was a sticker with a printed registration number.

'That's correct. BGY 397 – that's our vehicle.'

'Hired by whom?'

'I don't have the right to tell that.'

Broncks took the police shield out of his hand now.

'Are you finished checking it? In that case I ask you again – the last time I'll ask nicely – to tell me who hired it.'

The clerk looked at Broncks, then at the identification, then at Broncks. Then at a pile of papers in a letter tray with two shelves, ingoing and outgoing. He glanced at the man claiming to be a police officer while he leafed through the pile. He found the document he was looking for and scooted it forward on the counter.

'It's better if you read it yourself.'

John Broncks pulled the paper towards him. A car hire agreement with the petrol company's logo at the top and the text of the agreement spreading out over two pages. Partway down on the first page, the correct model and the correct registration number. A bit further down was another number, a familiar one – a personal identity number, ten digits he had seen before. And at the very bottom on a dotted line, the only thing that was handwritten.

Sam's signature in black ink.

A FAINT BUT distinct smell of smoke was clinging to the light wind. It came from above the house. For a moment it was as if he was imagining it, as if it only belonged to dusty memories – a smell that was always around him and Sam here. Mamma burning leaves and grass and Pappa burning everything else that was too unwieldy to lug with him to the Strängnäs dump.

John Broncks lingered, not moving, outside the pointed red fence. Dense, overwhelming darkness, the same as any evening during this season. The torch's beam hit the gate, which was properly closed. The latch, which never ended up in the right spot without effort, had been pushed down forcefully.

Sam Larsen

That was at the bottom of the car hire agreement.

A signature, which – together with the registry information about ownership of the Tumba house – linked his brother to the lorry's floor filled with over two hundred automatic weapons. When it was time to arrest Leo Dûvnjac, he'd have to arrest Sam also. He shouldn't have felt anything at all, seeing as they didn't exist for each other now, and hadn't for a long time. But – he felt it. Despair. It surrounded him. A gnawing, screaming, stabbing despair as unexpected as it was strong. He wasn't sure if it had to do with a not yet entirely extinguished brotherly love, or if it was the fact that he, Sam's own brother, would deprive him of his freedom a second time.

Already on the way out of the petrol station, Broncks started to call him, with no answer, each time drowned by a dead line. And when he was halfway – a little after the exit from Södertälje Bridge – he got hold of a neighbour on the island, who explained that he had seen Sam spring-cleaning earlier in the day but couldn't say where he was now. Not even the ferryman, who kindly added an extra trip between two departures, had seen him.

Spring-cleaning.

That's what the smell of smoke was.

When he walked up the slope that ended at their only remaining childhood home and followed the swirling wind to the back of the house, he saw it then. A red, almost orange glow in the middle of a pile of ashes in the same place where Mamma used to burn her garden waste.

The house was as dark as the evening.

The door was unlocked.

'Sam?'

Broncks called into mute rooms and his voice met no resistance. He tried to switch on the ceiling light both in the hall and in the kitchen but they didn't work. The electricity was shut off. It was so very quiet when the fridge was not even humming.

He swept the light from his torch up ahead, calling again in a voice that fluttered about between the cold walls.

'Sam? Hello? It's me, John.'

Then he understood.

Everything was gone.

The art on the wall in the entrance depicting stone walls, which had always hung there, was not there. The hall was completely empty. Even the little table that should have a red plastic shoehorn on it had gone – replaced by a layer of dust on the floor where it had stood, nothing else.

The kitchen, same thing.

Empty.

There were no Windsor chairs around a simple folding table. Only clear, slightly lighter squares on the wooden floor where the table legs had rested.

The small sitting room – the triangular sixties table, the rounded corner cupboard, the big television, the two floor lamps, the armchair, the rag rugs and the small sofa with the corduroy fabric frayed on the right side because that was where Mamma sat when she watched *Good Evening* and *News Report* and some debate programme – all gone. It was more evident than ever before how unevenly the floor was worn, which areas feet had walked upon.

His first thought wasn't particularly logical.

An upcoming house viewing.

Rooms that could be filled with something meaningful for the buyer, who would continue their life here.

His second thought was more relevant.

He slowly realised what actually had gone up in flames out there. Sam had burned up all the household furniture. And he had been wrong himself

– Sam did not intend at all to live there among his memories. He only wanted to say farewell to be able to leave them behind.

All the memories except one.

A single piece of furniture remained in the dark bedroom.

Broncks directed the torch beam towards it.

Pappa's bed.

The beam washed over the unmade mattress and what was lying on it.

The fishing knife. Broken point, bloodstained edge.

And he saw the silhouette of Sam's sinewy, young back, how he raised the knife and thrust it into their father's chest, again, again. Only the sound of muscle fibres tearing and ribs resisting.

He felt the anger, which the time before had become nausea. The anger he had locked inside for such a long time, and had consciously shut out because it was so pernicious. Anger blurred impulse control. Anger brought out a moment's actions that you had to live with for ever.

It was here now and he let it stay.

John Broncks rushed in to the narrow bedroom and grabbed hold of the wooden frame so that the knife fell to the floor somewhere behind the side of the bed. He dragged the thick, flabby, sagging mattress outside to the smouldering embers and dropped it down. He went back in and kicked the wooden frame to pieces of the right size to spread over the suddenly awoken flames.

Just the fishing knife left.

It lay so nicely in his open hand.

Fierce sparks from the embers played like flies above the mattress and bed frame, now catching fire on the sides. Suddenly the light was intense heat against the skin of his face as he stared into it.

Back then it had been him, the younger brother, who appealed to the big brother to save him. He had not asked Sam to stab their father but they both feared – when they held each other tight – that Pappa would sooner or later go too far and beat his younger son to death.

So Sam made his own decision.

To kill, instead of seeing his little brother killed.

But afterwards he, John, the one who was rescued, hurried to the green phone on the wall – which now lay in the fire, a piece of the receiver sticking up out of the ashes – and called the police. He gave up his own brother. Hadn't given him a chance. Without realising it, he had doomed Sam to a life sentence.

He must do it now.

He must give him the chance to avoid a new life sentence.

Before conducting the raid of the arms cache in the barn, before the arrest, he must reach Sam, talk to him and get him to understand that tomorrow it could all be over.

If, despite the warning, he chose to continue, to not believe what his little brother said he knew, then it would be his own decision.

Then it was Sam's own responsibility to live with the consequences.

But *he* had to give him the opportunity for that choice. That was *his* responsibility. And if his last route to contact stopped here in a burned-down dead end, he needed to try another one. The route that went through the man he decided to never again risk being humiliated by.

The fishing knife in his hand. He clasped it now.

He threw it into the flames.

IT WAS A RATHER BEAUTIFUL residential area, sandwiched between Tallkrogens centre and the humming national motorway to Nynäshamn, a Stockholm suburb that exuded the Swedish fifties for the Swedish middle class. Cars on almost every driveway. Manicured gardens on the border to being overworked, warm lights in every window. John Broncks wished that he could have managed to find himself in a reality of this sort, a context it seemed so lovely to sink down into and let wash over you. But it was not him. Somehow he didn't have a place here. He forgot how to live when everything was marked out and lay in ready-made piles.

He rang the bell at the front door with a shiny, oval, gold-coloured sign with AXELSSON on it. A monotonous signal was repeated in three equally long strokes.

He listened. Nothing. He looked in through the kitchen window, well lit, a pair of silver candles next to a pot of flowers next to a porcelain ornament. Still nothing.

A pile of ashes behind their childhood home. That was everything Sam had left.

There was no other message.

Broncks tried to resist, but the trembling that cut through his body was as insistent as it was foreign, a loneliness he had never felt before, so cold.

Sam had used the scorched-earth tactic. The idea was to destroy everything and only allow that which would weaken the enemy to remain. The idea was to demoralise. Poison the water of the wells, everything that was nourishment.

Like leaving a fishing knife in a bed.

Sam was his brother but was carrying that damn hatred. Broncks didn't understand, had never understood it – why he chose to define and treat his little brother as his enemy.

The trembling, ice cold through his chest came back, but despite all of Sam's fucking attempts to repudiate him, despite Sam's fucking hatred, it wasn't enough.

Broncks knew that he *must* meet him again, that he had to be able to give Sam a chance to make his own choice. And there was no other way left than to – once again – ring this doorbell.

Now, albeit faintly, he perceived what sounded like steps.

The little window at the side of the door darkened as someone blocked it while turning the lock mechanism.

A woman, with curly, strawberry blonde hair, watchful eyes.

'Hello, I am sorry to disturb you so late. I'm John Broncks and I am—'

'I know who and what you are. I remember you from the trial.'

Her tone was neither accusatory nor offended. She was simply making an observation.

'It is late. What do you want?'

He wanted to say *I remember you also – I remember how you sat at the very front of the high-security courtroom day after day, how you listened to the charges, one by one, formulated against your three sons.* And he wanted to add that he had seen it several times before, how close relatives chose to sit in exactly that place, the very front, to avoid the glances of people curiously turning around – as if it were easier to let them stare at your back.

'I'm looking for your son, Leo. This is the address given for him.'

'He isn't home.'

'In that case I would like to ask for your help. Ask that you call him. I assume you have his number? You should let him know I want to speak with him.'

The woman holding the door handle was watching him, her eyes still simply observing him – eyes that said I don't like your presence but you don't disconcert me, because if you, like me, have seen and experienced everything, you know no one and nothing shakes you up any longer. Or was it just a façade? Was that the reason she sat at the very front? After having got away from a man who wanted to knock her down and batter her to pieces, did she hope to avoid being struck and battered again by finding out that her three sons were serious criminals and were about to spend several years in various prisons? It's true – those who don't share in the reactions of others are not exposed to judgemental looks, they aren't vulnerable either and they don't fall down.

'You people were here yesterday at lunchtime, on his second day of freedom, and you brought him in for interrogation. At the same time you took the opportunity to turn my home upside down. So what is it about this time? Is he suspected of something?'

And then she did it again. She didn't yell at him, didn't slam the door, didn't even ask to see his police identification or other papers – she just watched him and attempted in a neutral voice to understand what was happening.

She refused to fall down.

'*If* I intended to arrest your son, I would not have come here alone. Your house would have been surrounded by armed police in order to disarm a person we classify as highly dangerous according to our risk assessment. From that you understand surely that this is not a formal investigation yet. Right now I'm not a police officer – I've come ringing at your door as a private individual.'

It was early April, and late in the evening, so rather cold for someone to be standing at the door in thin clothes. But it wasn't because she was freezing that she slowly crossed her arms. Broncks was sure of that.

'As a private individual? Then I understand even less why you want me to contact him. Because you surely haven't suddenly become best friends?'

He looked at her. He understood her.

But there was no good reply.

Because his hasty visit wasn't about her son at all but rather about a completely different man – about John Broncks's only living family member.

He was somehow still hoping his brother wasn't connected to the armed robbery. He was somehow still hoping to reach his brother, prevent him from participating in Leo Dûvnjac's arms sale and prevent him from being sentenced to a life term.

'It's like this, Britt-Marie. Is it OK, by the way, if I call you Britt-Marie? If I don't get hold of your son, if he and I are not able to talk and come to some agreement, then there will be more of that unpleasantness you felt during yesterday's house search, when it still only concerned a suspicion. It will be pure hell when he has carried out the serious crime that I know with certainty he is planning to commit.'

'No, it's not OK for you to call me Britt-Marie. Because you don't know me. If you did, you would know that I can't help you. I am his mother. I am not going to assist you in an arrest.'

'You won't be helping me to arrest him. You'll be helping me to *prevent* an arrest.'

He lied, again. He let her believe that it was *her* family member's arrest that the police officer on her doorstep wanted to prevent. He lied to her for fucking Sam's sake, exactly as he had lied to another shrewd woman who was also a skilled colleague. He wanted never again to experience the sort of disdain for himself he felt right now.

'I'm asking you to trust me, Britt-Marie.'

'I can't trust someone whose intentions I don't understand.'

'Intentions?'

'Everyone always has some intentions.'

Despair. A driving force that distorts intentions. It could have been his own mother who stood there protecting one of her sons. But he had no choice. He was forced to use what he wanted to avoid – the two other brothers. With them he could reach her. And she would reach Leo Dûvnjac.

'There are more people involved.'

'More?'

'Your son Leo is about to drag more brothers into this. Others who don't deserve this. He's done it before. Do you want it to happen again?'

'Felix?'

Broncks looked at her and saw the way his own despair became hers, while his self-loathing took hold and expanded.

'Do you mean it – Felix? Or, no, I . . . Vincent? Would he . . .'

'More brothers, Britt-Marie. That's all I can tell you.'

He wanted to shout it at her.

More brothers means my brother.

He wanted to, but he wouldn't. And then he could see it. How her stoic attitude, her power to resist falling dropped away slightly. Perhaps he was about to break through her protective shell.

'Call him.'

He held out his mobile phone.

'Britt-Marie, call him.'

'No.'

She was powerless. But strong enough to shake her head defiantly.

'Listen to me, Britt-Marie, you must . . .'

'Don't you hear what I'm saying?'

And she shouted.

'Vincent will never commit a criminal act again! I know that! I am his mother – *I know that!*'

And the words came from deep in her stomach and from her chest and passed through him and landed somewhere far away in the beautiful residential area.

'So I will never make contact on your behalf!'

And she flung out both her arms towards the driveway by the garage and the small illuminated road that led there.

'Will you kindly go now?'

And her voice was no longer shouting. It was as low now as it was sharp.

'Or would you like me to call one of the police officers who actually *is* on duty this evening?'

AFTER A FEW hours of aimless driving on deserted country roads, and perhaps the first sensible conversation they'd had as adults, Leo felt conflicted when he let his father out at the Dráva restaurant. He didn't like having two feelings simultaneously. It wasn't him. To be successful, all distractions must be peeled away. And colliding feelings distracted. There was of course delight. Broncks had taken the bait. His father had taken the bait. But while he was still sitting there in the driver's seat of the car and looking in the restaurant window, there was something else. Something dirty. His father walked up to the counter with light steps and chatted with the owner and ordered a cup of coffee before closing time. He looked pleased. Hopeful. It was hope that his eldest son had filled him with and would soon take from him.

Dirty.

Just as dirty as when, in another time, their father constantly did the same thing to three brothers – gave them hope and took it back.

It was necessary so that the plan would work. So that Broncks would be twenty or so kilometres away tomorrow when his own nest was raided by Leo Dûvnjac.

His father would naturally be disappointed. Hurt. But not injured. He would receive only one more telephone call and then not need to participate further. He wouldn't be affected by the legal consequences. After the fact, it would be obvious that he had been reduced to a pawn in the game that he so clearly suspected when they were in the barn. His father laughed out loud at something the restaurant owner said when Leo was forced to slide his eyes out of the restaurant into the car to make a U-turn over a solid line and drive around the corner – into Ring Road and down into the tunnel and straight into the car park under the large hotel.

Sam was waiting there when he arrived. Together they would continue over the old Skanstulls Bridge to Sullo's flat in Sickla and make the final preparations. Then his encrypted phone started to buzz in his jacket pocket. It was a number that only a few people had. He looked at the display. Mamma. Her home number. He didn't want to answer, didn't want to say farewell. He had made the decision that it was easier to simply disappear. But he didn't want to worry her either.

'Hello, Mamma.'

If she rang this telephone, it was important.

'Leo, can you talk?'

'I can talk.'

'Just now there was . . .'

She was not afraid. It wasn't that voice.

Upset.

Maybe even angry.

'. . . a policeman on my doorstep. He said his name was John Broncks. I recognised him. It was him.'

Broncks?

'He said that he has to talk to you, privately.'

A short while ago?

'He wants to come to an agreement with you so that more won't be affected. More brothers, that's what he said.'

There, at her house?

'More brothers, Leo – I have no idea what or who – Felix and Vincent, if he meant them. But I think you know what it's about.'

Broncks! Just now! At her house!

'I'll take care of it, Mamma. Don't worry.'

He pressed his mother's voice off with the button. Angry – would it sound like that the last time they spoke with each other?

'Your mamma?'

Sam smiled. Leo did not.

'No. Your fucking cop brother.'

When he recounted what the short conversation was actually about, it was as if Sam didn't hear what he said, as if he closed off a little more with each new word.

'John and I are the only ones remaining in our family. The only ones of the whole Broncks clan. Do you know that, Leo?'

As if he had already taken his farewell.

'And it doesn't matter. An adversary. That's how I see him. Have seen him for many years.'

As if they were talking about someone who didn't exist.

'An adversary – and the only one left. That's what he is.'

They headed left at the green light as they approached Gullmarsplan along Hammarby Road past Fryshuset and Statoil petrol station. Leo thought about how Sam was closest to him and he was quite convinced that he held the same place for Sam, at Broncks's expense. They were side by side on the way to the next phase in life where no one else could accompany them. But Sam had forgotten something – however hard he still tried to erase Broncks from his system, Broncks had obviously not erased Sam. There was no other reasonable explanation. Broncks was hoping for some sort of reconciliation. To be able to warn him about the impending arrest so that, when it was time to surround the barn, he would stand there with the weapons and Leo Dûvnjac but avoid his own brother.

Leo took the telephone out of his inner pocket again.

It hadn't felt good.

She answered directly.

'Is that you, Leo?'

'It's me, Mamma. I just wanted to say that I will drop by early tomorrow. To make sure everything's OK.'

He stuffed the phone back into the same pocket along with the words he couldn't say.

And, Mamma, to take a proper farewell.

They were getting close to Sickla and the area called Tallbacken and Sullo's flat inside the door marked number 25. He stopped in the space between two parked cars and then stayed seated while Sam opened the door and got out.

'I'll come in a little while. I'm just going to fix a small detail to do with tomorrow. Someone who I, just like you, also have to erase from my system.'

He nodded to Sam and rolled down the hill. It wasn't particularly far to Södermalm and Högalids Street. Fifteen minutes at the most.

You just made a fucking mistake, Broncks.

His anger gradually turned into rage, which he had not wanted to show in front of Sam the day before their big coup when all emotions must be restrained. It was no longer possible to keep it inside his chest.

You brought in my family.

The rage pressed out, struck out, and he shouted out loud, protected by the car's metal casing.

You threatened my mother with destroying my younger brothers' future.

He yelled again with the windows fully rolled down. He vented his frustration again and again. And it was almost pleasant.

260

IF JOHN BRONCKS PUSHED a little with the bumper on the car in front and a little on the car behind, he could just slip his own car into what seemed to be Södermalm's only available parking space. It was the same thing every time he came home late, right before midnight – driving around in confusion and looking through streets that were empty of people and full of vehicles. He had found this odd space at the top of Lunda Street, and then as he was walking homeward across Ekermansk Malmgård and Varvs Street and took the first steps on Högalids Street, the fatigue hit him. He really wanted to sleep. A short but good night and he would be rested enough to be able to keep going.

Broncks passed blocks of flats that were melded together in one long façade, all of them with four storeys and filled with small dwellings, all built during the first decades of the twentieth century. It was unusually dark, poorly lit. He thought about it first when he was approaching his own door, as if someone had turned off every streetlight. Only the light from the formidable church with twin towers on the other side of the street. Long shadows fell from a two-headed giant keeping watch. And then there were three strikes, the church bell's muffled clang, meaning a quarter to twelve. When he first moved here the plink-plonking four times an hour drove him mad and he unconsciously walked around and counted down to the next time – nowadays he liked the monotony, liked that the stately building did not give up. It stood there in the middle of a big city and announced that everything was still going on and was as usual.

But it was not as usual.

The despair that had turned into self-loathing was gnawing deeper and deeper, taking an even larger bite out of him. He was about to go too far, perhaps had already done so. He was not an easy-going person, not the sort people took easily to their hearts, but he had always had some kind of inner moral compass pointing in the right direction. Now it did not. It was as if he had ended up between two strong magnetic fields – between Leo Dûvnjac and his own brother. And that had made the compass needle stop and shake between two directions until it had smashed what was

261

him. Running around and calling himself – hiding behind – *private individual*? While he subjected others to lies? Hurt and shook up and even threatened for his own gain? Was Sam worth it – Sam who didn't want to have contact at all? Was he worth it regardless as to who or why someone held a fishing knife?

John Broncks had no answers right now except one. That he could not be that person very much longer.

The bunch of keys in his pocket was warm, in spite of the shiny metal encountering cold night. And as he was looking for the right key and the slot in the lock, it also became clear that the streetlight that usually illuminated the door was broken.

Suddenly he stopped moving.

He felt an unpleasant sensation, as if he were no longer alone.

As if someone standing behind him had sneaked forwards quickly and soundlessly.

'You and I, Broncks, will never be private individuals with each other.'

That voice.

John Broncks glanced at the glass pane on one side of the outer door and at what was reflected in it.

It *was* him.

'So the next time, *pig*, that you seek out someone in my family, you do it as a policeman.'

I reached out to you. But you preferred to choose the place.

Broncks turned around slowly. No gestures that could be misinterpreted. To stand with your back to the attacker was the same as being at a disadvantage.

'That's exactly what I tried to do yesterday in the interview room. It was you, Leo, who made it private when, uninvited, you tried to use Sam's and my history against me.'

'Uninvited? Sam chose to tell me in confidence himself. You do that for someone you trust.'

Then it went very quickly.

The man in front of him put his hand somewhere behind his back and pulled a pistol out of his waistband and pressed it against Broncks's left temple.

'And Broncks? This is *my* interview room. Because what you did this evening was something entirely different – you went to see my mother, frightened her and let her think I'm going to involve my brothers in . . .

whatever you think I'm doing. And you do it in some sort of fucking disguise!'

Even though the rounded metal mouth scraped his thin skin, he felt nothing – no anxiety, no fear.

'I don't understand your question, Leo. By the way, may I call you Leo? Your mother didn't like my using her first name very much and you might be the same. And I don't understand your question since you didn't ask one.'

Emptiness. That's all.

He didn't even think, just stared into a pair of eyes. Leo Dûvnjac didn't intend to do anything. It was a threat, not an action that he would follow through on.

'Because you know, Leo, that is what you do in an interview room. Ask questions in order to get answers. And don't you want to know why I visited your fucking mother?'

The pistol harder against his temple. The metal, which was just scraping before, was now digging a hole. Blood was running down his cheek.

'What did you say? What did you call her?'

'Then I'll give you the answer, Leo. To the question you aren't asking. Your mother. I visited her to get in contact – with you.'

Just as suddenly as when the pressure increased to the point where it meant instantaneous death if the trigger was moved only a few millimetres, it stopped completely. The gun dropped down and rested in a relaxed hand.

'And you got it. Contact. Next time I won't rub a red ring into your face. If you contact me one more time, *pig*, I'll shoot you.'

Leo Dûvnjac smiled at him and started to walk away.

'You know where Sam is!'

He had managed to get halfway across the street when John Broncks's voice reached his back.

'You had damn well better see to it that I meet him!'

He stopped right there, in the middle of the street. And he turned around.

'Go to hell, you cunt of a cop.'

Leo Dûvnjac smiled then, as before, and continued to walk away, as before.

'Call him! For fuck's sake, call him and tell him . . .' John Broncks ran, pursuing his voice and the fleeing back, '. . . that he and I have to meet!'

Then he caught up with him and they walked beside each other towards Långholms Street.

'Call! Call him! Help me arrange a meeting!'

'Broncks – do you even hear what you're yelling about? Why the fuck would *I* help *you*?'

Broncks had already realised he'd lost control. Despair and self-loathing that turn into desperation work like that. And he was so close to saying that. Screaming that.

You'll help me because you don't know that I know where your guns are. Because you don't know that I know what they are going to be used for.

But he didn't do that. Nor did he say, or scream, why it was so important to get to talk to Sam, why it was worth every metre of humiliation.

Because I'm going to catch you, you bastard. Because when I do it, I also have to catch my own brother.

'You don't know Sam, *pig*.'

Broncks almost stumbled over the kerb. His throat was hurting. He *had* shouted out that last part after all.

'You don't know him as well as I do, Broncks. If you did, you'd also know he'd rather take a bullet than be locked up again.'

Högalids Street turned into Långholms Street. And when Leo turned left towards Hornsplan, John Broncks turned also and they kept walking side by side, each with the person he perhaps hated the most.

'OK. Then we'll say this.'

There were more people out walking. There were ears and curious eyes and Broncks should have lowered his voice but he didn't.

'If you don't care about how things go for *my* brother – maybe you don't care about how it goes for *your own* brothers either?'

And then they both stopped.

'What the fuck do you mean by that, pig?'

Unlike the others, one streetlight seemed to be working and was shining on the asphalt in front of them. They had ended up exactly at the edge between light and dark and they stayed there, completely still. Maybe because Leo Dûvnjac had just made a threat without carrying it out, and next time he threatened, he also had to act upon it. Maybe because John Broncks would soon actually go too far, violating the limit of a policeman's powers.

'What do I mean, Leo? If you step into the light here so I can see you, then you can hear what the fuck I mean.'

Broncks himself took a decided step forward into the streetlight's beam, waving with his index finger towards the asphalt.

'Step into the light!'

'And I thought you didn't have any more dignity to lose. Go home and go to bed, Broncks.'

'Into the light, you bastard!'

'Come on now, you fine police officer. Go home and save your strength. Because I'm going to visit you again. When you least expect it. When I take away from you what you are most proud of.'

It almost sounded as if Leo Dûvnjac was laughing as he walked around the circle of light that stretched out into the street; quick steps as he vanished into the darkness.

'Then it's your choice, Leo! Your choice!'

Broncks, still taking no notice of the people moving around them, called after him.

'Because there's one thing you should be damn clear about – if you get my brother involved, I'll get your brother involved!'

NIGHT OUTSIDE HER window.

Elisa walked between the bookcase and the window, between the window and the bookcase.

She had many rules for how she should carry out her work. She liked that. Structure quite simply made her a better police officer. In her private life, on the other hand, there was only one rule – never ever return to a break-up, to a conflict. Men and women who touched each other mentally touched each other physically, and abusing the intimacy would only hurt again, more deeply the next time.

It could be easily applied to work life. A rule that her colleague was not at all familiar with.

For that reason, as some church bell was striking three times in the dark, she was walking about in her office in the police station like that clichéd policewoman she had promised never to become, who remained on the job instead of spending time with loved ones, who wouldn't even let go of an investigation for a moment of sleep. But there was a crucial difference. It was no longer just about a criminal bastard from the group of usual adversaries that should be locked up. This time it was also about a colleague.

She walked from the bookcase to the window and around the desk and the three piles constituting the investigation's three pillars. And she felt that with each new lap the frustration was increasing. *Alibis. For both, unfortunately.* He had looked at her with that devilish discordant smile. And right there, right then, she recognised when the distorted tone, which she still did not grasp, had come up for the first time.

In the interview room.

LD: Broncks – your little puppet and I have just been talking about how well people know their neighbours in a corridor.

She stopped at the pile on the far left, the one she called *You struck first, you bastard*. She had placed the transcript from the interview with Leo Dûvnjac there. Or rather, Broncks's interview with him.

LD: For example, there was a prisoner, can you imagine, who told me about how he stabbed his father to death in a summer cottage.

She read again about someone who knocked on the camera's lens with his fingertips and hit the microphone with the palm of his hand. He turned directly towards the man who was sitting in the next room and watching them on a monitor.

LD: Twenty-seven fucking cuts in his own father's chest.

About there somewhere Broncks had suddenly stormed into the room and interrupted the interview. Leo Dûvnjac had succeeded in provoking him. She had asked Broncks directly on several occasions about what actually happened, what Dûvnjac was talking about. And each time she met with the tone-deaf smile.

She didn't like gut feelings.

But the interview transcript lying in the pile in front of her contained facts.

There was something not quite right with John Broncks. And it was part of her job to find out what. Another lap around the room as the frustration slowly eased. It was always like this when the direction began to be clearer. From this moment on she must also follow Broncks's tracks, since he didn't know the rules. Never, ever return to a break-up, to a conflict. For a police officer that was the same as never catching the same individual twice. At least, not if you investigated him previously for a series of bank robberies and then sat in interviews with him for several months. You developed a relationship. You were no longer objective. You and the criminal had touched one another and one of you was going to abuse that closeness.

Elisa stopped at the pile of papers again.

On the line for additional suspects, she wrote Broncks's name in pencil next to Dûvnjac's and moved the printout to the next pile, which was lying in the middle of the desk and was called *You fucked up*.

Until she found an acceptable explanation for his actions during the

267

interview, John Broncks would also remain there. And if he weren't willing to provide it himself, she would, when the night turned into dawn and morning, have to find and speak to someone else who could – Leo Dûvnjac.

FAREWELL.

He had never even thought the word before. Old-fashioned, unnaturally grand, distancing. All the same, he was here for that reason, to say farewell. Not goodbye, not see you later. To close the door, not hold it open.

To take leave. For ever.

Leo had just put the key in the lock and turned it halfway when he stopped. Mere hours earlier the Broncks bastard had gone up these same steps to insult his family. He stared at his mamma's closed front door while in his mind he went through the eight stages of the plan's final step – its working title was *the police station*. It would be set in motion in just a few hours. The last stage meant leaving the country at exactly 19.00; the first one was to say goodbye no matter how bloody awful it felt inside – the precondition to be able to neutralise everything disturbing, to enter unencumbered, to avoid thoughts other than taking back what didn't exist.

During the long string of bank robberies, he had never had any problem opening bank doors and using a loaded gun to demand the attention of strangers. He never hesitated even while realising it meant danger and escape and other guns soon being pointed at him.

When he finished turning that key, he would have to open this door and look at her, at someone who in another world was all the love and security, and who wouldn't understand that it was the last time she would see him.

He took a quick look at Sam, who was sitting in the car in Mamma's driveway waiting, then a deep breath before he turned the key the rest of the way and opened the door slightly. The lights were on in both the kitchen and the hallway and there was the smell of freshly brewed coffee, despite the early hour. When they were young, Mamma packed her lunch bag, went to the nursing home in Sköndal in the evening, took care of the disabled all night and slept while her three children were at school. Now she worked days, and he heard the sound of spread-out pages of the newspaper being turned, time alone she hadn't had then.

She was sitting at the pine table in the kitchen, the seat closest to the window and the radiator, the seat that had always been Mamma's. Already dressed to go. The bowl of porridge and frozen blueberries empty. She wore red reading glasses, which she pulled down when she looked at him.

'Hi, Mamma.'

'Leo? I didn't hear you come in.'

The coffee maker was waiting lukewarm on the counter and he poured half a cup.

'OK if I take the last?'

'Go ahead. I'm leaving in a couple of minutes anyway.'

'Then I'll go at the same time. I have a lot to do, too.'

He leaned against the row of kitchen cabinets. He'd often stood like this, drinking a cup of coffee on the go, but it didn't feel like it used to. It was uncomfortable and the cabinet edges cut deep into his back.

'Mamma?'

'Yes?'

'I'm sorry about what happened last night. The idiot who frightened you.'

His mother folded her reading glasses and laid them carefully in a black case. Then she cupped her hand and gathered the crumbs on the table and dropped them on the plate.

'I wasn't afraid, Leo. Pensive, rather.'

'You don't need to think about it. The cop was talking shit. Do you hear that, Mamma? You shouldn't worry.'

She opened up the newspaper. She flipped past the culture section, the sports and the local section.

'Leo? Do you know how I read the morning paper these days?'

She flipped back to the pages with the national news.

'I always start here. Not with culture, not with sports or financial news or foreign news or Stockholm or entertainment. And there's a reason. I have to know if anything has happened – to be able to feel some sort of peace. Whether large robberies were committed. Maybe gunfire. Crimes. Pages I never looked at before. I started doing that when all of you were arrested. *Then*. After the bank robberies.'

Her fingertips glided over pages six, seven and eight.

'Every day something else was written. New charges, new pieces of evidence and witnesses. When finally after a few months I was allowed to visit you and I asked you about what happened, if everything they wrote was true – do you know what you answered, Leo? You said, "Don't worry, Mamma." Just like you said a moment ago.'

She held out the newspaper. As if she wanted him to take care of it, to take responsibility for it.

'Mamma, nothing is going to happen to Felix and Vincent. I promise.'

'But what about you?'

He held out his arms, smiling the warm, slightly lopsided smile he knew she liked so much.

'Mamma, I always get by.'

'So – look at me, Leo – why have the police already been here twice in the three days since your release?'

'Because they're like that.'

It seemed as if she was going to ask something else but then she changed her mind and got up instead with the glasses case in her hand. She smiled her Mamma smile as she turned off the coffee maker and passed him on her way out to the hall where she put on her coat and scarf and a pair of low leather boots with a zip.

Now. Now, damn it. That was what he was thinking.

'Leo, I have to go. Run, actually. There's rush-hour traffic and I start at eight.'

Now I should say it, what I've come for.

'Mamma?'

'Yes?'

'I . . . listen . . .'

'Yes?'

'I'll follow you out.'

She reached for her purse on the chest of drawers and then rested her fingers around the door handle.

'Leo, you're also leaving?'

'Yes.'

'So why did you come here?'

'Because I . . . told you last night I would. I wanted to check that everything was OK.'

'No, Leo, why did you *really* come here?'

She waited for an answer she didn't get. So she pushed down the handle and held the door, which was boosted by a lively morning wind. She let him go by, then locked up and walked towards her car, which was parked on the asphalt driveway and which took her each workday to the large hospital in Huddinge. Just as she was about to get in she noticed the other car, which was on the street and almost in the way of her being able to drive out.

'Who is that?'

A large blond man in the driver's seat. She guessed he was about forty, perhaps forty-five. She looked at him and he greeted her with a cautious nod. A few days ago she had observed the predatory car with police in it, the ones who later picked up Leo just when lunch was ready. This car also had something to do with her eldest son. She was sure of it, just as certain as she was that the man sitting and waiting was not Leo's enemy.

'Hey, Leo? Who is that?'

'Sam.'

'Oh?'

'A good friend.'

Britt-Marie quickly realised this wouldn't be followed by more information. So she turned off her car alarm, got in and started the engine. But when she was about to close the door, Leo caught it.

'OK then, Mamma . . .'

He clasped the frame of the side window uncertainly and leaned over the car door.

'Well, then . . . have a good day today.'

She pressed lightly on the accelerator to keep the engine running.

'And . . . listen, Mamma – don't worry now.'

Then she sat there – surrounded by the engine's insistent sound – and looked at him for a long time with a gaze that was neither reproachful nor resigned.

'Leo?'

'Yes, Mamma?'

As if she somehow knew that all she could do tomorrow was to continue reading the news.

'I love you.'

THEY HAD TWO CUPS OF black coffee and two ham and cheese sandwiches on a beautiful table made of some kind of metal. It was a fairly small café, empty at the moment except for the waitress, most likely the owner, behind the counter among the bulging piles of cinnamon buns and apple pies. And the two patrons sitting by the window facing Bergs Street and the police station.

'You should eat, Sam.'

'I can't. Can't get anything down. I can't fucking swallow.'

Sam poked a little at the plate and the untouched coffee cup as if to illustrate that he couldn't even touch them. He was nervous in a way that Leo had never seen him before, not even before the bankrolling robbery with a milk lorry as the only getaway car.

'I know there's not much time – but it's the time we have.'

'Leo – it's not about that.'

'Just a minute.'

Leo got up and walked towards the water pitcher on a separate table along with white napkins and shiny teaspoons. From there the view of the building across the street was almost better.

Kronoberg. An entire complex, the beating heart of the Swedish police, which pumped out uniformed police officers and marked cars to watch over the circulation of civil society. Fifteen paces away and absolutely none of them knew that he would be moving about in there in just a couple of hours.

He put the glass of water, filled to the brim, in front of Sam.

'At least drink something.'

'There should have been three of us, Leo. You were going to get a replacement for Jari. One of your brothers.'

Together they had followed the news about the Robbery of the Century on the television in one of the prison's assembly rooms. A series of reports over about a year. And he had hoped that it would drag out even longer before the judgement would be binding. But two weeks before his release came the fucking news. The Supreme Court would not take up the case. Everything changed with that. They had a deadline.

273

He knew that, according to the information he ordered from Sullo, the transport from the police station only went once a fortnight, every other Thursday, at 14.00. And the transport this time was unique – today, all the seized money from the largest robbery in Swedish history would be driven to Tumba paper mill to be burned. Because that was how it worked in the Swedish legal system. The banknotes had fulfilled their purpose as evidence in an investigation and therefore would be destroyed.

A once-in-a-lifetime chance.

'They said no, and I don't trust anyone else. We'll figure it out anyway.'

'The plan was to have one person outside to keep track of the real cops coming in. And two people on the inside. As it is, you'll be running around alone in there. It doesn't fucking feel good.'

'That's why it was all the more important that I conducted *the test* alone yesterday. I picked up a pair of sunglasses from some lousy investigation to try out the procedures and check the blueprints of the building. To measure the time. So that the staff saw me. And it went well, Sam! So easy! They couldn't imagine that anyone would be so brainless as to attack . . . in the station. In the basement beneath floor after floor of little fucking detectives who will try to anticipate how criminals like us would pull this off on the outside and arrest us *there*.'

Reaching across the table, he pointed out the window.

'Do you see, Sam?'

Sam had managed to take a couple of sips of water but they stopped somewhere in his throat again. And he really tried to follow Leo's index finger but he saw only more cars with more police.

'There, Sam. Two police vans. They are driving *away* from the place they think is the most protected. And there, do you see, four uniforms are *leaving* the building through the main entrance, laughing. Check it out, the one with the moustache furthest forward is saying something really, really funny and she, the one next to him, is laughing her head off. They're having a damn good time. And do you know why, Sam? Because they're only a couple of metres from what they have always considered to be their security – the fucking security that we're going to take from them for ever!'

He scooted the glass of water across the table to Sam who responded by shaking his head.

And that wasn't good at all.

There was no time for that sort of nervousness. To feel a little anxiety before a bank robbery or security-van robbery was always propitious. It

274

sharpened the senses. But it shouldn't take over. It didn't only affect movements; it made thought slow and impaired courage.

'Sam, the only thing you need to do is to make sure the empty suitcases are in the car as they should be and pick me up with the hand trolley and full boxes when I send a signal that I'm out again; from your vantage point you have an overview of the entrance to the police station on Kungsholms Street and the courthouse on Scheele Street the entire time.'

Leo reached out and put his hand on Sam's shoulder, as he had sometimes done with Vincent when he hesitated.

'So, Sam, *you* don't risk anything before we are finished and on our way. I'm the only one who can get caught on the inside.'

An old cowbell jangled. It sounded when the café door opened and closed, when customers came and went. Just then four new ones were arriving. The laughing police officers. They hadn't been on the way out to arrest anyone, they were going to eat buns and continue to laugh in here.

'OK, for safety's sake – have we thought of everything?'

Leo had lowered his voice even though the uniforms sat down at the other end of the café, right in front of the serving counter. He smiled.

We are sitting so close – and I am about to go through the checklist before the most audacious coup you'll ever hear about.

'Requisition slip is ready – with the signature of the right duty officer according to the schedule in the cop computer. Property reference number, ready – ten packages twenty-five centimetres high, thirty-two centimetres long and thirty centimetres wide. They need to fit in two large moving boxes with a little extra room. Uniforms – I wear one and you, Sam, plant the other, together with the real police shield, right after you drop me off at the courthouse.'

Then they sat in silence for a moment, listening to the laughing fools and to the large clock on the wall ticking so loudly. Finally Sam grabbed the glass of water and drank half of it. He even chewed a little on the ham and cheese sandwich.

'Good, Sam. Let's do it then.'

Leo had hung his leather jacket over the empty chair next to him. Now he took the mobile phone out of the inner pocket. He would only use this mobile for calling preprogrammed numbers. And he went out of the café for a while. While he was waiting for a connection, he looked at the police station, its yellow plastered walls oblivious.

275

There was just one policeman who *couldn't* be there at 13.45.

You arrested me, you bastard.

Only you would recognise Sam, and even recognise me – in spite of the lenses and shaved head.

Therefore you will find yourself far away from here. Therefore I am going to set the false lead into motion.

Then he heard the tone, which was repeated regularly and stopped when he got a reply from a familiar voice.

FOR THE FIRST time John Broncks had met his own death. The thought came that he would die right then. And he hadn't felt anything. He still wasn't sure whether that was good or bad. In the shadow of a church and in the gloom of a broken streetlight, without warning, Leo Dûvnjac had pressed a pistol – a Sig Sauer, the police's own service revolver, which strangely enough had been what Broncks focused his mind on – against his temple. It was sufficiently hard that it formed a round red ring in the sensitive skin.

He stretched. A small leather sofa was not the best place to spend the night.

It hadn't been possible to sleep afterwards. He had tossed and turned in bed, sweated and fought with the sheet and pillow for about an hour before he gave up, wide awake. And that had nothing to do with the death threat. The muzzle of the pistol had not frightened him. Dûvnjac had not frightened him. But Sam . . . a life gathered in a pile of ashes; a family, a childhood home in smouldering embers. This frightened him – a brother who refused to communicate or meet, who hated, and yet this was the only thing left.

With the sweaty sheet around his body, he got up and fetched a large glass of water, settled on the sofa and stared at TV channels broadcasting history documentaries about dictators, naval battles and royal psychopaths. And in the middle of a scene that was about the beheading of a nobleman who committed adultery, he fetched the bottle of whisky standing unopened on the bookshelf, which he had received as a gift from a colleague in connection with the Robbery of the Century – even though he never drank alone. He filled the glass halfway with the hard liquor instead. A few beheadings later he dozed off.

Until his telephone rang.

The stooped fellow on the ninth floor. The helpful detective at the intelligence unit office.

He advised him that he would send an audio file soon – the tapped telephone had recently been used a second time.

'Dad, I'll pick you up in three hours. OK?'

And Broncks recognised both voices well.

'Skanstull. In front of the restaurant.'

The older man, with a distinct accent, rumbling at the end of each sentence. The younger man with well-articulated authority despite the low-key voice.

> 'The buyer is meeting us there at a quarter to two. As I said yesterday, he wants to be sure we can deliver.'
>
> 'One thing before you hang up, Leo.'
>
> 'Yeah?'
>
> 'I just want you to know – yes, I was unsure about your damn idea at first. But during the night I saw it before me. It *is* a good business. Everyone will gain from it. The whole family.'
>
> 'It's great that you aren't hesitating any more because I seriously need your help.'

A little was left of the recording. The conversation had begun at 09.12 according to the black timeline at the lower edge. Altogether, it lasted eighty-seven seconds. Then the silence – which now was all that was heard – wasn't electronic. It was the father and son reflecting; they were going to sell the country's largest private arsenal in a few hours.

> 'And, Dad? I surely don't need to say that it's extremely important that you are standing out there in time, that you aren't late – like last time.'

Broncks looked at the clock hanging on the wall over the television. Quarter to ten. Only four hours remaining until their meeting with the buyer.

The time to be able to understand Sam's involvement was rapidly shrinking.

The time he needed to form the plan that would be implemented the very second Leo Dûvnjac received the payment.

John Broncks yawned and straightened his back.

When he sat on this sofa again in the evening, he would know if he had lost the only remaining member of his family for ever.

NOWHERE DOES TIME go so slowly as it does when you are moving through the corridor of a hospital.

Elisa first counted seconds, then steps, then breaths.

Whatever the method, her movements were frozen. It felt just as impossible to ever reach the other end of the eternally long passage.

It could be because everything was so monochromic. White walls succeeding each other, yellow linoleum floors growing together. It lacked focal points for your eyes. Or maybe it was about the internal focal points – the distance you have to walk to receive the news you fear. The helplessness it means to wait for information for which the likelihood of life and death is equal – the condition which once changed her for ever and which she never wants to go through again.

So she went there anyway.

To the end of eternity's corridor.

To the sliding doors, the entrance to the orthopaedic department K83, according to the sign on the ceiling, and it projected a calm that was the opposite of the department she herself had lain in that time. Here you were mended. Here the quality of life was increased. A patient most often left in better condition than he or she arrived in. And already a little way down this much shorter, much more colourful and cosier corridor, the woman she sought was standing, involved in a conversation with one of her co-workers, both of them in white coats and shoes with soft, thick rubber soles that were just as white.

'Hello again, I apologise that I . . .'

Britt-Marie saw her immediately, heard her speaking and stopped what she was engaged in. Elisa began walking to meet her.

'. . . came and bothered you here, Britt-Marie, but it is the daytime address you gave us, and since you weren't at home when I looked for you there and didn't answer your phone . . .'

'I saw that you called. But chose not to answer. Because I'm working now. And this is my free zone. My eldest son's activities don't reach here. I don't intend to talk to any police here.'

280

'I have only one question. And—'

'Good. Then we can talk while I follow you out.'

They passed identical rooms, each with four beds on wheels and framed by metal railings, all of them flanked by a minor forest of wheelchairs and crutches. And as soon as Britt-Marie opened the sliding doors and they stood on the very first plastic mat of eternity's corridor, she indicated with both her look and voice that the very short meeting must begin and end immediately.

'And what was it you wanted? Your *only* question?'

'Leo.'

'That is not a question.'

'I must get hold of him. It's important for me to do so. Otherwise I wouldn't be standing here.'

Britt-Marie's eyes – which were so determined – were suddenly tired.

'I don't know where he is.'

'When did you see him last? After all, your address is on his release documents.'

'That was your *second* question.'

Elisa tried to understand her unwillingness. She understood her frustration at the direction her sons' lives had taken. Her sorrow over preparing for detention hearings and prison visits instead of preparing for grandchildren. But she didn't understand why her unwillingness to talk was even greater now than it had been when they trudged in unannounced and turned her home upside down during a house search.

'Britt-Marie, I'm conducting a police investigation. I therefore ask you to answer – when did you see him last?'

The middle-aged woman was drowning in fatigue.

'This morning.'

'This morning?'

'Yes. He came home right before I was going to drive here. And he left again then, at the same time I did.'

'Did I understand you correctly? He came to your home early this morning – but only for a few minutes? Where was he going then?'

And then her gaze glided away somewhere, as if it was seeking a place to fasten, something to rest on, exactly like Elisa in the never-ending corridor.

'Britt-Marie? Look at me. Do you know where he was going?'

'No. I don't know. And I . . . Perhaps this sounds strange but I think . . .

I don't think he's coming back. It was a feeling I had. That he was saying farewell. He said it without saying it.'

White coat, white shoes, name tag on her chest: until this moment, her gestures, her charm had gone with the security her appearance conveyed. That wasn't so any longer. She stood there, flushed, broken. Almost passionate.

'And now *I* have a question for *you* that I demand you answer. Is this, your coming here, about the same thing as your colleague's visit was to my home late last night? Is that why you keep showing up all the time?'

'My colleague's visit?'

'Yes. Has something happened? If so, tell me about it.'

'Britt-Marie – *who* was at your house?'

'Broncks. He worked on the bank robberies. *Has* something happened?'

Elisa was silent.

'Answer me!'

John Broncks. Again? Without informing me?

'Britt-Marie, what did he want?'

'Now I am the one questioning you!'

'Help me now, Britt-Marie – what did he want?'

The confused mother was calming down a little. At least, the red in her cheeks seemed to fade.

'To be honest, I never really grasped what. The only thing that was fairly clear was that he was looking for contact with Leo. And the whole matter was that *I* should pass on the contact information. Why don't you ask him yourself? He works with you!'

Elisa's surprise that John Broncks suddenly found his way into their conversation began to turn into irritation, the sort that in turn becomes anger.

Broncks. What the hell are you doing?

'OK, Britt-Marie, I'm sorry. I can't explain why, but you have to help me here a little anyway. I *must* get something I can use to look into this further. What I now know is that Leo was at your home this morning. But how did he get there? How did he leave?'

'By car.'

'What car?'

'I don't know. A . . . car. Probably not his own. Someone drove him.'

'Drove him?'

'A man. A friend – he said that. Sam something.'

Anger was no longer sufficient to describe it.

Fury.

And it started deep, deep in her chest.

A friend. A friend named *Sam something*. She had pulled out the list of four names they should map out more closely, four candidates that shared prison time with Leo Dûvnjac and were now released. One of them was named Sam Larsen. One of two that Broncks insisted that he would investigate himself.

'Britt-Marie?'

Elisa had a link in her mobile to the current documents of the investigation. She found the right photo and held up the display in front of Britt-Marie.

'I want you to look at this.'

A portrait photo out of the correctional system's register. The most recent she had access to.

'Was it him?'

Britt-Marie's red reading glasses were hanging on a cord on her chest. Now she raised them to her face.

'Was it him, Britt-Marie? The friend in the car?'

She nodded.

'Yes. He looked like that.'

As Elisa returned through eternity's corridor, it went much faster than on the way in. She had other matters to think of than white walls and yellow plastic rugs – she had just got access to three new facts.

That her colleague was continuing to withhold information.

That a farewell to a mother heralded a big change.

And since she was convinced these two were linked and together they formed a new truth: that it was her task to put everything else aside and find out how.

THE TRUNK'S BARK was rough as he leaned his cheek against it. Pine. Next to birch, spruce and an occasional oak. John Broncks moved cautiously through dense, unkempt forest the one-hundred-and-fifty-metre distance to a deserted farm and a house on the west side of the plot, a dilapidated barn on the east side and a beautiful little grove of fruit trees between them.

From there he had a perfect view without being seen himself, just as on his previous visit.

He had parked his car on a secluded forest road about a kilometre away, moved the last stretch on foot and took the decision that he could only call Sam every ten minutes while he was waiting. Every new attempt was met with an electronic voice monotonously announcing that the recipient couldn't be reached. He called Sam's neighbour on the island five times, who explained that he hadn't seen him, and that the house seemed empty when he had peeked into it at Broncks's urgent request. And he called the ferryman three times, who in the end was just as anxious as he was himself, and with an increasingly quieter voice reiterated that Sam had travelled neither there nor back to the mainland during the last twenty-four hours.

He *must* keep looking.

He *must* keep trying to make contact.

It would not be too long before Leo Dûvnjac arrived to conduct his business.

The skin of his cheek began to get irritated and he moved slightly, leaning his shoulder on the next tree instead. And he looked around. The surroundings seemed so different in daylight. The desolation was even more present. A place just twenty kilometres or so from the city, yet ideal for someone who wanted to operate without any disturbance.

While he was waiting, he made yet another call.

To the head of the National Task Force, a man he met over seven years earlier in connection with the arrest of father and son Dûvnjac in a holiday cottage abandoned in the winter.

Broncks enquired about the availability of support for an operation that *could* be considered for that same afternoon, and got confirmation that it would be possible to dispatch the whole force in the current situation and that it could be in place within half an hour after the alarm, while regular police set up roadblocks.

He rested his gaze on the farm, on the poorly painted barn, which probably was once full of cattle, of life, and now contained a lorry filled with death. Nearly two hundred automatic weapons. But also an explosive device, a remote-controlled bomb constructed to detonate via a pulse from a mobile telephone.

John Broncks checked the time again.

The people he was waiting for should soon be at the entrance, according to the intercepted conversation.

One more call – the last one.

And it felt, somehow, like the same call he made to his big brother the summer between elementary school and gymnasium, when he made Sam listen to a terrified and desperate little brother pleading for urgent help. Then, the conversation led to disaster. But now, if he got hold of him, the outcome could be the opposite – to prevent disaster from being repeated.

He pressed the number, waited while the signal searched there somewhere in the air, and held his breath until he encountered the voice again, which explained mechanically that the subscriber couldn't be reached. Then it was as if his body began to tremble, as if he were very cold, the kind of shaking which can only be quietly waited out.

He knew then that he couldn't do anything more.

Other than to hope.

To hope that when Leo Dûvnjac and his father arrived and set off the alarm to the National Task Force, Sam would not be found there, by their side, and not be proved as involved as everything indicated.

COURTROOM 12, DIVISION 2. Leo leaned back on an uncomfortable wooden bench in a small and unassuming courtroom, so different compared with the high-security courtroom he and his brothers had sat in for many months, indicted for the country's most comprehensive series of bank robberies. He only realised now that he had never experienced a trial from this side of the railing. From the spectator seats.

And he was doing it in a police uniform.

The trial was that of a poor teenager who stole a number of randomly selected cars and was in a fucking bad position. According to the witness testimony of a forensic technician, the amateur had spread his fingerprints in every vehicle – fingerprints registered in the database since his previous indictment, when he'd also spread them in about the same number of cars.

Heavy walls panelled in dark oak. Big windows facing Scheele Street. Acoustics that amplified every scraping of feet and every nervous clearing of the throat. The perfect place for waiting.

Because it was here in this building, Stockholm's courthouse, that everything would begin.

From here, in three minutes and thirty seconds, he was going to initiate the final phase of a year's planning.

His mobile telephone lay on the wooden bench, very close to his right thigh. In the last few hours, he had monitored the location of the false lead and observed that Camera A, mounted on the fence at the beginning of the gravel road and now in daylight, registered a private car passing by with Broncks in the driver's seat. That was good, exactly according to plan. However, it was not according to plan that he was still acting alone. Not a single little elite police force had come to assist him. Little elite cops should be standing behind every bush around the barn, ready to arrest someone who didn't have any intention at all of showing up right there right this afternoon. He didn't understand why. But he couldn't wait any longer. He must begin now in order to reach what didn't exist as late as possible without arousing suspicions, but at the same time early enough to have time to finish the entire loading before the regular transport arrived at 14.00.

Leo got up just as the prosecutor, in his closing arguments, asked for a sentence of twelve months in prison for the teenager who spread his fingerprints in cars. He walked out into the stone corridor, which echoed power and subservience, and he continued down the wide staircase to the ground floor and on to the basement and the plate-metal door he had passed the day before when for the first time he walked through the underground passage of the police station without handcuffs.

BRONCKS'S OFFICE WAS empty. And it was just as well: it was still too early to pose a few questions directly to him. First she would look for the link between a policeman and a former criminal; between John Broncks, who should have been sitting there, and the man just identified as Leo Dûvnjac's friend, Sam Larsen.

Elisa continued to her own office, so impatient that she turned on the computer and sat down on her chair, the bag with the big sandwich still in one hand and a container with freshly squeezed orange juice in the other. Ordinarily she ate her lunches at the little café across Bergs Street with its view of the police station but also with a sort of distance, which for a brief time brought perspective and prevented her from being devoured. But today there wasn't time. She never endured going around with unsubstantiated feelings. And now, with such a strong feeling that one of the station's most respected colleagues was withholding information, she must investigate, delve and turn the feeling into facts. Circle a motive that made Broncks's bloody discord comprehensible. Like . . . like when you have a boyfriend you suspect of being unfaithful, and to be able to confront him, first you have to get evidence – a hotel bill, list of phone calls, a credit card statement. (The bastard had been so stupid that he bought lingerie from Victoria's Secret and denied it when she faced him in their shared kitchen with the Visa statement in her hand.)

Never defeated by a lie.

When she confronted John Broncks, she would not act emotionally as she did then with the idiot who drowned his mistress in lace underwear. This idiot, Broncks, would be unmasked more quietly and professionally, but of course he wouldn't get away with a well-formulated lie either.

Half of the cheese sandwich, half of the freshly squeezed orange juice.

Now, finally, the slow computer had opened the window to the police authority's criminal records and she entered Sam Larsen's ten-digit personal identity number.

And waited.

The computer continued to be painfully slow. Until it woke up and she leaned closer.

There, in the middle of the screen. The only hit for Sam Larsen in the criminal records.

MURDER – CHAP 1 § 3 THE PENAL CODE

IMPRISONMENT LIFE.
IMPLEMENTATION STARTED.

A crime.

An entire adult life.

COMMUTATION TO FIXED TERM SENTENCE 34 YEARS AND 6 MONTHS.
PAROLED.
REMAINING SENTENCE 11 YEARS AND 6 MONTHS.

She went on to the scanned-in first page of the verdict. The only facts that were available in addition. At the top-right corner, the oblong box explained that the verdict was reached in Eskilstuna district court.

A few lines down,

Accused: Larsen, Sam George.

Another couple of lines down,

Plaintiff: Broncks, Gunilla Ewa.

And it was as if at first she did not understand she had read what she had read. It was so truly out of place, so false, so . . . wrong, what was written there. For a moment she was convinced that she had allowed her frustration, which had turned into anger at a colleague's behaviour, to go to her head so that she had begun to see the name she was so upset about where it shouldn't be found at all.

She read it again.

Broncks, Gunilla Ewa.

Slowly she understood.

She wasn't imagining it. She wasn't thinking 'Broncks' there by obsession. He *had* kept back information.

Sam Larsen, who had served his sentence at the same cellblock at Österåker as Leo Dûvnjac, had murdered someone connected with a plaintiff named Broncks.

Who?

Why?

The rest of the verdict – just like the entire preliminary investigation – was stored in the City Police archive according to a note in the final line on the screen. The archive was located at the very bottom of the police station, in the corridor she most often visited when she had errands in the property room.

She stood up.

That was where she had to head now.

WHEN AN ACCESS card slips through the card reader, there's sometimes a squeaking sound that seeks out your nervous system and makes you shudder involuntarily.

That was how it sounded now.

And he shivered.

Or maybe it was the fact that the card worked a second time that gave him gooseflesh. The fact that the access card, which he had bought from Sullo and which belonged to a cleaning company, made the bolt of the lock turn around and the plate-metal door open to the passage connecting the courthouse with the police station.

13:35:00

He had twenty-five minutes left. At 14.00, the time the regular transport arrived at the seized property room, he would have to have returned here and made his way out through the entrance on Scheele Street and loaded the goods into the truck there.

He grabbed the handle of the trolley and began to roll the two some-what large moving boxes he had parked there while he waited for the starting point in the courtroom. The first steps into the underground passage were greeted in the same way they were the previous time, with sharp light from the bare fluorescent lighting and dry heat. Down here there were no seasons. Right at the first passage crossing after fifty metres, left after another at sixty-five metres. The first leg had taken him one minute and ten seconds when he went to pick up the sunglasses, plus another ten seconds in front of the identification camera. This time he would give it two minutes. That time, even before the first turn, he had heard the hard sound of shoes, a warning that others were close – two prisoners escorted by four prison guards and a uniformed police officer. Now only the whining of one of the trolley's thick rubber wheels was audible. He should have checked and lubricated them.

A little more than one hundred metres remaining to a heist no one had ever even considered before: stealing the banknotes that were to be sent to the Tumba paper mill to be destroyed. Burnt up. Notes emblazoned with blocked serial numbers that constituted evidence in a trial and were already replaced by the Federal Bank of Sweden with new serial numbers and new banknotes. Yet they were still worth exactly as much as the amount given on them and were still genuine. So later when a foreign bank contact – in his and Sam's case a woman by the name of Darya at the Russian Sberbank Rossii – would buy them at a discounted price and in turn sell them back to the Federal Bank of Sweden, the law gave the contact the right to receive one hundred per cent of their value.

Fifty metres. The first crossroads.

And a sense of unreality, as one of the country's most well-known criminals – and until Monday morning when he had been released, also the most dangerous of individuals thus classified – strolled freely around Sweden's central police station with the proper identification and dressed in one of their own uniforms.

It was so close that he laughed; it was bubbling up inside him.

Then Leo turned right at the passage crossing and didn't meet anyone at all. It was going more straightforwardly than he'd dared hope.

He knew the principle worked. The shortcomings of the system benefited those who thought a little longer. The agreement on the money's permanent value had been tested before in Belgium just a few years ago. It stated that banknotes and coins issued by a state's central bank always kept the value given on them.

The Belgian central bank had gathered in a billion two-euro coins for destruction, old coins that were to be replaced by new ones. Gold-coloured inside with a silver-coloured frame. Coin machines struck out the middle, flinging the gold section to the right and the silver to the left. Then the central bank sold the whole thing as scrap. The ones who had thought about it a little longer and used the shortcomings of the system were the owners of a Chinese company. They bought *both* parts of the scrap. They had their employees press both sections together again by hand. Two billion euros! They bought the metal scrap for nothing and then sent it back to the national bank of Belgium and said, 'Thanks, we'd like to have full value for our change.'

Sixty-five metres and the second choice – left at the next passage crossing.

It was halfway along the passage where the property room lay.

And the unreal was suddenly real. Over there, at the other end, the first

292

encounter was approaching. A lone individual. A woman, he was certain of it. She wore plain clothes and moved with purpose. She belonged here. If they both continued at their current pace, they would cross each other's path exactly at the camera outside his final destination.

Leo drew his hand over the shaved crown of his head. The thin blanket of stubble had begun to grow. Then he blinked a couple of times to ensure that his lenses sat properly, and so that the irritation to his cornea and the damn stinging would calm down. Finally, he steered the trolley next to the concrete wall. He wanted to leave plenty of room. They should be able to pass without thinking.

In just a few seconds they would look at each other, nod and continue. But – plain clothes? And with no other visible signs of the profession? Maybe he was worrying unnecessarily. Maybe she wasn't even a police officer.

He *hadn't* worried unnecessarily.

She *was* a police officer.

Of all people . . . *her*?

Dark, curly hair. A silver ring in each ear. And that look that refused to give way no matter how much it was provoked in an interview room.

Elisa something.

He had directed Broncks far, far away from here, being careful that the policeman who knew him and would recognise him the best wouldn't run into him. But he hadn't expected to meet her, here. She had picked him up in his mother's kitchen. She had sat across from him when he was intentionally unpleasant and defiant in order to get to Broncks. He had made an impression, an imprint she would remember.

And for the first time he doubted his disguise.

With three, at most four, steps remaining.

What if after the nod, after maybe even a collegial *hello* between two police officers, she was to recognise him?

What would he be prepared to do for one hundred million kronor?

Everything.

Then they met. Glanced at each other, and it was as if she saw him without seeing him. She seemed focused, on her way somewhere. He nodded and she barely acknowledged it.

And the moment was over.

She passed by just about as the whining from the trolley's wheel faded, as he stopped in front of the door to the property room and the security camera that would view and approve him.

A last look in her direction.

She stopped too.

Hell.

She turned around.

Hell. Hell!

But not to look at him – to take out one of her plastic cards and swipe it through the reader that opened the next storage door, a sign with ARCHIVE above it.

It wasn't because of him that she'd stopped.

She hadn't recognised him.

He breathed excessively slow and regular breaths to force his body to be calm. He tried to simply look into the camera and hold up his identification until he heard the buzz of the door's lock and went in.

13:36:40

He checked the time – it had taken one minute and forty seconds to reach the property room. Twenty seconds in the plus column.

The room was full of brown envelopes and boxes and empty of people; no one before him in the queue but no one behind the delivery counter either. He looked into the basement room along shelf after shelf with seizures from ongoing investigations. Just as oxygen-poor and dusty as at yesterday's visit. And then there was a sound from a little way back into the room, impossible to see but in all likelihood considerably larger, more of a hall, where most of the evidence envelopes were stored. A sound like scraping, only smoother and more crisp – corrugated cardboard against corrugated cardboard, boxes rubbing their sides against each other. The sound recalled hands, in an attic storage room that rose and ran over like dough, rearranging piles of rubbish that must give way to new rubbish.

'Sorry, I had to stay back there for a little while. So you have a pick-up again today?'

The same suit jacket as yesterday, with a red shirt in a shade that went better with the sweaty cheeks. Oscarsson. Leo hadn't had access to the storage personnel's schedule, but was equally relieved and grateful to be greeted by the same face.

'Yes, today again.'

'Eriksson, right?'

Leo nodded.

294

'Peter Eriksson. And I have—'

'Old crimes, Eriksson, have to give way to new ones. Do you know how many seizures an investigation averages today?'

'Surely it depends. On how many shots are fired. On how many participated in the crime. On how many—'

'Exactly, Eriksson! Exactly so. It's crawling with things that every fucking detective thinks are crucial for precisely his or her investigation, from the crime scene and perpetrator's home and victim's home and . . . It's clear as hell that most of my time nowadays goes on moving boxes around in there to try to find more room.'

Leo let the indignant, hard-working man drone on so as not to seem stressed; not to risk questions about the requisition he'd printed out from the same stolen police computer as for the trial pick-up and right now slipped onto the wooden counter between them. With the name of the day's duty officer on the top line and all the property reference numbers on the bottom line.

'And, listen, Eriksson, with the workload we all have today, I really get it – as soon as one investigation is finished, the next one is going to begin and people don't have time to run down here and sort out used evidence.'

Leo gently pushed the requisition closer to the storage room keeper, even turning it around to be easier to read, and let his index finger wander among the numbers corresponding to the property he was here to pick up.

'Then you're going to be happy now, Oscarsson, because here I come to create a little space for you – ten packages, all at once.'

Then it was Oscarsson's index finger wandering from evidence numbers 2016-0407-BG1713, the first, to 2016-0407-BG1722, the last, before he looked up, almost a little guiltily.

'Well, sure, I saw it yesterday, but . . . for the record. Your identification.'

Leo also turned the leather case around the right way, even opening it for him, service card for Peter Eriksson in one plastic pocket and the metal police shield in the other.

'Thanks. And these, Eriksson, all of them, are in . . . Rosengrens safes. So something valuable, one can imagine?'

'That's what is so good. That neither you nor I know such things, what envelopes and packages contain. You give out sealed exhibits and I transport them. And we avoid being tempted to do anything stupid. Isn't that so?'

In the end Oscarsson took the requisition, *finally*, and limped away into a passage between shelves. As soon as he vanished into the rather large hall, where the safes stood, Leo checked the stopwatch.

13:38:50

Twenty-one minutes in here seemed plenty of time when he made the plan. But not any longer. The relief that it was Oscarsson, who recognised him and could reasonably shorten the identification process, transformed to stress during the detailed account of the workload when he, on the contrary, lengthened it. What should have taken thirty seconds had cost over two minutes.

And then, in the silence that arose when the man in the storage room stopped talking, Leo listened for what was hopefully going on in there. No longer a smooth and crisp sound, it was mechanical and heavy and he recognised it well. The shiny, thick steel rods abandoning their fastenings in a safe. Rosengrens safes had stood in every Swedish bank during the time he used considerably more force to get at considerably less money. Hearing the metallic clunking, the very symbol of a heist he had dreamed of and which he had somehow been planning for his whole life, gave him a feeling he so rarely approached – pure happiness.

Be what you do.

Breathe and live the intoxication.

Control the adrenalin relative to risk – let out a little at a time and always have enough remaining.

'Here comes the first – damn heavy, I'm guessing twenty kilos.'

Oscarsson was walking towards the counter with the package, the length of a newborn baby. He carried it like that – in his arms and gently.

'Eriksson – what the hell's in them?'

Tightly packed banknotes. Don't you know that?

'I told you. Not a clue.'

And twenty kilos – if every five hundred note weighs 0.96 grams – corresponds to more than ten million kronor.

More than one hundred million kronor divided over ten seizures of just about the same size.

Oscarsson plonked down the package on the counter and headed back towards the shelves.

'I can only carry one at a time – nine runs left.'

Wrapped in brown paper and well compressed with just as brown packing tape.

Then Leo reached for the safe, held on to it and took back what didn't exist: banknotes that were to be burned and had already been replaced with new ones yet still held their value. Evidence in an investigation that John Broncks once led, solved and was acclaimed for.

He placed it down at the bottom of one of his two reinforced boxes – nine packages to go, yes, he had calculated correctly. They would all fit, with a little space left over.

13:41:40

The watch, again.

Sixteen minutes remaining of the time he allotted for this stage of the plan. With a rather old man, who probably moved more slowly and chatted more with each new package. The risk of standing here side by side with the regular transport, the ones who *had* been instructed to pick up ten pieces of seized property, was now more than a risk – it was probable.

But what if in spite of everything he was lucky?

In the best-case scenario, he would be out in the police corridors with a head start of only a few minutes at the moment the main alarm went off. And with the trolley's whining wheel weighed down by two hundred kilos of banknotes, he would move neither especially quickly nor smoothly when they pursued him through the underground passages, on the way back to the courthouse and the world beyond.

THE HANDLE WAS actually a wheel, or a steering wheel. When Elisa took hold of it and turned it sideways, the next section of shelves glided slowly apart and revealed two metal walls filled from floor to ceiling with completed police investigations.

A room filled with a silence she found nowhere else.

Folders and boxes and bundles of papers that, gently on the ears, muffled decades of crimes preserved in chronological order. The end of this section was marked 'March 93–June 93' in typewritten text, and when she walked into the narrow aisle, her irritation gradually subsided. It had begun with Broncks's duplicity and was reinforced by that bloody whining from the trolley belonging to a colleague on the way to the property room. Down here in this room, she was always simply present, alert. Others usually complained about the bad air and lack of daylight, but she observed and experienced something different – harmony. To her, the archive of the City Police was the same as peace and security, rows of preliminary investigations that brought order to often devastating events – violence and chaos examined, evaluated and explained.

There were seven levels of shelves in each section and she searched for the target number, which was B 347/9317 according to the documentation in Sam Larsen's criminal record. Almost at the very back and very top she found it. She fetched the rolling step stool parked at the entrance, climbed up on the rubberised surface and pulled down the rather heavy light beige archive box. She carried it to the little corner with two simple desks and began to flick through the bundle lying on top, the technical report. The first few pages depicted a simple sketch of the forty-seven-square-metre summer cottage, followed by twenty-eight pages of black-and-white photographs of various exhibits – a touch grainy as crime scene technicians' photos often used to be. Two of them caught her interest. One with the caption

Photo no. 5: North-east angle from the sitting room into bedroom 1. A bed is situated against the far bedroom wall. Sheets, blankets, mattress

298

```
and pillow heavily stained with the victim's
blood.
```

and the second, a close-up of a considerably smaller object, with the caption

```
Photo no. 14: Knife manufactured by Rapala.
Found on the floor. Grooved thumb grip, marked
finger grooves. Tip of the knife is broken off.
```

Elisa turned the lampshade away and redirected the light. The bulb was altogether too strong. It should have been forty watts, not sixty. She studied the close-up of the knife, which reminded her of those she had seen as a child when they scaled the single perch after several hours of fishing.

Was this what Sam Larsen committed murder with?

And why – what connection did he have with the murder victim and to a plaintiff named Gunilla Broncks?

The medical examiner's report was considerably thinner, seven pages.

```
Cause of death: multiple organ failure caused by
direct sharp-force trauma to internal organs and
massive internal and external bleeding.
```

A pathologist's explicit language filled the image with substance.

```
The torso shows 27 stab wounds in total, of
which 21 have sharp borders and 6 have the
character of lacerations with ragged borders.
```

A story of a murderer who repeated death again and again.

```
In one of the stab wounds with a sharp border,
a broken-off tip of a knife-like object was
found - lodged under the sixth rib in the
mid-axillary line. This tip measured 2.5 x 3 cm.
```

What was it about the victim that had incited Sam Larsen to this utter fury?

The judgement in its entirety was truly a tome, two hundred and thirty pages, which she skipped over. The summary she had already read up in her office was sufficient for now. However, the preliminary investigation, nearly as thick, might contain more answers. And she didn't need to read further than the introduction – the one alarm call – before the most remarkable week in her life in the police force became even more remarkable. There she found the answer to why her closest colleague had consistently broken the police profession's code of honour – both by lying and in deed he had deliberately obstructed their joint investigation.

```
'Hello, my name is John Broncks. I want to
report a murder.'
```

Two emergency calls had been made about the same incident almost simultaneously – one by the plaintiff, Gunilla Ewa Broncks, from a neighbour's house to which she fled. The other was from the scene of the murder itself, by a not yet sixteen-year-old boy.

```
'I understand. I am going to help you. What
number are you calling from?'
'Zero, one, seven, one. Then eight, four, zero,
eight, four.'
'Are you sure the person is dead?'
'Yes. The entire bed is full of blood.'
'Do you know who the dead person is?'
'My pappa.'
```

Elisa let the heavy bundle sit for a moment. She suddenly saw what she had always found missing in him. That neutral appearance that kept the violence at a distance. An investigator's eyes and voice and movements that didn't reflect what he worked with every day.

She understood now how Broncks had decided that it would never get to him.

```
'Are you alone?'
'My mamma ran to the neighbour's. My big brother
is probably here somewhere. He was the one who
stabbed him. Several times.'
```

```
'Now I want you to listen to me, John - because
I want you to run immediately to the neighbour's
too. And wait there until the police come.'
'I don't need to hide any more. Pappa is dead.'
```

Yet he hadn't succeeded in running from it any longer.

The violence *had* got to him.

It had caught up.

Elisa closed the thick preliminary investigation and put it in the archive box together with the judgement and the medical examiner's report and the technical report. Now she understood. Now she had her facts. But it didn't matter. The bastard had tricked her deliberately and sabotaged their investigation. Why was completely irrelevant. It gave him a motive – but did not free him from responsibility.

She climbed up on the rolling step stool and pushed the archive box into its place at the far end on the seventh shelf. The room she liked so much had once again widened her perspective. And now she was on her way out of there to continue a police investigation in which she fought and pursued *two* sides for the first time: the perpetrator, who committed the actual robbery, and her own colleague, who committed a different crime that in her eyes was just as terrible – treachery.

ELISA SOMETHING WALKED by out in the corridor between Oscarsson's seventh and eighth retrieval, heading in the other direction. Leo was able to follow her purposeful steps on the monitor placed on a chair on the other side of the wooden counter. She must be finished with what she was doing. The only person, other than Broncks, who could have recognised him. And he was still the only visitor to the property room. No one on behalf of another investigation had joined the queue to retrieve something from the thousands of pieces of evidence lying down here, packaged in brown envelopes or cartons.

Then, the loud panting.

That meant that Oscarsson was approaching, carrying the ninth twenty-kilo package in his arms. Bright red. Soaking wet temples, as well as forehead and neck, sweat forming a shiny film over the skin. Even the brown wrapping paper was damp from being pressed hard against the checked shirt. A thud when, without the strength to resist, he dropped the box onto the counter. The grey suit jacket had been lying there since the fourth run.

'The next . . .'

The man in the storage room was breathing heavily, clipping his words in the insufficient, dry air.

'. . . to last.'

In spite of his age and physique, he had so far kept a reasonable, steady pace. Once he stopped *talking* about how tough it was to work and actually started to work, each trip had taken him almost exactly one minute and forty-five seconds.

13:55:30

Nineteen of the twenty-one minutes Leo estimated for this part of the plan were used up.

'Fine, Oscarsson, then you can take care of the tenth straight away.'

If the man in the storage room didn't take a sudden break, if he also retrieved the final piece of seized property at the same speed as the others, and after Leo signed in the right spot and sealed his own considerably larger moving boxes, the time period would certainly have been exceeded – but not enough to run directly into the regular, scheduled transport.

A coup was still possible.

'Right, Oscarsson? While you are already moving, I mean. Then it's my job to drag them further.'

'All right. The la . . . st. The ten . . . th. When I . . .'

There was a Coca-Cola bottle halfway filled with water on one end of the counter. And the man in the storage room brightened up when he saw it, like a dear friend he had not seen since filling up in connection with the fifth package.

'. . . have emptied this.'

He started to drink, the seconds ticking away and anxiety throbbing inside Leo. Stress that could not, not, not be allowed to be seen on the outside. He had hurried Oscarsson as much as he dared without risking suspicion. He couldn't also urge him not to drink.

'Fluid out, fluid in. Isn't that right, Eriksson?'

The storage room man winked and just as he vanished for the last time into the passage between the shelves, Leo began to feel vibrating in his uniform jacket's one inner pocket. He answered.

'Leo, they're coming now! They are . . .' Sam. '. . . early. You must get out, Leo! Now!'

He heard Oscarsson rooting around and breathing heavily, far in there.
You must get out.

No.

Not yet.

If he were to break off now, with nine of ten pieces of seized property without signing for the receipt and saying goodbye, Oscarsson would sound the alarm immediately. That was an even greater risk than waiting for the tenth package. He turned away from the counter and whispered.

'I'm staying for the last one. I'll have it in less than one minute.'

He turned to the counter and the aisles between the shelves were just as empty as before.

He had lied to Sam. To calm him down.

'OK, Leo, then I'm off now, down to the underground.'

But he hadn't lied to himself. He heard that Oscarsson had just reached the safe and he knew how much time it took for him to lift it and carry it to the front.

In spite of this, he kept whispering.

'See you at the meeting place. Good luck.'

Then he counted the seconds so as not to come apart inside. Sixty-three until he heard the heavy panting. All the way to the counter, and it banged significantly when Oscarsson let go of the twenty-kilo package and allowed ten million in five hundred kronor banknotes to fall onto the wooden counter.

'And I sign – here somewhere?'

Leo hurried to pick up the pen and the storage room man's breathing was now so laboured that he couldn't speak at all. He just extended a white paper and a crooked, trembling index finger pointing to one of the blank lines.

Peter Eriksson.

The signature certainly looked about the same as last time.

Then he moved the tenth package from the counter and down into the last empty space in the top carton on the trolley. He folded and wove the four cardboard flaps together. Then a quick look at the watch.

13:59:10

One minute and thirty seconds over the time, while the regular transport had arrived five minutes early.

He had to get out of there.

'Can you be so kind as to let me out?'

Oscarsson nodded, as silent as he was tired. He pressed the button on the wall until the thick metal door to the corridor clicked. The two moving boxes sat firmly together thanks to the weight, and two hundred kilos helped the whining wheel to stop whining. Leo pushed the door open with his back, then a powerful jerk of the trolley over the sill and a last look at Oscarsson, who was resting, leaning forward onto the counter with the whole weight of his body distributed on shaking arms.

He was alone, again.

In the middle of the corridor on the first of three legs.

The first crossing was waiting up ahead about forty metres. Right, and no one in this corridor would be able to see him any longer – the real transport always arrived via the west entrance. And it was so easy to walk. Once, with a hand trolley he had prised a four-hundred-kilo kitchen boiler out of a renovation project and over an uneven garden. This was half the weight and fully pumped-up tyres on even concrete made the motion less unsteady. It felt as if he was flying forward.

Until he heard footsteps.

Just before he was going to turn off right and vanish behind the concrete wall for the next leg.

He turned around. And there, at the other end of the corridor – he guessed eight or nine metres away – were two uniformed policemen, also with a trolley.

They would be there in less than a minute. And in about another minute – after a procedure at the wooden counter with exactly the same request for ten twenty-kilo packages, which one of their colleagues had just now given out – the alarm would be sounded.

JOHN BRONCKS MOVED cautiously three, four, five tree trunks forward, still hidden, in order to see without being seen. Fifteen minutes earlier, all the anxiety, tension and anticipation made his heart beat out of rhythm – he couldn't move and his chest cramped up when he couldn't release the accumulated discomfort. That was when Leo Dûvnjac and his father should have arrived at the poorly painted barn over there filled with automatic weapons. When he should have found out if Sam was involved to the extent he feared. When he should have called the head of the National Task Force and requested an immediate emergency response.

Emptiness, that's what he felt. Disappointment. Like a child who waited and wished and counted down to the present in shiny paper and curled ribbon, which was then opened and didn't contain what it should have.

Something wasn't right.

The Leo Dûvnjac he'd pursued for such a long time, who confounded the entire Swedish police corps – the whole of Swedish society – began a bank robbery exactly at the planned moment every time and carried out a job in exactly the estimated time. And his greatest job ever was there in the barn, military weapons for a reasonably large army, which would also bring in more than ever when they were sold. The Leo Dûvnjac he analysed and interrogated would never come unprepared or let the buyer wait.

Then there was a chirp in Broncks's ear.

'To all units.'

In the earpiece connected to the communications radio hanging on his belt.

'Suspected robbery at the property room Kronoberg.'

And he stood entirely still.

A robbery – inside the police station?

'National alert issued at 14.01.'

Emptiness. Disappointment.
It was slowly starting to gain meaning.

'Perpetrator in his thirties, height 190, brown eyes and shaved head.'

A major crime, an aggravated robbery, about twenty kilometres away, being committed at the same time Leo Dûvnjac should have committed a major crime, here.
This was a modus operandi Broncks recognised.

'May be wearing police uniform and possess forged police identification in the name Peter Eriksson.'

That was why he didn't arrive in time for this job, Broncks thought, because he was on time for a different one. I found out only because *he* wanted me to find out. The guns in the barn are here only so that *I* am here.
Diversion. False lead. Decoy.
Just like when he planted a bomb at the Central Station, lured the police there and at the same time robbed two banks many kilometres away.
And brown eyes, shaved head, police uniform, police identification?
Disguise. Façade. Escape as if by magic.
Just like when he parked two cars, one on each side of a community, and forced them to search in two directions.
Leo Dûvnjac.

THE FINAL STEPS to the plate-metal door. Leo leaned the trolley temporarily on its two feet and it stood both upright and steady while he drew the access card through the slot of the card reader.

Nothing.

No blinking green light, no metallic click of the door's lock.

Shit.

He drew it through one more time, but the door separating the police station's passage from the courthouse was still shut. He rubbed the piece of plastic against the fabric of the uniform jacket and drew it through again.

Fuck. Fuck. Fuck.

The regular transport had only half a corridor left and then the ID check and they would be let into the property room, then confusion, then a mistake becoming clear.

That fucking card, it has to work.

He turned around. Still no one behind him. His movement through the last two sections of the passage had been entirely without any encounters and also quick as the trolley – thanks to the heavy load – rolled silently on the concrete.

A new attempt.

The access card into the slot. Swipe.

And now the blinking green light.

The metallic click.

His back pushed against the plate-metal door as he opened it, both hands on the trolley, and with another jerk over the doorsill, which was slightly wider than the one in the property room. He was inside. On the right side of the underground entrance to the courthouse.

The lift was not particularly large and it was crowded with two huge boxes. He took off the police uniform, revealing blue overalls. The cap had been in one pocket and now he unfolded it; PORTER in capital letters on the peak. There were two floors between the ground floor and the main entrance of the courthouse, a sufficiently long ride in a lift to be able

308

to hide the police uniform in the box on top. He stepped out into a sombre, echoing stone building, kept walking to the heavy iron door and out into daylight and fresh air. A deep sigh of relief while he looked around, searching for the lorry that should be parked there just outside.

He had made it to the meeting place.

But there was no one to meet him.

Rapid glances, first towards Kungsholms Street and the underground entrance in that direction and then towards Bergs Street and the underground entrance that way.

Sam – where the fuck are you?

BRONCKS WALKED OVER the last tufts of grass, then a jump over the marshy ditch and still another over the simple wooden fence to the gravel road.

He tried to shake it off; the thought that got stuck was now moving around inside him with each new step. *Suspected robbery at the property room Kronoberg.* The thought connected to this exact point in time, Thursday at 14.00, and also to the point in time fourteen days ago when the judgement in what was called the Robbery of the Century had become binding. The two points in time were linked – bound together by one hundred and three million kronor that were no longer needed as evidence and in a few hours would be destroyed.

You bastard.

You took my brother and manipulated him into committing crimes that carry sentences up to life. You took the robbery loot that in some way became my redress as a policeman.

Then you led me on a wild goose chase to this place. Dressed as a policeman, in my *security and pride, in* my *clothes, you attacked both the heart of* my *family and the heart of* my *profession with a single blow.*

And that was enough right there, right then that he couldn't walk any longer.

So John Broncks started to run.

Towards the fucking barn.

THE MONOTONOUS HONKING increased in intensity the closer the lorry backed up towards the façade of Stockholm's courthouse. While Sam lowered the tail lift, Leo grabbed both handles of the trolley, rolled it on board and pressed the button for it to glide up again. The two reinforced boxes filled with five-hundred-kronor banknotes were identical to all the other brown boxes already placed in the truck's cargo space. Then he jumped out again, closed the back door and opened the door to the driver's cab on the passenger side.

'Drive.'

Slowly along Scheele Street, left at the first crossing onto Hantverkar Street, towards the city. He guessed a quarter of an hour, perhaps twenty minutes in inner city traffic to the multi-storey car park, then the same distance to Värta Harbour.

'You were late, Sam.'

'I was *delayed* because the underground train was late. One train at the platform while the next one was waiting in the tunnel. I couldn't throw away the bag with the other police uniform before both were gone.'

A nearly full bus halted in front of them and a long queue of passengers at the bus stop were making things difficult and taking their time while they were boarding and trying to find a seat. But Sam sat patiently as they had agreed and waited without trying to overtake it.

'But what about you? How did it go for you?' he asked.

Then the bus finally closed its doors and they could continue, past City Hall and the white archipelago ships with their reflection in the waters of Lake Mälaren.

'How did it go?' asked Leo.

'Yeah?'

'There are two hundred kilos of banknotes back there.'

JOHN BRONCKS RAN along the deserted gravel road, aware that he was lured here and that weapons in the red barn constituted the bait. Just as on the previous occasion, he opted to bypass the large doors with the heavy-duty padlock and kept going to the smaller entrance on the long side. The same rebar lay on the border where gravel became grass. He used it to prise off the metal hoop the smaller padlock was fastened in, jerked the door open and went in.

Everything looked as it did the day before. Nothing appeared to have changed.

He approached the lorry and took away the rubber cord holding the tarpaulin in place. And the cargo were untouched. The terracotta tiles covering the bed and walls of the lorry were still there, just as were two hundred stacked automatic weapons, decorated on top with a bomb in a wooden box.

'Underground station Rådhuset temporarily closed off.'

A new warning.

He took out the earpiece and unfastened the communications radio from the belt to be able to hear better.

'Police uniform located on the track adjacent to platform.
Perpetrator likely inside the underground system.'

He wasn't the only one completely taken in. Those who found the uniform and shut down train traffic, and who were now reporting it on the radio, were also utterly duped. They didn't know what he knew – that Leo Dûvnjac's criminal mind operated just like this. That it wasn't a robber escaping in the underground system that they were chasing, but rather someone who had shed his skin and become what he had always dreamed of – someone who carried out the grand heist. That they were looking in the wrong place, where he *wanted* them to search, where he *allowed* them to find the shed skin.

Broncks picked up his mobile telephone to call the directors of the various task forces in turn, who now must know who they were looking for and that they should therefore continue in a different direction.

But he never managed to call the number. Because his own telephone rang first.

And for a moment the emptiness that became violation that became anger turned into emptiness again.

You? Now?

He nearly shouted his name.

'Sam!'

But he got no reply.

'Sam, for fuck's sake, say something. I *see* that it's you! If you only understood how happy I am. I have tried to reach you lots of times, and I—'

'I see that. It's on the screen of the mobile, Broncks. Forty-three missed calls.'

That voice? On Sam's phone?

'And so you still haven't understood that your brother doesn't want to talk to you?'

The voice belonged to Leo Dûvnjac.

'And when *he* doesn't want to – I get to do it instead.'

The noise of city traffic. He heard that.

John Broncks pressed the handset harder against his ear.

The other telephone was in a car – that muffled sound that always comes from a badly insulated car.

'And by the way, Broncks? If we are going to talk now, I want us to see each other. Eye contact. If you turn half to the left and look up at an angle to the corner above the doors, you will find a camera.'

John Broncks did it. And there was a lens of a very small webcam.

'Good. Now I can see you, Broncks. You seem to have lost weight. And you're unshaven as hell. Aren't you well? Perhaps a bit much to do?'

Provocations. He didn't give a shit about them. He couldn't afford to be provoked. He knew that more would soon be coming that required his strength and that the piece of rubbish on the other end of the line didn't call to insult him.

'And since you've got all the way to my little truck, I assume that you have also realised that I'm not likely to come to meet you today. That I've had something else going on. And it's too late for you to do anything about it.'

John Broncks stared into the lens, the eye representing another eye. Only now he saw that its shell was painted red in the same shade as the rest of the barn wall.

'But you shouldn't be sad about it, Broncks. Even though you didn't get to meet me, you're going to get to keep all the guns I let you find. That is, if I don't happen to see anything in the camera that I don't want to see, or hear something on the police radio that I don't want to hear.'

Broncks wondered if Sam was sitting there next to Dûvnjac in the car, whether he was also listening to this, also watching him.

'So I don't want to hear either my name or Sam's name on the police radio. If there's a fucking police message, the guns will be destroyed. If the camera is turned off and the monitor goes dark, the guns will be destroyed.'

A calmness turning into unpleasantness. The same calm that every security guard and bank official described they were addressed with during robbery after robbery.

'So now, Broncks, you son of a bitch, you'll do what you liked so much before: acting as a private individual and not as a policeman.'

A brief clicking sound, followed by electronic silence. He had hung up.

John Broncks stood with the telephone in his hand, staring at a barn wall. And maybe he should feel as annihilated as the calm voice assumed.

But he didn't.

Because during the absurd monologue, in which demands were stipulated and guidelines drawn up, a new thought was beginning to take shape. How he could respond to it. He would not do what the man watching him through the camera lens expected.

THE FRONT OF the lorry was very close to the patterned concrete wall with gaps wide enough to see through – the NK building's brown façade. The pavement and street could be seen down below if they leaned forward.

That's what they saw from the top level of the multi-storey car park, level 6, in the heart of Stockholm. The higher up, the fewer the vehicles, and so the fewer car owners who might risk encountering something they shouldn't. Behind the truck, they changed from the blue work overalls to regular jeans, shirts and jackets – clothes that would blend in on the journey across the Baltic Sea. In the lorry's cargo space, the contents of the two full moving boxes were divided between four large suitcases. Then they moved the suitcases to the next vehicle, a grey Volvo – a car that would blend in for the trip between the city centre and Värta Harbour. While Sam held tightly onto the wheel and steered around and around on a narrow roundabout taking them level by level down to the ground, Leo sank down in the passenger seat and checked the webcams. Empty. Both on the outside and inside of the barn. When he looked at the last recorded sequence, from thirteen minutes ago, he saw Broncks leave the farm and disappear. The cop bastard had done exactly as he had been instructed. He hadn't spread the forbidden names over the police radio, hadn't sabotaged the camera and hadn't called for backup.

They were down and drove out of the concrete merry-go-round into the daylight and afternoon traffic and shopping tourists who were getting in the way of stressed-out suits.

Four and a half hours until departure.

To a new life.

THE NEWLY VARNISHED parquet floors no one had tramped on; the chalk-white ceilings that absorbed the light nicely; the walls, which still had no stories to tell – Vincent liked the feeling of being in an entirely freshly renovated flat and able to hand over a normal new start. It was so completely different from starting over in a prison cell, or after a prison sentence in a transitional flat arranged by a consultant at the Probation Office.

He drove here for the very last time to ensure that he hadn't missed any details in any of the rooms or forgotten improvements. Then, unable to go, he stood there in a place that would soon be furnished with smells, lives and movement. Love and conflicts had not yet reached these rooms and taken root.

And he knew why it was so difficult to go.

Out there, beyond the windows of the flat, the opposite was residing right now.

A little while ago he heard on the radio that a robbery had been carried out *inside* the police station, a unique robbery presumably involving large amounts. A heist. Leo had always talked about this and, over the last few days, had tried to get one of his younger brothers to participate. He even sat right there on a toolbox to badger him about it.

Vincent ran two fingertips over the knuckles of his right hand, which were still sore and discoloured.

A final look at the shiny new place before he locked the door with the keys he would hand over tomorrow. When he was on his way down the stairs, he heard footsteps on the way up. He cursed that he'd stayed a little too long; now he would run into the couple who owned the flat and who perhaps were here to look and plan and mentally move in. He wasn't in the mood for that, for small talk, not today.

It wasn't the middle-aged childless couple. It was the neighbour, the old man with his hair in a ponytail, smelling of turpentine and oil paint. They had seen each other nearly every day since he started work and not a word the entire time. They mutely nodded to each other for the last time.

316

His van was where he usually parked it, in one of the spaces belonging to the housing cooperative. As he approached, he saw someone standing there leaning on the bonnet of the van. A man in his forties. Leather jacket and jeans. A face he recognised even though he hadn't seen it in six years.

'Hello, Vincent. I tried reaching you by phone. You didn't answer. So I thought I'd come here.'

John Broncks.

The cop who led the investigation of the bank robbers popularly called the Military League.

'I don't answer if I don't recognise the number. And hey – you're crapping on my car.'

'It doesn't matter. Because you aren't going to use it right now. You're coming with me.'

'I'm not going anywhere with you. I did my time. And I haven't committed a bloody crime since. You know that. At least your cop colleague does, who came around here fishing for alibis.'

Broncks struck the side of the van a couple of times with his hand.

'You work here?'

'Yeah.'

'And it's going rather well? For you? For the company?'

He hit the metal of the van again, this time clearly on the logo, V CONSTRUCTION.

'Yeah.'

'In that case – would you rather we come here and pick you up with uniforms and a marked car? Do your customers know your history?'

Fucking idiot.

Leave me in peace.

He wanted to scream. Or to sit in the van and back over the fucking cop who was threatening the one thing that couldn't happen in a job built on recommendations.

'Listen – that's not OK. What the hell are you doing?'

'That's the sort of thing you get to enjoy when you've done time. Sometimes you get to ride in a patrol car and answer questions. Routine. Ask all your buddies from the slammer.'

Back over him, drive forward again and back over him one more time.

'What's this about?'

'We'll talk about it in the car.'

'No – *what's it about?*'

'Your brother. Leo.'

But a scene that attracted attention tomorrow at the formal handover of keys and the final bill . . . that didn't feel good at all.

'I'll just make a phone call.'

Vincent took a step away from the car and pressed one of his few preprogrammed numbers on the keypad.

'Hey – you fucking better not be calling your brother. If you are, you'll be guilty of a crime, you understand that, right?'

Then he held up the mobile close to Broncks's face so it would be easy to read MAMMA on the screen.

'Is that a crime too?'

He turned around, waited for the signal to be sent and lowered his voice.

'Mamma?'

'Yes?'

'I don't think you should count on me for dinner this evening.'

'No? Vincent – why not?'

'I'm sorry.'

'But I told you that Leo isn't coming. You don't need to feel the way you did about the lunch. I understood that, and that's why it will be only you and me.'

A step further away and now he was whispering.

'Mamma, something feels . . . not right.'

She didn't reply. Perhaps she didn't hear.

'Listen, Mamma, this, it—'

'What? Vincent, what doesn't feel right?'

'I'm . . . standing here with a policeman. In front of my workplace. That's why I can't come. He wants me to go in for an interview.'

'What do you mean a policeman?'

'The same one who investigated the bank robberies.'

She hesitated again. He could hear her breathing and knew she was upset.

'I don't understand at all. You've done well. Paid off your reparations and taken your prison sentence. They should . . . they should leave you in peace!'

'It isn't about me.'

318

Now he was the one breathing audibly, hesitating.

'It's about Leo.'

The gigantic passenger ferry was still in the water at the quay, furthest out at the new pier at Värta Harbour. Four hours until departure. Three hours until they could go on board and step into a luxury cabin on the upper deck with a clear view as the Baltic Sea came to an end. They were going to spend the time in between at the hotel located just a few hundred metres away, in front of which they were now stopping. At a reception desk deserted in the afternoon, they picked up the room key and continued to the lift. They stood together in it on the way up, a space reminiscent of the cramped cell where they'd planned the heist and felt the hunger. It was even more pleasant surrounded by four suitcases loaded with banknotes.

The car turned right at the crossing at Fridhemsplan towards Drottningholms Road, not left towards the police station at Kronoberg, where they should be heading.

'Where are we going?'

'I told you. You're going to answer some questions.'

Vincent turned around so he could see more. It was the first time he'd been in the front seat of a police car and could move freely. He had been handcuffed and in the back seat on every previous occasion.

But it felt just as wrong.

'Yes. You are going to interview me. *At the police station.*'

John Broncks shrugged his shoulders. The bastard actually did that.

'As you perhaps know, a thing or two happened there today. It is roped off and rather in confusion.'

'Well? Sure – I heard it on the radio. But we are on our way *out* of the city.'

'Yeah, we are.'

Vincent looked around at both sides of the road when somewhere past Thorildsplan, they turned onto Essingeleden, the motorway going south.

'This isn't right. What the hell do you think I've done? Tell me! And

319

I'll give you an answer right away! I have kept a journal with entries for every hour of my parole, which ends in less than a month. You will never get me!'

He turned to Broncks. The policeman had sat there in the driver's seat, silently staring straight ahead since they left the building with the newly renovated flat.

'That's good, Vincent. Smart.'

When they came out of the first tunnel, he accelerated.

'But it won't help you one bit now. This is about the crimes you committed long before you started to keep your journal.'

A waiting room, that's what the hotel room was. Temporary shelter in the final stage of a robbery getaway as they waited for the departure of the passenger ferry, which they could see through the window.

Leo was sitting on an orange sofa, tucked in between a wardrobe and an oversized floor lamp. He took both the ferry tickets out of the inner pocket of the jacket intended to blend in and put them on the coffee table. The name on the first one matched a driving licence used three days ago when the milkman Johan Martin Erik Lundberg sailed through a roadblock, while the name on the second ticket matched a police identification used late that afternoon when the uniformed Peter Eriksson picked up ten boxes of evidence at the police station's confiscations room. Then he pulled out of his trouser waistband one of the police service pistols he'd bought in a cold basement from a fixer called Sullo, which he had later pressed against the cop Broncks's temple when the church clock approached midnight and which he had just carried unseen during the entire duration of the robbery.

While Sam drew the curtains to prevent anyone looking in from windows on the other side of the street, Leo reached for one of the suitcases, opened it and took out the police radio wedged in between two packages of bundled banknotes. And he listened. Constant radio traffic revolving around a robbery inside the police station. The entire area around Kronoberg was closed off and the hunt was now focused on the underground system, where a police uniform was found on the rails in an easterly direction.

The time to departure had shrunk, and so had the distance to the ferry.

Champagne would soon be rolled into Cabin 571, uncorked and toasted with.

'Here. All the way, Vincent. This is where I want you to stand.'

John Broncks waved with both hands to Vincent, who was still standing at the doorway to the barn.

'Then take a good hold on the tarpaulin on your side of the lorry, as you help me to pull it up.'

'I still don't understand what we're doing here. What you're up to. What kind of fucking police work is this?'

'The best kind. When you even have evidence and can send down the criminal.'

'Listen, if you want to interrogate me at a fucking farm, I can go along with it, if it gets you going. But do it, dammit! So I can get back. I have dinner plans this evening.'

The late daylight seeped in through the many cracks that time had carved out, but, in spite of the play of light, the barn was nearly dark in places and Broncks switched on the makeshift ceiling light.

'Come on now, Vincent, aren't you at least a little curious about what's on the floor of the lorry? That's what we came here for. That's what I wanted to show you.'

'Do you think I'm stupid? I don't fucking plan to put my fingerprints there.'

Broncks smiled as he loosened the plastic rope alone and threw up the back part of the plastic tarpaulin. A curtain was lifted and a scene revealed. Since Vincent was in the line of sight, with a clear view of the lorry, it was easy to read his reaction. He understood exactly what was lying on the floor of the lorry stacked in a pile.

'Nearly two hundred automatic weapons, Vincent, that you and your brothers stole but were never charged for. So they're lying . . . here. And can you imagine? When I randomly chose one of them and dusted it with my zephyr brush, it showed traces from you! So you don't need to worry at all about fingerprints. We already have them.'

Quiet. Not a word.

Vincent's body seemed entirely at rest, if it were not for his eyes, pupil and iris, which conveyed information when he realised what he saw. The weak odour, which he smelled already as he stood at the barn's doorway: guns oiled to protect them against moisture and time.

'And now, Vincent, we are going to pose the questions we came here for. But not to you. To your brother.'

———

Leo turned the volume down on the police radio – the voices running around tunnels he had directed them to, even more lost than they had a clue about. And when he went on to a new inspection of the webcams monitoring the other false lead, he saw that Camera A registered a vehicle. Heading *to* the barn. He played the sequence again. Broncks's car. Broncks in the driver's seat. And next to him – another person.

Another cop.

Broncks, for fuck's sake – it doesn't fucking matter how many colleagues you take there. You have already lost me. And now you are going to lose your weapons trove.

With the mobile still in his hand, he dialled up the eight-digit number that didn't reach another subscriber, but rather the telephone at the same place as the Broncks bastard himself. It was coupled to a battery that would release a thermite bomb. One key left. The green phone icon. But before he pressed it, before the explosion, he took one last look at Camera B for a clear image of exactly where the two cops were moving so as not to risk injury.

Broncks was standing next to the lorry and had just loosened a rubber rope and revealed its bed. He was talking to someone. It wasn't possible to see the other cop, but for some reason they were lingering at the doorway beyond the reach of the lens.

Broncks was standing too close to the bomb.

Leo rested his trigger finger in the air. He had to wait for him to move. Which happened only a couple of seconds later, as Broncks started to walk towards the other cop on his way out of the picture.

Now, Broncks, you are going to experience how it feels when three thousand degrees melts two hundred automatic weapons down to metal paste.

His thumb was hovering over the final button – when the telephone rang.

On the display the image from the security camera changed to the name that shouldn't be there.

You?

He could almost feel a long embrace in a newly renovated flat with someone who had hit his knuckles until they were bloody.

'Vincent?'

Breathing.

'Vincent . . . little brother? Hello? Well, say something . . . Why are you calling now?'

'He's not the person calling.'

That voice. On Vincent's phone?

'I told you . . .'

The voice belonging to John Broncks.

'. . . if you get my brother involved, I'll get your brother involved.'

Leo saw Broncks come into the picture again, a black pistol in his hand. He was pressing it against the back, between the shoulder blades, of someone who was also on the way into the picture.

Vincent.

'As you perhaps see on your camera, Leo, I'm standing here with your brother. I just arrested him for a crime of terror with a probable life sentence.'

Four metres, if Leo were to guess. From Broncks and Vincent to the lorry.

Sufficient safety clearance for detonation.

'You understand, Leo, that his fingerprints are on every single weapon. Yes, like yours. As are your middle brother's.'

So in ten minutes there'll be no evidence left.

'No other police officers at all are aware of this place. Or that we are here. So I can imagine, Leo, removing both your brothers' fingerprints and only keeping yours.'

Because now, Broncks, I'm holding my fingertip above the icon again.

'If you also come here, that is. If you give yourself up.'

'Hey, Broncks, you bastard?'

'Do it and I'll let your little brother go.'

'You know there's a bomb in the car, right?'

'Yeah. And I'm certain you won't set it off as long as I'm standing here with your little brother.'

I'll press it down now. The tip of my finger. And, Broncks, it's no ordinary bomb like you think. It's a stationary melting furnace. A bomb to live through – not to be killed by.

He pressed the green phone icon down.

He watched the image on the mobile telephone's display.

And – nothing happened.

He pressed it again. And again. But the lorry remained, still intact. No

323

biting light from hot thermite raining down over the guns out of the container on the roof.

The only change in the picture was when John Broncks came close to the camera lens and looked right into it.

'You have a decision to take, Leo. Your little brothers – or you.'

––––––––

'Leo?'

A dud.

'Leo – what the fuck are you doing?'

Sam was able to catch up with him in the short hallway, just before the hotel door.

The bomb should have detonated. A chemical reaction between aluminium, hematite and iron oxide should have given off heat sufficient to eliminate the false lead.

Something had gone really fucking wrong.

'Hey, Leo? We agreed to stay here until the ferry's departure.'

'I have to go there, Sam.'

They had both seen and listened to the same sequence of images – nothing of what just happened needed to be explained.

'I *have to* go there and detonate the bomb manually.'

Mamma wanted them to tear apart the bonds. He had done that and said farewell, but all the same it didn't happen.

They were never broken.

'Otherwise my brothers will get life.'

'You *can't* leave here!'

'I'll make it in time.'

'I understand how *my* fucking brother thinks. Fuck you. Fuck you with the guns. Fuck you with the guns when you escape with the loot from the Robbery of the Century. He'll exchange it for your brothers every day of the week. If you go now, Leo, it will go to hell! And you won't come back!'

Leo looked into the hotel room, past Sam's broad body. He'd placed what he needed there on the table.

'You're right, Sam.'

A few rapid steps and he picked up the ticket then the pistol.

'You go on board the ferry when they let down the bridge. I promise I'll come knocking on the cabin door.'

He left and Sam no longer tried to stop him. That's why he turned around in the hotel corridor. It seemed as if he was obliged to say it.

'Sam?'

'Yeah?'

'I'm sorry. But I can't guarantee your brother will be alive when it's over.'

LEO STOPPED FOR the first time to check the cameras when he had come so close that he could see the abandoned farm from the gravel road. Camera A, mounted on the fence, showed nothing. So no police reinforcements had arrived via the entrance for cars. Camera B, from inside the barn, was black. Broncks had taken it down or covered it over. The head start had been lost the moment Vincent was put on display.

He left the car to go the last section on foot. In a wide circle he passed through surrounding forest and approached the barn from the back, making certain that no police reinforcements had arrived from that direction either.

He would destroy the past so that the past would not ruin his brothers.

The final stretch, to the area of the barn without windows and doors. He was now certain that Broncks was acting on his own. Not just because there was no sign of other people here – but also a decision, taken by the Swedish police command, which legitimised an arrest built on his younger brother being used as blackmail material, could never happen.

It was quiet outside, and when he laid his ear against the wooden wall, quiet in there too.

This operation was one hundred per cent John Broncks's own. And alone, man to man, Leo was convinced that he would win every time, with or without weapons. But with Vincent as Broncks's life insurance, and a bomb that would have to be triggered manually so that no traces would remain, all under the same roof, the outcome was not as obvious as he let Sam believe. Also, as the clock was ticking towards the ferry's departure, there was no time for rational plans. That's why he simply walked around the barn and opened the door.

'I'm here now, Broncks.'

It looked just as it did when he left the place for what he had assumed was the last time. A single enormous space with a small loft at the very back and a lorry parked in the middle.

'And *I* am here – behind the truck.'

That really was the cop's slightly cheerful voice coming out from the other side of the vehicle's body. Leo pulled his arm back, his hand under his jacket, fingers against the pistol's grip. And while he slowly moved forward, the bead, the sight post sticking up a little at the tip of the barrel, was chafing against the skin of the curve of his back.

'Where is my brother?'

'You'll see him if you walk around the truck.'

He let go of the gun and the front sight continued to chafe. He must take in the whole picture. Vincent's position. Orient himself and then act.

He walked cautiously around the vehicle.

He saw Broncks first, sitting in front of the simple workbench that he himself had sat at while making the thermite bomb. As he kept on for a few more metres and went around the front of the lorry, he also saw Vincent standing next to the passenger door, unnaturally still.

A chain ran between his little brother's right hand and the handle of the lorry door.

Locked.

Near the truck and the evidence Leo had come to destroy.

'Just do as I say. Then everything will be fine.'

Broncks spoke calmly, with even breathing. He had the upper hand so far. Vincent was staring, bent forward towards the barn's worn floorboards. He didn't meet his eyes and was showing no emotions.

'Put your hands behind your head, Dûvnjac. Then walk slowly to me.'

The pig held the service revolver in the hand he raised above his head. A clear gesture to instruct and at the same time note that the visitor should give up any potential plans to do anything not well thought out.

'Vincent, brother . . . How is it going?'

Leo tried to make contact with Vincent's evasive eyes. They left the floor and met his.

'Listen, Vincent – you'll soon be out of here.'

Visible anger. Anger, not fear.

'I promise, Vincent.'

Leo turned again to Broncks.

'Hey you, *John* – how the fuck had you imagined this would go?'

While he was waiting for an answer, he glanced cautiously at his little brother and the lorry. Cutting the chain of handcuffs would be difficult without the right tool. It should be possible, on the other hand, to simply prise loose the lorry door's handle with the appropriate weapon.

A weakness. That's what he was looking for now.

The weakness that always reveals a clear possibility in the moment and that you don't know you have before it arises.

'You promised that my little brother would go free. Can you guarantee that?'

The policeman raised his pistol, still without speaking, and pointed it right at Leo's chest.

'Broncks, what the hell – do you intend . . . to shoot me? Then you'd have to shoot Vincent too. You already have quite a lot here you're going to have a problem explaining. Are you going to add two corpses to that?'

John Broncks seemed to smile a little as he got up and pulled another pair of handcuffs out of his jacket pocket.

'There won't be any shooting here at all – if you just kindly put one cuff around your right wrist.'

He tossed the cuffs through the air in a wide arc.

'You'll fasten the other cuff to the door handle I have locked Vincent to.'

Two brothers chained to a vehicle containing an unexploded bomb. All that was needed for everything to go to hell was an electrical impulse, which in turn would set off a chemical reaction that generated heat – an incredible amount of heat that melted down iron and burned skin and tissue. A white shock of several thousand degrees.

'If you want to get me alive, Broncks . . .'

Leo let the handcuffs fall and they thudded lightly on the soft wooden floor.

'. . . let my brother go, and explain to me how you thought you'd hold him outside the investigation.'

John Broncks moved closer and stopped when he reached Vincent.

Halfway.

'When *you* are handcuffed too – then I'll let him go. But he can't go directly from here. First he is going to help me unload all the guns. Then he and I, together, are going to wipe down barrel after barrel, stock after stock, trigger after trigger. Except for the very last one, which you'll leave your fingerprints on. You have my word, Dûvnjac.'

'Your . . . *word*?'

'My word. And my brother. Right? You know I'm alone here. And you've likely figured out why. Because right up to the end I thought I could prevent Sam from working with you. And so I have committed a shitload of violations.'

'Mistakes, you mean?'

'Call them whatever the fuck you want.'

'Mistakes that could cost you your job and which now you want to exchange for my brother? My silence for your silence?'

Leo bent down to pick up the handcuffs.

'So you think that's fair, Broncks? That I'll be doing life while you keep your job?'

He tossed the cuffs and chain back to John Broncks, not in a wide arc, but rather in a straight line. A projectile at the face. In a reflex motion, Broncks raised his hands up to protect himself, enough of a distraction for Leo to get the chance he had waited for since he stepped into the barn.

He crouched like a predator to hurl his body against the policeman's legs, with his strength gathered. All the force, all the weight and all the explosive power would hit the target, overthrowing the man who stood in the way of his escape plan, while he himself was in the line of fire during the whole process.

The subsequent motions came automatically.

He struck the gun out of the policeman's hand and pounded his head against the floor until he lost consciousness. Then he got up and pulled his own pistol out of his waistband and pressed it against Broncks's unconscious brow.

He had decided. He would shoot.

'No!'

Vincent jerked his own body back and forth like a tethered dog, while the chain between the handle and wrist rattled.

'Stop, for fuck's sake!'

'He has to be out of the way, Vincent! He'll never give up. Never! I don't plan to do life for *his* sake!'

Vincent tugged and pulled to get to his brother.

'Leo – it doesn't matter what you do! This shit will always find us! Me and Felix and Mamma and even Ivan! Your fucking actions always find us, and if you run, they'll come to us instead – do you still not get that? Everything will still be there! Nothing vanishes, *everything will still be there*. You aren't going to shoot! Then you force me to be a part of it and I don't want to be any more!'

Vincent pulled at the handle, kicked with his shoes, tugged and yanked until the whole lorry shook.

'Come on now, Vincent, I haven't forced anyone!'

'We were born into the same fucking family! No one forced us then either! No one!' Tears were running down Vincent's cheeks. 'I try to wash away the shit, don't you get it? I do it every day, a little at a time. But, Leo, it wouldn't be possible to wash this away. Not if you shoot him.'

His little brother pulled at the chain without coming free.

It was the last time.

At that moment a vibration made its way from the door handle through the vehicle until it reached two cables connected to the terminals of a small battery.

A simple ringtone to a relay earlier should have caused the cables to make contact with each other. For some reason the signal didn't work. But Vincent's anger and grief, as he kept on jerking the chain, did.

Leo didn't hear it at first. The filament was heated up in the thermite mixture of iron sulphate and aluminium, which lay in the container on the roof. The intense, bright white light whirled and gobs of fire were spat out that vaporised the thick plastic in just a few seconds. The crackling sound increased at the same rate as the thick, pale yellow shower of fire struck the stack of weapons below.

Leo threw himself away from the tsunami of heat coming at him.

After the first wave he looked up.

Vincent's body was hanging, heavy and without any motion in his arm and wrist. Chained to the door handle, like a bag full of organs.

The heat abated just as quickly as it had started, but was still crackling among the gun parts lying on the thin bed of the lorry between thermite and petrol.

He looked around the barn floor. There, under the workbench, was a grooved piece of iron that had once been an essential part of something. He prised the door handle free easily and carried his little brother out of the barn in his arms.

Vincent's skin was warm, his fingers moist and sticky.

Leo laid him carefully down on the grass, checked for signs of life and saw that his neck was charred and soft, as if it had been cooked.

And he heard the powerful bang.

The thermite had eaten its way down to the petrol tank. The explosion's glow was less severe now and the fire less intense, but the sound grew and practically threw itself out of the barn.

That was why he didn't notice the footsteps until, in the corner of his eye, he glimpsed a hand raised somewhere behind him.

John Broncks's hand. And it held a pistol.

The butt of the pistol struck the back of his head.

He felt nothing.

From blazing fire to subdued darkness in an instant.

Golden Thread

THE SCHOOL'S CORRIDORS remind him of the hospital's corridors, the ones leading to Mamma's ward and her steel bed. He had never thought of that before. The cold lights, the polished linoleum floors. How the sound travels around when you walk, in front of your face and without losing strength. It's flying back and forth right now, mostly from the shoes of the director of studies, hard heels casting their presence around. The Monk, as he's called, and he serves part-time as director of studies and part-time as a woodworking teacher. Hard as nails and strict. A grey fringe around the monk's tonsure. But Leo has always regarded him as decent – without being certain whether that is connected to being one of the few given the highest marks in woodworking at the end of the term. In that and in English. At their individual meetings, the Monk described a student who was both handy and good at solving problems, and the student very much liked hearing that. He's the only teacher Leo doesn't want to disappoint, but who will soon be disappointed – in a big way. That was why the Monk had recently knocked on the classroom door when the physics lesson was in progress and explained that Leo Dûvnjac must leave the classroom a moment and that he should follow him so he could meet someone. He knows. He knows that one of his best students was handy and solved problems when he broke into the school and café with a hammer and chisel and stole all of Friday's profits.

Every time a foot is put down anew, *clap* is followed by *thud*, as they approach the hall – the sound is stark since they are both silent, and besides, it's very quiet as it simply is in a school when no one is on break.

He is going to meet 'someone'.

The police.

Leo already saw them in the morning, two cops in uniform standing at the hall's vent window and investigating. Then at lunchtime he walked by when the caretaker was changing the lock on the door to the pantry and replacing a cracked window frame with a metal one that wouldn't be possible to prise open again. And he had already understood that the notice

Leisure-time Lena taped up at the counter announced that the café was closed today because of a break-in.

How the hell can they know it was me?

'Someone' is sitting at one of the hall's oblong tables, the one furthest away. A man in a grey suit wearing a blue tie, with an open brown brief-case on his knee. No uniform. Leo has met this sort before, like those who investigated the fire and sent his father to prison – superintendent or inspector.

Felix. It was him. The goddamn snitch.

'I spoke with Agnetha.'

The suit extended a scrawny hand.

'She explained that I could find you here, in school, even though all three of you are on leave. My name is Per Lindh, and I am a lawyer.'

A lawyer? Do I need that too?

'I can't afford that.'

'Sorry?'

'A lawyer.'

'You don't need to worry about that. The public pays my salary when I represent your pappa.'

Pappa's lawyer? Not mine?

So Felix had kept his mouth shut.

'Then I'll leave you here, Leo. With Per. So you two can talk undisturbed. And then I think you should go home to your younger brothers. You don't need to be in school after what happened. Not this week. OK?'

Leo nods and the Monk clumps away, clap thud, clap thud.

'Your pappa asked me to come and find you.'

They are alone in the large hall, on either side of the table, where he is usually one of the many students who play cards during breaks. Chicago. They started playing that in Year 7. And it feels almost more deserted now than it did during the night when the café's cupboards were still full.

'Your pappa wants to meet you all.'

'Us? All three?'

'Yes. He asked me to convey that to you, so you can arrange it.'

'It won't work. Felix will never come along. And Vincent has no real idea of what happened.'

'And you, Leo?'

The wig and the ciggie, in a bag under the sink.

'What do you want to do? Do you want to visit him?'

336

And they will stay there. I promised Felix.

'I sincerely think, Leo, that it's you he wants to meet. He wants to tell you why he did what he did.'

'It's not necessary. I saw what he did because I was there.'

The lawyer Per Lindh nods and roots around in his briefcase as if he is searching for something important and finds it after a while. A box of chewing gum.

'Want some?'

Leo shakes his head as the lawyer takes out two pieces and begins to chew.

'Your pappa has described in detail what happened when he came to you all. When he entered the flat. It was a good thing you were home, Leo.'

'I got between them.'

'And I think that's what he wants to tell you, so that you know that too.'

'I saved her life.'

'And if you want to hear him say that to you, Leo, there isn't much time. Because your pappa will be moved soon to a different remand prison, in a different city.'

THE POLICE STATION in Falun is shaped like half of a black horseshoe on the outside; inside it reminds you of the hospital, and of the school, since all public buildings seem to be an extension of one another. They look alike, sound alike and smell alike. They even have the same temperature and the same air pressure. Worthless knowledge you can't get the highest marks in – but Leo is learning it these days.

Long, shiny corridors. Dismal doors that lead somewhere.

But the employees' clothes, the hospital's long white gowns and the school's suit jackets and blouses, are at least exchanged here for different uniforms. Black ones. After having been escorted through the whole building to reach the remand section, Leo realises that it is absolutely quiet. Not a sound is heard from within the corridor, and the cells in a row there. And the visitors' room, which a friendly detective ushers him into, is soundproof.

He really likes these kinds of small locked spaces where he can hide himself and shut the world out. But there's a difference here. Someone else has done the locking, from the outside. He even has to press a red button if he needs to pee. The correctional system inspector stressed that before she turned the key. Others make the conditions that govern the closed room, not him.

A claustrophobic room only becomes claustrophobic the minute it's not your choice.

Leo has waited in locked visitors' rooms before. Twice, before the long sentence for the firebomb, his father was in prison for aggravated assault of people outside the family. Leo visited both times – but never in the remand section. He knows that because the difference is striking. The remand section he's in now is darker, more confined. Prisons are certainly surrounded by a high, thick grey wall but daylight is encountered everywhere. This room is too small, the paint on the walls is too shabby and the fluorescent light on the ceiling lacks a plastic cover. That's probably why it feels different. Unless . . . Maybe, maybe the difference instead lies in the fact that here no one has been sentenced yet? That people have

338

more hope? And they are more frustrated when they long to be out? That *could* be what creates the ugly, claustrophobic impression. In prison, it's clear that it's about adapting and holding out while the time passes.

The room has two plastic chairs, a wooden table and the door with its large pane of glass so that the staff can see in. A built-in window that can't be smashed. They can look in and he can look out at the blue shirts going by. Correctional system personnel. But he doesn't hear them – the sound has also been locked out – so he doesn't hear the footsteps he knows so well either, Pappa's footsteps, right in front of the remand guard's.

Newly shaved. A gaze as clear as water. That was how he sometimes looked long ago, when everything was fine and he had promised Mamma not to drink or fight.

And he smelled of soap.

But grief is hidden in that clear gaze. Pappa can look sorrowful without becoming smaller. Most people shrink. Now he is standing there and observing his son, who is already sitting. He watches and smiles. And it seems wrong. It does not belong in the cramped space.

'Where is Vincent?'

Pappa is wearing blue trousers, a white T-shirt with sleeves that are too long, and some kind of slippers on his feet, which have probably never felt anything other than brown dress shoes.

'Leo – where is your youngest brother?'

Even though Leo arranged with the lawyer to come alone, he had hoped to avoid this – and had made a last attempt to lure his two little brothers into coming. Vincent didn't even respond and just lay on the bed, staring at the wall.

'He didn't want to come along.'

'And Felix?'

Felix surprisingly calmly explained how he had gladly visited Mamma no matter how many bloodshot eyes she had, and he would come along to the hospital any time, but would never visit Pappa. Leo hadn't nagged. He understood.

'He . . . Well, you know how Felix is sometimes.'

Pappa looks away, off somewhere. As if he is still there, at home.

'I never saw him, when I came in, I mean . . . I never saw Vincent.'

'He was standing behind me. Then, when I got in-between, he ran off with Mamma's nurse's bag.'

'Nurse's bag? What do you mean?'

339

'He locked himself in his room with it.'

The shame. Now the clear gaze is filled with grief. It's the shame Pappa always exhibits when he has struck someone and realises it, afterwards. And it's as if the room is shrinking even further. They don't have space any more, him and Pappa and the shame. It's not possible to breathe. The metal door is closed and tightly sealed. He has never been locked together with Pappa in a room that lacks air. He will remember how it feels right now, and make sure that he never ends up like this with him again.

'Is there . . . well, another room we can meet in? A little bigger? It is so . . .'

'I haven't had any other visits. So I don't know. And my own cell, five square metres, doesn't even have a window.'

Suddenly Pappa leans forward and lays a rough hand on his son's shoulder.

Leo winces, without knowing why.

But Pappa notices, regrets it and takes his hand away immediately. And Leo regrets it too; he didn't mean to wince.

'Being confined isn't so bad, Leo . . . but to be confined *in here*.'

His father presses his hand against his chest.

'No one wants that. So I was forced to do what I did. Do you understand that? Why I came home to you and your brothers and . . . your mamma?'

'No. I don't understand. I saw that you came in to beat her to death.'

Pappa's instinct is to rage and attack. Leo is sure of that. Even though he is sober, he sticks out his chin and stares at him with lowered eyes that pierce through him when they make contact.

'I thought that was why you wanted me to come here, Pappa. At least that's what the lawyer said.'

Pappa doesn't attack him. Just as quickly as he was ready to do so, he relaxes, he draws his fingers like a comb through his Elvis hair and his expression softens.

'So you don't understand it? That I had to?'

He gets up from the rickety chair, which is groaning under his weight, and walks to the glass on the door and studies the blue shirts going by. And for a moment it seems as if he is choosing between breaking the windowpane and pushing the red button to call the guard to say the visit is over.

'It's like this, Leo.'

He doesn't smash the unsmashable glass and doesn't push the button.

'Do you know how you weave an absolutely authentic rug, my son? Not that factory shit you buy at Ikea – a real one, made by hand.'

He waves his arms at an invisible loom.

'You place one thread in at a time and press it against the other threads.'

A rug? What is he talking about? And he smells like soap, not wine, Leo notices.

'Every day, Leo . . . is a new thread. Which you weave into your rug.'

Now he turns back towards the table and sits down again.

'Three hundred and sixty-five threads, day in and day out, year in and year out.'

He illustrates with sweeping arm movements. He slips in the pretend thread and presses the pretend beam of the loom.

'Often the thread is grey and dull, and not a thing is happening. You eat, shit and sleep. But sometimes, Leo, it's red or green, when you are doing something you like. And sometimes, like when I came home to you all, the thread is as black as a fucking Bible.'

Leo is observing a father who so often spoke like this, allowing a lot not only in his voice but also in words. As far back as Leo remembers, his father tried to explain what solidarity was, forming a clan of their own together – about wild geese who fly away and repent and instead land among their family; about Cossacks who dance the Bear Dance and defeat great armies; and about thin sticks that can't be broken if they are laid tightly together in a row – and he had learned how to look interested without listening. That isn't working now. Right now his father is sober and his voice doesn't slur. It ensnares.

'But occasionally you also add a golden thread. Genuine gold as you sit weaving your life! And right before you die, you see your *entire* rug, the pattern of different coloured threads. Imagine Hitler's rug, Leo, pitch black! And Mother Teresa's, gold, gold, gold. Her rug is gleaming! Other rugs are like ours. Mostly grey, a little green and red and Bible black – and here and there a little gold thread.'

His hand is against his chest again and he hits it.

'You know, life can be hard to live.'

Leo has been sitting, leaning back ostentatiously, at the greatest possible distance, especially since the hand on the shoulder. Now he leans forward without being aware of it.

'But . . . some days, Pappa, can there be two different threads next to

341

each other? Or what if they are twined together to make one? As he continues speaking, he puts both elbows on the table, like Pappa. 'Because, well, your thread is black. What you did to Mamma. But my thread, at the same time, maybe had gold in it. When I . . . you know, they said it . . . if I hadn't been home, she would have been dead.'

The strange smile that he doesn't understand. That doesn't belong in this room.

'Leo?'

'Yes?'

'Don't mix our rugs together now.'

Leo recoils. It wasn't a good idea to sit close. And the room shrinks a little more.

'If I had wanted to kill your mother, I would have done it.'

Because if he stayed where he was, it would have been like with his mother's face.

'Do you get it, Leo? I had to do what I did – but I did it under control.'

Each word feels like a blow.

'Do you seriously think, Leo, that I would kill your mother right before your eyes? Have you not listened to anything I said?'

Yes. I've listened. And I don't care about your fucking rug. And your fucking threads. I hung onto your fucking shoulders so that you couldn't hit her any more.

'The other night,' starts Leo.

Black as a Bible. So is that how you want it?

'Felix and I were at school. With a big rubbish bag. We filled it. We took a strongbox with money.'

Now he is the one striking. And the strange smile is gone.

'I broke it apart when we got home. Full of coins. And a lot of banknotes.'

Mamma was angry. But Pappa shows no sign and doesn't say anything. He just walks to the unsmashable window and looks out.

'Full of coins, do you say? And a lot of banknotes?'

'Yeah.'

'Was there . . . uh, anyone who saw you?'

'What do you think? I have control.'

Pappa reaches his hand out to the red button on the wall and presses it.

'You should go home to your brothers.'

'But Mamma thinks I should return it all. All of it, Pappa.'

The metal door is opened by two guards in blue shirts. As Pappa starts to walk between them, the soft slippers glide over the stone floor.

It's silent again.

Until he stops and turns around.

'Leo?'

'Yeah?'

'If no one saw you, then no one knows about it.'

HE HAS BEEN to only one funeral in his life, and when he left the church it felt exactly as it does now, leaving the semi-curved building of the police station. He draws deep breaths and is dizzy, alive and the opposite of coffins and black threads.

If I had wanted to kill your mother, I would have done it.

What did the old man mean? Did it not mean anything that he got in between them and made him stop beating her?

If no one saw you, then no one knows about it.

Was it good that he opened the window and door and cupboard and strongbox with a screwdriver, chisel and hammer? It was as if his father first took something from him but then regretted it and gave back something else.

Leo is walking slowly along the asphalt when suddenly his legs begin to run of their own volition, over the bridge and the stream, which divides central Falun and every year is flooded with meltwater.

Gave? Or took? Fucking gold thread or fucking black thread?

He lengthens his stride and runs faster. He doesn't care which it is and has decided not to become like Pappa, but to be better than that, better than someone who escapes to a claustrophobic room because he doesn't dare to remain in his own body.

The town centre starts on the other side of the bridge and he hurries past the library, towards the pedestrian precinct where H&M is and a grey jacket with a hood put on a mannequin in the middle window.

He has a wig and a ciggie. Now he'll get the rest.

He goes in and takes the escalator up to the men's department. He already knows where it's hanging – in the far corner to the right, on a steel rack with large signs for this year's autumn jackets. There are about six of them. He skips over the large, small and medium sizes. He grabs the hanger with the last one in XL. Light grey with a hood just like the one in the shop window. Not a hoodie, but a real jacket for men who go into the forest and pick mushrooms and need to pull up the hood to protect themselves from the rain and hear the drops landing while shots from the moose hunt are falling in the distance. He goes past the empty fitting room. It isn't going to fit anyway and he puts it down on the counter and waits for the shop assistant who is folding the sleeves so neatly.

'This is extra large, you know that? And the item runs rather large – it won't fit as you might expect.'

She isn't very old. He guesses twenty-five. Her gaze is intense as she assesses his narrow shoulders and lanky body.

'I know. It's a present.'

Her smile is beautiful.

'Well . . . would you like it wrapped?'

'Wrapped?'

'If it's a present, I mean. I'd like that. If it was for me.'

'Yeah . . . that'd be fine.'

He watches her fingers as they fold the paper, which is the same shade of red as her nail polish, and curl the ribbon.

'That'll be ninety-nine kronor and fifty öre.'

He nods, a little nervously. Has he convinced her? Is she still wondering? But he decides then that it doesn't matter. He'll dye it and fill it up with wadding.

She puts it in a plastic bag and he pays for it with money from another plastic bag, which is in his pocket and is as big as a tennis ball. She smiles the pretty smile again.

'Piggy bank?'

'Piggy bank.'

————————

He's on his knees in the bathroom, resting his chest against the edge of the bathtub and dipping an outstretched arm into the ten-centimetre-deep lukewarm water.

He had gone on from H&M with the gift-wrapped autumn jacket to the sewing shop on Holm Street. He explained that his mamma asked him to buy padding, some finished pieces for filling out shoulders and some of the sort that feels like vacuum cleaner filters and is sold by the metre. Three metres, that should do it, and a little dye – the dark green shade. He paid for it with one-krona coins, the last ones from the parking meters.

Leo stirs the lukewarm water with his hands protected by Mamma's rubber gloves, the ones she uses to prevent rashes as she scrubs the floor or does the dishes. He doesn't care about rashes but wants to avoid dye

345

residue on his skin, which can't be scrubbed away and so can be easily identified. He stirs with his hands like with the ladle in the semolina porridge, round and round, until the dye is dissolved. The instructions describe how a garment should be processed in the washing machine so that the dye will be distributed evenly over the fabric but he doesn't want it to be even. He wants it to look crappy. So he empties the contents of the glass jar into the bathtub and lays down the light grey jacket, washes it around and rubs the fabric against itself so that it will be blotchy and unevenly dark. When the material has absorbed what he thinks is enough dye, he rinses it under running water. He wrings the water out of it like out of a wet towel, hangs it up on an inflatable plastic hanger and starts to dry it with a hairdryer.

'What are you doing, Leo? That noise.' Felix at the bathroom door. 'Turn off the dryer – I can barely hear the TV.'

'Forget about that. But bring the map.'

'What? What map?'

'Your map. The same one as before. Just get it.'

Felix gets it – and Leo finally switches off the hairdryer and instead folds out the map on the toilet lid. The paper reduces reality to a scale of 1:5000. He leans over it and studies the details.

'What are you doing?'

'The cycle paths.'

Felix creeps up beside his big brother. The last time it was lying like this, on Vincent's floor, it had been about the cycle paths from the ICA shop. *Escape* routes.

'You shouldn't do that. You promised.'

'You don't need to worry, little brother. I can do it without you.'

'Alone? Against Click?'

'Felix, do you remember what you said? "Vincent is a damn mummy. And Mamma's in hospital. And Pappa's in custody. And now are you also going to get arrested?" That's precisely why. Although not the last thing. Don't you get it? It's just us left. Only we can fix it.'

'We? I said I wouldn't come along. Because it's an idiotic idea. You got it, again, when you visited Pappa, right? You two . . . There's always something with you two.'

All of a sudden Leo leaves the bathroom with the map still on the toilet lid. Felix looks out into the hall and sees a box being pulled out and his big brother returning with a pen in his hand.

346

'Here.'

Leo draws a cross on the open map, not far from one of the cycle paths, in the green field designating forest.

'OK, Felix. You don't have to do anything you don't want to. But don't tell me that my idea is lousy because it fucking isn't. I'm going to do it. No matter what you say.'

He draws a line from the middle of the cross to the nearest cycle path, and continues, a blue line of ink all the way to the square. To the ICA.

'I'm going to tell Mamma if you do it.'

Leo freezes. He rarely gets angry, at least not with Felix. He is now. But not in the way Pappa gets; Leo gets angry so that he is on the verge of crying, as if he is sad at the same time.

'Dammit, Felix!'

He screams loudly, not caring if Vincent hears it.

'We are brothers! We never, ever, ever tell on each other! You know that!'

And Felix knows that it's in earnest.

'OK. I *won't* blab.'

And that it reaches deep inside.

'But it's still a crap idea.'

Vincent has heard. Now he's standing there and looking at them. Bandaged. The chocolate-coloured part at the mouth has come loose entirely and is hanging and wobbling about. The arms scribbled with ink are even more scribbled on. He has found the green marker too and green veins are winding around all over the gauze bandages.

'OK. *He* gets to decide if my idea is lousy or not.'

'The mummy, Leo? Is he going to decide?'

'He's the little brother of both of us. Of course he gets to decide.'

He puts his hand on one of Vincent's shoulders, as their father did in the remand centre. But Vincent doesn't wince.

'What do you think, Vincent? Should I, or should I not, hoodwink Click?'

The bandaged boy looks alternately at his two older brothers who are waiting for his answer. So he does that. He answers.

'Yes. No.'

He pulls on the bandage, which trembles around his mouth, alternating between up and down.

'Yes. No. Yes. No. Yes. No.'

347

Until Felix starts to clap ostentatiously.

'You hear him. He says no.'

'He says yes. And no. He's just being silly.'

The hand on the shoulder turns into a hug.

'Vincent – this is serious. You get to say only *one* thing. If I should – or I shouldn't.'

This time their little brother hesitates, as if he is taking the time for a well-considered decision. He takes hold of the stumps of bandage around his mouth and pulls them up to his nose.

'You should.'

Now it is Felix who freezes.

They are waiting for him. And they have to wait. Then he shrugs.

'Well. Now we know. Mummies prefer crap ideas. But when it's over, Leo, you have to buy me a brand new map. You've ruined this one with your fucking pen and your fucking crosses.'

'If you turn me in, I'll turn you in'

THE SMELL OF oil, always evident lower down in large vessels, seemed completely gone here on the upper deck for first-class cabins, and the hard floors were replaced by soft carpeting. But it was just as cramped. The cart with the suitcases bumped against the corridor walls and ventilation pipes as Sam looked for the cabin door, number 571. It even swayed slightly, as always on the sea, even though he was still at Värta Harbour with barely an hour until departure.

559. 561. 563.

Just a few doors left before he could swipe the plastic card through the card reader and walk into the suite for the escape's final stage.

He was enveloped by the odd calm that sometimes crept in through the skin and locked itself in the chest, forcing his tense body to relax. The calm only came from the feeling of knowing you have done everything you can and thus can do no more. What will happen will happen because you no longer affect the outcome. The agitation, the pursuit and the adrenalin had increased further and made his racing heart thump out of rhythm when Leo decided to turn and drive back – *If I have to, I'll kill your brother, Sam, but I'll come back.* Suddenly it was as if all that never existed. A temporary, nameless visitor he had already forgotten. Going quietly into the luxurious cabin, putting the suitcases with one hundred and three million down on the floor and checking to be sure the champagne was precisely as cold as it should be. Right now this was his entire world. Here, in one of the armchairs upholstered in reddish brown leather, he would sit and look out through the window facing the sea while he hoped that Leo was on the way back. That their shared journey would have a shared ending.

Unlike him, Leo had someone to lose.

He had turned around and risked everything because of that. Leo had brothers and parents who would miss him and he would miss them. Leaving for ever meant so incredibly much more to him. As for himself, Sam didn't miss anyone. And no one missed him.

He abandoned the sea view for what stood on the trolley. He caressed an expensive bottle with the tip of his index finger. Dom Pérignon. Neither of them had experience of how this particular champagne tasted. The important thing was that it was the most expensive on the ship's menu. *No. We aren't free, yet. When we are sitting on that goddamn boat. On the way to Riga and St Petersburg and Sberbank Rossii.* He picked off the glittery metallic paper around the neck of the bottle, which he then pressed entirely down into the bucket of ice. He turned the drinking glasses up. Then, *in the suite, we'll drink. Bring in a case of champagne.* Then *we'll be free, Sam.* And he remembered how difficult it had been to offer Leo a drink in the little cottage's kitchen before the first robbery.

Two knocks.

He listened, holding himself back.

Two more knocks on the door of the cabin.

He took a quick look at the clock radio on the nightstand by one of the beds. Six thirty-three. Twenty-seven minutes until departure.

You made it back in time.

Sam turned the round doorknob halfway and let the door glide open.

It wasn't Leo.

'Hello, Sam.'

It was his brother.

'Your accomplice isn't coming.'

His own brother.

'You see, right now he's sitting in the back seat of a patrol car in hand-cuffs, on the way to Kronoberg remand centre.'

John.

'The same complex where he got one hundred and three million today. And I know he did it with your help, Sam.'

John?

I don't understand.

It shouldn't be you standing there.

'Accomplice? I don't know what the fuck you're talking about.'

His voice sounded steady, Sam was certain of that. Even though the bits that should present reality in front of him didn't fit together at all.

'Sam, are you going to let me into your fucking cabin?'

Further off in the narrow corridor, other voices were audible, more passengers looking for the right cabin number. To attack John here, now, was too great a risk. So he stood to the side and let him come in. He noted that beneath the unbuttoned leather jacket, which he had also worn at the unannounced visit to the island, a dark brown holster with a service revolver could be seen.

'Champagne, Sam? Not bad.'

In spite of the first-class ticket, the cabin wasn't particularly large. Now it became even smaller. Wherever they positioned themselves, they stood too close to each other.

'A pity there isn't anything to celebrate any longer.'

Sam watched his younger brother wiggle the champagne bottle until the pieces of ice scraped against each other just as much as they scraped against the metal bucket. He watched him study the suitcases on the floor and try to decide whether they were large enough for ten boxes of bank-notes from the confiscations room. At the same time he held up a ticket identical to the one Sam had himself – Leo's ticket.

'I couldn't stop you then. From killing our father. But I can stop you today. Today I'm the one who decides what the ending is.'

The swimming bottle was as cold as it was wet when Sam fished it up and pulled out the cork.

'OK, John – how does it end?'

A single blow.

His hand was tight around the neck of the bottle while the light and frothy amber fluid ran over his fingers.

A single blow with the thick bottom against John's temple and I decide the ending, again.

'Like all fairy tales. Happily. You take your suitcases, which I assume contain one hundred and three million kronor, and accompany me to Kronoberg.'

'You didn't stop me then. You aren't going to stop me now. You're here alone, John. If you planned to arrest me, you'd have brought along a whole army. So down deep you've already decided.'

'Sam, I *have* decided. But I had a hope that it could end . . . in a digni-fied manner. That's why I came alone. To give you a chance to surrender. If you don't do that, now, they are going to be standing there on the other side of the Baltic waiting for you – and then it won't be particularly dignified.'

'So you're going to tip them off? About me? Again?'

'If you don't give me any other choice.'

Sam took a step forward and the room shrank even more.

'You know, little brother, I have stabbed a family member to death before when there wasn't *any other choice*. It would be the easiest thing in the world for me to stab to death another family member who doesn't give me another choice either and leave him lying in a bed exactly as I left our father lying in one. And then when I stroll across the gunwale in Riga, a cleaner will find you on those white sheets just as fucking bloody as he was.'

'I know you aren't a murderer. And you know that, too.'

They looked at each other, for a long time. The expensive bottle remained hanging in Sam's hand, so much heavier than a serrated fishing knife.

He couldn't kill someone for money.

Just as he wouldn't have killed then for his own sake.

'I put a stop to our father – otherwise you would have ended up dead, John. You wouldn't be standing here. So now you'll look away! You owe me that. You owe me twenty-three years.'

Sam had taken a step just before that shrank the distance. Now it was John who came closer.

'You're wrong, Sam. Yeah, it *was* me, then. But it's a fucking long time since I was afraid of beatings. Of someone standing in front of me and threatening me. Sure, you're the big brother. You're thirty kilos heavier. And you have everything to lose if you come with me – and all the same you don't fucking scare me. It was you who held the knife. Chose to hold the knife. You'll never escape it.'

'That's exactly what I'm saying, John! It was you who called me, back then. And *you* will never escape that! Don't you remember? *You have to come here, brother. Pappa is going to kill me. I can't take it any more.* You must remember that! I fucking came. For your sake. Stabbed him twenty-seven times for your sake. And then, John – fuck, John! – it was you who called the cops! I saved you and you called the police. I didn't do anything wrong, John! You did something wrong. You owe me this! Live with it, brother.'

If either of them were to take another step, they would crash into each other. So they stood there and stared. Closer than they had been in twenty years – close enough to be able to feel each other's breath and follow each other's eye movements.

Then the ship sent a tremor moving upwards from the engine room. Then a loudspeaker announced that it was fifteen minutes to departure.

'Give me that.'

John Broncks nodded towards the champagne bottle hanging with its neck in Sam's tightly clenched hand. When nothing happened, he reached over and coaxed it out of Sam's grip. And then he poured some into the glasses, which bubbled over, and he gave one to Sam.

It tasted like golden apples and toasted bread with a hint of citrus. It even remained at eight degrees – but neither of them experienced it.

It was a drink shared by strangers with memories in common, a farewell for ever to the past.

THE FLATSCREEN TV on the shelf over Dráva's long, narrow bar lacked sound, but it didn't matter. Out of the moving puzzle of events without voices, a strange slide show emerged.

Ivan smiled as the excited cops in helmets with black visors and automatic weapons in their hands ran after each other in a long line. They looked like the tail of a large rat slinking down into the underground station next to the police station. At least fifteen, maybe twenty of them.

What the hell were they doing down in the underworld?

It was up there things seemed to be happening.

From multiple angles, video cameras showed the Kronoberg police complex was blocked off and the entrances were barred. Uniformed cops guarded flapping plastic – like a large package no one was allowed to open before the crime was solved.

A smell of tannic acid was being spread from the percolator behind the coffee machine and the bottom of the glass coffee pot was covered with black film. Neither Dacso nor his wife had filled it and now they were gone. There was no one behind the counter, and not a living soul could be seen through the little round window in the door leading out to the kitchen and the big work surface.

The restaurant was empty apart from the woman sitting a few tables away in the corner, where it was a little darker. Her thin fair hair was nearly invisible but formed a hairstyle that didn't really agree with the orange-yellow face and the dry lips. She usually sat there, at the same table, every day, and drank a demi-carafe of the house white wine.

He made an effort to ask her if she had seen the owner of the restaurant, but changed his mind. People alone at places like Dráva were always looking for a chance for a drunken conversation, and it never stopped but ground on and on. It was still possible to see that she had been beautiful, though she was doing her best to spoil it. But her self-image was likely still there, in which she was probably still just as beautiful. That was how she smiled and moved, unaware of how years of daily consumption of alcohol had carved away at her at the same time and created a false image

356

that was so easy to hold onto. He too had been close to being caught up in it before he took the decision to change.

The plastic-wrapped police complex on Kungsholmen had been replaced by a bombed house on the West Bank. How something could look so black when the sky in the background was so blue . . . He couldn't bear wars that had been around longer than his sons. Instead he was heading in behind the checkout to the kitchen door, to look for Dacso and his fucking coffee beans, when he noticed that the sky on the TV changed again and now it was as grey as lead. The news report from the West Bank had switched to pictures of a Swedish plot of low-growing spruce forest around a bumpy gravel road.

And the feeling bit him on the neck. Again.

And deceit's ice-cold blade landed. Again.

And it had to do with Leo. Again.

He reached over the bar, looking for the bloody remote control. He recognised that particular gravel road and knew it ended at an abandoned farmhouse and a barn with its large doors hanging on rusty hinges.

Now.

Now he *must* hear what the voice had to say.

But the oblong box with little buttons in various colours and strange icons here and there was gone, just like the coffee and Dacso. He had to continue staring at a mute screen. The barn – which he recognised as he had the gravel road – was burning. It was burning! The reddish yellow fire was devouring the wooden walls and climbing further up to the sky as black smoke.

It was in there that Leo kept his tools.

What am I doing? Planning our future. You said it yourself – if you can change, I can change.

All they needed to build everything anew was in the lorry. Father and son. Together.

It's great that you aren't hesitating any more because I seriously need your help.

Now it was burning down. Leo had stood so close to him, displaying everything, explaining.

Everything was being consumed by red and yellow flames.

The telephone was always in the inner pocket of his suit jacket. Their own pathway of communication, just between them. He pressed the button for the preprogrammed number, as Leo had taught him, and waited . . .

357

no signal. Nothing. Leo's telephone was switched off. Their line, broken off.

Leo? Was your brother right?

Are you using me?

Ivan closed his eyes and tried to remember. What had Leo actually given as an answer to his question? No, he didn't remember. Or was it that he didn't want to remember the sentence that had sounded so convincing at the time?

Yeah. I mean what I'm saying.

'Coffee?'

It was burning on the screen, burning and burning.

'Do you want some, coffee?'

Everything . . . everything is a lie and is burning up, he thought. A big, fat fucking lie. Everything you attempt, everything you accomplish burns sooner or later.

That's how it is. It burns.

It turns into flames.

It turns into soot.

That's why you didn't come to pick me up. I was on time and you didn't come.

'Hey, Ivan? Coffee?'

'What?'

'I just put on some fresh coffee.'

Dacso. He had come back, from somewhere.

'No . . . no coffee.'

Leo had used his own father. Ivan didn't know how or why but he was certain that Vincent had been right – that he had been reduced to a pawn in some kind of fucking game. A little green plastic soldier, a game piece. With no understanding of what it meant in the big picture. He felt it in his neck, chest, stomach, and it felt as if there was only one way to stop the pain gnawing him inside and out.

'Give me a bottle of wine.'

The grip fell on his neck, the second time in one week. Once too many – and the reason Ivan Dûvnjac could no longer manage what he'd promised himself.

'But you . . . you don't drink? Wine, I mean.'

'The bottle, for fuck's sake!'

Dacso shrugged.

'OK. You're a customer. You can do as you like. It'll cost two hundred and twenty-five kronor.'

The fine row of bottles stood next to the loudspeaker on the shelf circling the bar. Dacso pulled one of them down, a bottle of red.

'And you're sure about this, Ivan? Even though you've stopped.'

'The bottle.'

Dacso slowly pulled out the cork and reached for a fresh glass.

'Two hundred and twenty-five. If you want the whole bottle. Or sixty kronor by the glass.'

A promise to yourself, what the fuck is that?

Nothing.

Because it can't change other people.

'All of it. The whole bottle. And you can take it out of the money you got from Leo.'

'I didn't get any money for wine from your son. But he paid in advance for the dinner you are going to eat here.'

If I can change, you can change.

Even that was a lie.

It burns, like everything burns.

'Yes, that money. For the crap food we haven't eaten and aren't going to eat at your dive.'

'Your son said I should hold onto it until *he* came back.'

'My son isn't coming back!'

Ivan pulled the room temperature bottle out of Dacso's hand. It felt better to fill the glass himself. *Egri Bikavér*, bull's blood in Hungarian. He knew fucking well what it meant. As he swallowed the first lukewarm drops, he saw Dacso putting five-hundred-kronor notes, four of them, on the bar. Money that belonged to his son and now he would drink it up. And it felt so pleasant in his throat, in his whole body, like an old friend you've hated for two years, who suddenly makes you laugh again.

OUTSIDE AND INSIDE.

John Broncks had only had such a strong experience once before – back then his pappa was lying in a bed with a fishing knife in his chest.

Everything simply continued to go on around him. A young woman walked by their window eating ice cream. Two older men sat down on the pier, fishing for perch and drinking bottles of pilsner.

The same feelings, the same motions now – alone in a car in the police station's underground garage while his colleagues ran around on the other side of the vehicle's sheet metal in another reality, pursuing an answer he already had.

That was why he was incapable of getting out. He must decide whether he would bury the answer for ever or open the car door, snap his fingers and freeze their motion, shouting, *I have the solution.*

Only he had the correct information.

Only he could channel the energy buzzing about out there and direct it towards two robbers.

Only he knew that the plunder taken from here a few hours ago was right now packed in four suitcases on board a ferry that would dock in Riga's harbour early tomorrow morning.

Outside and inside. The world and me.

He had lacked the strength to arrest Sam himself. But he could, with just a few words, see to it that someone else did.

John Broncks put his hand on the door handle and let it rest there. Should he once again send down someone who sacrificed twenty-three years for his sake?

Then he pressed down the handle, opened the door and stepped out towards the other world, but not into it.

Should he hand over someone who saved his life?

He started to walk slowly through the huge garage and nodded to colleagues without taking in who, aiming for the metal door that led to the lift and stairs to the investigation division.

It wasn't about the fact that they were big brother and little brother. Not about blood and loyalty.

Maybe it was about – after all – a debt that had never been paid off?

That was why he stopped visiting Sam over the years. Every time they were silent, each on their side of a rickety table in a visitors' cell, the debt had sat next to them and whispered: *He saved your life, but in a little while only you will walk back out into freedom.* Eventually Broncks stopped coming – how many times can a human being abide hearing the same thing repeated?

He opened the door to the lift and pressed the button for the third floor but changed his mind and took the stairs. They took a little longer to walk up.

Long enough to be able to be certain it was the right decision to let a debt that didn't exist cost exactly one hundred and three million kronor to redeem.

THE TURMOIL was so strong she was breaking apart, and combined with ten minutes of standing still and waiting, it was quite simply impossible. So to endure it, Britt-Marie walked two full turns around the Kronoberg police complex in the falling evening darkness, alongside something she'd never seen before – all the buildings had been encapsulated behind the sort of blue-and-white barrier tape that the police usually put up *away from* the police station. The entrance on Bergs Street looked exactly like the entrances via Polhems Street and Kungsholms Street and Police Station Park. The entire police operation was a single big crime scene. Even the underground to it had been blocked off and the buses had been diverted. She had got the same version from a couple of the many curious onlookers gathered side by side with journalists and photographers. Some kind of rather large crime had been committed *inside* the police station itself. Someone had even whispered excitedly that there was information about the largest theft in Swedish history.

After the second lap, she stopped at the low stone wall forming the boundary with the courthouse. She had an appointment to meet there with the same young policewoman who had first picked up Leo and turned her whole house upside down, and later showed her a photo of the man in Leo's car at the hospital – a workplace that should have been off limits. Elisa. An unusual first name, but a pretty one.

And there she was, coming out of the entrance to the police station. She lifted the thin plastic tape, walked under it and zigzagged through the pack of onlookers.

'I only have a couple of minutes, unfortunately. As you can see, it's a little chaotic in there.'

Britt-Marie nodded and smiled as best she could while she tried to find a comfortable position. Just as she hadn't been able to stand still, it also was impossible for her to let her hands hang loose. So she secured them by crossing them over the upper part of her winter coat.

'Vincent called me. He's my youngest son. I think you've also met him? He was upset. A little scared. He said he'd been contacted by a police officer.'

Elisa turned towards the group of onlookers. Someone who had tried to go over the barriers was turned back, politely but firmly.

'Excuse me, I had to . . . What did you say, Britt-Marie? Had he been contacted by police? By us?'

'Yes. That was what he said. Do you know anything about that?'

'No. I've met your son Vincent on only one occasion, and that was yesterday at his place of work. He seemed calm then. A police officer? Did he or she say what it was about?'

'Only that it had something to do with Leo. And that he was urged to accompany a police officer – the same one who investigated the bank robberies before the prison sentence.'

Elisa was forced to engage with the increasingly vocal crowd again, assisting the two deployed security guards in a discussion with the photographers who had pushed their way to the front. And while Britt-Marie stood there at a distance waiting for her reply, she turned over what she had actually heard herself say just now.

A police officer demanding that Vincent do the one thing he didn't want to – take part in an investigation of his brother.

'I apologise again, Britt-Marie. It's starting to resemble the atmosphere of a riot over there. Reporters demanding answers because the editors who sent them are demanding answers. A crime inside the police station is evidently tantalising. But now I'm back.'

Vincent, who decided never again to commit crimes, never again to have anything to do with the police.

'And as for your question, Britt-Marie, about your son Vincent, unfortunately I can't help you. I have absolutely no knowledge about him right now. But I promise to look into it right away.'

Nevertheless, she simply knew: Vincent had been drawn into exactly what he feared.

And he had been right – this did not feel good at all.

HE HAD NEVER been afraid of the dark. Quite the opposite. It protected, just as silence protected.

But not this time.

It was only now, after the decision about Sam, and with the ceiling light and desk lamp still off and thus alone in all that was nothing, that he dared to feel the unbearable heat and the intense white light.

A firebomb.

None of them had had time to scream.

He had not grasped what scorched skin looked like right afterwards.

John Broncks pushed, almost threw open one of the office windows, which looked out onto the courtyard of Kronoberg police station, and let the evening chill rush in. He closed his eyes. Slow breaths. He leaned out into the swirling wind.

It made no difference.

The fire from the roaring explosion shattered the silence, just as the white light penetrated the safe darkness.

He had never killed or even injured anyone. During his entire adult life, he had worked with the violence of others without ever using it himself. He had investigated the hellish consequences of violence again and again, but always after the fact. Now he had also experienced the very moment of death as a professional. When violence took a life. It had even been lying on the ground in front of him.

And he knew why.

For the first time in his service, he had acted as a private individual, not as a police officer. And the decisions John Broncks had taken as a private individual had now brought consequences for the policeman John Broncks.

It had always been the other way round.

The violence that he hated so much had forced him, evening after evening through investigation after investigation, to become sharper and more interested – a force that involved him and kept him there. Until the culprit who sat in a remand cell four floors up.

364

As he leaned out of the window even further into the icy wind and cold air, he perceived from his clothes that he even *smelled* of the consequences – burnt hair, scorched skin, phosphorus and gunpowder. And he realised that whatever he tried, no matter how far he leaned out, this day and the decisions that led to the explosion – and death – would never leave him.

So he must, from that moment on, escape it.

Just like all others who were responsible for the aftermath of violence and took flight from him in investigations. He must reshape the truth and carry the anguish without it being seen from the outside. He would never be able to tell his colleagues about what had happened. About what really happened.

He let his office remain dimmed.

And he opened the other window too so that the wind would play freely.

ELISA LIFTED THE thin plastic barrier tape that was flapping in the light wind and crouched down as she ducked under it towards the east entrance of the Kronoberg police station. Someone in the front of the crowd called after her – *What happened in there? When will we get information?* – and she turned around to see who it was, her eyes fixed instead on the woman a bit behind the curious onlookers, at the mother of Leo and Felix and Vincent Dûvnjac.

Britt-Marie had sat down on the low stone wall. She seemed so fragile. Elisa could still feel her anxiety and worry about her son.

Urged to accompany a police officer who had investigated the bank robberies.

That fucking Broncks.

He was the one she should be calling on her mobile, which she pulled out of her jacket pocket, to get the answer to the question the anxious mother had asked. But you didn't call people who withheld information – you confronted them. For the moment, she had to use an alternative route and dialled an entirely different number.

'Duty officer.'

Even though she was well aware that the duty officer was fully occupied with the catastrophe in the confiscations room.

'Hi, Elisa Cuesta here. I need help with an immediate search for a Vincent Dûvnjac, spelled D-Û-V-N-J-A-C. He's in our records, photo and description out to all patrol cars.'

'How much of a hurry? What priority?'

'The highest.'

She had not even reached the stairs to the investigation division's corridor when he called back.

'Elisa, we got an immediate response.'

'Yes?'

'One of our cars responded to an alarm south of the city a few hours ago.'

'Yes?'

'The person you're enquiring about, Vincent Dûvnjac, was found dead.'

366

THE INVESTIGATION DIVISION was slumbering in darkness. After six o'clock it usually looked like this. Colleagues had made their last calls to forensic technicians and fingerprint experts, finished listening to the day's final interrogations and put the printouts of the most recent witness testimony back in the correct file. But this evening, everyone, just like herself, had orders to remain on duty – either down in the basement and corridors leading to and from the property room, the crime scene, or in the area around the courthouse's underground station, where the last and most current evidence, a police uniform, had been located out on the rails in the tunnel.

Halfway down the corridor, the dark became cold – as if somewhere the wind was blowing straight into the building. Elisa noticed that one of the doors stood open and moved a little in the draught. The door to John Broncks's office.

Broncks had vanished from the police station in the morning and since then had been impossible to find.

She now knew Broncks had his own agenda.

Broncks had secretly contacted a person she met and posed questions to as recently as yesterday, and who was now reported dead.

She increased her stride by the coffee machine – no shit silver tea in a paper cup – and headed straight to his office. Without knocking she pushed open the rattling door and saw him sitting there at the desk with the lights dimmed and both windows wide open.

'I want you to come with me to my office. I'll show you something.'

'Elisa, not now.'

'Right now.'

It was difficult to see his expression, with his face dissolving into the blackness of the office, but his unmistakable sigh was audible.

'I can't cope with talking about investigations. It's not the right circumstances. I must ask you to leave me in peace.'

She wasn't certain but it could have been that he was smiling at the same time. And not just the discordant grin; it was that marginalising and arrogant I-stood-and-watched-you-while-you-slept smile, which he had used when he invited her to investigate together with him.

She switched on the ceiling light.

'Elisa, for fuck's sake, now just get out of my office—'

'No.'

The bright fluorescent lights drowned them.

'John, you are coming with me to my office. You and I are going to talk to each other. And we'll begin with someone extremely central to our *joint* investigation, but about whom you have failed to give me all the facts.'

She had been right and she saw it now – it was that fucking smile.

'Sam Larsen. Your brother.'

A VIEW OVERLOOKING Birkastan, the black roofs looking like a hilly landscape of sheet metal. The sky above was much clearer when the light wasn't reflected in the snow that slid down during the day. Or maybe the wine made sure that brain cells moved more lightly, more freely, so that he perceived the stars as more sparkling, as if they were not so far away.

Ivan supported himself with his hip against the balcony railing. He reached out his hand with the glowing cigarette in it and he could almost touch them. It wasn't light years to them, but rather an arm's length. A couple more drags and he tossed the butt towards the empty filler tin and it landed among the others, easily four hundred of them, a pack a day for four weeks. It would be even more if he counted Vincent's. He actually didn't like it that the youngest of them smoked, but the feeling of belonging when they both stood out here together, father and son, had made him refrain from protesting.

Vincent should be here. But the radio hadn't been on, the bloody heroin music that all young people listened to, and all the lights in the flat had been switched off. With the moving in tomorrow, he had to come soon.

Ivan shut the balcony door again and it felt good to walk through the sitting room and see a professionally painted ceiling, and to know that he still was just as quick as the young blokes and also more skilful. Uneven and sloppily applied paint was always irritating. He was convinced that Vincent wanted to work with him on the next flat as well – not just to continue to get to know his pappa but also because it was damn difficult to find a better painter.

The wine bottle stood on the kitchen counter. He had parked it there while he was listening for the heroin music. Bull's blood, straight out of the bottle. He swallowed fast – he didn't want the taste, only the feel of the heat in his chest. As he placed it down on the metal counter again, an odd double ring arose.

Ding-dong. One more time. Ding-dong.

The front door.

Someone was ringing the bell.

369

'Come in. Enter.'

He moved the bottle to the empty pantry. Maybe it was the neighbour – she was always complaining – or the owner coming to see how nice it had turned out.

'Come in, come in.'

A woman. It was possible to tell from the footsteps, light and tentative.

'Vincent?'

It wasn't the neighbour. And not the owner of the flat.

Her? What the hell is she doing in the hall?

'Are you here, Vincent?'

The mother of his three sons. Britt-Marie.

He opened the pantry door and let three large gulps fill his chest. When he was done, she was standing in the kitchen and observing him.

'Two years.'

Just as surprised to see him as he was surprised to see her.

'Two years, Britt-Marie. But now it is over. I am not sober any more.'

More large gulps. He held out the bottle.

'Would you like some, Britt-Marie? Egri. Bull's blood. That's what it means, in Hungarian.'

'I'm looking for Vincent.'

She looked around and seemed to be listening for something.

'He should be working here. That was what Vincent said anyway.'

Ivan made a sweeping motion with his arm towards the newly painted kitchen ceiling and the newly painted walls and the new tiles between the sink and the cabinet doors.

'Do you see how nice we've made it? Your youngest son and I. Everything is perfect. Vincent is so careful. Do you remember how he laid the pencils in a row when he was little? He is still like that. Everything in its place.'

'Can you answer my question? Where is he?'

'Why are you looking for Vincent?'

'He called me this afternoon. He was upset. He had had contact with a police officer and said that it was about Leo. After that I haven't been able to get hold of him. I'm worried, Ivan.'

Fucking TV.

A large area was blocked off about twenty kilometres outside Stockholm. At the same time around the courthouse and the police station inside the city.

Ivan hadn't understood how, or why, but he was certain that he had been used, one of those pawns in Leo's plans that Vincent talked about. That in some way it had to do with what was on the television. But would Vincent have also been dragged in? No. He didn't think so. Vincent had decided. And he had seemed clear about it.

'You know, Britt-Marie, I have got to know Vincent now that we work together, and I can assure you, you don't need to be worried. He would never commit a crime again.'

She smiled but it wasn't a friendly smile.

'So you don't know where he is either? You have, as usual, not a clue, right?'

'He's coming soon. Don't worry. What do you mean, not a clue? What did *you* know, Britt-Marie, when they were robbing banks? They left you out. Leo came to *me*. We were sentenced together!'

She shook her head slightly. As she sometimes had done before. Sadly. With resignation.

'I believed . . . that they would split up. Hoped that, so fervently. That the splitting had finally begun. That the insane, absurd bonds you forced on them as children, the twisted family loyalty – *us against the world* – that the bonds would have broken there in prison, that the sentence would have torn them apart and that our three sons were heading away from each other.'

Up until then she was nearly whispering. Now she was gradually raising her voice and would soon be shouting.

'Vincent didn't even want to come home and eat lunch with Leo. He was afraid, Ivan, to be pulled in again. Do you understand that? I so wished that he would be here. But he isn't. So he's on his way there – where he doesn't want to go! And it's your fault, Ivan! The fault of your fucking bonds! The fault of that fucking loyalty! Everything you stand for is destroying my children, everything you ever—'

Her head felt so small in his open hand as his blow hit the entire left side of her face. From the temple to nose to jawbone. He could even feel his fingertips sink into her scalp. And if she hadn't fallen down, the next blow would have been with his fist.

But there were no more.

She didn't scream, didn't run, but just sat there on the newly sanded kitchen floor with the blood running out of her nose and looked at him.

Then he reached for the bottle. There were a couple of gulps left at the bottom, enough to ward off the feeling that was starting.

A single blow was all that was necessary to break apart all the fucking change and become himself again.

'Hey, Ivan?'

She was still looking at him as she got up.

'The last time we saw each other in a flat, our sons cleaned up after you. Wiped up fresh blood.'

Then she walked towards the hall and front door.

'Now you get to do it yourself.'

John Broncks wasn't sure, but he guessed that was the vending button she usually chose, black coffee with a little milk. His own drink didn't correspond to any number – regular hot water taken from a special tap to the side of the drinks machine for the others in the investigation division.

He'd succeeded in delaying the conversation in Elisa's office for just over fifteen minutes now. He had been forced to hurriedly gather his thoughts to construct a lie – she had new information that threatened his entire existence, both as a policeman and as a private individual.

He now knew how the lie should appear and be best presented. As an interrogator, he had learned that skilful liars always begin with the truth and only truth can cover over what the liar wants to hide. Quite simply, a lie must be true enough for the recipient to believe it.

The last drops of coffee went down into the paper cup, and on the way to her office he did what she had done two days earlier on the way to his – held the slightly rounded lips of the cups to avoid burning himself.

'Knock, knock.'

He repeated Elisa's movements again, this time raising the cups as an explanation for the audible knocking, before he came in and put down her steaming coffee between a couple of large piles of paper.

'One for me, one for you.'

Start with the truth.

For this particular lie, that meant – if there wasn't another way out – to admit to what she now knew for some reason. That Sam was his brother. And he should add that it was a mistake not to talk about it. But he would never confess the crime or the guilt or the fact that he failed to fully act as a police officer. He had not only let his own brother go, in spite of an armed robbery of a security van with a deadly outcome, but also he had let him escape with suitcases containing one hundred and three million kronor, stolen three floors below the chair he just now sat down on.

'Seriously – coffee?'

'Yeah?'

'John, coffee? Haven't you understood that the one thing that we abso-lutely *won't* do now is have a coffee break together?'

Elisa took the paper cup and carried it to a gap between the binders on the bookcase in a corner of the office.

'I'll drink it cold – when you've gone.'

Then she let her hand wander among the three stacks of papers on the desk and patted them gently, as if they were alive.

'These piles, John, are my own system of investigation, which you have never been particularly interested in. Because what separates you and me is that I work with facts, not gut feelings. Each pile is built on facts. This one, for example, to your far left, I call *You struck first, you bastard* and in it are always the conditions that shaped the moment of the deed.'

She pulled out a sheet randomly from somewhere in the middle. One of the forensic technician's photographs of a pile of cartridges under two ATMs.

'For example, like . . . well, a photo of ammunition – the precondition for entering the scene of the crime. Where did it come from? The Swedish defence. What gun can it be matched to? An AK4, stolen from a military armoury. What does that give me in the investigation? Facts, John, to link to a suspect.'

Elisa drew out another sheet, just as randomly.

'A second example so you'll completely get it. Here we have another photo. Of an entirely ordinary registration plate. According to the estab-lished report, the plate was stolen, as you know, the night before the crime. And it was placed on the vehicle that the surviving robber drove from the scene – the precondition for being able to pass as one of Arla's milk lorries. Facts, John, to link to a suspect.'

She placed her two examples aside and took a stapled pile of papers from the top of the stack – now it wasn't random any more and Broncks guessed that it was seven, maybe eight documents.

'But the strange thing is, John, that in the same pile there is something that can be linked to . . . you.'

And she pushed them along the surface of the table to him.

'A district court verdict. Twenty-four years old. A murder – a father stabbed to death by his son. If you look here . . .'

Her index finger searched along one of the lines at the top of the first page of the bundle.

'. . . you see the murder victim is named George Broncks. Your father. And here, in this line, John, you see the convicted murderer's name is Sam Larsen – your mother's maiden name. A name previously changed from Sam Broncks.'

That verdict.

On *her* desk.

Elisa had done exactly what no one should ever have the right to do again. She had dug up his family's business – a father who abused, a mother who looked the other way, a big brother who murdered for the sake of his little brother and a little brother who turned him in.

'What the fuck is that to do with you? You stand in front of your fucking piles and . . . throw it in my face! That has nothing to do with me today.'

She pretended not to notice his flushed cheeks and loud voice. If she even noticed them. She was so focused on what she had begun to demonstrate and prove.

'So you are in the first pile. The facts show the precondition for a crime – that you and Sam Larsen are brothers. Then if we look a little at the next pile, the one in the middle that is called *You fucked up* in my system and defines when crimes become clues, you are there too, John. Because in that pile, there's this.'

She handed him the sheet on top, which only had four handwritten lines and which he had scribbled on when they'd stood in his kitchen.

'Four names to check. Four inmates who did time at Österåker in the same cellblock at the same time as Leo Dûvnjac. You were quick to circle the name of Sam Larsen. And to explain that we should follow up on two each, alone, because of shortage of time. You did not say a word about him being your brother. Not a word about his description matching the robber we both sat and examined on the video sequence. The only thing you said, John, was that he had an alibi. An alibi I have never seen.'

Then she moved her hand to the third stack.

'I usually call my final pile of papers *You can't fucking think you'll get away.* When clues become the perpetrator. And in that one, John, is this report.'

It was also on top.

'Recorded by a patrol from the Eskilstuna police I sent out to your brother's registered address. It shows that in a recent fire at the back of the house, still with smouldering embers under the ashes, remains of

375

furniture, clothes, books and even photographs were found. The fridge and freezer were emptied out and the electricity was shut off. Although a neighbour saw him there as late as yesterday.'

Fifteen minutes. That was all he'd had for the lie.

'Do you hear what I'm saying, John? All that taken together shows that your brother left for good.'

He had used the better part of the time to make a call from his office telephone to someone he hoped would be his lifeline.

'Dammit, John – did you let that happen?'

So when he leant back, it was to play the one thing he didn't feel – ordinary.

'Elisa, you're right. I made a mistake.'

Even though inside he only wanted to run out of there.

'Of course I should have immediately told you that we are relatives. But our ties have never been especially strong. We have only seen each other a few times in twenty years. Blood doesn't mean shit to us.'

The judgement from childhood still lay in front of him and he grabbed it and held it up. Up to this point he had given her the truth, in order to now be able to continue with a lie.

'You've read it yourself, right? In that case, you know I was the one who turned him in and saw to it that he was arrested. And I wouldn't hesitate to do it *again* if he committed a crime. But he *hasn't*. Since he *has* an alibi.'

The lie she would evaluate right now and test whether it held up.

'Then I want you to give it to me, John. So I can check it myself.'

He had managed to make a telephone call.

'Do you remember you said you'd gladly help if there was a problem?'

To a lifeline.

'I remember.'

'I need your help now.'

'There's a man named Bertil Lundin. He works as a ferryman on the car ferry that connects the mainland with the island we lived on back during that judgement you were waving just now, the island where Sam lived after his release. The ferry is the only link over and back, and Lundin will confirm – when you contact him – that Sam was on board the car ferry at 16.30 on the day of interest, heading *to* the island.'

Broncks browsed in the middle pile of papers without asking for permission. He was looking for the photo of a masked robber running to a milk lorry and waved it as she had waved it before.

'*At the same time* this photo was taken.'

———————

He had been lucky; the ferryman had been just as easy to talk to as he had hoped.

'*At 16.30, did you say?*'

'*Yes. The trip over.*'

'*In that case . . . your brother could certainly have been on board. And I would be able to know that because he stepped out and waved to me in the control room as he always does.*'

'*Thank you. And the surveillance camera?*'

'*Unfortunately it is going to be out of use. Broken. And it has been for a week.*'

'*Thanks, again. And I'm sorry, but I simply can't say why.*'

'*You don't need to. I should have helped you long ago. When you were little.*'

———————

John Broncks got up with his untouched silver tea in his hand. He had placed his lie on her desk and he started to walk towards the corridor, away from the questions he lacked the strength to continue to answer.

'Now you have something to check and place in your little piles, while I go back to my office and switch off the lights and open the windows again, because I prefer to have it that way.'

He was able to get about as far as the doorway when her voice managed to catch up.

'Not yet. There was one more thing. Vincent Dûvnjac.'

He stopped but didn't turn around.

'Yes?'

He couldn't sit in front of her fucking papers again. He hadn't prepared for this. A lie requires that the liar himself understands what happened. And he didn't know if he wanted to do that, yet.

'He's dead.'

'I know that.'

'You were there when it happened.'

'Yes.'

'How is that, John? And even more interesting – how is it that Vincent was there with you?'

'That will be made clear in the report I'll submit to the leader of preliminary investigations tomorrow. Good evening, Elisa.'

A single step over the threshold was as far as he managed to get this time.

He didn't see, but he heard her free yet another document from the third and last pile of paper.

'While you delayed coming in here to me, John – and I can't swear to it, but I think it sounded as if you made a call – I also took the opportunity to make one. To my contact at one of our telephone companies. The operator Vincent Dûvnjac signed his contract with. The paper in my hand contains the list of the telephone numbers that called him today. A couple of them are especially serious. That verifies a statement from Vincent's mother: that a police officer – who previously investigated the brothers – contacted her youngest son and pressured him to accompany him for the sake of her eldest son.'

She left her desk and walked up to him, took hold of his shoulders and forced him to look at her.

'John – I'll say it one more time. I've dubbed the third pile in my system *You can't fucking think you'll get away.*'

And her eyes were burning.

'Leo Dûvnjac is in it. He is not going to get away. Your brother, Sam Larsen, is there and he won't get away either. I'll search until I find him and get him to talk. Because now you are also there, John, and I will fucking send you down. You know I don't care if I make enemies in this station as long as I am right. You will never, ever, ever get away with this.'

JOHN BRONCKS NEVER switched on the lights in his office that evening, that night.

Nor did he close the two windows.

If you don't want to return to the past when all debts are finally settled, if you don't want to stay in the present and encounter the unbearable heat and the intense light from a bomb, only one alternative remains – to continue forward.

To do that, you must know how, and to where.

He would be able to remain sitting in the dark and icy cold until dawn, when the fog lifted in the harbour of Riga.

Then he must know. Then he must have made a decision.

Then it would be over.

EARLY DAWN. The light had just begun its journey across the sky. And the corridor through the Kronoberg remand centre did not seem as dark.

He would soon cut a deal with the devil.

But the devil didn't even look at him. He just sat there on the cell bunk with an empty gaze.

'Should I open it?'

That was the second time the sleepy young prison guard with the bulky bunch of keys repeated the question.

'Not just yet.'

The little square opening in the cell door framed Leo Dûvnjac in a way that made him seem almost small. John Broncks considered for a moment meeting his blank silence with closing the square opening again and leaving. But he had no choice. Someone who wants to start negotiations with the devil can't expect an invitation.

'Now you can open it.'

There was rattling when the keys scraped against each other and mechanical clicking as the parallel bolts of the lock were released from the doorframe.

'Thanks. Close it when I've gone in and then leave us.'

'Are you sure about that?'

John Broncks nodded impatiently.

'Yes. I'm sure.'

'You want to be in there alone? Without an alarm?'

'Give me the alarm and go.'

The remand centre guard took a small black plastic box out of his trouser pocket and handed it to Broncks.

'A slight pressure on the button in the middle. That's all you have to do.'

The guard left them and, through the opening in the closed door, they could both hear the rattling from the large bunch of keys fall silent, the squabbling metal fading as he walked away.

The remand cell was not particularly large. An unmade bunk, a table

380

attached to the wall, a dripping washbasin. It became even smaller with two men and their mutual hatred. After being quiescent and stable for six years, it had escalated over a few days to *if you get my brother involved, I'll get your brother involved.*

'What happened yesterday . . .'

John Broncks had somehow hoped to never be forced to put Vincent Dûvnjac's death into words beyond a police report – and especially not for the person sitting now in a closed room and staring at him.

'. . . should never have happened. Your . . . Vincent, he—'

'*You* don't say a fucking word about my little brother.'

Leo Dûvnjac had not yelled at him. It would have been simpler if he had. Even though a sound is waves requiring air to make their way, his despair echoed in the oxygen-poor space.

'And now I think you should use that fucking assault alarm. I don't want you in here.'

John Broncks stayed there, still. Standing near someone who hates you is easy when you have no alternative.

'Leo – I want you to listen to me.'

'Go.'

'Give me two minutes.'

'Just go.'

Broncks did it. He went. But only one step, to the thick metal door, which he opened slightly, then pulled closed again.

'This is a conversation that only concerns us. Not between a policeman and a suspect – between two individuals who, each in his own way, have gone through a truly horrible twenty-four hours.'

He left his hand on the door handle, as if to signal that it was properly closed.

'Not that I understand what it meant for you – but the last time we saw each other here at the police station, when I let you out, you turned and called out something like: "Today, John Broncks, was a fucking black thread for you."'

For the first time it felt as if Leo made eye contact. The hollow stare filled with something that might be life.

'And I imagine that what we should talk about now is precisely such a thread.'

He was observing, as if attempting to decide what he saw.

'You'll get your fucking two minutes.'

Leo Dûvnjac reached out his hand, with the palm open.

'If you give me the alarm.'

Broncks understood what he said, what it meant. But he right away searched in his trouser pocket for the little black plastic box and laid it in the waiting hand.

'And if you don't say anything within two minutes that makes me look at you in a different way, Broncks, I'm going to crush your head against the concrete wall behind you.'

Leo Dûvnjac got up and the narrow cell became narrower.

Broncks glanced at the closed door and realised that, if the pent-up fury of the man in front of him found no reason to subside, in less than one hundred and twenty seconds there would be only one man alive in the cell.

'Because you understand, Broncks, that a bastard of a black thread more or less doesn't matter. You used Vincent to get to me and it all went to hell – you're responsible for his death.'

Leo Dûvnjac was more than ten centimetres taller than Broncks, so when he leaned forward, he also leaned down so that their eyes could come really close as he whispered.

'Can you hear it, too, Broncks? The second hand. Tick tick. Tick tick.'

John Broncks heard it. And he felt it, inside. It was almost pleasant knowing that the next moment would decide everything. No matter how, or what, it would soon be over and he didn't need to prepare himself or wonder any longer.

'So here it is: I am the only police officer who knows *exactly* how everything that has happened the last few days fits together.'

'Tick tick, Broncks, tick tick.'

'That it was you who staged the robbery of the security van that my brother and the dead man, Jari Ojala, carried out – *criminal offence aggravated robbery*, eight years in prison. That you and my brother together conducted the robbery in the basement of this station, the one all my colleagues are trying to solve right now – *criminal offence aggravated robbery*, ten years in prison. That you stored two hundred military-grade automatic weapons in a secret room in your own residence, *criminal offence crime of terrorism* – life sentence.'

'Tick tick, tick tick.'

'And I repeat – right now I'm the only one who knows it. But other police, skilful police, have begun to dig, attempting to see the links I've already seen. So you have a choice: you can choose to tell them everything, or you can choose to do what you and I both know you are bloody good at – keeping your mouth shut.'

John Broncks felt Leo Dûvnjac's hand stroking his temple. The man who hated him so much had suddenly jerked his arm forward, as if to highlight how easy it would be to carry out his threat.

'One minute left.'

And then he patted the cold, hard concrete surface next to the back of Broncks's head. Clear language. But John Broncks didn't move away and didn't stop talking; on the contrary, he leaned closer and rested against the concrete.

'I've also lost a brother today.'

As if he wanted to show that he accepted the agreement – *it's your right to kill me if I don't succeed in convincing you.* He stayed there too when Leo struck with an open palm, again near Broncks's cheek. It landed with a loud smack on the concrete wall.

'What the hell are you talking about! You don't have a fucking clue what it means to lose a brother.'

'Yesterday evening, I sat with *my* brother in a luxury cabin on a ferry that was about to depart. I drank out of the champagne glass he filled for you. I could have made certain he was arrested then. I can still arrange for him to be arrested when he reaches Riga harbour in a few hours. I can also not do that. If you do what I want.'

A few seconds. Maybe more. Then Leo lowered his arm, dropped his gaze from the wall and didn't even count down the seconds, didn't tick any more.

'It was like this when Sam, your brother, and I met – in a cell with a closed door at Österåker. When I thought that he was running your errands.'

John Broncks was certain he had succeeded in subduing the rage for the moment. He had been able to capture Leo Dûvnjac's interest.

'So what the fuck is it you want, Broncks?'

'That you don't confirm for anyone, at all, that Sam was involved.'

'And why shouldn't I do that? Why shouldn't I take the opportunity to send you to prison too – the person responsible for Vincent's death?'

'There is nothing that connects me to *his* death.'

'You lured him there! You locked him to the lorry door with your fucking handcuffs!'

'The same handcuffs I moved to your wrists before my colleagues came.

For every outside analyst, your presence there is so much harder to explain than mine. Isn't that so? Because in my version there would be an explanation of what the metal clump now lying there actually is. Where it came from. What the entire trail of clues looks like. So . . . if you don't verify it, *I* won't verify *your* involvement. And we would be able to stand out there on the pavement in five minutes' time, never to see each other again. You would be able to look for my brother and the suitcases he has with him, precisely as you once planned.'

'Fifty million? Listen, you bastard Broncks, Vincent is still dead.'

The only thing Broncks was sure of was that his two minutes were over.

'But yes, I . . .'

And the alarm, which was in Leo Dûvnjac's hand, was given back now.

'. . . will do it for Sam's sake.'

They looked at each other as their hands met.

'The interesting question, Broncks, is who are *you* doing it for?'

John Broncks took the black plastic box and opened the cell door and yelled to the young remand centre guard that it was time to lock up. Then he left without answering the question. It would have seemed too small, too sad to say it – *for my own sake.*

THE BLUE-AND-WHITE plastic tape fluttered a few metres from the entrance to the police station on Bergs Street, so light and fleeting in the April wind. Leo pulled up the hood of his jacket and passed the first uniformed police unnoticed. When Broncks grabbed the barrier tape and lifted they looked at each other one last time, a quick, cold glance before they continued in different directions – Broncks back into the building and Leo slowly towards Hantverkar Street and the city centre.

A short distance away on the pavement, he couldn't help but turn around and contemplate an entire police complex embedded in plastic. Scandinavia's largest robbery had been carried out *inside* the police station not very many hours ago, by the man who was now leaving it.

He had succeeded in taking back what didn't exist.

At the same time, he had taken from Broncks what he had been so proud of and acclaimed for.

It meant nothing.

The only similarity between being released now and being released earlier in the week was that Vincent was not there. Four days – the time it had taken to lose everything.

He saw Mamma in front of him that first evening, so steady, so balanced on her feet, just as she stood the times she defied Ivan. *Whatever you do, Leo. Don't get your brothers involved.* She had looked at him and caressed his cheek.

He continued walking alone through the early morning in Stockholm.

He encountered stressed-out people walking to work, cars honking angrily at each other and buses groaning their way forward in hectic traffic. But he didn't see them. There, somewhere, midstride, he couldn't hold out.

That is how it is.

Sometimes you close off because you love too much.

Then when you open yourself again, you realise that grief is a creature that feeds on memories.

It was as if, without being able to know it, of course, he was embraced by all the people who through his actions were forced together in order to be able to tear apart bonds; Mamma and Pappa in an empty flat; John Broncks and Sam Larsen in a first-class cabin on a ship; himself and his beloved little brother in an abandoned barn.

Forced together to bring about an end.

And he, who never cried, did so now.

Eye of Steel

THEY ARE STANDING on the cross on the map, exactly in its centre, out in the forest that corresponds to the map's green field and slightly away from the cycle path corresponding to the line Leo drew with the blue pen.

Felix is sitting comfortably on a huge, egg-shaped rock that resembles a giant's head. He dangles his legs and slides down to be able to press his heels deep into the soft moss. He wants to come closer as Leo empties the contents of two plastic bags.

And it's too late.

Felix regrets it from head to toe but can't back out.

A promise is a promise.

Vincent decided. The crap plan would be carried out. But then, when everything was ready, Leo suddenly explained that he didn't need any help at all and that he would rather carry out the plan by himself. And for that very reason, quite strangely, Felix began to nag. *I want to do it now.* Almost crying. *I want to.* He does not even understand himself how his own no also became a yes. Yet deep down, he knows exactly why he changed his mind. Not because he wants to – but so Leo won't go to prison.

Leo went through everything at home in the kitchen, explaining that he chose the cross on the map – the pine grove they are standing in now – because no one can find them in it. He had already checked it out, with the same carefulness that Leo always checks things. On a chopped-off tree in the grove, he had hung a hockey jersey – Leksand's blue and white, colours that don't belong in the forest in autumn. After that he cycled by on the path ten times. The jersey did not emerge a single time out of September's garb. So the grove was ultimately designated as the starting point – the place where a fourteen-year-old would be transformed into Druggie-Lasse and Druggie-Lasse would afterwards be transformed into a fourteen-year-old.

A figure lies before them on the ground: the jacket with uneven green colouring, the wig with shoulder-length hair and the wrinkled pack of John Silver cigarettes. And cut-out, pieced-together padding in various shapes.

389

The most important piece will fit on the stomach. Leo is especially pleased with it, four layers of padding combined with an additional two at the bottom. A pot belly. He sewed it together by hand, big stitches, and it will be held in place with a rope.

'Tie it.'

The pot belly conceals his thin stomach, reshaping it.

'Felix? Tie it at the back, here.'

His little brother does so. He pulls the rope, and ties it with a bow. He shakes his head when he sees the result.

'You've dubbed him Druggie-Lasse. It's all wrong.'

'That's his name.'

'Druggies never have stomachs like that.'

'Druggie-Lasse drinks, too.'

'They're thin, like threads.'

'He's a binge drinker, mostly beer. A good deal of vodka. A fucking lot of carbohydrates.'

Then the breastplate, with padding that makes him seem thicker, while the shoulder pads sculpt him broader. Both of his upper arms are provided with a layer of rolled padding, which Felix tapes on instead of tying them on.

'What is it?'

Leo tries to catch Felix's eye. He's been too quiet for too long.

'Hey . . . Felix?'

Then he realises that protesting about whether or not Druggie-Lasse has a pot belly is hardly about fatness. Rather, his little brother was hesitating and maybe even trying to stop it.

'Hello, answer me – what's the matter?'

Felix tears off the last bit of tape and the right arm is ready.

'I've never pinched anything before.'

So here comes stage two: the attempt to prevent. Since the first one didn't work.

'But isn't that good, Felix? Then it's believable. You *will* get caught.'

In the outer pocket of the jacket is a mirror with a wooden handle. Leo holds it in one hand while he primps with his free hand – like Mamma when she makes herself look pretty. He prepared at home, rubbing a thick pencil on a rag, a worn pillowcase Mamma saved for polishing windows. Now he rubs the dark graphite on the rag onto the area under his eyes and his cheekbones.

'Ten minutes to six, sharp, Click will discover you. Remember to shoplift as goddamn miserably as you can.'

Finally, he adds a thin layer on the jaw to look more tired, hollow.

'Afterwards, when Click has grabbed you, he'll take you into the office. You'll sit there a while. He'll ask you where you live and what your mother's name is. First you don't reveal shit. You keep quiet and are as sulky as hell. Then maybe you say something, anything at all, that it's a mess at home now, that sort of thing. Then nothing else happens – you are underage. The important thing is that you go into the office. A scolding behind closed doors and I'll take care of the rest. Click will be dealing with you when the woman goes to the bank with the cash. OK?'

The wig is pulled over his short blond hair. Then he puts on the jacket, which fits now, thanks to all the padding. Last of all, he pulls up the hood.

And Felix sees someone else. Surely not his big brother.

It's Druggie-Lasse. Even the bloody wig under the hood looks like real hair straggling.

'Shit. It works.'

'Told you so. Now repeat what you're supposed to do.'

Felix ostentatiously holds up his wrist with the watch on it and starts to walk without a word towards the square and the ICA shop. Then halfway through the grove he turns around.

'I'll shoplift so damn badly that Click takes me to the office.'

'Good, little brother. And what time?'

'Exactly ten to. Not earlier, not later.'

LEO PUTS ON the brakes and jumps off the stolen cycle, all in one motion. It's easy even though he looks big. Because a stomach, chest and arm muscles made of padding don't weigh a thing. But he's sweating. A river and a couple of streams are running under his jacket and form a lake at the end of his back, and on his forehead, where the wig touches the skin, it itches, and especially under the band tightened to hold his hair in place, it itches so badly it's driving him mad.

His goal is waiting behind the next crest and he gets off the cycle path. Branches and twigs are stuck between the spokes of the wheels. It sounds like when he was younger and fastened the king and queen of clubs onto the bicycle fork with clothes pegs. When he is sure no one can see his bike from the asphalt trail, he leans it against a tree and starts to walk briskly, zigzagging between crooked birches and straight pines while the lake of sweat around his body overflows.

There.

Right there the forest ends and the city centre begins.

It's right at the end of the trees, where the vegetation gives way to the stone of the square, that Druggie-Lasse will stand and feel very nervous while he chain-smokes, cigarette after cigarette, to get up his courage. That's what Leo wants the police to conclude afterwards. The false lead: five cigarettes that were smoked beforehand at home at the kitchen table until they shrivelled to butts and were saved in a plastic bag to be strewn now out over the moss.

THE ANTI-SHOPLIFTING mirror looks like a mastodon's eye of glittering steel as it hangs in its obvious place on the ceiling and observes as he passes the aisle for juice and jam, heading for the sweets shelves.

An eye that sees everything: everyone who comes in empty-handed and goes out with full shopping bags; everyone who passes through the sliding doors and the uniformed guard standing next to them, between the autumn wind outside and white lighting inside.

Quarter to six.

Five minutes left. Felix checks the watch against the big square clock on the wall between the checkout counters. Will Click arrest Leo then? Even worse, what if the police car glides by, just like that, right when his big brother runs up and snatches the leather bag? Leo wouldn't have a chance. That's why Felix's legs are shaking so damn much. Soon it will start. No one knows how it will end.

He looks up in the mirror and realises that he can be clearly seen from all directions.

The steel eye.

That's perhaps why he thinks of her.

When Click has caught me.

When I sit across from him in his office, then I must say what Mamma's name is.

That's how it works.

He's come to the sweets shelves, close to the first checkout and the sliding doors that Click spies from. Four minutes and thirty seconds left. Until then he is going to pretend to be choosing chocolate bars, which according to the sign weigh 100 grams each and vary between milk chocolate, whole nut and Swiss nut, and the kind Mamma likes with fruit and almonds.

Mamma's name. So she will find out what I am about to do.

Tomorrow when I'm sitting by her hospital bed, her eye and the red deep in it, burst blood, will stare at me like the steel eye on the ceiling.

And I, who told on Leo, will become the thief now and she will look at me like she looked at him.

393

No.

He won't fucking do it.

He'll leave the chocolate bars there on the shelf. Forget it and just go home. Avoid sitting first in the office and then by a bed as someone he doesn't want to be.

Right then the woman with the leather bag steps out of the stockroom, and when he glances up into the mirror, events are distorted. He is visible, the woman is visible and Click is visible – but upside down, and somewhat skewed.

The steel eye sees everything and nothing looks as it should look.

Felix feels he is shaking all over. The woman with the leather bag is on her way to the exit and the square and the bank on the other side. If Leo snatches the money, and Click is standing where he is now, his big brother will be arrested. Like Pappa.

He has to. He has to pinch the blasted chocolate.

Felix reaches for the shelf and closes his eyes when he grabs the first, best, one hundred gram bar – and immediately drops it. It makes a sound when it hits the floor.

His hands are even shaking so much that his fingers are useless.

Once more. His right hand. Whole nut, even bigger, two hundred grams. And in a second he pushes it down inside his trousers. One more, just as big, and his belt is pulled so tight that both chocolate bars are broken in half.

And then – pain.

A bite of a dog's drooling chops around his shoulder.

Such fucking pain.

'And you haul those up again as quick as hell, lad!'

Click, with a grip that feels mechanical, a claw clutch that can't be turned off.

'Open your jacket and show what the fuck you're hiding there!'

Click is bellowing. At the same time the woman with the leather bag is bellowing outside. Her scream gets Click to release the claw clutch somewhat and turn his eyes towards the large shop window.

When the scream is heard again, he goes closer to the window to get a better look and find out where it's coming from and what it is associated with. On his way there, he drags the eleven-year-old shoplifter behind him, the soles of his shoes sliding along the ICA floor from the heavy tugging.

Now the shop window is like a television, like at the hospital when Leo screened off the world between his shoulder and the doorframe. It gets ever bigger, and the outside becomes distorted in the same way and seems less real.

The picture depicts a woman.

She is sitting on the ground with her hands over her mouth while her shriek forces its way out between her fingers. She is crying and the TV window's sound reproduction is perfect. It is easy to grasp the eight words she is repeating: *He took the bag. He took the money.*

At the same time, in the left corner of the picture, someone is rushing away from her. A large man dressed in a dirty green jacket with the hood up. Click sees it just as clearly as Felix while he presses him up against the wall, hard.

'You stay here! Do you get that, you piece of shit!'

'Yeah.' His voice is shaking so much that the shoplifter doesn't even hear it himself. 'I get it.'

The last thing Felix sees before the screen goes blank is the guard in his uniform leaving the ICA shop and hurrying across the square.

In the direction Druggie-Lasse disappeared.

HIS LEGS MOVE freely and effortlessly past bare trees and leaf-covered moss, as if he is floating forward, and in his hand he's holding onto the leather bag, hard. But not as hard as she held it when he pulled it out of her grip. It took three strong tugs before she collapsed.

All that remains are the cries his light steps are taking him away from.

He couldn't stand them. She screamed for her bag, yet his mamma kept quiet during the entire beating.

They are surely the reason he hears something else. Behind him. Someone else's breathing. Twigs snapping beneath heavy black guard boots.

Click. Shit. *Shit.*

How the hell can he be so fast?

Soon – just past the next grove, the next moss-covered stone.

Soon – the tree with the bicycle.

Leo throws himself on the saddle and pedals. It's fairly slow. Wandering branches find their way into the wheels and he stands up, pressing the pedals down, while the guard's uniform is coming closer.

Roll, roll, roll, you bastard of a bike!

A dip, an uprooted tree, a thicket. He glances back again – just as Click reaches out his fat arm and his fingertips brush the metal basket.

'Stop, you son of a bitch!'

A small grab, enough to slow the momentum – Click has got hold.

I'm caught.

But in the jolt that occurs when two forces meet and pull in opposite directions, the guard's tired legs get tangled. He stumbles, loses his grip and in the same motion shoves the bicycle down.

Leo lands softly in the blueberries; Click rolls twice, hits a rock and begins bleeding heavily from his forehead. Nonetheless they both get up – at the same time.

The bastard doesn't give up.

He has to grab the bike again, roll, pedal, roll, pedal, before the guard can get to him.

There, only a few metres away, the cycle path is waiting, a downhill stretch.

His last chance.

FELIX RESTS HIS hands on his knees, letting them carry the weight of his whole upper body. Leaning forward, breathing heavily. He has to stand like this outside the door until he is breathing normally. It can't be noticed when he passes Agnetha's door on the second floor on the way up the stairs.

He did as Click said – he waited inside ICA's sliding door, in front of the wide noticeboard. The guard hadn't actually needed to say a word. Felix couldn't move anyway. Paralysed, he had observed through the shop window Click pursuing Leo across the square and into the trees, while a lot of people gathered to help the ICA woman up and console her. In the confusion, he decided to run. Not in order to escape, but to avoid seeing the guard come back out of the forest with a kicking, yelling Leo.

It took fifteen minutes to run home. He isn't tired, even though his heart is pounding and the soles of his feet are throbbing. There's a small chance that Leo will get away, that he's already here. It's much faster on a bicycle.

He can hardly contain himself. He throws open the door, trips up the stairs and rushes into the flat.

'Leo!'

He checks behind every door and peers into every room.

'Where the hell are you!'

Finally, Vincent's room, and before he can even ask, their little brother shakes his head so that the loops of bandage fly in a storm.

'Leo isn't home. Not yet.'

Shit. Click caught up with him.

Leo is on his way to the same police station and the same remand centre that Pappa's in.

And Mamma's questions will come.

How the hell will he answer them when he doesn't know the answers?

He thinks of the radio. Radio Dalarna, the station she always listens to, local news every half-hour. He runs to her bedroom and the radio standing on the night table and he tunes it to 100.2.

398

Crummy music. But it's just a few minutes until the next newscast, and he lets the crappy music continue so he won't risk missing the start of the programme. He doesn't notice Vincent until the mummy dance begins. Vincent climbs up on the bed and jumps, with the gauze fluttering.

'Stop!'

'No!'

The news is starting now. The first item.

'Stop, you idiot!'

His little brother looks offended and even hurt, but there isn't time to care about that.

'You sit still and keep your mouth shut while I listen!'

The news item is over and the newsreader's voice is as pleasant as it is serious when she begins the next item.

'Half an hour ago – right before closing time – a robbery was carried out at a shop in the Slätta district when a courier was assaulted and robbed of a large sum of money.'

Felix is even more frightened on the inside and therefore even angrier on the outside, so when Vincent jumps up on the bed a second time, he yells at him loudly. When that doesn't help, he wallops his upper arm, where it hurts most.

'Wha . . . what . . . Felix, what the hell are you doing!'

'Surely you don't feel a thing – you have bandages on your whole body.'

'But it hurt.'

'So wrap more bandages on yourself. And leave me alone!'

'Witness statements relate that a lone man was seen leaving both the scene and the victim of the robbery, first running and then on a bicycle.'

That was it. The news voice explains that they will come back to the robbery at the shop on the next newscast when they know more, before she continues with an interview with the local Falun commissioner, something about the budget deficit. Everything while Vincent jumps up on him again, a third time, and lands more heavily than before.

'Vincent, I said . . .'

But when Felix turns around to wallop him a second time, he encounters a different face. Visible traces of smeared graphite under the eyes and along the cheekbones.

His big brother has sneaked in through the front door without being noticed.

'Are you home?'

'Are *you* home?'

They don't hug. But it feels as though they do, all the same.

'Yeah. I took off, Leo. When Click chased you.'

'Did you say your name?'

'What?'

'Was there time for you to say your name?'

'I was going to. Then she screamed. And you ran past with the bag.'

Leo smiles and bends down towards something on the bedroom floor. He lifts it up onto the bed.

'I snatched it. I ran like hell. And I rode away from the fat bastard guard when he lay whimpering in the ditch.'

The brown leather bag! It's really it.

'So why . . . in that case are you coming home *now*? If you rode the bicycle? If you managed it? Don't you get it that I . . .'

Leo places the leather bag between them.

'Felix – wait.' He yells towards the hall. 'Vincent, come here too. I'll show you something.'

Time passes. When Vincent answers, his voice is low and morose as it gets when he is irritated or crabby or angry.

'I don't want to.'

Or possibly all at the same time.

'Come and you'll see.'

'I don't want to! Felix is fighting. He hit me.'

'Come on, Vincent. Look at this. You've also been a part of this. You were there and decided that we'd do it. And that was important.'

Shuffling through the hall. Just as curious as he is wary.

'Come. Up on the bed. With us.'

Vincent hesitates and tries to meet Leo's eyes first and then Felix's. Felix beckons him, which means he should come.

'Sorry. Do you hear? I shouldn't have walloped you. Come on.'

Vincent pulls distractedly at one of the loose gauze bandage bits, as if he is fixing them and fastening what came off in the mummy dance, and jumps up on the bed.

'Good. Now we're all here.'

The brown leather bag is closed with a zip. Leo pulls it and widens the opening with his hands. He moves so that Felix can peer down, and when he is finished, he moves so that Vincent can look down into it.

'When the banknotes are lying packed in, they don't look like so much. But I counted. After I buried the clothes and the wig and covered them over with leaves.'

Sweeping, exaggerated lip movements as he forms one number at a time.

'Thirty. Seven. Thousand. Eight. Hundred. And. Fifty. Kronor.'

One more time. Faster.

'Thirtyseventhousandeighthundredandfifty.'

Three brothers. Together. In Mamma's bed, sitting around a leather bag full of banknotes. One common breath and the local radio are audible. More crummy music in the empty space before the next newscast. Music and . . . feet. From the stairwell. More than one pair. And they stop at their floor.

'The cops, Leo!'

The doorbell rings. Twice. Someone who doesn't seem to have time to wait.

Leo flings himself off the bed with the leather bag in his hand and flies to the row of built-in wardrobes. He chooses the one in the middle, the one for bedding and towels.

The bag goes right between the pile of sheets and the one of pillowcases.

'You two stay here.'

The doorbell calls a third time while he's in the bathroom washing his face clean of graphite. He dries himself and hurries to the front door. He glances towards the gap in the doorway of Mamma's bedroom and Felix forms the word *cops* with the same exaggerated lip movements as Leo's just now.

Leo closes his eyes, counts to three and turns the lock.

The social services lady. And behind her, to one side, Agnetha.

Not the cops.

They say hello and make it clear that they want to come in. The social services lady is without her coat, so they must have been sitting down at Agnetha's and have talked already.

'Do you have your brothers at home too?'

Leo nods towards the partially closed bedroom door.

'In there. In Mamma's room.'

The social services lady doesn't ask for permission before walking in, and Agnetha follows, and Leo follows Agnetha and sees what they see: one little brother lying on half of the bed with a dirty, loose bandage; another little brother lying on the other half of the bed with his ear tight up against a radio broadcasting the local news. The social services lady starts to speak, as if she is in a hurry.

'Your mother.'

Or she doesn't actually know *how* she should say it, only that it seems better to get it out right away.

'She isn't coming home, here, yet.'

Felix takes in what she's saying with one ear, while the other one is filled with the next newscast, which also begins with the shop robbery in the district of Slätta. It seems he wants to tell, as if so much would be simpler then, but he can't, because he was involved too. What they did is about as far away from coconut balls and juice packs as it's possible to be.

Thirtyseventhousandandeighthundredandfifty times ten kilometres away.

'I think . . . She thinks, that is, your mother, that it will take two more months.'

Now he's listening to the social services lady with both ears.

'Two . . . months?'

'Yes, Felix. First, she must heal on the outside. And then heal on the inside. She is going to see many doctors, with different expertise. But after two months, when she is healed both on the inside and the outside, she'll come home to you.'

Two months. Eight and a half weeks. Sixty days.

Felix thinks about an eye, Mamma's eye, which looked tired and was shining red where it should have been white. Now he knows for sure that it is true. Burst blood is better than black gaps. Burst blood heals faster than black gaps.

'You will all be staying with a family.'

The social services lady smiles when she's speaking, as if it's about something pleasant. It doesn't seem particularly genuine; more as if she feels sorry for them.

'A good family, who will help. In Hosjö. You'll stay with them for the time being. Until your mother is back again. Only for that time.'

Leo doesn't care for her smile at all.

'I don't understand. It's working really well with Agnetha. She can come here when she wants to.'

402

'We already talked about it a couple of days ago, Leo, didn't we? That Agnetha was a temporary solution.'

'Temporary? What a bloody word.' He turns to Agnetha instead, who isn't smiling so damn much. 'But . . . what do you think, Agnetha? Isn't it going well? Can't you tell her about it, so that she understands?'

Agnetha tries to look at the social services lady just as much as at Leo and his two brothers.

'Well, yes, it has gone well. You are fine lads, all three of you. But I have a full-time job. Two months . . . it simply won't work, Leo. I think you'll understand that, if you just try to.'

The social services lady attempts to put her hand down on Leo's shoulder, or neck, and he ducks so she'll miss. She doesn't know him well enough to know how little he likes it. So she nods towards the hall instead.

'Come with me over here. We need to talk, just you and I.'

She carefully closes the door after them and looks for words that perhaps for the first time will define the sort of dilemma she is now facing and has never before had to solve – what it means to be in the vacuum that arises when two parents disappear at the same time and two little brothers are trying to survive with a fourteen-year-old who has been schooled in resolving life through dancing with bears.

'Listen to me, Leo. I think . . . that you aren't doing OK, even though you say you are. I don't think Felix is OK, no matter how many times he says so. And I don't think that even you, Leo, think that Vincent is doing especially well, right? His entire body bandaged – still. He must be offered some help. And right now that help is not here with you in this flat.'

SUNSET OUTSIDE THE WINDOW, an orange sky shining brighter still as Leo adjusts the Venetian blinds.

Clothes. Schoolbooks. Exercise equipment. Toiletries. And a small number of the hundred kronor banknotes, which belong in a bank depot but are wedged in between sheets and pillowcases. He packs enough for two months in a sports bag and two plastic bags.

'Vincent refuses to get his stuff ready.'

Felix chose a single bag, his mother's suitcase. The one he is now holding in his hand.

'He refuses to even say what he wants to have with him so that *I* can pack for him.'

The taxi is coming in an hour. The taxi that will pick up three brothers and drive them to a house in Hosjö.

Leo doesn't sigh as he goes to Vincent's room. He understands why those bags in particular aren't ready – a small rucksack and some sort of gym bag lying empty in the middle of the floor – while Vincent busies himself with constructing the roof of a Lego aeroplane. Or maybe it's . . . nothing. Just pieces that are attached together and don't belong together at all.

He sits down next to him. Big brother and little brother, close to each other.

'Vincent? You have to stop building . . . well, whatever it is you're building. And pack instead. Felix and I don't know what you want to have with you.'

Vincent continues to press Lego piece onto Lego piece onto nothing.

'The social services lady and Agnetha said so. We are going to another family. To where all the fine houses are.'

A round red piece on top of a green, oblong one.

'You heard it yourself. That's why you're sitting here and sulking, right? But it'll go quickly. Mamma will be back soon, and then it'll be back to normal.'

A flat blue piece on a wide black one; two yellow ones side by side with four white ones.

404

'Vincent?'

Leo puts his hand on the stack of many-coloured Lego pieces and forces his little brother to look at him.

'Please, please, Vincent?'

He stays like that until he gets an answer.

'Maybe.'

'Maybe, what?'

'If you promise, Leo, that she's coming back. That we're coming back. Here.'

'I promise.'

'Scout's honour?'

'Scout's honour. If *you* promise something else. That none of them – not the social services lady and not Agnetha, and not the other family, that none of them, Vincent, can know that a mountain of coconut balls was under your bed. Or that there's a lot of money in the leather bag in Mamma's wardrobe. Not ever. OK?'

His youngest brother has always been one of the smart ones. There has always been something going on in that little head, and as quick as hell. But after Pappa's blows, after the bandage, it's working incredibly slowly.

Lost thoughts have to take their time.

'OK, Vincent? Thumbs?'

His thumb was never wrapped in the gauze bandage. It was always free. Now it meets first Leo's thumb, and then Felix's.

'Thumbs.'

'And Vincent – this is the only time. With the leather bag in the wardrobe. Leo has promised. Right, Leo? The *only* time.'

Felix observes Leo, waiting him out. It was directed only at him.

'The only time. I promise both of you.'

Leo pretends to swear on an imaginary Bible and gestures something like the sign of the cross. Vincent smiles a little, and it has been a long time since the last time. Now, maybe it'll work now.

'And Vincent?' Leo reaches out and gently grasps two partially bandaged hands aiming to continue to build on nothing. 'Listen, when we knock on the door of the family, you can't look like this. You *have* to take off the lousy bandage. Otherwise . . . otherwise they'll send you somewhere else, and you won't get to be with us. Don't you understand that?'

He tries to make contact with Vincent's eyes, the eyes that usually are so present and alert but have fallen down these last few days into deep holes.

405

'Now, Vincent, we're going to loosen your left hand. Only a tiny bit.'

He catches hold of the dangling piece and unravels it, two turns and more skin can breathe.

'See, it's going well. Now your right hand, and just a little again. OK?'

Loosened bandages are soon hanging from both hands, like the shed skin of a snake. Leo reels them in carefully, carefully. The arms are de-mummified. The upper body comes next, dressed in a total of three rolls of gauze, with bigger gaps, more skin gleaming through. Another two lengths have been used to reach from the upper thighs to his ankles where they are tied with simple knots.

'Vincent, trust me. One more turn – now the bandage around your neck is gone. Do you feel the air on your skin? Now we're rolling this off. I promise it won't hurt.'

When half of his body is freed from the once white fabric, things change. Vincent starts to pull on it himself and pushes away his big brother's hands.

'*I'll* do it.'

Just as methodically as he wrapped himself up, he unwraps himself, letting the discoloured, floppy bandage fall in a twisting pile on the floor.

Leo smiles at what is surely *life*.

And he does so entirely certain he was right.

They hadn't fucking needed to pack their bags and move to another family for two months – he can take care of things, just as he'd said. This, and whatever might happen. You can take care of things if you think. If you plan. And then don't do what others think you're going to do.

He looks at Vincent, who's sitting close to him, without bandages; at Mamma's bedroom across the hall, with a wardrobe that hides a bag with more than thirty thousand kronor; at Felix who's going to understand, when he's older, that in order to weave in a golden thread you sometimes have to first weave in a black one – and that his big brother really meant it when he promised that it was the only time. That *if* it should happen again, it wouldn't be for at least several more years. And that *if* it happens again after that – again, it isn't going to happen for many years.

That is how he's thinking as he sits on the floor of a boy's room with his brothers, one on each side of him.

He can't know then that these autumn days, when he will remember them much later, will always remain happy days.